S0-AKO-801

A RESOUNDING CHORUS OF PRAISE FOR LORI HANDELAND!

BY ANY OTHER NAME

"[*By Any Other Name*] will make you aware of things you may never have known and, in the end, will make you think, feel, and understand. Ms. Handeland has created a remarkable story."

—*Rendezvous*

"Lori Handeland takes the violence of our history and makes it a powerful setting for an even more powerful love story. The pain of choosing between a vow of hatred and a vow of marriage is hauntingly vivid within Lori's words."

—*The Literary Times*

"Ms. Handeland's way of weaving historic characters into the backdrop of the story is outstanding. The love story is at once enthralling and believable . . . a keeper for any historical romance reader."

—Calico Trails

FULL MOON DREAMS:

"This is my kind of story—a tortured hero redeemed by love. The circus setting adds sparkle; the hero and heroine provide the sparks!"

—Madeline Baker, bestselling author of
Feather in the Wind

MORE PRAISE FOR LORI HANDELAND

FULL MOON DREAMS:

"...a fast-paced, exciting and chillingly delicious tale...Fans of both the supernatural and historical romance genres will rhapsodize over *Full Moon Dreams*!"

—*Affaire de Coeur*

D.J.'S ANGEL:

"*D.J.'s Angel* is a dazzling romance...resplendent with heart-stopping emotion and vibrant in its passion!"

—*Rendezvous*

CHARLIE AND THE ANGEL:

"Ms. Handeland delivers an uplifting story that will warm your heart with a man well deserving of the title 'hero.' "

—*Romantic Times*

SHADOW LOVER:

"...an insightful insight into the mind of evil. A terrific book, start to finish!"

—*The Paperback Forum*

MORE THAN FRIENDS

"I'll miss you. I've always wanted a friend." Julia admitted, staring longingly into Ryan's deep blue eyes.

The whisper of her words fell between them. Heat flared in his eyes like lightning through the sky. He stepped toward her, wrapped his arm about her waist and yanked her against his large, hard body. Her breath caught in her throat. She didn't know what she'd said, but whatever it was, her words had released a stranger.

"I don't want to be your friend," he growled.

Her gaze searched his but she found no answers there. "Then what?"

"This."

His lips crushed hers, as hard as his body, as warm as the night. Every sane thought fled from her mind; insanity took possession. She could think of nothing beyond the languid heat that seemed to infuse her blood, even as her heart thudded ever faster. Her head spun with uncertainty, her body swirled with need, and her mouth begged for more. Though she'd never been kissed, she instinctively knew this kiss was life altering.

Other *Love Spell* books by Lori Handeland:
FULL MOON DREAMS
CHARLIE & THE ANGEL
SHADOW LOVER
D. J.'S ANGEL
SECOND CHANCE

BY ANY OTHER NAME

LORI HANDELAND

LOVE SPELL BOOKS   ✦   NEW YORK CITY

*For my sons, Andrew and Alexander, who have taught
me many things, the most important of which
is how deeply I can love.*

LOVE SPELL®

March 1998

Published by

Dorchester Publishing Co., Inc.
276 Fifth Avenue
New York, NY 10001

If you purchased this book without a cover you should be aware
that this book is stolen property. It was reported as "unsold and
destroyed" to the publisher and neither the author nor the publisher has received any payment for this "stripped book."

Copyright © 1998 by Lori Handeland

All rights reserved. No part of this book may be reproduced or
transmitted in any form or by any electronic or mechanical means,
including photocopying, recording or by any information storage
and retrieval system, without the written permission of the
Publisher, except where permitted by law.

ISBN 0-505-52252-7

The name "Love Spell" and its logo are trademarks of Dorchester
Publishing Co., Inc.

Printed in the United States of America.

By Any Other Name

Chapter One

Julia Colton stood in the doorway of her home, caught between two worlds. In one lay a dream—sunshine and warmth, the scent of earth, grass and water, life and freedom. In the other lay reality—shadows and damp, the stench of herbs and medicine and sickness, death and drudgery.

Guilt flooded her, as it always did when she began to feel sorry for herself. Her future at least held the promise of life. Julia glanced back at the still shape upon the bed. Her mother's held only the certainty of death.

"Mama, I'm going down to the creek to get some fresh, cool water. It'll help your fever."

The shape on the bed shifted, moaned, and then swallowed the sound of pain, of weakness. Elvira Colton's gray, bone-thin face appeared from the nest of blankets, and her feverish eyes met those of her daughter.

"Go on ahead, darlin', I'll just sleep awhile. Why don't you take a little time in the sun? I'll rest better if I'm alone."

Julia gave a quick nod and grabbed the bucket from its resting place next to the door; then she turned away and plunged into the sunshine before her mother could see the tears spill from her eyes.

Mama would not sleep. The pain and the fever would not let her. At times she fell into an exhausted state that resembled death, and when she awoke she was always weaker than before. Whenever Julia urged her to rest, her mother would say, "I'll be restin' for eternity soon enough," and since Julia could not argue with that, she did not argue with Mama at all.

Mama had been bedridden since Julia was a little girl. Too many births, too close together, had weakened her. Then, a few years back, while the boys and her husband had been off harassing the Kansas folk, she and Julia had been caught in a burning cabin. Though Julia had awoken and dragged her mama outside before they both died, Mama's lungs were burned from the smoke, and the doctor said it was only a matter of time until they gave out completely. Julia had never forgiven herself for sleeping too deeply that night, nor forgiven the Hell-sent Jayhawkers for burning the cabin in the first place.

Her mother's admonition to take a little time in the sun made Julia's guilt throb harder and hotter in her stomach. Mama knew she'd been aching to get outside, and in her typical, selfless way, had given Julia a reason to go. Though she felt it was her duty to stay inside and do what she could for Mama, Julia took the gift of freedom and ran with it to the creek.

The day was a surefire keeper—too early in the year to bring the stifling heat common to a Missouri summer, and a cool breeze that smelled of new grass and just-sprung flowers rippled the shiny surface of Colton Creek. Julia put down the bucket and stepped closer. Through water as clear as glass, she watched fish shadows dance along the multicolored bottom rocks.

"Ho, there!" The distant call of her father to the plow horses made her start and jerk her head in that direction.

With her four brothers gone to join the renegade Confederate militia, Sam Colton had more work than he could handle. Not that he begrudged his sons the fight. The Coltons had been Jayhawker-haters since the word was invented, and since the immigrant Irish, abolitionist Murphys had gone and bought the land on the other side of Colton Creek, her father's hatred had become an obsession.

The Murphys' farm, which had once been Colton land, had been sold many years back when times were particularly rough. The fact that the land had not only left Colton hands but had later become a part of Kansas made Julia's father nigh on to obsessed with getting it back, through any means—legal or otherwise. The rumor that the eldest Murphy son had ridden with the group of Jayhawkers who had burned Sam's farm and maimed his wife only made his hatred for the family that much more fierce.

There were always arguments and fistfights whenever her father and Shamus Murphy met up, not to

11

mention an ongoing history of malicious mischief on both their farms. There was even occasional sniper fire from the tree line on the creek. Thus far no one had been seriously injured, though a bullet had once gone through the fleshy part of Julia's oldest brother's hand. Didn't hurt him much, just served to make him madder and meaner.

Since the boys had gone off with Quantrill, Julia's father, who had never been an easy man, had become downright nasty. These days the depth of his anger at the world, and the Murphys in particular, frightened Julia. He had become a hard man, and he would not be happy if he saw Julia malingering at the creek.

Julia reached for the bucket, then hesitated. Mama had told her to stay awhile, and her father was too busy to leave the field before sundown. He'd only come looking for her if she didn't bring him his dinner at noon. A glance at the sky revealed she had at least an hour before then.

In a rare moment of youthful abandon, Julia turned her back on the bucket, pulled off her shoes and stockings, hoisted her skirts and stepped into the shallows.

"Eeek." A short, sharp squeal of surprise escaped her lips when the water, still cold from the winter melt-off, captured her feet. But after the initial shock she began to enjoy the tingle of the cold and the lap of the waves against her calves. Her toes scrunched into the smooth stones, and fish flitted just ahead of her as if leading her onward to a secret, special place.

Mama always said Julia was a dreamer. The life she led had made her so. Mama, a teacher before she'd become a wife, owned a trunkful of books. Julia blessed those books every day. If it hadn't been for those books, Julia would never have believed there were men in the world who did not thrive on murder and mayhem, who did not dismiss women as servants, who did not speak to them as though they were fools. Just once she'd like to meet a man who was strong on the outside but gentle on the inside, a man who could listen and learn, a man who could protect a woman and love her.

Her brothers loved her in their own way, she was certain, and they would protect her with their lives. She had fond memories of their youths together, though the men they'd become bore little resemblance to the children she had known. Their father and the times had produced hard, rough, dangerous men who no longer seemed to have any patience for a sister who did not understand them any more than they understood her.

Julia sighed. She put aside thoughts of the past and an uncertain future. She became so enthralled with the game she played with the fish that she didn't realize she was no longer alone until she laughed at the antics of a particularly brave fish and someone laughed with her.

Her head jerked up. A gasp stuck in her throat. Her heart began to thud with uncertainty, then fear. A man sat on the opposite bank of the creek—the Kansas side. His clothes consisted of bits of Union blue combined with mismatched confiscated pieces. He had Colts in his belt, ammunition strung across his chest and two rifles in the spider scabbards strapped to his horse. There was no question. He was a Jayhawker— part of the renegade Union militia.

13

Trouble.

Julia started backing toward the Missouri side of the creek, but where before the stones had seemed smooth and easy to walk upon, they suddenly became sharp and shifted beneath her feet, causing her to stumble.

The man stood, watching her with a smile that made the water run colder and the sun shine less brightly than before. Julia could hear the frightened rasp of her breath, at odds with the peaceful lap of the creek against its banks. She'd seen his type before, when they'd burned down her home. Now, again, in a single instant, looking into the eyes of this Jay-hawker, she saw all that was bad, and it was coming toward her.

"Well, howdy do?" He began to advance, stepping into the water, his boots causing ripples in the creek, ripples that became bigger and bigger as he waded toward Julia. "And what might you be doin' out here all alone?"

"I-I'm not alone. M-my father's just over the hill."

"Over that hill, you say?" He pointed to the swell of ground behind her. Julia nodded. "Well, that'd make you a Missouri gal, a Bushwhacker woman. Wouldn't it?"

Julia didn't answer. Calling her a Bushwhacker was an insult, but she knew she wasn't in any position to take offense. Why, oh why, had she wandered so far downstream? "H-he'll be coming for me if I don't bring his dinner."

The man's smile widened, though it never reached his eyes. "It's not dinnertime yet, missy, so I believe we've got time for a visit. First me and you, and then, if you like,'' he snickered, ''or even if you don't, you can visit the same with my friends over the Kansas hill yonder.''

All the time he had been advancing, Julia had been retreating. Her heel hit the creek bank, and she stepped out of the water. ''Th-that's mighty nice of you, but I have to get home.''

She hiked up her skirts higher and dashed for the safety of the Missouri hill. If she could get in sight of her father, he could drop the Kansas varmint with a single shot. She hadn't taken two steps before he was on her. She went down hard in the red Missouri dirt. The skirts she'd tried so hard to keep from getting wet tangled with her legs and ground into the blood-colored mud.

She drew in a deep breath to scream, and he shoved her mouth into the dirt, making her see bright, shiny points of light when her nose and teeth met the unyielding earth. The sound of rending cloth and the sudden trickle of cool air across the back of her legs alerted her to the loss of her skirts.

Though she'd spent a great portion of her life nursing her mother, Julia had been raised with four brothers. She knew how to fight, and she knew how to win. Her first elbow jab connected with his ribs.

Sour breath exploded across her cheek, followed by an *oomph*, and he released his hold on her arms. She rolled quickly onto her back and instead of the common knee jab, she drove the heel of her hand into his nose.

Blood spurted and he howled. Then she used her knee, and the howl became a shriek. She was free.

But only for a moment.

The degenerate's screams had brought his friends at a run, and though Julia had been halfway to freedom, the click of their rifles being cocked brought her to a stop. She turned to meet the stares of three more pairs of evil eyes, and she knew her fate was sealed.

Julia swallowed and fought tears. She would not give them the satisfaction of seeing her cry, nor of watching her beg. Though she was twenty years of age and should have been long married, the war and her home situation had left Julia both unmarried and uncertain of men and their intentions. And what she saw in the eyes of these men terrified her.

This was her punishment for taking a selfish minute to herself. She should have known better. As her father had told her often enough, her purpose in life was to care for Mama. Julia had no other duty upon this earth, and if she forgot that, God would punish her for certain.

Julia stood on the banks of Colton Creek and watched the three men carefully ford the stream, keeping their rifles fixed on her. It didn't take them long to splash through the creek and join the first, who had recovered enough to stand. They circled her like a pack of mad dogs. She thought she'd seen all of Hell's fury in the first man's eyes, but now she realized how wrong she'd been.

One reached out with his rifle and poked her in the stomach. She winced but did not retreat. How many times had she fought all four of her brothers and won? Though they were tough and mean, they probably weren't very smart. She knew how to bide her time, wait for an opening and then strike, or run like hell.

The back of her skirt was grabbed and tugged; she

spun in that direction. To her left a flash of movement, then to her right. She began to feel dizzy, sweaty, panicky. She could not catch her breath. A shove from behind made her stumble forward, directly into the arms of the man whose nose she'd bloodied.

"Enough playin'," he snarled. "She knows how to fight, and I don't aim to let her get another shot at me. Let's have done with this." A bloody hand reached for the front of her dress. Rabid eyes glared into hers. "You're gonna beg to die, Bushwhacker bitch." Dirty fingers gripped her neck. She closed her eyes and said a prayer.

I need a hero. A knight with the bravery of Lancelot. The strength of Hercules. The wisdom of Solomon.

Rancid breath filled her mouth and nose. She flinched and her captor laughed.

Or anyone you've got right now will do.

KABOOM!

The gunshot froze them all. Julia's eyes snapped open, and she peered hopefully toward the Missouri hill.

"Help?" she whispered, but all eyes had turned toward the Kansas side of the creek where there stood a single man, his horse and his gun.

Ryan Murphy kept his rifle and his eyes trained on the four men surrounding the girl. They wore the uniform common to the Kansas Jayhawker in 1863—part Federal soldier, part guerilla fighter—but these men were not behaving like soldiers.

"Get away from her," he ordered.

They stared at him as if he'd lost his mind. The one with blood all over his face and his dirty hands all over the girl snickered. "You want some, too, boy? We'll be glad to share. After."

"Back away or I start shooting."

The man's amusement died. "You ain't gonna be able to get all of us with one rifle, boy. If I was you, I'd do the backin' away."

"I might have one rifle, but my men have one each. If you don't get out of here, they'll blow you to Hell and gone."

He put just enough conviction into his words to make the four glance uneasily at the brush, where the tips of several rifles glinted in the sunlight. The leader's eyes narrowed and he scowled at Ryan.

"You aren't a Federal. No uniform. Is you with one of the other Jayhawker bands?"

"Who I am isn't important. Just move on."

"What's the matter with you, boy? She's just a Bushwhacker. We kill women like her every damn day. Or is you one of 'em, too?"

Ryan hesitated. The girl was a Bushwhacker. Perhaps he should just ride away. His family hated the Bushwhackers like no one else—even more than his Irish ancestors had hated the cursed English. The Missouri guerillas had taken his mother's life and his sister's mind. Those tragedies had in turn changed the father Ryan loved into a man whose sanity he questioned more with each passing day.

Ryan risked a glance at the girl and blinked. She was beautiful, even with dirt smeared across her mouth and cheeks and her hair tangled and trailing free of its pins. She was near his age, slight but tall, with creamy skin, wide light eyes and hair of a strange color—black with red streaks the shade of Missouri mud flashing in the sun. Something about that hair sparked his memory, as if he'd seen it or hair like it before, but he could not bring the rest of the thought forth and shook off the strange feeling that he knew the girl.

How could he? He had barely spared a glance for women in the past; he didn't have the time or the inclination. He had no room in his heart or his mind for anything but fulfilling his vow of vengeance. But this beauty, in the space of an instant, captivated him. He'd never seen a female fight like a she-cat. Though he knew he should despise the Bushwhacker woman, he couldn't help but find her fascinating.

Ryan forced his gaze from the girl and back to where it belonged, on the leader of the Jayhawkers. "I'm no Bushwhacker," he snapped. "You cut across my land to get here. I want you off. Now."

"If that was your land, then you're a Kansan. One of us."

"I might be from Kansas, but I don't hold with Jayhawker ways."

"Well, ain't you hoity-toity? At least we're fightin'." The man's lip pulled back into a sneer. "You just stayin' home to protect *your* land?"

Ryan didn't answer. He knew better than most what a Jayhawker band could do. He'd been one himself not long ago. He couldn't say he was proud of that. He was ashamed of what he'd done and what he'd allowed to be done. He had left them and never returned, though he couldn't take back what had happened. As far as he was concerned the Jayhawkers were as bad as the Bushwhackers. Both were simply in it for blood.

"Whatcha care about her for anyway?" the Jayhawker asked, looking peevishly at the restless girl.

Why did he care? Ryan wondered. Maybe because the fight in her eyes and the defiance in her stance reminded him of women he'd loved before.

"I don't abide abusing women, no matter who they are. Now get."

The men considered him for a long, tense moment, and Ryan fought not to let his unease show. He had spent the past several years dealing with men worse than these, and he had learned the quickest way to lose control of a bad situation was to let your fear show.

Sweat trickled down Ryan's back as the Jayhawkers looked first at him, then at the rifles poking through the brush. He considered giving the signal for a warning shot but waited. He feared if a single shot was fired, all Hell would break loose. He would wait until he had no other option.

"Aw, shit," the leader cursed. "I don't have time to be standin' out here in the sun arguin' with a boy. Let's go."

He shoved the girl. She stumbled, her feet tangling in her torn, trailing skirts. Lurching forward, she managed to regain her feet, her hands coming up in front of her, clenched into fists as if she meant to fight them all. But they had already turned away, to splash back across the creek and trudge toward their horses. Ryan shot a glance at the brush and jerked his head, ordering an escort to follow and ascertain that they left Murphy territory immediately. The brush rustled, a single rifle barrel withdrew and Ryan turned back to the girl.

She still stood with fists raised, her gaze narrowed on his face. Her skirt and petticoats ruffled in the breeze, the torn ends hanging free to reveal bare legs. Ryan's gaze flicked to the long expanse of creamy flesh and stuck there. He'd never seen a woman's legs before, at least in the light of day, and these were mighty fine. His interest trailed upward over rounded hips, slim waist and an impressive swell of breasts beneath the muddied, bloodied bodice of an ugly gray gown.

"Well?" she snapped, and his eyes returned to hers. There, anger and fear warred. Despite her fear, this woman was ready for a fight. A spark of admiration lit within him—a spark he quickly doused. Bushwhackers were the enemy, even a Bushwhacker woman. They had no conscience, no mercy, no hearts and no souls. They had murdered his mother and for that they would all pay.

"Well?" she said again. "What do you plan to do?"

"Do?"

"Kidnap? Rape? Murder? What?"

Ryan took a moment to return his Spencer to the scabbard on his saddle. His horse danced a bit, then lowered its head to drink from the creek.

He considered the girl. "Why would I do any of that?"

"You're a Murphy," she sneered.

He narrowed his eyes as a memory tugged at him. Could she be—? Ryan glanced at the Missouri hill, then back at the girl. No. The Colton girl was a child.

21

Too young to leave home alone. That's why no one ever saw her.

"Yes, I'm a Murphy. A Kansan. What of it?"

"Bad through and through. Yankees. Thieves."

The girl had more guts than was good for her. Or perhaps she'd just been pushed past her endurance. His own sister had retreated into silence, maybe when they were in danger, Bushwhacker women just couldn't shut up.

"My pa says the same about Missourans. You're all evil, vile, murderin' savages. Bushwhackers."

At last she dropped her hands. Her back straightened, and she yanked her skirts into place. She stared him straight in the eye, and indignation had burned away the fear. "I am not!"

He stared at her for a long, silent moment. "Neither am I."

Then he turned his horse and left her standing by the banks of the creek.

Julia watched him go, glad he'd ridden away before she'd said something hateful. The man had saved her honor, if not her life, and she should be grateful. Even if he was a Murphy, he'd risked himself and his men to save her. Just like a hero from one of the stories she read to Mama at night—except the heroes in her books never wore the face of an enemy.

She squinted against the sun's glare toward the low brush lining the Kansas side of the creek. She watched the rifle barrels withdraw, one after the other, retreating in perfect precision down the line. After a short rustle of brush near the area of the last rifle, hoofbeats pounded away into the distance.

Julia frowned. She had heard just a single horse. How odd.

Her rescuer must be the eldest Murphy boy, the one she was supposed to hate more than the others because he had hurt Mama. Or so her brothers and her father said.

She'd never actually seen any of the Murphys. The night their farm had burned, the renegades had been mere shadows in retreat as she'd pulled Mama from the burning house. She didn't even know either of the Murphy boys' names, having only heard them referred to as "them damned Murphys."

In a proper world, Mama would be mortified with Julia's lapse of manners in not thanking the young man for saving her life. But their world was neither proper nor sane. How could she even consider exchanging a kind word with the man who had caused her family such pain?

At the thought of her mother, Julia emitted a moan and spun about to race along the creek bank. She grabbed her shoes and socks, then retrieved the bucket, dunked it in the shallows and hurried toward home, not caring how much water sloshed down the front of her skirt. The dress was ruined, and even if it wasn't, she'd never be able to bear wearing the garment again.

Julia glanced at the sky, shoving her damp and tangled hair from her eyes. She had just enough time to change her dress, tend Mama and take dinner to her father. If she didn't dawdle. Still, she took a moment to breathe deeply, hoping to calm her racing heart and stop her hands and knees from shaking. She had been terrified back there. Really terrified for the first time in her life. If that Murphy boy hadn't come along when he had—

Julia broke off the thought, alarmed at the way the memory of the Jayhawker's face and eyes and hands suddenly made her want to weep. She had no time for such things right now.

Julia stepped into the house, careful to keep quiet, but she needn't have bothered. Mama was already awake.

"Lord above, Julia Colton, what happened to you?"

For a moment Julia considered telling her mama everything. Then she saw the gray tinge to Mama's skin and the purple circles beneath her eyes. It would be too much, and there was no point in telling her. "I-I fell. Down into the creek . . ."

Her mother's eyes narrowed. "And tore your dress, too?"

"Y-yes, Mama."

"And climbing out, you mussed your hair and muddied your face?"

"Y-yes, Mama."

Julia couldn't look her mother in the eye now that she'd lied. Instead she busied herself packing a dinner pail for her father. She should have known Mama would not be so easily deceived.

"Come here, child."

"I-I've got to take this to Father. He'll come looking for me otherwise."

And though her father had never yet raised a hand to her, she'd always seen a dangerous glint in his eye. Their relationship, never warm, had gotten worse since the Jayhawker raid. He seemed to blame Julia for Mama's worsening health, berating her for not hearing the Jayhawkers sooner and for not protecting the farm and Mama better than she had.

"Let that set a minute, child, and come here."

Julia sighed. She and her mama were as close as any two people could be. Her mama had carried Julia within her body and given her life. Before Julia was full grown they had reversed roles. Now, they were with each other every day, nearly every hour. She could hide nothing from her mama. Why had she even tried?

Turning away from the pail, Julia crossed the room and sat on the chair next to the bed. Her mother's gasp made her look up from a rapt contemplation of her clasped hands.

"What's the matter?" Julia asked. "Do you hurt worse?"

Her mother's gaze was fixed on Julia's bodice. "There's blood on your dress, child."

Julia looked down and almost groaned aloud. Bloody fingerprints marred the gray cloth. There would be no lying her way around this, even if she had been a decent liar. But perhaps she could make the story sound a bit better, less frightening, if she tried.

"There were some men at the creek."

Mama's ashen face paled further. "Did they hurt you?"

"Not as much as I hurt one of them."

Her mother raised her eyebrows at that. "How did you get away?"

"A man came. . . ." Julia paused as she remembered the burnished gold of the Murphy boy's hair,

25

the way his eyes had shone blue against the sun-darkened skin of his face. Though he had never gotten down from his horse, the length of the stirrups made her think he was taller than any man she'd ever known, well over six feet. The memory of his hands, sure upon the rifle, and the command in his voice when he'd ordered the Jayhawkers to leave caused an odd, shaky feeling in the pit of her stomach that she desperately told herself was hate.

"A young man," she amended, then met her mother's curious gaze. "He was like a-a knight from the storybooks we've read. He rode up on a horse, not white, gold, like his hair. He faced four men older than him, and they listened." Julia didn't add that his men were covering him from the brush. He'd still ridden to her rescue alone.

She smiled at her mother, but her mother did not smile back. "What else, child?"

Julia had hoped she would not have to tell the bad part, but her mother knew she was hedging.

"He said he was a Murphy."

Mama looked into her face for a long, searching moment. The way she stared made Julia's cheeks burn, though she did not know why. Then her mother sighed and leaned back against the pillow. "You must never see him again," she whispered, the sound ancient, defeated.

"What?"

"The Murphy boy. Never again. Your father would—" Her voice broke, almost as if she was near tears.

"Mama!" Julia went down on her knees next to the bed and grabbed her mother's hands. They were ice cold, despite her fever, and they shook beneath Julia's own. "You're sicker. I'm sorry I stayed away so long. I-I couldn't help it."

Suddenly her mother's fingers turned, grasped hers with surprising strength, and her eyes, as green as her daughter's but fever bright, captured Julia's with their fervency. "You must not see him again. Promise me."

"But Mama, why would I see him? He came by and helped me is all. Besides, I think he's the one who hurt you. I hate him! I do."

Mama shook her head. "I saw your face just now when you spoke of him. I heard your voice. You're young, beautiful, and you've been trapped here with me. You dream of heroes and knights and things that aren't true and can't ever be. The forbidden calls us all. I should never have let you read all those books. Your father always said they'd make you crazy as me—wishing, hoping, praying for dreams to come true. I know about temptation, Julia, and the disaster it can bring. Not just on you but on everyone you love."

"I don't understand."

"You don't. I know. I've never explained to you what happens between a man and a woman. Love and hate, passion and pain. You can ruin your life, Julia, for a few moments' pleasure. When you're young you don't think beyond right now. You believe you'll never die. You never think about consequences or guilt or blame. You only think of those things when you're old." Her hands fell away from Julia's to lay listlessly at her side, and she turned her face to the wall. "Like me."

Julia didn't know what to do. She reached out and pressed her own shaking fingers to her mother's brow, wondering if Mama was delirious. It wouldn't be the first time. But the flesh beneath her fingertips felt cooler than before and damp with a light sweat. The fever had broken. Mama should be better, not worse.

Her mother jerked her head away from Julia's fingers. "Go tend your father. I'm not out of my head. Leastways not the way you think. I should have known something like this would happen. The sins of the fathers . . ." Her voice drifted off.

Julia stood, staring down at her mama's face. A tear traced one cheek. That tear frightened Julia more than anything else. In all the years of pain and illness, she had never seen her mama cry. "Mama? Don't cry. I won't see the Murphy boy again. It was nothing. I just thought to tell you a story is all. I didn't want to scare you."

Her mama didn't answer, and Julia turned away to take her father his dinner. She needn't have bothered. Her father filled the doorway.

His dark, furious gaze swept over her disheveled, torn dress and unbound hair. His mouth tightened and he roared, "What Murphy boy?"

Chapter Two

Julia swallowed and glanced at her mother, who had struggled up onto her elbows to stare at her husband. Two bright spots of color flamed in the midst of her mama's sheet-white cheeks. Her lips were pursed together as if in pain, and Julia took a step toward her. Her mother shot her a glare. Julia stopped, hovering between her parents, feeling an odd tension between them and unable to understand its source.

"It's nothing, Sam. The girl just fell in the creek. No cause to get upset."

Julia nearly gaped. Mama had lied. She'd never known her mama to lie, and since she must have a reason, Julia kept her own mouth shut.

"I heard her say Murphy. It's bad enough them damn, thievin' Yanks bought the land that was mine, but they call Colton Creek, Murphy Creek. It's been

Colton Creek since my daddy's daddy was a baby.''

"I know, Sam." Mama sighed and eased back on the pillows. She was no longer able to sit up for longer than a moment.

Her father stepped inside, and Julia had to fight the urge to step back, her fear of him washing over her as he glared into her face.

"I'll ask ya one more time, girl, what Murphy boy?''

Such anger, such hatred filled his eyes, Julia found she couldn't talk even if she'd wanted to. His hands clenched, as if he wanted to strike her, but a glance at his wife made his face tighten before he stepped away.

"What happened, Vi? Why is she all torn and dirty and bloody? I protect my own. Ya know that. I'll have the truth. If not from you, then from her.''

"I told you what happened. She fell. Now leave her be. Take your dinner and go or you'll never finish for the day.''

Sam Colton's pale skin, tinged pink from the sun and the heat, darkened to red. He moved forward and Julia, despite her fear, put herself between him and her mother. He ignored her.

"You're lying," he hissed. "Ya swore ya'd never lie to me again.''

Mama didn't answer, and Julia turned to see if her mother had fainted. But Mama's eyes were wide open, staring at her husband in shock and anger.

Suddenly Julia's arm was grasped so tightly she winced.

"Sam!" her mother shouted, then began to cough.

Julia tried to go to her, but her father yanked her

about. "If your mama won't tell me the truth, you will. What Murphy boy? Was he on our land? What did he say to you? Did he do this?" He indicated her torn, muddy, bloody dress.

Julia didn't know what to do. Her father looked mad enough to hit or to kill, but her mama had lied to keep him from knowing about Julia's rescuer. If Mama had lied, whatever her reason, Julia must do the same.

"No, Father. I-I didn't see anyone."

He grabbed her by the shoulders and shook her until she thought her teeth might rattle out of her mouth. "You lie. You're as much of a liar as your mother. I should have known ya'd end up just like her."

"Sam! You swore you'd never hurt her!"

He glanced over Julia's shoulder and snarled, "And ya swore ya'd never lie to me."

The room became silent, the only sounds Mama's labored breaths at war with her husband's and her daughter's.

Julia's father turned back toward her, and in his eyes lurked fury and purpose. "If neither of ya will tell me the truth, I'll find it out my own way."

He strode from the room, dragging Julia behind him.

"What happened to the wee colleen?"

Ryan's brother, Jason, cantered up on his apron-faced mare, startling Ryan from his thoughts. And a good thing, too. His thoughts had been stuck on the girl since he'd left her at the creek. Something about her bothered him.

He glanced at Jason and shrugged. "I reckon she went on home. Where she should have been in the first place."

Jason nodded, though his grin and the knowing, annoying look in his eye made Ryan think he meant to say more. Before his brother could open his mouth, Ryan tossed him two rifles. Jason had to use both hands to catch them and his knees to keep his horse under control.

"Hey, what'd you do that for?"

"I'm not carrying your rifles as well as mine. Jayhawkers leave?"

"Uh huh." Jason's grin, never absent for long, returned. "You sure were right about settin' our rifles up in the brush to look like there was more of us. They didn't even argue with you, Ry. I wish I could stare men down like you do. You'll be an officer for sure, if we ever get to join the real army."

The usual exuberance that lightened Jason's voice disappeared with the last sentence. Raised on the stories of their grandfather's exploits in Ireland against the English, they had played at soldiering since they could walk. They had wanted little else in life but to be in uniform. Ever since their mother's death in a Bushwhacker attack five years ago, when Ryan was fifteen and Jason was eleven, they had lived and breathed vengeance along with their da. Soldiering had become a means to an end.

A year after their ma's death, the Murphys moved south, away from the heavy fighting that had crisscrossed their first farm and made living there impossible. No sooner than they had bought this farm, their father and Sam Colton had taken one look at each other and hated on sight. Their ancestry—Irish and English—had made the hatred natural. Even the land over which they argued made the fight reminiscent of the one that still raged across the sea—the English coveting the beauty of the Irish countryside for their own just as Colton coveted the more prosperous Murphy farm.

Still, they might have avoided a family feud but for one thing: Ryan's desperate need to keep his vow of vengeance. Grief-stricken and guilt-plagued he had run off and joined a Jayhawker band, believing that any fight was a good one if it was against those who had hurt his ma. But he'd learned differently one night when the Jayhawkers had slipped onto Colton land. The boys and Sam weren't there, but the old lady and the girl were. Their screams still rang in Ryan's head.

Thankfully neither had been killed, but the injury to Mrs. Colton had turned the minor skirmishes and fistfights between the Coltons and the Murphys into something much deeper. The Coltons were out for blood, and the Murphys had no choice but to be bound for the same.

Torn, Ryan had turned his back on the Jayhawkers and joined the Border Patrol. The sanctioned Kansas militia seemed his best chance to help keep his family safe from the marauding Coltons. Even when true war was declared and Ryan could have joined the Union and become the soldier he'd always dreamed of, he had remained with the Border Patrol. Family came first, and Ryan could not abandon them to the revenge of an enemy he had provoked. But now that the Coltons had run off with Quantrill, he found little or no hostile activity to defend his family from. Ryan ached to wear Union blue and fight the real war—for real reasons.

Ryan's thoughts returned to the present as he and his brother rode into the yard. Sliding down from his horse, he glanced at the sky. Just past noon. He and Jason could take dinner out to Da in the fields when they returned to work and save Kathleen the trip. They'd have to work harder and longer to make up the time they'd lost, but Da had been insistent that they patrol the area. They had to be especially careful with Kathleen the way she was.

Ryan and Jason took care of the horses, then turned them loose in the corral. Together they walked toward the house.

"Think Da might let me go back with you when your leave's up?"

Ryan shrugged. Da had needed help getting the spring crop in, and with the leniency of a farm community, the patrol allowed each member leave to help at home if needed. He had to return to his unit in a week.

"So what was she like? The Reb colleen?"

Ryan glanced sideways at Jason and frowned. Though their father spoke with a brogue, Jason and Ryan had been born and raised in the New World. They called their father by the Irish endearment *da* at his request, but Jason always seemed to work a bit of the Irish into his speech, an affectation that annoyed Ryan to no end. Most likely it was meant to.

Despite Ryan's scowl, Jason just grinned and winked. "The Reb colleen, Ry? Remember?"

For some reason that wink made Ryan mad. "She was a girl is all."

"Not just a girl. A right beautiful colleen, as it were. Did you see those legs? That hair? Whooee! She was a looker, even all dirty and bloody. I'd like to see what she looks like prettied up."

Ryan stopped and grabbed his brother by the shirt-front, yanking him close. "You won't be seein' her no way, Jase. You leave that Bushwhacker woman be."

Jason's grin widened. "I think you like her."

With a grumble of disgust, Ryan shoved his brother and turned away. Before he'd taken a step, Jason tackled him from behind, and they went down hard in the dirt.

Why Jason always insisted upon wrestling him Ryan had no idea. Ryan was older, bigger, and Jason just didn't have enough mean in him to be a good fighter. But he did love to wrestle.

Ryan flipped Jason onto his stomach, straddled him and yanked his arm up between his shoulder blades. "Take it back," he ordered.

Jason laughed. "No. You liked her. I saw your face when you looked at her the first time. You not only liked her, I think you loved her!"

Ryan gave his brother's arm a sharper yank. "Take it back."

"Never."

Before Ryan knew what he was about, Jason executed a new maneuver, leaning into his captured arm and bucking Ryan sideways. Ryan slammed onto the ground hard enough to grunt, suddenly blinking at the sunny sky. He scowled as Jason straddled him, pressing a forearm into Ryan's throat, just enough to make his eyes water.

Jason smiled, his big white teeth ablaze beneath joyous blue eyes and hair as red as fire. "Say you liked her."

"Can't—talk—" Ryan wheezed, and Jason, who had no subterfuge in him, lightened his hold enough for Ryan to lift his knees and fling Jason over his head.

"Umph." All the air in Jason's lungs rushed out when he landed on his back in the dirt.

The two of them lay there awhile, getting their breath back. Ryan closed his eyes against the sun's glare, but when a shadow fell across his eyelids, he opened them to find Kathleen staring down at him.

He looked back at her, uncertain these days of what to say, what to do, when it came to his big sister. She'd once been pretty, in a tall, strapping way, her strawberry hair and blue-gray eyes striking and her full-throated laugh as joyous as Jason's grin. But now, her hair threaded with gray, her eyes dull with pain, and her clothes hanging from a too-thin frame, she looked years older than the twenty-eight Ryan knew her to be.

Kathleen looked from Ryan's face to his dusty clothes, then flicked a glance toward Jason. Her lips twitched, and she rolled her eyes heavenward in a perfect imitation of their mother's disgust over her boys' fights. This was the first sign of emotion Kathleen had shown since her husband's death.

Ryan sat up. Jason did, too. They glanced at each other and smiled. Perhaps Kathleen would be all right after all.

"Hey, Katie," Jason said. "Wanna go for a ride later?"

The momentary expression that had lit her face disappeared, and the blankness returned. Kathleen turned away and headed for the house. Since her husband, Stan Simmons, had died the year before, she had not spoken. Her eyes still screamed in terror whenever a soldier came too near, and she never went any farther from the cabin than necessary. Even her trip to the field to bring them dinner each day left her shaking and pale. She would run all the way home once she'd done her duty to the family.

Ryan watched his sister disappear into the cabin, and the burn in his stomach grew. The pain had been his constant companion since he'd buried his mother so many years before. He wanted to make every last Bushwhacker pay for what they'd done to his mother and Kathleen. Standing, Ryan offered a hand to his brother. "What'd you go and say that for, Jase?"

Jason's sigh was as close to sadness as Jason ever showed. He took the proffered hand and lurched to his feet. "I don't know. I just thought, maybe, she was better. Maybe she'd answer me. Be her old self."

"I don't think her old self is there anymore."

Jason sighed again. "I think you're right."

They were silent for a moment; then Jason gave him a sideways, uneasy glance, and Ryan tensed. Jason rarely felt uneasy about anything. When his brother spoke again Ryan understood why Jason looked like ants crawled in his pants.

"You aren't any better. Since Ma died you've changed. You used to be fun. You laughed. You joked. I could talk to you and you listened. But now all you think about is war and revenge. You're worse than Da sometimes. I miss that other brother. I'm lonely, Ry.''

The burning flared hotter in Ryan's gut. He had changed. He'd watched evil men do evil things and been unable to stop them from killing what he loved. He and his ma had been close; they had shared dreams, spoken easily of what was in their secret hearts. They had shared a hope of freedom for all men, and her joy in finding a country that shared her dream. Though most Irish despised the Negroes, fearing their freedom from slavery would steal jobs from the immigrants, Ryan's ma had seen only the injustice. She had wanted to help change the world. She had encouraged Ryan's dream of following in the footsteps of his grandfather, making the life of a soldier his own, protecting and serving the country his ma had taught him to love with all his heart.

She had thought him a hero in the making, and he had wanted to become that hero with all the passion his youth and innocence had to offer. When she died, his open, gentle heart died too, giving birth to a young man with a closed, angry, vengeful soul. The only way to make the guilt, the burn, go away was to make the ones who had destroyed his life pay, yet the things he'd done to enact vengeance had only made the pain worse. Because in some ways he'd become as bad as those he sought to destroy.

''You tellin' me you don't miss Ma?'' Ryan demanded. ''You don't look at Kathleen and want to hit something, or someone? You don't hate every last Missouran for what they did to them?''

"The entire state of Missouri ain't responsible for Ma or for Kathleen."

Ryan felt betrayed by the one he trusted the most. Furious at Jason's calm face and disgusted with the truth that lay in his words, Ryan clenched his fists and lowered his voice. When he spoke the softest, he meant it the most. "Of course they're to blame. It's their hate and their greed that caused this war. They killed Ma just because of who she was, where she lived."

"So we should do the same?"

"You defending them?"

"No. But I'm not gonna let hate eat me alive from the inside out. If you do, then they've won. If you can't admire a pretty girl or imagine kissing her in the sun, simply because of where she was born, then you're already dead, Ry. Don't you see?"

Ryan did see, but he had hated too long and too hard to stop now. He didn't know if he even wanted to try. If he didn't fulfill his vow to make the enemy pay, would the pain in his stomach ever go away? Would he ever be able to sleep without the nightmares and the memories? Would he ever be able to forgive himself for not being a hero when a hero was needed the most?

"You don't want to join up then?" Ryan asked.

"Of course I do. That's my dream. Yours too. We've talked about it every night since we could talk at all. But there's a difference between joining up 'cause it's the right thing to do and joining up to wipe out every man in Missouri, hoping we get the one who killed Ma. She wouldn't want that, Ry, and you know it."

39

Ryan had no answer for that. Still, he couldn't stop himself from despising men such as the Colton boys, who spread terror wherever they rode just for the pleasure of it. Taking care of men like those would be his duty—even if he hadn't watched them kill his mother. But he had hurt theirs. Was an eye for an eye the answer?

The two of them stood there, shoulder to shoulder, until the sound of approaching hoofbeats made them trace fingertips across the grips of their pistols and turn toward the road.

A man rode into the yard. He was their father's age, with salt-and-pepper hair, a ruddy complexion and the clothes of a farmer; it wasn't until he yanked his horse to a stop that Ryan recognized the old man as their enemy. As the fury flared in his belly, he saw the girl clinging to the saddle. Her face shone pale and stricken beneath a tangle of hair, the mud still smeared across her nose and mouth. Confusion mixed with his hate. What was she doing with Colton?

Ryan's brow creased and he looked into her eyes. Hers were wide and frightened. She shook her head at him frantically, as if trying to tell him something, though he couldn't figure out what. His memory nudged him again, a thought just beyond his reach—a younger face, frightened eyes, hair a strange shade in the dancing light of flames, a mouth too young to shout the curses that had risen above the crackle and burn to follow him off into the night.

As Colton drew his pistol and pointed the weapon at him and then Jason, Ryan inched in front of his brother, though Jason tried to shoulder him aside. They both froze and stared when the man spoke.

"Which one of ya boys attacked my daughter?"

The word *daughter* made the image-memory that had been haunting Ryan's mind become clear. Four years had made her a woman, but in her eyes he caught a glimpse of the girl who had screamed curses at his back as he'd fled the scene of his second worst nightmare.

"Daughter?" the young man mumbled, a multitude of conflicting emotions warring in his eyes.

If Julia hadn't wanted to dig a hole and crawl into it before, she certainly did now. Obviously he hadn't known who she was or he'd have let those men hurt her. She should have expected no less from a man who had reputedly burned her home down about her ears not four years past.

Julia hadn't known what her father meant to do when he'd dragged her from the cabin and ordered her to ride with him. She'd fought at first, but the madness in his eyes had stopped her, frightened her into stoic compliance. Now she wished she'd done anything but accompany him. The Colton-Murphy feud was alive and well and about to explode before her eyes.

"Well?" he shouted. "Which one of ya is going to own up to what ya did? Be a man, now."

"Father, please," she whispered, mortified.

He ignored her horror, keeping his gun pointed at the two young men—one, the man who had helped her, the second, a younger boy she'd never seen before—though the matching shades of their blue eyes assured that they were brothers, despite the differing hair colors and expressions.

"Colton, we didn't do anything but help your girl," her golden-haired rescuer stated in the deep, commanding voice that made Julia think he was much older than he looked.

Her father was not impressed. "I came home to find her lookin' like this with the name Murphy on her lips. Just look at her and tell me ya didn't touch her."

The young man glanced at her, the guilt she'd seen in his eyes gone, a reflection perhaps, not the truth, replaced by a disdain that made her cringe. He thought she'd brought down her father's wrath upon him. She wanted to die.

"I didn't touch her," he said, staring into her eyes all the while.

"Liars. Thieves. All of ya." Julia's father glanced back at her. "Get down, girl. Show 'im closer the mess he made of ya."

"No, Father," she whispered. "He didn't—"

"Don't tell me no," he shouted and shouldered her from the horse.

She landed on her hip in the dirt, and her hair swung forward to cover her face. She let the strands hang there to cover her tears and her confusion. Her father had never liked her, but he'd never been mean before. He'd just ignored her existence, treating her more like a nurse or housekeeper than a daughter. But today's events seemed to have sent him sliding past an edge of reason she had not known he tottered near.

The scrape of a boot nearby made her glance through a small opening in the curtain of her hair.

Dusty boots and dusty brown trousers appeared. With a shaking hand, Julia smoothed back her hair and stared up into the solemn blue eyes of the young man. His mouth a thin line of anger, the hand he held out to her stayed steady and sure.

She took his hand, and her eyes widened at the tingle of awareness that seemed to begin at the tips of her fingers and flow all the way up her arm. He pulled her to her feet, but he did not let go of her hand. Instead, he continued to hold her fingers in his as he stared into her face with a bemused expression. It was as if he felt it, too, this strange connection, and knew as little as she what to do about it.

"Get away from her, ya Yankee bastard," her father thundered, cocking his gun.

Another gun clicked nearby, and the young man released her to spin around. "Jason, put that gun away," he ordered the red-haired boy.

"Not until he does." Though his eyes had laughed when Julia first saw him, Jason's eyes were not laughing anymore.

The sound of hoofbeats made all the guns swing in that direction, all the eyes focus on the rider fast approaching. A man the same age as her father, the red of his hair faded with age, the blue of his eyes a match for those of his sons, stopped the horse, yanked his rifle from the scabbard and jumped to the ground.

"Boys, just what is goin' on here?" The charm of his Irish brogue was spoiled by the scowl on his face.

Julia's father slid to the ground, too, and closed the distance between himself and the eldest Murphy. The two men stood as near as their rifles, cocked and trained on each other, would allow. "One of your filthy get put his hands on my girl. From the way he's pawed her so far, I'd lay odds it's your eldest, and I wouldn't put it past him, since harmin' Colton women is his specialty. Why's he here, anyway? The Border Patrol too tough for him? He had to run home to Daddy?''

Murphy's bushy, sandy eyebrows drew together over his nose, and he threw a glare at his son. ''What's he talkin' about, Ryan?''

His name was Ryan. Julia grasped that information as the young man sighed and turned away, as if he could no longer stand to be near her. When he approached the two older men, his brother stepped up beside their father, pistol ready in his hand.

Unease trickled down Julia's back. Her father was outnumbered and outgunned. His unreasonable anger had brought them here; would his irrational beliefs get them killed? If the Murphys wanted to, they could kill both Julia and her father, bury them on their property, and no one would be the wiser. Certainly Mama might guess where they'd gone and could tell her sons when they returned, but by then it would be too late for Julia or her father. Dead was dead.

''Da. Colton. Put up the guns before someone gets killed.''

They ignored him, continuing to glare at each other for so long that Julia held her breath. If one decided to shoot, would they all end up dead? Most likely. Her breath rushed out in relief when at last they uncocked their rifles and lowered them. Jason reholstered his pistol, and the air in the yard seemed to cool.

''What are ye doin' on me land, Colton?''

''Ya heard me. Look at the girl. Someone tried to

ruin her. I know ya don't have much for conscience, but even I'm surprised at this.''

Julia couldn't keep quiet any longer. "Father, he never touched me. He helped me. He didn't know I was a Colton at the time, and probably would have ridden on by if he knew, but he made those other men go. Why won't you believe me?''

She took a deep breath, having lost all her air along with the words that had tumbled from her mouth as quickly as she could speak, wanting to get them out before her father silenced her again. Her heart began to hammer against her breast when he stepped close and leaned forward to face her nose to nose. "Shut your runnin' mouth, girl. Not another word or I'll shut it for ya. Got that?''

Julia swallowed and nodded. When had her father's eyes taken on that wild, unfocused look? She stared into them, fascinated, reminded of a rabid farm dog they'd once had to shoot before it ran mad amid the others.

Ryan Murphy continued to argue. "I didn't touch her, Da. All I did was stop some Jayhawkers from doing something a lot worse than touching her.''

Her father spun away; the suddenness of his movement made Julia flinch, her reaction causing a frown to appear upon Ryan's face. The frown remained as her father approached him.

"Nice try, boy, but I saw the way ya pawed her when she fell, the way ya looked at her. Ya expect me to believe ya didn't violate her? After what ya did to my wife and my farm I know ya have no conscience, and ya don't care who gets hurt.''

Ryan lost his temper for the first time. "I didn't

touch her," he shouted. "Hell, I never even crossed Murphy Creek."

That was the wrong thing to say to Sam Colton. His face flushed purple and his eyes flashed fire. "It's Colton Creek, ya sad excuse for a man, just like this is Colton land and will be forevermore. On my side of the border, less than this is cause for a shotgun."

Ryan's father scowled and stepped close enough to Julia's father to bump chests. "Are ye tryin' to get me boy to marry yer old-maid daughter?"

Her father took a step forward, shoving Murphy back a foot. "If he were anything other than a yellow, Kansas bastard—but she's better off dead than a Federal whore."

Murphy growled low in his throat and tackled her father around the waist. They went down in the dust, rifles falling away as they punched and kicked and shouted. The two boys looked at each other, shrugged and started to shout encouragement to their father. Julia ran forward and then jumped out of the way of the roiling mass of legs and arms at her feet.

"Aren't you going to stop them?" she shouted over the scuffles and curses.

"What for?" Jason yelled back. "Let 'em get it out of their system."

Which they did. The two older men pummeled and pounded each other until they were both bruised and bloody. The fight didn't end until her father rolled close enough to his discarded rifle to pick up the weapon and aim it at Murphy.

An instant later two pistols were cocked and pressed against her father's head. "Don't do it, old man," said Ryan.

46

Julia's father hesitated. Then he cursed and threw the rifle aside. When the two Murphys moved back, he got to his feet. The elder Murphy followed. The two were breathing heavily and simply glared at each other.

"Well?" Colton asked.

"Well, what?"

"What are ya gonna do about your son ruinin' my girl?"

"I—never—touched—her," Ryan said through his teeth.

"If ye don't want him to marry her—not that I'd allow it, mind ye—then what d'ye want?"

Her father smiled, a thin, nasty smile she'd never seen him use before. "Satisfaction."

Murphy didn't seem to like the smile any more than Julia. He frowned. "What d'ye mean?"

"Just return my farm and move along. Then there won't be any more trouble."

"I paid fer this land fair and square. Ye lost it long ago through no fault of mine. And what would ye be needin' another farm for anyway? From what I hear ye have enough trouble workin' yer own since yer boys up and run off."

"They wouldn't have had to run off if it weren't for the damned Yankees and their Oaths of Loyalty and Enrollment Acts."

Murphy smiled. "I heard how the Federal soldiers took yer crop and yer cattle when ye wouldn't swear their oath. Lucky they didn't burn yer house t' the ground like the last time. Right nice of them, too, t' let ye stay out of the fight t' take care of yer sick wife."

47

Her father's fists clenched at the insult. "It's your little bastard who made her near death in the first place."

"If ye'd been home protectin' yer own, nothin' like that would've happened."

Julia thought her father might have apoplexy right there and then. Murphy had touched a sore spot with those words. Her father had been plagued by guilt over that horrible night. Sometimes Julia wondered if his increasing disgust with her these past few years had been a reflection of his disgust with himself. She knew for certain that the feud had worsened because of the raid and the guilt-fueled fury all the Colton men carried because of that one night. She wondered how Ryan felt.

"If I could do it again . . ." Sam's voice shook with anger and so did the hands he'd clenched into fists at his sides. "I'm not afraid. Of you or any other Yankee bastard. Now what's your answer? Do ya return what's mine or do I send a message into the brush?"

"This land is Murphy land. There'll be no givin' nor any takin'."

"Then there'll be trouble. A lot of trouble. Once I tell the boys on my side of the border what yours did to my gal, there'll be trouble like ya never dreamed of, Murphy."

"Go t' Hell."

Her father smiled his new, nasty smile and answered, "You first."

Julia looked at each of the four men in turn. They were at an impasse. She had to do something, and even though she'd tried before to no avail, she tried one last time to tell the truth.

"He didn't do anything, Father. I swear."

"Shut up, girl. I wouldn't believe ya if ya swore on the Holy Book. Now we'll let them think on this, on what might happen, and we'll get on home." He turned and walked toward his horse, throwing a final taunt back over his shoulder. "I'll deal with ya there."

Julia did not want to go with him, but she had little choice. She turned to follow. A touch on the arm made her pause. She looked up into the eyes of Ryan Murphy. In their blue depths she saw both confusion and anger. It was as if he didn't want to touch her, to help her, to comfort her, but couldn't seem to stop himself. Perhaps he did feel just a little bit bad about what he'd done in the name of his cause.

"Will he hurt you?" he asked.

"I-I don't know. I don't think so." Julia took a deep breath. "No, he won't."

Ryan glanced at her father, then back at her, and his voice lowered to a whisper that made Julia's insides go warm and fluttery. "You're sure?"

Julia stared into his eyes, and she saw something she'd never seen before, something she couldn't identify. Compelled, entranced, tempted, she wanted to learn what that look meant, and she wanted to learn it from him.

But since his name was Murphy, she knew she never would.

Chapter Three

The trip home was silent. Julia would rather have walked, anything to avoid being near her father, but when she'd suggested it, he'd snarled at her. So she remained where she was, holding on to the back of the saddle, clutching the horse with her legs as her torn skirts flapped in the breeze.

Her father pulled the animal to a stop several hundred feet from the house and put a hand on his rifle. Julia leaned sideways to look past his shoulder. Horses milled through the yard.

"Mama," she whispered, and jumped to the ground.

"Hold, girl, some of them's your brothers' horses. They must be back from Texas." With a whoop and a holler he kicked his horse into a gallop, leaving Julia to follow on foot.

Her father might be happy to see his boys, but she wasn't. The number of horses meant they'd brought their partisan friends along. That Frank James made her nervous, and the two Bills, Quantrill and Anderson, were downright frightening. Cole Younger wasn't so bad, but more often than not he wasn't with the guerillas when they came to call. Right now, Julia would like nothing better than to hide in her room, but she couldn't leave her mama alone with this rabble.

Julia was surprised to see Jesse James, who at fourteen had been told by Quantrill he was too young to ride with them, on guard outside of the house with his brother, Frank. Since the partisans had been away for the winter, Jesse had most likely come to meet up with Frank. Neither of the James boys acknowledged her approach but kept their gazes focused on the road and the bushes.

Julia slipped into the house where her brothers, father and the two Bills stood about. None of the men even noticed her entrance. Mama still lay in bed, and at the sight of Julia, a tiny bit of color seeped back into her pasty gray face. Julia smiled and nodded to reassure Mama, but her smile froze when she heard what her father was saying.

"It's not bad enough what he did to your ma, but just look what that Murphy boy did to your sister. He's gonna pay. They're all gonna pay. Time's come to get serious about this feud, boys. Dead serious."

Julia's four brothers—Abner, Ben, Clark and Delbert—replicas of her father in diminishing age and ascending size, turned their black zealot's eyes upon her. They had taken to their pa's teachings like birds to the air, hating the Kansas folk even more than he, if that were possible, and the Murphys most of all. They, too, felt guilt at not having protected their mama better, and that guilt was magnified by their pride; they hated none so much as those who burned their farm and stole their self-respect.

Even Del, the youngest and the biggest, whom Julia thought might have an ounce of compassion left in him, hated with a ferocity that was terrifying. She had practically raised Del these last few years and had loved him very much. But even her love hadn't been enough to keep Del from becoming mean and hateful just like the rest. He followed wherever they led, which had been straight into war.

When the Union government, to which the state of Missouri pledged allegiance in word if not in spirit, had ordered all able-bodied men between the ages of eighteen and forty-five to join their army, the four Colton boys had slipped into the bush and found another way. In Quantrill's Raiders they'd discovered men as vicious as themselves and gone about turning their hatred upon the enemy. Now she realized with growing horror that their father meant to use her mishap to turn the wrath of his monstrous creations, along with their vicious comrades, upon the Murphys.

While a day earlier she would have shrugged and let them go, today she'd been aided by a Murphy. She owed a debt. Though she'd lived her life with men whose sense of honor swayed in any meager breeze, she'd spent her dreams with men whose honor was legendary. She preferred to think her sense of honor had been molded by the latter. She would not rest easy until her debt was paid.

Julia hurried past her brothers and the rest to stand

in front of her father. "No, Father, you have to stop this! He didn't do anything but help me. There were Jayhawkers at the creek, and they would have hurt me if he hadn't stopped them."

Her father scowled into her face, then spat at her feet. Julia flinched at the crudity but did not lower her gaze; she had learned long ago that to show weakness in her house was to surrender completely. When she didn't back down, her father dismissed her with a sneer and turned toward the men sitting at the table, the two Bills, the leaders. "She keeps sayin' that. I think he's turned her head, which is all the more reason to kill him. Though I've been wantin' that one dead since he rode with the bunch who torched my place."

Bill Quantrill nodded in solemn agreement or perhaps consideration of her father's words, Julia knew not which. Quantrill would never have been taken for a guerilla fighter if seen on the street. Tall and slim, with sandy blond hair, a thin boyish mustache and blue eyes, he looked more the schoolmaster he'd been a few years back. But he was no longer a teacher. A self-styled colonel, he was one of the most vicious rebel leaders in Missouri.

As tame as Quantrill looked, his companion, Bloody Bill Anderson, looked the opposite. His straggling black beard, flamboyant dress and renowned habit of attaching human scalps to his horse looked rational when compared to the feverish gleam that burned in his eyes. He did not speak now either, he merely looked into Julia's eyes and smiled.

The world wavered, and Julia fought against the bright spots of light in front of her face. The two Bills might frighten her, they wanted to, but as much as she disliked what her brothers had become, the fact remained that she was safe in their presence.

That knowledge gave Julia the strength she needed to speak. "Colonel Quantrill, there were Jayhawkers at the creek not more than a few hours ago. They attacked me, and I'd appreciate it mightily if you went after them."

Anderson scowled when she addressed Quantrill instead of him, but Julia knew better than to reason with a rabid animal. Quantrill was on the edge, but he hadn't dove into the deep. Yet.

Quantrill frowned at her, a frown of concentration, not anger, and Julia held her breath. If he said so, the entire band would go after the Jayhawkers, or they would descended on the Murphys—just like her father wanted.

"You say there were Jayhawkers at the creek. Your pa says these Murphys are the enemy." Though studiously polite in tone, Quantrill's flat, Yankee voice, so different from the southern lilt of her family and their friends, always startled Julia, reminding her that Quantrill came from Ohio, not here.

"The Murphys *are* the enemy," her father snarled. "That damned kid crippled Vi."

What her father said was the truth, or as close to the truth as they knew. Julia had screamed her fury at the backs of their attackers, but their faces had been shadowed by the night. Maybe Ryan Murphy had burned her home and crippled her mama, and maybe he had not. Perhaps that rumor had been put about by her father in an effort to justify his feud for the land he would forever covet. Either way, she lived, unharmed, because of Ryan Murphy, and that she could not forget.

"Father's just looking to use you, Colonel. He wants the Murphy farm. He told them they had to turn it over or he'd send you over there."

"Shut up, girl, or I'll shut ya up." That threat had been snarled at her so many times today, Julia didn't give it much thought. She wondered momentarily what her brothers would do if her father gave in to his anger and slapped her, as the twitch of his fingers revealed he wanted very badly to do. Most likely they would do little, since he *was* her father.

"Hmm." Quantrill studied her, then narrowed his eyes at her father. "It's not a bad ambition to want the Kansas land, Sam, and I can understand your being mad about your wife and gal, but I can't let you use this troop for your own personal feud. We've been down south all winter, and there's other things for the boys to do now. Important, military things." He turned his pale gaze back to Julia. "But if we get the chance, we can pay the Murphys a visit later."

A sob from the bed made Julia forget the problem at hand. She forced away any lingering fear and hurried to her mother's bedside.

"Mama?" she asked, going down on her knees next to the bed. "Are you feeling poorly again?"

Her mama beckoned her nearer. "Did your pa hurt you?" she whispered in Julia's ear.

"No, Mama."

"He fought with them."

"With Mr. Murphy. Yes. It was ugly, Mama."

Her mother laid back and closed her eyes, her lips, tinged blue, pressed into a thin, tense line. "Forget it.

Forget them. There's nothing you can do. Now go upstairs and change your dress before these animals get it in their minds to go wild.''

Julia had forgotten her torn dress and ramshackle appearance. Her legs were visible through her torn skirts. Her chemise spilled from the rip in her bodice. She wore no corset: she never had since she had no one to lace her into the contraption each day and had found herself unable to manage on her own. She must look like a harlot or worse, a bad image to present in the presence of the rough men who comprised her world.

Julia glanced over her shoulder at the others. They were all drawn into a circle, whispering their wicked plans. All but one.

Bill Anderson's dark, evil eyes met hers and, like before, he smiled. She was reminded of the men at the creek. The way they'd leered at her, the way the one had touched her. She swallowed the thick, foul lump at the back of her throat, stood, and then backed away, keeping her eyes on Bloody Bill all the while.

Never turn your back on a madman, she thought.

She fled up the stairs to the second level that had been added when they rebuilt after the fire—the room that had become her sanctuary. Once inside, Julia shut the door and breathed a sigh of relief to be away from the oppressiveness of Anderson's gaze. She'd have to be careful. That one would not care about her brothers' protection. He would do what he wanted and deal with the consequences later—or perhaps before. He would kill her brothers, every one. She'd been raised to put family first, country second and herself way on down the line, so she would make sure she gave Anderson no chance or reason to hurt that family.

Julia spent the next half-hour scrubbing herself, but no matter how hard she rubbed, no matter how deeply the lye soap burned her skin, she could not erase the feeling of violation from her body and her mind.

Nothing worked until she thought of Ryan Murphy's hand on her arm. The firmness of his touch, his deep, commanding voice and the strange, secret look in his eyes had made her feel like a woman and not a child. Why did the gaze of a man who was her enemy make her feel safe, while the gaze of Anderson—whom her family considered a friend—chilled and terrified her? Perhaps it was because even though Ryan was an enemy he was not evil. She could see that in his eyes. He had helped her despite her birth; he had helped her despite her name.

She should have the courage to do the same. She owed Ryan Murphy a debt, and that debt she would repay. To do so, she would need to see him again.

Though the very idea should frighten her body and soul, anticipation filled her heart.

Ryan spent the next two days plowing and planting until he thought his back would break. The thick brush common to the area, combined with the red earth and stone, had made clearing the field an already difficult task. Keeping the fields from being overtaken by weeds took time and untoward energy every year. Planting a crop once the field was clear took even more. The work was hard, but the fact that they needed to get the bulk of it done before Ryan returned to the Border Patrol made each day an eternal nightmare of heat and exhaustion.

If he could have slept well at night, perhaps he wouldn't have felt so vicious all day long. But whenever he slept, clouded images came to him of his mother, his sister and Julia Colton walking down the same dark path. The three of them in the same dream confused the hell out of him. What did the three of them have to do with anything?

Ryan stood at the edge of the yard, holding his sweat-soaked straw hat in his hand and contemplating the sun as it drifted toward the western horizon. Covered with dust and stiff with sweat, his hair didn't even move in the slight breeze that blew across the land. He glanced at the wash barrel outside the back door.

"To hell with it." He tossed his hat aside and stalked toward the swimming hole that fed into Murphy Creek. He was going swimming, clothes and all.

As he neared the water, the smell enticed him. He'd heard tell that cattle would stampede at the first scent of water after crossing a desert. He understood that completely. He yanked off his boots and his guns and ran for the water, jumping off the bank and landing in the middle of the swimming hole with a splash that would have made Jason proud.

Ryan held his breath and drifted to the bottom; the cool, wet sift of the water soothed the heat and sweat and dust from his skin and hair. He drove upward, bursting through the surface, spraying droplets all about, and swam to the shallows. He yanked off his shirt, shucked his pants and tossed his clothes toward land.

Lying back, he swam with strong, sure strokes upstream where the creek deepened from the shallows farther south, and he gazed at a sky painted both sunset and moonrise. Kansas was home and he loved it here. He remembered little of the East, where he had been born, beyond constant noise and dust and too many people. He remembered far better his father's tales of Ireland, the beauty and the pain, and his mother's words of love for their land in America. The freedom here, the promise, called to Ryan just as it had called to his parents.

The Murphy family had come to Kansas in 1854 in an effort to keep the territory from entering the Union as a slave state. Taking up residency in order to vote, they stayed on with their daughter and sons. The years that followed had brought such tragedy that the Murphys' original purpose, to further the abolitionist cause, had been practically forgotten. Ryan wondered if his father had ever been as devoted to the cause as Ma, or if he'd taken up her banner merely from adoration of her. What would it be like to love someone so much that when they died everything that gave you joy in your life died, too?

His father had been a different man years back: gruff but loving. He had adored his daughter, seeing in her the wife he loved, and he'd been as proud of his sons as any man could be. His wife's death had changed him—anger ruled his life. When Ryan had run off to join the Jayhawkers, whom his da had always called scum, Da had praised him for doing the right thing. When Ryan had left them, come home and joined the Border Patrol, his da had never said a word, but Ryan had felt his disappointment even so. Last year when Kathleen had come home, silent and skittish, Ryan feared his da's anger had begun to lean toward madness. The entire family was falling into ruin and Ryan was helpless to do anything to stop it.

Ryan sighed and kept swimming, the lull of the water and the quiet of the creek soothing away the aches of the day. His gaze wandered, lighting on things as he swam by—brush, tree, duck, Julia.

He blinked, foundered, sank and came up sputtering and choking, only to stand in the chest-deep water when he discovered she was real.

"What are you doing here?" he spat, brushing wet hair out of his eyes. "Didn't you learn anything last time you were out alone?"

She sat on the grassy Missouri bank, shadowed by the encroaching night. Her hair gleamed with russet streaks painted by the last rays of sunset, and her scent, roses and the damp, salty drift of tears, wafted over the water, addling his mind.

"Last time I wandered south, off Colton land, kind of like you've drifted north, off Murphy land." She held up a very large pistol. "This time I brought Granny's Dragoon."

Ryan narrowed his eyes on the gun and thought of his own, back near the swimming hole and too far away to grab, even if he hadn't been naked as the day he'd been born. He'd never felt more exposed in his life. From the look on her face, she knew it, and she enjoyed it. He sank up to his chin in the water.

He contemplated her, considering his options. The water would not protect him if she chose to shoot. Neither would the air if he chose to make a run for it. She continued to stare at him, a slight smile playing on her lips, the gun not pointed in his direction at all.

She didn't seem bent on killing him. At least not right now.

"You know how to use that thing without taking someone's head off?"

The smile that had been tugging at the corners of her lips blossomed into a grin. "If I want to take someone's head off, I could with this thing. But yes, I do know how to shoot. My granny taught me."

"Bushwhacker women," he muttered.

Her smile faded, and Ryan cursed himself as the cause. He had not seen her smile before, and she had a lovely smile. He cursed himself some more. What ailed him? It was bad enough he dreamed of her every night, he didn't have to covet her smile. She wanted something, most likely to ask him if he'd been one of the men who'd raided her farm, hurt her mama.

He sighed. Best get this over with. "What do you want?"

"I never thanked you." Her voice seemed loud in the sedate hush of the expanding evening.

Surprise made him blurt, "For what?"

"For saving me. I was stupid to come out alone, unprotected. To drift away from home and not keep my wits about me. I knew there was a war on, but . . ." She shrugged. "I didn't realize how bad things had gotten. I thought I'd be safe here."

"You weren't." He tilted his head, considering her. Was the depth of her innocence real? "You aren't," he concluded.

"I wanted to see you."

Here it comes, he thought. *The question. If I answer truthfully, she'll shoot me just as I deserve. And if I lie, she'll probably shoot me anyway, and I can't say that I'd blame her.*

"See me for what?" he asked.

"I had to warn you." She stood and he tensed, but she tucked the heavy pistol into the pocket of her dark blue skirt and twisted her empty hands into the folds of material. "My father told my brothers about you. About what he says you did to me."

Ryan stilled, forgetting for a moment other questions, other nights. Her brothers were back. He was surprised they hadn't already been over to visit—with their guns.

Unease bit the back of his neck. Or maybe they were here, with her. She said she wanted to thank him, but should he trust her? Just because she was a woman, a beautiful woman, didn't mean she wasn't as much a Colton as the rest of them.

He started inching toward his own land, his own guns, as he kept her talking. "I'm not afraid of your brothers."

"You should be." Not seeming to realize it, she walked downstream alongside him. "I am. And if the Coltons don't scare you, Quantrill and Anderson should."

"They're back, too?"

"Yes, and while he was in the mood, Father told the two Bills his fantasy about you. I tried to tell them they should go after those other men instead."

Ryan scowled, his pride pricked. "I don't need your help."

She scowled right back. "Quantrill said they might pay you a visit someday."

"I'm sure they will." Ryan would make sure his

patrol camped close to his home until Quantrill and the rest moved on.

They'd nearly reached the bank where he'd left his clothes and guns. Now Julia was out of her territory. While Ryan should feel more at ease, he did not. He liked her being in danger even less than he liked himself being there. All of his earlier soothing, pleasant feelings had vanished like the sun. This entire situation made him twitchy, though if her brothers had been hidden in the brush they'd have shot him long ago.

"Why did you tell me this?" he asked. "Aren't you betraying your family?"

Her hands twisted harder in her skirt, and she stared at her feet. "They'd probably think so. I believe in paying my debts."

"A Colton with honor?"

Her head came up; her chin tilted higher. "You think that's impossible?"

"I've never met one."

"Have now."

"So . . ." He considered her. "We're even?"

"Aren't we?"

Not even close, but since she did not seem to want to ask the question that lay between them, he would not answer it either. To do so would get him maimed or killed. Perhaps he deserved that, but he still had a vow to keep. "All right," he said. "We're even. Though I didn't help you to put you in my debt."

Her hands stopped moving. "Why *did* you help me?"

"That's the question." He shrugged, unwilling to voice his private torment to a stranger, the dual guilts that made him the man he was and not the man he'd hoped to be. "I couldn't let you be hurt, even though you're the enemy."

"Most wouldn't care."

"I know."

They remained silent. Ryan wanted to get his clothes on. The pleasing coolness of the river had turned chilly with the sun's desertion. He had to get rid of her first, and he knew just how. "So where are your brothers now?"

She laughed out loud. "None of your damned business, Ryan Murphy. I'm not that much of a traitor. I'll tell you only that they're not home, so your skin is safe for the moment. And so is mine."

"It was worth a try."

"Well," she said, gathering her skirt in one hand, "I'd best get back."

"Me, too."

She turned and meandered along the creek bank toward her home. She disappeared into the silver-streaked darkness, and Ryan winced at the return of the burn to his stomach. It was an ache he'd lived with since his another had died, an ache that had faded while she'd been near.

Ryan shook his head. The exhaustion and the moonlight were making him mad. The girl had paid him a debt she believed she owed him. He admired her sense of honor, shown in telling him of her father's scheme, and her devotion to family, revealed when she would tell him nothing more, but she was still the enemy. He had no business thinking of her smile and her laughter and the scent of roses that followed wherever she went.

Ryan swam through the swimming hole and hoisted himself out of the water. After using his shirt to dry off, he reached for his pants, then froze at the sound of a voice.

"I come down to the creek every night at sunset for dishwater," Julia said.

Ryan spun about, holding his trousers in front of his privates. The opposite bank of the swimming hole was empty, but the sound of her voice and the scent of her skin followed him home and down into his dreams.

Julia berated herself all the way back to the farm. Why on earth had she hidden and watched him climb out of the creek? Mama would be mortified. Father would—She didn't even want to think about what her father would do.

Since the fateful day she'd met Ryan Murphy her father had ceased to speak to her. He acted as if she no longer existed. Sometimes at night she'd hear her parents arguing—something they'd never done before. Her father had always treated her mother with tolerance, if not with affection. She'd borne him four sons and for that she deserved his respect. She'd lost her health because he'd not protected his own, and for that she'd gained his devotion. Sam Colton had never argued with his wife, never raised his voice, never behaved with anything but strained politeness—until now—and that only proved how far removed he'd become from the man he'd been.

Julia asked her mother what they argued about, but she would not say. She would only begin to cry, silently, horribly, and Julia stopped asking.

After pushing aside the confusing, sad thoughts of home, Julia couldn't keep herself from remembering the long, tall, muscular slide of Ryan's body from the water. His shoulders had bunched enticingly as he'd lifted his lower, equally enticing half from the creek. The light of the moon had cast silver shadows over the golden flesh of his back and danced across the lighter shade of his buttocks and legs, unkissed by the sun's rays.

Her heart had sped, her throat had closed, her tongue had thickened while she watched him bend for his shirt, then rub the cloth over all those firm muscles and that endless expanse of skin. She hadn't meant to speak, shouldn't have, but she had. And when he spun toward her voice, she'd ducked into the brush and focused her attention on the new view of his broad chest, sprinkled with hair, and his firm waist blending into hard hips. There her perusal had stopped for he held his pants before him in stunned silence.

The night air brushed cool against Julia's heated face. He would think her a loose woman, if not for watching him, then for the assignation she had suggested. She was embarrassed, but she could not be sorry.

She had meant to ask him if he'd truly been there when the Jayhawkers had hurt her mama. She knew her father, knew he was capable of spreading that rumor without any truth to back it up. But when she'd been in Ryan Murphy's presence she'd been unable to make herself ask that question.

If he had been there, she should despise him. She should want him dead. She should kill him herself. Those thoughts were more than she could bear, so she'd chosen the coward's way and let the question hover silently between them, never being voiced. What she did not know could not hurt them.

During the time she'd spent with Ryan Murphy the ever-present, aching loneliness that was a part of her, body and soul, had eased. She wanted to see him again, to try and understand how a man she should hate intrigued her so much she could think of nothing but him through every day and long into every night.

Chapter Four

Even though Ryan spent the next day believing he would not meet Julia Colton that night, when the day waned, to the creek he went, berating himself all the way for being ten times a fool.

What if she had set a trap for him for her brothers or planned to do him in herself? That thought made Ryan take his horse and check his guns, just in case. He told himself he could not miss the opportunity to gain some information about Quantrill and the rest from something she might say, even though he doubted she would let anything slip. What he did not do was admit that after a night spent dreaming about her, the memory of her voice lured him back like a siren's call.

The splash of his horse through the creek made him flinch. His gaze searched the brush and found no one, though if the Coltons were here he would not have seen them before they blew him to pieces. He was such a fool.

His horse pricked forward its ears and blew out a snort of welcome. Ryan yanked his Colt free and trained the weapon on the now swaying brush. Julia broke through and gasped at the sight of him, dropping her bucket and putting up her hand to her chest.

"You scared me," she accused, bending for the bucket.

Ryan holstered his weapon, got down from the horse. "You didn't think I'd come?"

"Not really." She moved past him to the creek, dipped the bucket into the shallows and out, then leaned forward to draw her finger across the surface of the water. Ripples spread like wind across a field of wheat. "I was foolish to tell you I'd come. I figured you wouldn't be as foolish as me."

"You were wrong."

Her hand stilled, though she didn't get up or turn to face him. "If my father knew we were here—"

"I know," he interrupted. "Mine, too. We're asking for trouble."

"Yes." She straightened, then turned to face him. The setting sun lit her hair from behind and shadowed her face, but her voice was heavy with a confusion that called to his own. "So why are we here?"

"We like danger?"

Her head tilted to the side and she studied him. "Maybe you do. I like peace."

"Funny thing for a Bushwhacker to like."

She stiffened. "I'm not a Bushwhacker."

"What are you?"

She sighed; her shoulders sagged. "I have no idea."

She walked past him to sit on the grassy area between the creek and the brush. He caught the scent of roses and followed it, sitting down at her side, close enough to touch her, though he dared not. Something strange had come to life between them. Something he should put a stop to but could not. He wanted to be with her, to talk to her, to understand her and whatever hummed between them like heat lightning in the night.

"You don't agree with your family's stand in this war?" he pressed.

"I don't agree with war. Killing, burning, maiming. For what?"

"For what's right."

"What could be right enough?"

"Unity, freedom, the country."

She gave him a considering glance. "Is that why you rode with the Jayhawkers?"

"No," he said, shortly. She had come too close to the question that would force a confrontation he did not want to have. Once that question was answered there would be no more peaceful meetings in the night, and right now he needed this oasis of calm in the storm of his life.

Before she could press him, he pressed her. "What about your brothers? You're loyal to them, you love them, even though they live by the code of violence. They're renegades who'll be shot if they're captured."

She cast him a suspicious glance. "They're hard to

love sometimes. But they're my brothers." She looked up at the sky. "I wish . . ."

Her face reflected the fervency in her voice, and Ryan found himself drawn to her even more than he had been before. He wished for many things, too, in the secret silence of sleepless nights. It had been a long time since he'd spoken of wishes and hopes and dreams. He had not realized how very much he'd missed sharing that part of himself—until now.

"What do you wish?" he whispered.

She glanced at him as if she'd forgotten he was there, then ducked her head to the side so he could not see her eyes. "This is silly. I know you came here to try and get information from me about my brothers. Let me tell you now, even though I know they're vicious and I know they're killers and I despise that in them, they're my brothers, my kin. They'd protect me to the end from anyone and anything, and I'm not going to betray them, even though—"

She kept her face averted, and finally Ryan reached for her chin. At the first touch of his fingers on her skin she started. He felt the jolt, too, throughout his body, but he held on and gently but firmly turned her to face him.

Her eyes, wide and startled, stared into his. Her tongue darted out to wet her lips, drawing his gaze to the moist path. "Even though what?" he asked.

Crickets called; fish jumped; his horse stamped at a fly, but between them silence stretched.

"Julia?" he asked, a different question now, a question that pounded in his blood, in his head, in his loins. This was insanity. She was poison, yet he could not seem to let her go.

She saw the change in his face and removed herself from his touch, though her gaze still captured his. "Mama says I'm a dreamer. I've read too many books and admired too many fairy tales." She tilted up her chin. "But I know what's real. I believe somewhere in this world there has to be a man who honors his word, who can be both strong and gentle, who doesn't live by a code of violence and vengeance. A man who can learn from his mistakes and move onward."

Her final words broke the spell between them. Ryan stood, walked away from her warmth and her scent, the turmoil she brought to his body and the peace she brought to his heart. He couldn't be the man she dreamed of. If he honored his word, he was bent on vengeance—for his mother, his sister and everyone who had died by the hand of a Missouri madman. His destiny lay in his vow, not here with a girl who dreamed impossible dreams. No matter that her dreams called to a part of himself he'd buried long ago. He might have turned his back on the Jayhawkers, but he had not given up his vengeance nor his vow. He could not and still live with himself.

He heard her stand. "Ryan?" She came closer. Her hand grazed his shoulder, and he stiffened against the rush of need such a tiny touch produced. He had not realized how much he'd missed the caress of a woman until this moment. A sudden memory came to him of his mother, her gentleness supported by strength, and loneliness swept through him as painful as it had been the moment she had died. He cursed the weakness he tried so hard to deny, but which always crept up on him in the dark peace of the night.

Julia's hand retreated, and he spun toward her, causing fear to flare to life on her face. Stifling a curse, he caught her hand and held her still when she would have pulled free and run away.

"Calm down." He shifted his hold from a prison to a caress, rubbing his thumb along her palm, soothing her as he might soothe a terrified horse in the midst of a battle. "You don't have to be afraid of me. But you shouldn't trust me either. I'll do whatever I have to do to keep my family safe from yours and to make sure men like your brothers go to prison or worse."

The fear in her eyes lingered, though she quit fighting to be free. "You don't have to hate like that."

"Yes, I do."

"Why?"

"I took a vow, and if I break my vow everything I've lived my life believing is a lie. Right becomes wrong, honor is just a word, and the bad men win."

She stepped closer, staring into his face all the while. He still held her hand and she used her free one to cup his cheek. The tenderness of her touch reached all the way to his toes.

"My family would say I'm bad to be here with you."

"I don't think so."

She smiled softly, sadly, then withdrew one hand from his cheek, the other from his grasp and stepped back. "Which just proves, bad is in the eye of the beholder."

While he contemplated her statement, she retrieved her bucket and walked toward home. Just before she disappeared into the brush, she turned. "Tomorrow?"

He nodded, unable to deny his need to see her again. She had bewitched him with her voice and her scent and her gentle caress. Talking to her soothed him in ways he hadn't been soothed since his mother had died. And even though the lines between wrong and right, good and bad were becoming blurred in ways he'd never considered before, Ryan knew he would continue to meet Julia Colton at the creek no matter the danger to them both.

Their clandestine meetings continued. Julia came to depend upon them for a tiny bit of joy in her usually bleak days. Ryan's imminent return to the Border Patrol made each meeting that much more precious.

While he sat at the creek with her, she could delude herself into believing that he was not her enemy. She never called him anything but Ryan. The name *Murphy* never left her lips. They spoke of many things, but never anything that might bring the tentative peace crashing down about their ears. They met in a make-believe world where no one had ever died, or been hurt, because of their name.

To Julia, Ryan was an interesting young man who spoke to her as if she was something more than a nuisance or a necessary nurse. He valued her opinion. He wanted to know her dreams and her hopes and her wishes, and she wanted to know his. They talked of the future, not the past. She spoke of peace and he listened, though he did not agree. Still, she sensed his heart was not evil, like the hearts of all the other men she knew, and she was drawn to him as she'd never been drawn to anyone before. They shared, they talked and they tried very hard to ignore the simmer of something more that threatened to boil over in the midst of every accidental touch.

Because when he left her he would become the enemy once more, and their days in the moonlight would be all she had left. Simply memories of the friend she'd never known she wanted but had come to need far too much.

One night Ryan was late and Julia became worried. She paced the banks of Colton Creek, considered wading across, then realized she would only end up pacing the other side. She could not approach his home any easier than he could approach hers.

That thought made her shiver despite the humid, pulsing heat of the early evening. A thunderstorm threatened, though not close enough to break. Still, the tension of the storm pressed upon her, making the anxiety within her grow.

Why did she keep meeting him like this, courting disaster? It would be death for him and a beating for her if they were caught. They both knew it, yet had been unable to stop. And for what? An hour each day with a man she could never even kiss?

Kiss? Where had such an idea come from? She had never thought of a man in such a way before, but with Ryan Murphy she thought of little else. Was Mama right? Had she been tempted by danger? Was flirting with death the only way she could feel alive? Or was Ryan himself calling to a part of her that had been sleeping all of her life?

Her thoughts returned to Ryan. How the sun turned his hair gold and the moonlight made silver glow through the strands. His hands, though rough and callused, touched with a gentleness that made her breath catch and her heart race. His voice, deep and commanding, brought gooseflesh to her skin, and every night when she left him, his scent—a mixture of man and soap and sunlight—haunted her dreams.

A murmur of annoyance rumbled in Julia's throat. There would be no kissing for her with Ryan Murphy. What had begun as a debt had evolved into an odd sort of friendship. Their conversations had given her a chance to convince him to let peace bring about change rather than violence. She was a sensible girl, with a sensible outlook, even if her dreams were not sensible in the least.

Ryan appeared from the darkness that shrouded the Kansas side of the creek, and Julia sighed in relief, but her relief was short-lived. "I have to go back tomorrow."

She caught her breath and tears burned her eyes. "Ryan, don't go."

He seemed as surprised as she was by her reaction. A frown marred his brow. "I have to. You always knew I would have to go."

"I hoped you wouldn't."

He shook his head, confused. "Why wouldn't I?"

"I don't know. I'd hoped you'd see that this war won't solve anything. Not for you or anyone else."

"Maybe not. But I can't stay home and do nothing."

She stared at her toes while she admitted the truth, her weakness. "I-I'll miss you. I've always wanted a friend." She looked into his face. "You're my first."

The whisper of her words fell between them. Heat flared in his eyes like lightning through the sky. He stepped toward her, wrapped his arm about her waist and yanked her against his large, hard body. Her breath caught in her throat. She didn't know what she'd said, but whatever it had been, the words had released a stranger.

"I don't want to be your friend," he growled.

Her gaze searched his but she found no answers there. "Then what?"

"This."

His lips crushed hers, as hard as his body, as warm as the night. Every sane thought fled from her mind; insanity took possession. She could think of nothing beyond the languid heat that seemed to slow her blood, even as her heart thudded ever faster. Her head spun with uncertainty, her body swirled with need, and her mouth begged for more. Though she'd never been kissed, she instinctively knew this kiss was life-altering.

She pulled back for a moment, needing to know one thing before her mind went south completely. "What is *this?*" she whispered, her breath mingling with his.

His eyes, thickly lashed, the brilliance of their blue shadowed by sadness and perhaps a tinge of guilt that Julia understood all too well, stared into hers. "Trouble. Should I stop?"

Julia smiled, refusing to allow the clamor of warning in her mind to ruin the wonder of her first kiss. "No. Kiss me again. Just kiss me again."

The shadows haunting his gaze fled, replaced by the heated, secret look she had dreamt about. His lips returned to hers, and for an instant she saw through every look he'd ever given her. She knew blasting heat from within, mirroring the lightning in the stormy sky above, a chill down her back, not the wind but a promise. Secrets in the night, fantasies she did not understand. Julia gave herself up to the madness.

He savored her, nibbling her uncertain, untutored mouth. Startling her with his boldness, he tasted her, running his tongue against the seam of her lips. She gasped in surprise, and he delved within, learning the contours of her mouth with his own, enticing her tongue to dance. Though she should be shocked at the intimacy he taught her, she wasn't. Instead, she wanted nothing more than to continue the lesson. She'd never thought a mere kiss could be like this—consuming, mind-numbing, earth-shaking.

She followed his lead. She knew no other way. When he groaned her name and drove his hands into her hair, scattering the pins and freeing the tresses to tumble down across her shoulders, the sudden ferocity of the movement brought a sliver of sense to her ad-dled brain. She moved her hand to pat the weight of her gun, still in her pocket.

But he did not hurt her. Instead he thrilled her, the momentary wildness she'd sensed calming until he touched her face gently, then cupped the back of her neck, making her chest ache with a desire she had never experienced until now.

How many times in the solitary darkness of her room had she wondered what it would be like to be held with such tenderness and need? To know what it was like to feel something other than loneliness and fear and guilt? She felt something different now, though she could not name the strange yet wondrous feeling. Somewhere between fear and excitement she hovered, her breath hard and fast, her breasts swelling beneath her chemise, an odd, heated tingling starting deep within the most secret part of her self.

When his fingertips brushed the buttons of her gown, he hesitated, his mouth hovering above hers. He muttered a curse and pulled away, standing near, yet touching her no longer.

"I'm not your friend, Julia. You shouldn't think of me that way. You have to remember what my name is."

The gilded glow of her first kiss faded as anger rushed through her, fueled by embarrassment. He was still, and always would be, the enemy. "Were you remembering my name while you kissed me and touched me, Ryan? Or would any woman do? I think you're lying, to me and yourself. You kissed *me*. And you didn't give a damn that I'm a Colton."

He moved toward her, his tall, muscular body crowding her, suddenly too close, too angry and too male. She took a single step back but allowed herself no more. She would not run, no matter what.

"I give a damn," he murmured, the softness of his voice belied by the hardness in his eyes. "But just because I want you doesn't mean I'm going to let you and your sweet voice and your tempting body sway me from a cause I believe in, the vengeance I must have."

The devil caught her tongue and kept her talking when she should have shut up. "If you're so all fired set on your cause and your vengeance, then why are you riding with the baby Border Patrol? Join the real army. Get in the real fight. Or are you as yellow as my brothers say you are? Are the rumors about you true?"

Eyes narrowed, he looked as mean and as tough as any raider, and she recalled their first meeting. If those four men who'd meant to hurt her had fled from him, they, too, had heard the power in his voice; they had seen the steel in his eyes. This man was dangerous, even if he could be gentle. She'd lived the past few days in a dream, thinking she could tame the tiger. But she should have known neither men nor tigers could be turned from what came naturally—vengeance and violence.

"Why don't you ask the question you've been wanting to ask since we started this, Julia?"

She swallowed, opened her mouth, but she could not seem to make herself speak.

He answered her anyway. "I was there."

She didn't move, terrified that if she did he would stop speaking. Suddenly, though she'd not wanted to hear the truth before, she needed to now.

"I was sixteen years old when I joined the Jayhawkers, though they didn't let me raid. I held the horses, or I made the cook fires; sometimes, if we got caught in a bushfight, I loaded the guns. But I was there that night."

He paused, swallowed and looked away into the distance. Julia listened to his words and watched the play of emotions across his face—anger, horror, guilt and fear.

"I watched them set fire to your home, and I didn't do anything to stop them. I didn't know anyone was inside until I heard you cursing as we rode away. By then you'd dragged your ma out and were safe. The next day I rode away and I never went back. But your brothers were out for blood. Can't say I blamed them, but I couldn't let them hurt my family because of me. I joined the Border Patrol to stay close and get help. But I was there, Julia. I was there.''

The silence stretched between them, heavy, damning. This man who fascinated her, who thrilled her, who'd given her her very first kiss was one of those who had hurt her mama and ruined her life. Her face flushed with heat and her eyes filled with tears, anger and pain at war. Julia turned her back so he would not see her weakness and let the angry words spill from her mouth. "Go," she spat. "Go back to your Border Patrol. Pretend you're doing something to help your precious cause. You're no better than my brothers or my father."

"I never said I was."

The fury seemed to drain out of her at his quiet admission. He'd owned up to what he'd done, recognized how wrong he'd been. No doubt he lived with his guilt every day and had tortured himself over his mistake for years. He was different from her brothers and her father. They hurt whoever they wanted and never looked back.

Quiet stretched between them. The night pressed upon them. The words they'd spoken and the kiss they'd shared hung over them. At last Ryan broke the silence.

"You're right about one thing."

Something in his voice made her ask, "What?"

"If I'm going to live my life by a vow, I've got to do it. If I believe in the cause my ma died for, I have to act, before it's too late."

She spun about. That wasn't what she'd meant. But he'd already started to walk away. "No, Ryan—"

81

She took a step after him, meaning to argue some more. But he swung back, swept her up in his arms and kissed her again. As before, her mind went south; all she could do was cling and kiss him back.

He broke their kiss, his breathing as labored as hers. "This was a bad idea, wasn't it? I should never have kissed you. Now I'll never forget you."

He left her standing on the banks of Colton Creek. She cursed him for a long time. Then she cursed herself.

Fool that she was, she'd never forget him either.

Ryan followed through with his intent to enlist early the next morning, riding out before dawn and completing his task before noon. On the way home he turned his horse toward a building perched upon a distant hill. The tall spire reached toward the clouds, shadow against sunlight, peace within a world of war.

He left his horse at the hitching post and walked from one world into another. Cool air soothed his heated cheeks; muted, colored light eased his aching eyes; intense quiet calmed his racing heart. He breathed deeply of the scented air as his eyes focused upon the candles that flickered and danced in a mysterious breeze, their golden light playing with the sunlight that streamed through the stained-glass windows behind the altar.

Ryan walked toward a curtain at the side of the room, his boots thudding, his spurs clanking against the marble floor. He removed his hat and tossed it onto a bench, then pushed aside the curtain and stepped forward.

When the curtain fell closed behind him, the darkness became complete. Alone, yet not alone, Ryan took a deep breath and began.

"Bless me, Father, for I have sinned. It's been . . ." He broke off, thinking, then gave up trying to remember. "A lifetime since my last confession."

"Surely not a lifetime."

"Feels like one."

"And what sin do you have to confess today?"

The voice, solemn yet amused, made Ryan smile in the blackness surrounding him. He had needed this—a sane voice amid the madness within him and without.

"I kissed a girl."

He heard a snort, like laughter quickly stifled, but before he could question the sound, the voice continued, "And she didn't wish to be kissed?"

"No, she wished to be kissed, all right."

"Then where is your sin?"

"Her name."

"Her name is a sin?" Confusion laced the voice.

"To me."

"Explain."

"Her name's Julia."

"A lovely name."

"Colton."

The hint of laughter in the air died, replaced by a heavy, horrified sense of shock. "What?"

"Julia Colton."

"Are you insane?"

"Yeah. I think I am."

"Her brothers will kill you."

"If her father doesn't get me first."

"What were you thinking of?"

83

Ryan couldn't sit still any longer. He yanked open the curtain and stepped into the deserted church. The second curtain flashed back to reveal his companion. Ryan scowled. "You can quit talking to me like I'm a child. You're not much older than I am. I've known you since you wet your pants."

Connor Sullivan's mouth curved slightly, his version of a smile, but as usual, the expression did not reach his eyes. The black robe of his profession complemented his blue-black hair and gray eyes. Connor had been a handsome young man, even in their youths, but it had never gone to Con's head. The fifth son, Con had been sent to study for the priesthood while he and Ryan were still boys. There was some mysterious compulsion there, family legend, vows taken in blood, superstitions born in Ireland long before Con or Ryan had been conceived. Con had been bound by them just the same. So he had gone to study at St. Mary's Seminary in Baltimore, and by the time he had returned, a priest, his family had been wiped out by Bushwhackers.

Sent south by the diocese, he'd been appointed to the church on the hill when its ancient priest had died. It was Con, knowing how much they needed to get away from the horror in the North, who'd sent word to the Murphys four years ago of the vacant land in his parish. Though Ryan had felt a foreigner here, Connor's presence had helped to soothe his initial distress.

"It's good to know that no matter how high I climb in the Church, there'll always be you to remind me where I came from."

Ryan shrugged. He shouldn't tease Con so much.

But he always hoped if he tried hard enough he'd bring a spark of life back to his friend's eyes. He hadn't seen anything but heartache there since Con had gone away all those years ago.

The unusual silence coming from Con drew Ryan's attention. He glanced at his friend to find him staring in horror at Ryan's blue uniform. Slowly Con raised his gaze to Ryan's. "What the hell is that?"

"Hell? Are you allowed to curse?"

"Stop it, Ryan. This isn't funny. You've joined the army?"

"This morning."

"Jason, too?"

Ryan looked away, flooded with guilt again. "No."

"What about the promise you made to join together?"

He'd known this question would arise, but he'd made his decision and he could not go back now. Ryan met Con's eyes. "I can't wait any longer. I have to keep the vow I made to Ma."

Con sighed. "So you break one promise to keep another?"

"Jason will understand."

"Will he? Maybe he'll just run off and join up, too."

"He's too young."

"Both sides are desperate for men. He'll lie about his age. Many have. Or he'll take your example and join the Jayhawkers."

Ryan scowled. "I'll drag him home and kick his butt."

"How can you when he'd only be following your example?"

Ryan hated it when Con was right, and he so often was. "Aw, hell. Just leave me be, Con. It's done now. They aren't sendin' men East anymore, so I've been assigned to the force occupying Bates County. I'll be able to keep a closer eye on the farm, Jason, Da and Kathleen if I'm in the county, and I'll have more men and bigger guns to back me up."

"And why would there be the need for you to keep a closer eye on the farm than you've kept so far with the Border Patrol?"

"There's been trouble with Colton again. He thought I touched his daughter."

"You just confessed that you did."

"I didn't then. Not how he thinks." Ryan let out an exasperated sigh. "Anyway, like I said, it's done now. I'm in the army. I'll be able to do more to stop Quantrill and the Coltons if I'm wearing the blue."

"I suspect you're mighty happy about this. You've been begging to become a soldier since you were old enough to walk and talk."

Ryan nodded. "It's all I ever wanted to do. Especially after Ma." He looked up at the multicolored glass window above the altar that depicted the Virgin crying over her dead son. He returned his gaze to Con's. "After Kathleen."

Con's gaze skittered away from his. "I know. What happened wasn't your fault. Every time I see you my heart breaks, remembering how you were before—"

"I'll never be that way again," Ryan interrupted, "so stop remembering." He was not prepared to listen to Con's usual sermon on this subject. He always ended up with a stomach on fire when Con got through with him. "The Bushwhackers killed the boy

I was when they killed my mother. I couldn't do anything to stop them from murdering her. But they'll pay. I vowed to make every last one of them pay. I made a mistake joining the Jayhawkers, but the vow still stands. I should have gone before, but to be honest I was—''

He broke off, unwilling to give voice to the secrets in his heart. But when talking to Con it did little good to hold back. Con always knew when there was more. And he would calmly question you until you broke down and told him everything.

"You were what?" Con prodded.

Ryan cursed. Con merely waited.

"I was afraid, all right? Afraid of what I'd do if I let all the anger out again. I was sorry about joining the Jayhawkers and horrified at what happened to the Colton women, but to be honest, a tiny part of me relished the Jayhawkers' viciousness because a tiny part of me felt it, too. The Border Patrol is pretty tame. The army is a different story.''

"But you joined anyway. Why now?"

Ryan thought of Julia's taunting words, her accusation that he was yellow. He hadn't joined to prove her wrong. He'd merely heard the truth in her anger. Vows were meant to be kept, not broken. Causes meant to be won, not abandoned.

"The vow, Con. I've let too many years go by without living up to it. Now I have my chance.''

"I was always taught that to break a promise to God or man is the worst thing a body can do. I've lived my life by that belief.''

"And you're right.''

"Am I? Sometimes I wonder. If keeping a promise

hurts more people in the end, is that right? When you went off with the Jayhawkers, didn't you make things worse? For your family and for yourself?"

When Ryan didn't answer, Con shrugged and sighed. "Let's hope you *live* to regret whatever you do." Con looked deeply into Ryan's eyes. "I understand you feel that you have to do something to make up for not being able to save your mother. But no matter how many Bushwhackers you kill, your mother is dead. Forever. No matter how hard you try to take the blame, it wasn't your fault."

Ryan flinched. "Trust you to rip out my heart and stamp on it," he said.

Con merely raised his eyebrows and shrugged. "My job. Life does strange things to people. Sometimes you just have to forgive, forget and let those you love live their life the way they need to live it."

"Even if they might die?"

Con stared at him for so long Ryan squirmed. His friend might be one of the youngest priests in the state, but Con had a way of looking at him that made him feel like his grandfather was taking him to task for lying. He always wanted to tell Con everything. Con had said it was his gift, and his curse.

"Yes, Ry, even if their way of living is self-destructive, sometimes you just have to let them go."

"You're talking about me."

One side of Con's mouth tilted upward. His idea of a smile. "Smart man."

Ryan thought back to the heated kiss he'd shared with Julia Colton in the moonlight. He wasn't smart. "Not by a long shot," he said, then he picked up his hat, nodded to Con and strode toward the door. He should have known Connor Sullivan would not let him leave with the last word.

"I'd stay away from Julia Colton if I were you."

Ryan turned at the door and grinned at his friend. "Of course you would. You're a priest, Con, and a damned good one."

Then he slipped outside before his friend could reply.

Chapter Five

Ryan stood outside his tent and watched Jason approach in his brand-new Union Blues, a bright grin on his young face. His little brother had found him in two days.

Jason stopped and saluted. Ryan scowled, refusing to return the salute until the grin faded from his brother's face.

"What are you doing here?" Ryan demanded.

"I'm your new orderly, Lieutenant."

"Wonderful." Ryan stalked away. Jason scurried to keep up.

"Where you goin', Ry? I mean, sir?"

"To tell the recruitment officer you're sixteen years old."

Jason stopped dead. "If you do, I'll join one of the Jayhawker bands."

That statement caused Ryan to turn and contemplate his brother's ghost-white face. Damn, Ryan hated it when Con was right. "You wouldn't. They're not soldiers, they're renegades. Murderers of the worst sort. I told you what happened when I rode with them. You're not making the same mistake I did."

Jason shrugged. "I want to fight. If you won't let me fight with you, I'll go my own way."

Ryan looked deep into his brother's eyes and saw the anger there. Jason was never angry, especially at him. "Why, Jason?"

"You lied to me. Promised we'd go together, then went off without me."

"I know. I'd waited too long already. I couldn't stay in the Border Patrol on the outskirts of every battle when I knew that if I was in the war I could help win it. I need to help win it. I made a vow. To Ma."

"You made a promise to me. We'd join together. You always said a man's only as good as his word."

Ryan sighed. He had said that. Many times. "Fine," he spat. "You can stay. But you stay by me. You hear?"

Jason's grin returned, and Ryan gritted his teeth to keep from swatting his brother across the top of the head. This wasn't a game.

"Does Da know where you are?"

Jason's grin froze.

Ryan cursed again. He wouldn't put it past the old man to come after them, too. He'd been making noises about fighting the good fight for the past several months. But his concern for Kathleen had kept him from acting on his wishes, and Ryan's insistence that Jason was too young and the Coltons were too near had helped as well. Now, the Coltons seemed to have forgotten the Murphys in their enthusiasm for the real war. Kathleen seemed to improve with each passing day, though she wasn't and probably never would be again the woman they'd known, and since Ryan and Jason had run off, Da would have no reason to remain on the outskirts of the skirmish. The way he'd been acting since Ma died, he would relish diving right into the fray. Sometimes Ryan wondered if Da wanted to die just so he could be with his wife once more.

Guilt burned Ryan's belly. If anything happened to Jason, or Da, or Kathleen, for that matter, it would be his fault.

He returned to his tent, ignoring Jason's excited chatter. He was exhausted, not just from the military maneuvers, but from the continuation of his dream-filled nights.

Since he'd kissed Julia his confusing dreams of her walking the same path as his mother and Kathleen had changed to dreams he had no trouble understanding. Now he dreamed only of Julia in ways that left him hard and aching, then awake and sweating.

God, he missed her, in every way a man could miss a woman. He missed her face and her voice and her laugh and her touch. Most of all he missed what he had never had, could never, would never have—her body beneath his.

He'd enjoyed their talks, relished their time together. Those few days had given him a glimpse back at the young man he'd been before the Bushwhackers and the Jayhawkers had changed him. But every second in her presence he had burned with the desire for more than words to be between them. When she'd called him friend he'd been unable to stop himself from showing her how unfriendly he felt.

He never should have kissed her, never should have altered their inappropriate friendship to illicit lust. That was all it was between them, he assured himself, lust. He hadn't had a woman in far too long. And Julia was a woman, despite her too-trusting innocence—a very beautiful, desirable, warm-hearted woman.

A groan escaped him as the memory of her response caused his body to tighten. The thought of her responding in such a way to anyone but him made him furious. He wanted to take her away from her life with her vicious brothers, sick mother and crazy father, which only made him crazy, too. He was responsible for the life she led. Now that he'd admitted that, she would probably hate him forever. And that would be for the best.

He was a soldier. She was the enemy. He had to remember that. He *would* remember that.

Ryan drifted toward sleep and the sound of Julia's voice.

Julia went to the creek every night, but Ryan didn't come back. She continued to go anyway. She told herself she did so to keep her father from thinking she'd been up to anything during the days she'd been with Ryan. The truth was, she went there to relive every second they'd shared. When she went to the creek she felt so much closer to him—even closer than when she kissed him each night in her dreams.

She should hate him. She'd told herself that many times. But every time she tried to, she remembered his face when he'd told her of the last night he'd been a Jayhawker, and all she could feel was sad.

News was the war had become more vicious. In late May a party of Federal soldiers approached the Samuel farm—the home of Jesse James, his mother, stepfather and sister. When Dr. Samuel would not tell them the whereabouts of Frank and Quantrill, they hung him, then took a bullwhip to Jesse. The soldiers succeeded in sending Jesse, at the age of fifteen, off to join Quantrill for good. Dr. Samuel survived, though his mind was not right. Jesse's and Frank's anger fueled a guerilla rampage into Kansas.

Had Ryan Murphy, in his new blue uniform, been at the Samuel farm? If so, and Jesse had seen him, Julia did not hold out much hope for his life. Truth be told, if he were capable of such atrocity, she could not mourn him. Yet she could not believe he would do such things, he who had turned away from such viciousness in the past. She had been close enough to see truth in his eyes, and though there'd been sadness and guilt, even hatred at times, she had not seen the evil and murder, the soul-consuming hatred that lurked in the eyes of her brothers and their friends. Ryan might think he hated like that, but he deceived himself.

Nothing changed at home. Her father worked day and night in the fields. Her brothers showed up there and here, helped a bit and then rode off. Julia continued to care for her mama, though their close relationship had changed. Julia could not confide what she'd done. She could not tell her mama she had kissed the enemy, let alone that she wanted to do it again.

Finally, in June, there was to be a dance at the nearest friendly farm to the Coltons. Despite all of the horror going on about them, sometimes Missourans needed to pretend their life was normal. The dance would be held in a barn built to replace one that had been burned to the ground by the Federals, and Julia smiled sadly at the irony.

"You go on now and have a good time. Don't worry none about me," Mama said as Julia packed a basket of food to take along.

The sound of horses outside made her tense. Federals? Raiders? Or worse?

Julia went to the window and peeked out. Worse. Her brothers.

"Who is it?" Mama asked.

"Ab, Ben, Clark and Del."

Mama groaned and turned her face to the wall. Julia had to agree.

Her father ducked into the room. "Get your things together, girl. Your brothers are here to take ya to the Turners."

Julia blinked. This was the first time he'd spoken to her directly since the incident with the Murphys. "I thought you were taking me," she said.

He frowned. "And who would stay with your mama? Did ya think I'd just leave her alone to take ya off for some fun? I swear, since that Murphy boy got a hold on ya, you've lost all family feeling. Maybe ya should stay here. I can't trust ya out of my sight."

"No, Sam, let her go. They need the help. I need the rest."

"She don't need to stay for the dance. Such goin's on'll only turn her head."

"I'll be fine. And if she leaves before the dance, how will that look to the Turners?"

"If she meets a beau, decides to run off, who will take care of ya, Vi?"

Mama winced. She hated to be reminded of how helpless she was. The nightly arguments between herself and her husband had stopped, and she no longer cried every day, but Julia had been unable to get her mama to tell her what the fights had been about. From the way her father had been avoiding her and the way her mama looked at her now, Julia had to think the arguments had been about her.

"She deserves a life of her own," Mama said, with a touch of her long-lost spirit.

"Her life is not her own. Remember that. She's alive to take care of you." He spun about so fast, Julia took a step back. The anger had returned to his eyes. "Ya remember how ya were raised, girl. Loyalty—to family first, then your country. Honor your mother. You're to care for her until the day she dies."

"Yes, Father. I will."

He scowled. "Take your basket and get out of here before I change my mind."

Julia didn't wait to be told twice. She fled—to her brothers—but sometimes one devil was better than another.

She wore her best gown. A bit frayed, perhaps, but all she had these days. Mama said the pink fabric brought out the red in her hair, and the roses embroidered along the hem made Julia feel truly feminine. Since she didn't own a hoop, Julia had filled out the skirt by wearing every petticoat she and her mama owned. She'd be warm in the sun, but at least she'd dressed like a lady for this one day.

Del helped her into the wagon, then climbed in beside her and took up the reins of the plow horses. They had no extra riding horses since the Federals had come the first time. Her father counted them lucky the plow horses hadn't been liberated.

"Why are you here?" she asked Del. "Doesn't Quantrill have someone for you to burn out or murder?"

Del reached over and yanked the hair at the base of her neck. "Ouch!" Julia yelped, rubbing the spot. Ab, Ben and Clark snickered. Julia narrowed her eyes and plotted vengeance.

"Mind your mouth, Julie." Del clucked to the horses, and their group trotted from the yard. "Pa says you've gotten soft on the Yanks."

"Have not."

"Doesn't matter anyway. Pa wants us to raid at the Murphys. Wipe 'em out. But Colonel Quantrill heard the old man is alone with the girl. Seems the yellow brothers finally joined up."

Julia swallowed as she remembered her taunting words that had made Ryan do just that. Now Jason, too, had gone to war. "What girl?" she asked.

"Sister, I think. Touched in the head."

"Probably met some of you all. That'd frighten anyone out of their wits."

Del laughed, pleased. "I sure do hope so."

Julia stared straight ahead and tried not to remember Del as a little boy. She'd practically raised him, though she'd not been more than a child herself. He'd been a sweet baby. A good boy. She'd loved him and he her. But he'd gone bad along with the others, and her heart ached with the loss. How could innocence go so wrong and love turn to indifference with such ease?

They reached the Turners, and Julia was surprised to see many of the area's menfolk, who had faded into the brush with the guerillas rather than join the Federal army.

She jumped from the wagon without waiting for Del's assistance, then glanced up at him with a frown. "Aren't you afraid the army will hear of this illegal gathering and come on by?"

"We aren't afraid of anything," he sneered, "let alone their army."

She looked at him for a long moment and tried one last time to reach the little brother she mourned. "They'll kill you if they find you, Del. No quarter for partisans. No prison. No chance anymore to swear allegiance like Frank did, then slip away into the brush later. They'll shoot you or hang you, right here and now."

Blood rushed to his face, from anger or fear she did not know which. "Don't you think I know that? I swore to die for the cause. I will if I have to. They're the invaders, Julie, not us." He looked away from her, out over the milling throng of people already at work on the new barn. "You haven't seen what I've seen out there. The horrible things they've done to old folk and women."

"And you haven't done the same in Kansas?"

His mouth turned down, offended. "Not me."

Julia reached up and put her hand over his so he

would not drive away before she finished. Perhaps she had one last chance to reach Del, to make him understand what kind of men he rode with. "If not you, then the others. The two Bills. Jesse and Frank. What about George Todd and Archie Clement? They say Archie's insane. A murdering lunatic. And you ride with him, Del, so what does that make you?"

He sighed, his shoulders slumped, and for a moment Julia caught a glimpse of her little brother in the downward curve of his mouth. Then those lips tightened, and he stared at her with the eyes of a stranger. "A patriot. A soldier. A man protecting his land and his family."

Before she could argue further, he yanked his hands from beneath hers and drove the horses and wagon away, joining his brothers at the edge of the woods.

Julia watched them dismount and set up guard. The way they prepared, she doubted they were as unconcerned about a Federal raid as they made out. One of the Turner boys rode with George Todd, so no doubt the guerillas had sent some men to help the Turners today. The others were most likely raiding at the border to keep the army occupied elsewhere. But if you wanted to stay healthy in Missouri, you never let down your guard. Not with the enemy, not even with a friend, and that made life pretty lonely for everyone.

"Where ye goin', boyo?" a voice with an Irish lilt called out.

Halfway out of the tent, Ryan paused and gritted his teeth. He'd thought Jason asleep, worn out from a day of chasing partisans through the brush. But he seemed awake enough.

"Go back to sleep." Ryan kept his face toward the night.

"You goin' out to spy?"

"Would you hush?" Ryan turned around, and his brother's eyes widened, then he hooted with laughter.

"What you got on your face?"

Ryan's lip twitched as the reminder of his disguise made the horsehair mustache tickle. The straw hat of a farmer combined with tan trousers held up by suspenders, a flannel shirt and work boots completed his transformation, or so he hoped. He didn't plan to get close enough to be seen in the light and recognized.

"Never mind me," he snapped. "Go back to sleep. That's an order."

Annoyance killed the teasing lilt in Jason's voice. "Just because they made you a lieutenant don't mean you can tell me what to do, Ryan Murphy."

"Yes, it does. That's exactly what being a lieutenant means. Now shut up and go back to sleep."

"No way. If you're goin' spyin', then I'm goin' too."

"Dammit, Jason, you are not. Even if I have to hogtie you, you're staying here. This isn't a game."

The urgency in Ryan's voice reached his brother at last. Jason scowled and settled back on the cot. "At least tell me what you're doin'."

Ryan twitched his itching lip and sighed defeat. "We had word some of the partisans are at a barn raising in Bates County. I'm going to the dance."

Jason sat up again. "And if they're there we'll attack?"

"No. There'll be too many women around. I'll try

to hear something useful. Then maybe tomorrow or the next day . . .''

Jason's eager face crumpled. ''I'd like a shot at 'em tonight.''

''So would I.'' Ryan understood his brother's frustration. They'd spent the entire day chasing ghosts through the woods. Ducking sniper fire. Hiding amid the trees and brush. But every time they got near the partisans, the bastards slipped away. It was useless chasing Bushwhackers through their own backyards. The brush and woodlands were their home now, and there was no way a Federal army would catch guerillas when they went to ground there. So the Union had resorted to spying. And Ryan had volunteered to be the spy.

Though his face was known to those he would spy upon, his knowledge of the area was unmatched. In fact, he'd demanded to go despite the danger. For a different reason. Even if he only saw her from afar, he had to see her one more time. Poison he'd called her once, and poison she was. She'd be the death of him yet; he didn't care.

''You stay here,'' he told Jason. ''I can't do this if I have to worry about you, too. Understand?''

Thankfully, Jason nodded and lay down. As Ryan slipped into the night his brother's voice followed him. ''And ye'll be careful now, boyo, or I'll know the reason why.''

''I always am,'' Ryan muttered, though when it came to one Reb girl he was not very careful at all.

Riding from the Federal camp toward the Rebel party, Ryan's life took on a dreamlike quality. It was as if he watched himself, unable to prevent what would occur, be it disaster or success. Some things were fated, and this night was one of them.

Alone he went into enemy territory. Disguised as one of them, he approached the music and the laughter and the light. Unchallenged, he hovered outside, looking in, and he saw her.

She danced in the arms of another. His enemy. She was everything he'd tried to convince himself she was not. Beautiful, graceful, brave and true. A woman to admire. A woman he could not have. A woman he should never have met, let alone touched and kissed.

A mistake, for the unacceptable attraction he'd felt the very first time he'd seen her, dirty, bloody and terrified, had become a full-blown obsession after kissing her in the moonlight and dreaming of her. Now seeing her in the glow of the lanterns, amid many who would kill him for being here, let alone for kissing one of their own, he wanted her more than ever before.

If he didn't know better, he'd think he'd fallen in love with her that first day. Ryan shook his head, trying to clear the hazy, dreamy whisper of fate and doom from his mind. He was so confused and he had no one to talk to—not since he'd walked away from Julia at the creek that day. Con would be no help with questions about women or love, and this particular woman made seeking advice from his da or Jason an idea to laugh at.

Ryan slipped about the newly constructed barn from door to door, keeping her in sight, keeping himself from the sight of others. He heard her laugh, saw her smile, swore he caught a drift of roses on the heated night air. His mission forgotten, he watched her until a hand clamped his shoulder and a voice hissed in his ear, "What are you doing here?"

He froze, afraid to turn and discover who touched him for fear he'd find ten guns pointed at his head. If he died tonight, so be it, but he did not wish to die in front of her.

His dream disintegrated and harsh reality cleared his mind. He stared straight ahead and tried to think of a way out of the trap he'd landed in. The hand shook him. The voice spoke again. "You idiot. Have you no sense?"

Ryan nearly collapsed with relief when he recognized the voice. "I could ask the same of you, Father. Since when do Yankee priests come to Bushwhacker parties?"

Con growled, stepped up next to him and elbowed Ryan in the ribs. "Their priest was killed. They asked me to bless the barn."

"And you came?"

"It's my job. God is no partisan."

Ryan turned his face slightly, keeping Julia in sight while he contemplated his friend. "And you? What are you, Con?"

Con scowled so fiercely, Ryan was impressed. "I'm a priest."

"You don't hate the folk who killed your family?"

Con's jaw tightened. A muscle leapt in his cheek. "No."

"Somehow I don't think I believe you."

"Believe whatever you want. What are you doing here?"

"My job."

"Which is?"

"None of your damned business, Father."

"Quit calling me 'Father.' " Ryan heard Con's teeth grinding together.

"Gladly." He smirked. "Father."

They continued to stand side by side, watching the swirl of dancers. The scene looked peaceful for all its movement and music and mirth. The night was the stuff of memories, of dreams, a world that had vanished come back to life for a single evening.

"Do you ever dream, Con?"

His friend shot him a sideways, contemplative glance. "Sometimes."

"And what do your dreams tell you?"

Con snorted. "That dreams often lie."

Ryan focused his gaze back upon the single dancer who occupied his dreams. "I dream of things I shouldn't."

"That's why they're dreams."

"But dreams can come true."

"Sometimes."

Ryan hesitated for a moment, uncertain if he should voice what bothered him. Somehow talking about them made his dreams all the more real. But he had always taken his troubles to Con, even when they were children. Ryan gave up trying to hide his worries.

"Since I joined the army, I wake up every morning feeling as if the future hangs over me. As if something has begun, something I can't stop. Something tragic."

"If you don't get out of here before someone discovers who you are, your future *will* be tragic. And very short."

Ryan straightened as Julia said good-bye to her

dance partner, a young man who couldn't have been more than fifteen, though he wore a gun. She waved her hand in front of her face, as if too warm, and headed for the open door on the far side of the barn.

"You're right," Ryan said as he moved away from Con. "Time to go."

Con grabbed his arm before he could escape. When Ryan glanced at his friend he was surprised to see sadness in Con's eyes. The sadness made him hesitate as anger would not have done. "You were always the one to chase down danger," Con said. "Even when we were kids. You were the one who dove into the deepest part of the stream. You were the one who crept up on a rattler lying in the sun."

"And I ended up swimming better than anyone and wore a rattle on my best hat."

"Someday your luck's gonna run out."

Ryan turned his head just in time to see a swish of pink skirt vanish into the night. "Not today."

"Is she worth dying for?"

Ryan pulled his arm from his friend's grasp, but instead of just striding away, he put his hand on Con's shoulder and gave him a nod of thanks for the concern.

"That's what I have to find out," he said, and went to do just that.

Julia escaped—from the barn, the noise, the men and the boys. Once she would have reveled in such an evening. Music and laughter, dancing and joy. Especially now, when such things were so rare. But all she felt tonight was trapped. She kept looking for another face, a face she knew could not be there, must not be there. Yet she continued to hope it was.

She hurried away from the barn into the star-bright night. Nearby she could hear the murmur of voices, her brothers and their comrades, walking a picket line between the farm and the woods, waiting for a raid she prayed to God would not come. What would she do if a horse broke from the trees, rode her down, its rider set to kill her? Would she turn, look into death's eyes and see the man she could not get out of her mind? Julia shivered and shook her head against the image.

It could happen. Had happened before, and her mama had suffered. Would Julia be the one to suffer next?

All those stories she'd read to her mama over the years had addled her brain. She'd dreamt of a golden knight, a hero, a savior, and he had come. Since she'd seen him her dreams had changed. Instead of the golden, faceless knight, she dreamt of Ryan—in ways that made her blush.

The weather had turned humid; summer had arrived. It seemed even nature hovered heavy above them all, waiting for something that had begun and could not now be stopped. Something tragic.

"Julia?"

The voice was so close, for a moment she saw again the enemy bearing down on her from the darkness. She gasped, spun about, and the enemy was there. She closed her eyes to make him go away, yet when she opened them again he remained.

A quick, furtive glance about revealed that they were alone, at the edge of the north woods and hidden from view of those in the barn and beyond by the house. She had wandered too far away from the others to be safe. Where was her mind these days? She could as easily be dead or kidnapped by the enemy. Or perhaps she was about to be, since the enemy stood right here.

Julia hugged herself against a sudden chill that assailed her despite the heat of the night. Though she'd dreamed Ryan would be there, hoped but not prayed, the fact he was there made her remember her strange, furtive, secret dreams.

"Are you crazy?" she whispered, putting herself between him and the music and the light.

He smiled, the silly mustache he'd grown covering the corners of his lips. He was so handsome, even with a crushed hat, frayed suspenders and a smudge across his cheek. Her heart did a funny sort of dance, and she pressed her knuckles against her chest to make it stop. This feeling she had for him would not do. She was too old to believe in fairy tales. Love at first sight was a myth and, in most of the stories she'd read, brought terrible trouble to those who believed in it. Trouble she had enough of already.

Ryan's gaze dropped from her face to her hand, then lingered upon her breasts. His eyelashes lifted and his eyes met hers. The mirth had disappeared, and the blue deepened with the dark, secret look that made her quiver.

"I think I am crazy," he said, his voice harsh and low. "Crazy over you."

A flush crept up her neck to her cheeks. "You shouldn't say that. You shouldn't be here."

He stepped closer, crowding her with his large, warm body. Instead of a desire to flee, all she felt was desire. Her head tilted back, and she became captured in the depth of his eyes. "I know I shouldn't be here, but I am. You can't tell me you haven't thought about me. That you haven't thought about our kiss and wanted more. That you haven't burned in the night. Dreamed of me, dreamed of us. You have, haven't you?"

She should admit nothing, say nothing, but when the wind shifted and the music drifted toward them, an enticing, enchanting tune that called to the awakening need in her own heart and soul, she could not stay silent nor remain still.

"Yes," she whispered, "I have."

She swayed into his arms and he caught her, pulling her against him almost roughly, then touching his cheek to her hair with such gentleness she swallowed again, against a rising tide of tears, not confessions. She had wanted this, wanted him, all of her life it seemed.

He stepped sideways, taking her with him, and she stumbled, for a moment not realizing he meant them to dance. She sighed and relaxed in his arms.

They danced beneath the stars, removed, yet not alone. Their families were there, the hatred and the strife hung in the air above them, dancing with the shadows of tragedy that awaited. Still Julia could not bring herself to tear free of the magic. She stared into his eyes as she danced with him, and if her heart had not been lost before, it was lost for certain now.

The music stopped suddenly and so did their feet, but he did not release her. Instead he held her closer, his hands, restless at her waist, smoothed over her hips in a scandalous way she should put a stop to but could not.

"Julia?" he whispered, as if in saying her name, he could remind himself of truths they should remember.

"Hmm?"

"I need to kiss you. Please, may I kiss you?"

She did not answer. Instead she lifted her arms to encircle his neck, pressed her body and her lips to his. The kiss was familiar, yet new. Their first kiss was tinged with anger and fear, but this one was a conscious choice taken despite the danger to them both. She forgot everything when he took her mouth and showed her she had been a child all of her life until this moment.

The embers they had fanned that day by the creek roared out of control. What lay between them was sudden, unexplainable, unacceptable, but undeniable, and it had not gone away, despite the questions, the confessions.

Julia opened her mouth at his urging, allowing his tongue entry, matching his caresses. Her hands seemed to have their own will, tangling in the hair at the nape of his neck, knocking his hat free to bury her fingers in the thickness and draw him closer. His palms rested at the juncture of her back and buttocks, pressing her against a hard ridge that pushed at her stomach and made her moan with confusion and need.

She broke the kiss, staring up at him, shocked at the maelstrom within her. His mustache hung sideways, obviously a fraud, and her lips twitched. He frowned, and she reached up to pull the mustache loose. He took the fake and shoved it into his shirt pocket, then leaned his forehead against hers and sighed.

"I'll have to go to confession again," he said wryly.

"Have you sinned?"

He lifted his head and stared at her mouth, desire plain in his eyes. Then his lips quirked. "Give me my sin again."

This kiss went deeper, harder, longer. He traced her collarbone with his thumbs, the thrill of his touch making her hot and cold all at once, and Julia lost herself in the wonder of Ryan. His smell, his strength, his heat, the contrast of soft lips and hardened body. She wanted to run her hands over every inch of him and learn every difference. She no longer knew herself, and she did not care.

Her body strained for knowledge, for completion. Her mind cried out his name as her lips drank from his.

Then her ears heard the cock of a gun, and her heart burst into a thousand shards as her brother's voice shattered their enchantment.

"Turn her loose, Murphy. It's time to die."

Chapter Six

Ryan tore his lips from Julia's, lifted his head, stared straight into eyes as cold and deadly as those of the rattler he'd bested all those years ago. That day he'd had the advantage—a gun in hand and no one but himself to worry about.

He tried to move in front of Julia, but she clung to him like a burr to his horse's mane. "No," she hissed. "He'll kill you."

"If you don't move, he'll kill you."

"He won't." Her lips thinned. "He wouldn't dare."

Before Ryan could comment she turned to face the intruder, her fingers clutching Ryan's as they crept toward his gun.

"Go away, Del. Mind your own business."

The man stepped from the shadows into the shaft

111

of moonlight, and only then did Ryan recognize him as the youngest Colton, Delbert. His youth made him no less dangerous.

"You'd better move your butt, Julie, or I'm gonna come over there and move it for you."

Ryan tensed. "Don't touch her."

Del scowled. "She's my sister. I'll do whatever the hell I want to." He approached; his face twisted with hatred. "You get your filthy Federal hands off her. Pa said she was sweet on you." He shot a glance at Julia so full of venom her fingers clenched about Ryan's. "But I couldn't believe she'd let a Murphy lick her boots, let alone kiss her. I never figured her for a whore."

Julia's gasp of surprise and pain made Ryan see red. When Del reached for her, Ryan yanked the pistol right out of his hand. Luckily the kid did care about his sister some and he'd uncocked the gun. For a solitary second Del stared at his empty hand, then reached for his second pistol. Before he could draw, Ryan shoved Julia to the side and hit her brother as hard as he could on the jaw. The kid went down, and he did not get up.

The sound of footsteps made him draw his gun and step in front of Julia, who was unnaturally quiet and white-faced. A figure approached and Ryan cocked his gun, then hissed, "You'd better stop right there or pay the price."

The figure hesitated. "Ryan?"

Ryan swore. *Con.* Why couldn't his friend ever mind his own business? But then, his business *was* everyone else's business.

Con stepped forward, then stopped with a start, his

gaze traveling from a still unconscious Del Colton, to Ryan's gun, to Julia. His lips tightened and he approached her. "Are you all right, Miss Colton?"

"Y-yes, I-I—" She shook her head as if to clear it, gave Ryan an odd glance, then frowned at her brother. "This is my fault. I should have known this would happen."

"Don't blame yourself," Con soothed. "You're where you're supposed to be. Ryan, however, isn't. And he'll be leaving now, won't you, Ry?"

Julia glanced from Con to Ryan. "You know each other?"

Con hesitated again, then gave a short nod. "Ryan, say good night."

"I'm not leaving until I'm sure her brother isn't going to hurt her or make her life miserable because of me. I'll just wait until he wakes up and have a little man-to-man with him."

"You should have thought of that before you came here."

"Shut up, Con."

Con's thoughts were plain upon his face. He believed Ryan used Julia to obtain information about her brothers and their comrades. Once he might have—before they'd spent those hours at the creek, before he'd admitted what he'd done to her mother and been taken back into her embrace just the same. Their time together had been magical, something to treasure, something apart from the world and the war and the feud. He could not take her trust and twist it for his own purposes. Though if he followed his vow and his duty he should, if he believed in honor, he

113

could not. If he did not believe in honor, he was no better than those he despised.

Ryan stifled a groan. Why did everything have to be so complicated? He turned his gaze to Julia and found himself captured by the green of her eyes. He remembered the softness of her lips against his, her murmured moans, her shy yet strong hands touching him, making him nearly wild with desire. He should be concentrating on his mission, but all he could think of was her.

The sound of voices fast approaching brought Ryan to his senses. His gaze met Con's over Julia's head. "You have to go," his friend urged.

"Yes, go," Julia agreed.

"No. I'm not leaving you with him. With them."

"Dammit," Con swore, sounding very unpriestly, "you know where there's one Colton there's more. If they catch you here, with their sister looking like she's been thoroughly kissed and their little brother unconscious, you'll not only die, you'll die slow."

Con was right, but Ryan wouldn't run away and leave Julia to face whatever Bushwhackers did to women who kissed the enemy. What kind of soldier would he be then? What kind of man? If he hadn't learned anything from his past, what reason did he have to go on?

"I won't leave her," he blurted.

Julia let out a choked cry and grabbed him by the suspenders, yanking him close. "Leave," she snarled. "Now. I can handle my brothers. I haven't survived twenty years as a Colton without knowing what to do with them. Do you think I want to see you shot full of holes right in front of me?" She kissed him, hard and furious, then shoved him backward with all her strength. "If you die, I'll die with you. Is that what you want?"

He stared at her, amazed. He had never seen such strength, such conviction, such passion in a woman.

"There's someone over here!" A shout went up from just beyond the house.

Julia flinched, and her eyes went from angry to agonized. "Go. I swear I won't let them touch you. I'll die first."

She meant it, and knowing her brothers, they wouldn't hesitate to oblige her. Ryan holstered his weapon and backed toward the darkness of the trees. "Father, I'm leaving her in your hands," he said.

Julia's chin went up and her eyes flashed fire. "I can take care of myself, Ryan Murphy."

"You can, I'm sure. Still, as long as Father's stuck his nose in here, he can watch out for you."

The last he saw of her, she bent over her prostrate brother, helping him to sit up as she whispered into his ear. Her face a white circle against the indigo night, whatever she said to Delbert made his face go even whiter.

Ryan smiled, seeing she could hold her own with the rabble, then slipped through the trees to find his horse.

"Say a single word about what happened here, Del, and I'll make certain Bloody Bill finds out about you and his sister."

Though Del was still groggy from Ryan's punch, he understood what would happen if she followed through on her threat. From years spent as siblings he knew Julia did not make idle threats. She could not have survived in their household if she had.

His face drained of color, and he stared up at her with their father's eyes—full of anger and disgust. She had betrayed the Colton code.

"He'll kill me if you tell."

Julia fought the sadness the loss of her little brother brought to her heart, but she knew what she had to do. She looked straight into his eyes and murdered the last vestige of softness that lay between them. "I know. A life for a life. That's the deal. Agreed?"

Just then Ab, Ben and Clark burst from the night, pistols drawn. Several other partisans followed close behind. The priest stepped in front of Julia. Since her brothers would not hesitate to shoot a man of God if the need should arise, his courage was impressive. He took his promises seriously, it seemed.

Ab frowned at the scene, his gaze sweeping the trees for a sign of the enemy. "What's goin' on here, Del?"

Julia turned her gaze back to Del and waited. If he decided to call her bluff, they could both die. She did not pause to wonder why a few days of clandestine meetings with Ryan Murphy had made her willing to die for him, but she was. Del saw the truth in her eyes and gave a short nod. She stood, helped him up and faced the mob.

"Del and I had a little disagreement. Father tried to smooth it over, but . . ." She shrugged and spread her hands wide. "I had to flatten him."

Her brothers relaxed at the explanation. She'd flattened them many a time. They holstered their weapons and came over to slap Del on the back and take him off for some good-natured ribbing. Before he left, Del glanced at her with narrowed eyes and mouthed, "Traitor."

Julia shivered. Del would not forget this, nor should she. When she looked at the priest he studied her with curiosity.

"What did you say to him?"

"A secret. I keep his if he keeps mine."

"And all for a kiss from your enemy? Is it worth risking the love of your brother for a moment's pleasure?"

When put like that, Julia felt foolish. "What would you know of it, Father?"

He flinched, then looked away. "More than most," he said.

"Would you rather I'd let them murder him when I could do something to stop it?"

He returned his gaze to hers, lifted then lowered one shoulder. "Guess I'm confused. All I've heard since I came to Bates County is that the Bushwhackers hate the Federals. Your brothers are as Bushwhacker as they come, and the Murphys are mighty loyal to the Union. There's that to hate, even if there wasn't the feud between your families. And then there's the truth of Ryan's time with the Jayhawkers."

Julia's gaze slipped from the priest's as he continued. "I see he's told you that. Yet you just risked your neck for him, a man who admittedly made a mistake and regrets it, but who hurt your mother nevertheless. A man who has vows to keep and causes to fight, which most likely sent him here to spy on these people, your people, and betray them if he could.''

Julia blinked, swallowed. She hadn't thought of why Ryan was here, only that he was. Her joy in seeing him again had overshadowed the truth she should have recognized. He had not come here for her. He'd come to spy. And she'd saved his sneaking life.

How could she have forgotten the uniform he wore now, even if he hadn't worn it tonight? It seemed every time he kissed her she lost more of her mind. Yet she couldn't believe he'd kiss her with such passion, touch her with such gentleness, and not mean it.

But what did she know of men, besides her brothers? They'd do whatever they had to for the cause. Why would she think any less of Ryan Murphy? Now he wore a uniform that gave him the legal right to do whatever he could to hurt those who had hurt him. How many times had she sworn hatred for those who had hurt her mama, yet now that she'd come face to face with one of the culprits, all she could do was think of reasons to forgive and forget. She and Ryan had more to hate each other for than to love.

Why then could she think of nothing but love when she looked into his haunted blue eyes?

Ryan waited, for hours it seemed, still in the night, hidden in the brush, until he heard the sound of horses, a wagon, the voices of men. Then he waited awhile longer, until the horses rode north, taking the men with them, leaving the wagon and one rider behind.

He crept from hiding, slipping through the shadows

118

that danced with the descending moon. He tried not to hear the clamor in his head that told him he should be on his way back to camp, to relative safety with others of his kind. He should not be here, alone, with the enemy.

But from the moment he'd seen her tonight in the golden glow of the lantern, he'd been unable to think clearly, let alone act with any sense. Whenever he was with her, the incessant throb of hatred he'd nurtured for so long, the ache and the burn of guilt in his gut faded, and a strange sort of peace took its place. He was drawn to that peace, just as he was drawn to her. He could no more deny that need in himself than he could deny his vow. He had become two men—one who craved the peace brought by her presence and the other who sought the death of all she held dear.

On the second story at the back of the house a window glowed with candlelight. Ryan slid along the tree line, his gaze focused upon that window. The upper floor must have been added later, for the window opened out onto the roof of the main structure. As he watched, someone pushed aside the curtain and a figure appeared. The light of the moon fell upon her face, illuminating Julia, hair unbound, the silver glow from the sky painting traces of white through her hair and making her shift seem made of moonbeams.

She leaned her elbow on the windowsill, put her palm to her cheek and stared up at the sky. For a single instant he wished to be a glove upon her hand so he could touch her cheek, and then she sighed. "Ah, me."

Just the sound of her voice, sad though it was, made some of his pain recede. Ryan moved closer.

He was beginning to understand why a moth flew into the flame of a candle, lured by the warmth and the light to its death.

"Why does it have to be him who makes me want what I can never have?" she murmured. Though she spoke softly, the stillness of the night brought her words to Ryan as if she whispered them into his ear.

"I'm a Colton. My purpose is to take care of my mother. To help my father. To be loyal to my family and their cause. Why does his touch make me want to deny my father, refuse my name?"

Ryan left the shadow of the trees and moved swiftly across the open area between the brush and the house until he stood directly below her. So caught up was she in her discourse with herself, she did not hear or see him. He held his breath as she went on.

"What's in a name? If he were anyone other than a Murphy, would these feelings I have for him be so bad?" She sighed. "Yes. Who he is goes deeper than his name. It's what he believes is right. Who he believes is wrong. Those he calls friends, and those he calls the enemy. He's a Federal soldier now. Even if he wasn't a Murphy, he'd be poison to me just the same."

"You can call me whatever you like, if that helps," Ryan said, just above a whisper.

A startled intake of breath and a shuffle of movement from above proved she'd heard him.

"Who's there?" she demanded.

Ryan moved away from the wall into the moonlight. "My name makes me your enemy, so I won't speak of it."

Her eyes widened, first in surprise, then in fear. She

leaned forward through the window, heedless to her state of undress. "What are you doing here?" she hissed. "If someone sees you, you're a dead man."

Unable to concentrate on her words at first, his attention focused upon the provocative presentation of her breasts in the low-cut shift. He started when she snapped, "Ryan, if they see you, they'll kill you."

For some reason, the danger and Julia made him feel more alive than he'd felt for a very long time. He grinned in the face of her fear, slipped free of his boots and climbed up the side of the house.

"What are you doing?"

Slowly, carefully, he made his way across the roof until he knelt just outside her window. Now her eyes were wide with suspicion, and looking down, she gasped, then crossed her arms over her breasts. She began to back away, but Ryan reached forward and touched her. One gentle slide across the heated flesh of her forearm, then away. That one touch was enough to make him bite back a moan.

"Don't go," he said. "I won't hurt you."

She hesitated, then as if a moth herself, drawn to the flame of disaster, she stayed. "I'm not worried about me. They will murder you." She said the last four words slowly and clearly, as if she was speaking to an idiot.

Perhaps she was. Ryan couldn't seem to make sense out of anything he'd done lately. "They aren't here," he pointed out. "I heard them ride away."

"My father is."

Ryan spread his hands wide and looked around. "Where?"

"Inside. Downstairs, asleep with Mama."

"Is he a light sleeper?"

"No. He sleeps so hard the house could fall in, and he wouldn't wake up till morning."

"Then if we're quiet, we'll both be safe." She frowned and crossed her arms tighter. "Just for a minute. Please?" Ryan held out his hand. She stared at it, crossed her arms in the other direction, shifted her hips. Finally a groan of defeat escaped her lips and she placed her fingers in his. She sat down next to the window. Inside. He did the same. Outside.

"You shouldn't have listened to me before. I was trying to make sense of—of—this. Whatever this is. What I said was meant for me alone."

"You were talking about me."

"About, not to."

Ryan nodded. "I'm sorry. I didn't mean to listen. But I was here and you were talking." He waited a moment, savoring the warmth of her hand in his. He'd never sat and held hands with a woman. He had missed a lot. "We have a problem, Julia."

She sighed, from the depths of her heart, it seemed. "I know."

"I've never felt like this about anyone. I think about you all the time. All I want is to be with you. Yet I've gotten my fondest wish; I'm a soldier. That's all I ever wanted to be. And you're the enemy."

"I'm not your enemy."

"No?"

She pulled on his hand until he looked into her eyes. "No," she said firmly.

Ryan looked away. This situation was impossible.

"Were you one of the men at the Samuel farm?"

Ryan frowned and looked back at her. "No."

122

A held breath rushed past her lips. "I knew you couldn't do such a thing."

"I agree they went too far, but I could just as easily have been there, and I would have had to take orders like they did."

"Hanging old men and whipping boys? I can't believe you'd allow such a thing."

"I'm a soldier. I do what I'm told, when I'm told. I agree what happened to Dr. Samuel was a disgrace, but Jesse James is not a boy. I doubt he was ever a boy."

"Well, you all did it now. He's gone to Quantrill for good, and he's mad."

"I know. There'll be hell to pay."

They remained silent, thinking of all that had happened and all that might happen with them on opposite sides of an impossible war. Sometimes it seemed the war was only Kansas versus Missouri, just a larger, more vicious version of the blood feuds that had existed here for so long. The rest of the country was so far away and uninvolved in the struggle between the two territories become states, a struggle that would go on even when the real war ended.

"Did you come to the dance to spy?" Julia asked. "Or to see me?"

The hope in her voice near broke his heart, but he had to tell the truth. "To spy."

She looked away from him, across the open fields to the north where her brothers had ridden. "And are you here now for the same reason?"

He tugged on her hand until she looked into his eyes. "No. I'm here now for you."

123

Instead of the smile he'd hoped for, the one that made his pain fade, her lips turned downward. "How do I know you're telling the truth when you're a spy?"

"I'll swear," he said, then looked about. "By—" His gaze turned upward. "By the moon."

"No," she blurted. "Not by the moon, which only appears at night, then disappears at dawn. If you swear by the moon, will you and your truth disappear, too?"

"What should I swear by?"

She stared into his eyes, searching, and then at last she did smile, the smile he'd dreamt of. "Don't swear by anything. All I need is your word and I'll believe."

"Why?"

"You told me the truth once without my even having to ask. Why lie to me now?" She pulled her hand from his and came up on her knees so she could place her forearms on the windowsill and lean toward him. "Come here," she murmured.

Fascinated, bewitched, he shifted onto his knees so he faced her through the window.

She slanted further forward; a soft breeze picked up her hair and whisked a strand across his cheek. He smelled roses and tears. "Kiss me." Her whisper surrounded him, enticed him, lured him forward.

Gently, touching only her lips with his, he kissed her until the rest of the world faded from his mind. How could a mere kiss make him feel as if she'd touched him everywhere with those soft, strong hands?

She broke the kiss, but her mouth hovered near his. Her eyelashes lifted, and she stared into his eyes.

"Your lips don't lie. You feel the same as I do. I'd never lie to you, Ryan. I couldn't. So I have to believe you'd not lie to me. You never have."

A soft cry from inside made her stiffen and jerk away. She turned her head toward the sound. "Coming, Mama," she called, then swung her gaze back to him.

"You have to go," she hissed. "Now."

She began to stand, but he grabbed her hands in his. "If you need me, for anything, you can get word to me through Con."

"Con?"

"The priest. At the church on the hill."

"Why would I need you?"

"I don't know. But I hate to think of you here all alone with them."

She laughed. "I've been alone with them all my life."

"You're not alone anymore."

Joy lit her face, and she squeezed his hands, then kissed him once, hard on the mouth. A woman's voice called her name from downstairs.

She winced. "Go. Quickly."

He did, sliding over the edge of the house and letting himself down onto the ground as quietly as he could. He shoved his feet into his boots and risked one more glance upward.

She still stood in the window, watching him, and he was struck again by her beauty, shining both from within and without.

"What is this between us?" he asked.

"I don't know." She smiled, sad and soft. "But God help us."

Chapter Seven

Ryan slipped into his tent as dawn tinted the East. Just as he lay down, hoping for an hour to rest his mind and body, Jason popped up and began to talk.

"So, what happened? Who did you see? What did you hear? Are we goin' to get 'em today?"

Ryan moaned and turned away, pulling a blanket over his head. But Jason, never one to be deterred by anything, let alone a flimsy army blanket, reached across the few feet separating them and yanked the covering not only off Ryan's head but off him entirely.

"Jason . . ." Ryan growled as he turned back to face his brother.

Jason held the blanket out of Ryan's reach and grinned like a fool. "Answer me, now, boyo, and I'll leave ye be."

"Nothing happened. I saw no one. Heard nothing. We're going nowhere today. Now give me that blanket before I make sure you sleep for the rest of your miserable life."

He reached over and tried to snatch the cover from Jason's fingers. Jason was quicker and yanked it out of the way. His face collapsed from cheerfulness to disappointment. "You were gone all night and you didn't learn nothin'?"

"Nothing." Ryan leaned forward, and this time succeeded in snatching the blanket. He settled back and closed his eyes.

"Was she there?"

Though his voice was quiet, Jason's words fell between them with the intensity of a thunderclap, followed by a waiting silence.

"Who?"

"You know who. The Colton colleen."

"Why would she be there? Why would I care?"

"Uhh, you've said her name." Jason cleared his throat. "In your sleep."

Ryan groaned.

"Ry, when I teased you about her that first day I was only jokin'. But since then . . . Well, you've been different. More like you were before Ma—" He broke off with a sharp intake of breath.

Ryan narrowed his eyes and glared at Jason. He didn't like the way this conversation was headed. Jason saw too much, too often. "Why would you think the Colton girl would have anything to do with me changing? If I have changed, which I haven't."

"I just remembered how Da always used to say he was a regular cantankerous coot till he met Ma."

"And I'm cantankerous?"

Jason sighed. He never liked to hurt anyone's feelings. "You're the best brother there is, you know that. You saved my life, more than once. But since Ma went away you've been nothin' but cranky, and that's to say the least. Your eyes are cold, unless you're lookin' at me or Kathleen, and your mouth . . . well, you hardly ever smile anymore, Ry, and you had a right good smile."

"Anything else?" Ryan growled.

"That for one."

"What?"

"Your voice. You snarl at everyone. Now that's all right for the army, me boy, but it got to be a bit tryin' at home with the family."

"I see. So what are you saying?"

"Since you met that Julia girl, you've been more like the brother I grew up with. I just thought maybe you really do like her, just like I teased you about."

"And if I did?"

"It'd be a problem. Da'd have a conniption, that's for certain. Her brothers'd most likely shoot you, if her father didn't first."

"True."

"But if you do like her, Ry, and she likes you . . ." His voice trailed off.

"Yeah?"

"If I was you, I'd do whatever I had to do to be with her."

"You would? Well, what about Da? I don't think he'd agree, even though Ma meant everything to him. So much that he's never been the same since she died."

"Neither have you."

"And should I be? Should I pretend Ma's death never happened?"

"No. I'm not sayin' that. But did it help to join the Jayhawkers? Did it make you feel any better to be just like the men who killed Ma, who hurt Kathleen?"

Ryan's mouth tightened and Jason rushed on. "I'm just sayin' if you like the girl, you shouldn't let anything stand in the way of bein' with her, if she makes you happy again. Maybe she'd be good for you, Ry."

"What if being with her meant giving up everything I ever wanted or loved? The army, the farm, the family."

"Your vow to Ma?"

He turned on his side and stared at his brother. "What do you know of it?"

"I might only have been eleven, but I wasn't stupid. Ma wouldn't want you to get yourself killed for her. She was a gentle soul."

"Who didn't deserve to die the way she did."

"No, she didn't. But I just bet she's turnin' over in her grave, seein' what's happened to you. She doted on you. She depended on you."

"Look where it got her."

"Are you ever goin' to let that go and get on with your life?"

"I don't know if I can. I took a vow. I have a duty."

"Let it go, Ry, just let it go."

"How?"

"Maybe the Colton colleen is a step in the right direction."

"Or a step toward Hell."

Jason sighed and lay back on his bedroll to stare at the top of the tent. "I'll love you no matter what, you know? No matter what you've done, or haven't done, if you keep a vow or break it, you're my brother, and I'll always love ye. Forevermore."

The persistent agony in Ryan's stomach faded to a dull throb, but his eyes burned with a strange sort of heat. He blinked hard and fast to clear the strange wavy lines from his vision, and as he did a drop of water fell to his cheek. Frowning, he glared at the roof of the tent, then threw off his blanket as the bugler sounded reveille.

"Damned tent's got a leak in it," he grumbled and shoved his feet back into the boots he'd so recently removed. On the way out the door, he swiped the remaining "rain" from his eyes, hesitated as unspoken words and feelings welled up inside him, then he shook his head sharply and burst outside without voicing any of them.

Julia spent the rest of the night with her mama, who'd started another fever. The fevers were getting higher, lasting longer and leaving her weaker and weaker. The joy Julia had felt after spending the brief time with Ryan disappeared bit by bit while she bathed her mama's face and chest with cool water.

Her father kept looking at her strangely. Did her guilt show in her eyes? On her face? Had a scarlet letter appeared upon her chest? Hers a *T* for traitor, rather than the *A* of Hawthorne's tale? Del had not told, or her father would be doing more than staring, but all the same Julia's unease increased. When her father went to the fields at last, she breathed a long sigh of relief.

"How was the dance, child?"

Julia turned to her mama with a smile. She would not let her see how very worried she was this time. "Wonderful, Mama, just wonderful."

"I'm glad. You deserve to have some good times."

"I'm fine, Mama. I like to stay with you." Julia busied herself cleaning the table so her mama would not see her face heat at the lie. Once she had been content to stay with Mama, though she had dreamed of a world beyond. Now she only thought of the next time she might see Ryan Murphy. Alone.

"Who did you dance with?"

Julia's gaze flicked to her mama's, then away. Sometimes Mama saw too much. "Lots of boys."

"Any one in particular you liked?"

Mama definitely saw too much. "Not really, though Ted Chandler is a good dancer. Polite. For a boy of sixteen." Julia couldn't help but compare Ted's stuttering compliments and gangling young body to the deep, commanding voice and hardened strength of another.

"He join with Quantrill?"

Julia started at her mama's question, lost for a moment in the memory of blue eyes and searching lips. "H-he talked about George Todd. I think he's with them."

"You're hidin' somethin', child."

In the midst of wiping the table for the third time, Julia froze. "I don't know what you mean."

"I think you do. You've never lied to me. But now I can't get you to look me in the eye. I know your life hasn't been easy. I know your pa isn't the lovin' sort, and those boys . . ." She sighed. "If I hadn't birthed 'em, I wouldn't think they were mine. But livin' with them, here, you've become a strong woman. A smart woman. Or at least I hope you're smart. Are you smart, Julia?"

Julia raised her gaze to her mama's. Mama's eyes, so like her own, filled with tears. "Damn," she said, and swiped the back of her hand across her eyes. After a moment she regained her composure and beckoned Julia closer. "Sit." She indicated the ever-present chair at her bedside.

Julia sat.

"Your brothers are your brothers, no matter that your pa has made 'em into killers. They're no worse than the Jayhawkers who did this to me—" Julia fought not to wince or to weep. "Or the ones who would have hurt you at the creek. The only reason we haven't been attacked more often, hurt like the Samuels and the others, is because of how vicious your brothers are. If we didn't have them, we'd be in a fix for certain."

"I know, Mama."

"Do you? Do you really? You remember that, if you're ever tempted to turn traitor."

Julia remembered Del's lips forming the word *traitor* and was unable to control her wincing this time.

"Uh huh," Mama said, watching Julia closely.

"I wouldn't ever hurt my family."

"Hmm," her mama said. "You know, I was in love once."

Julia blinked at the sudden change in subject. "With Father?"

Mama snorted. "No."

"Does Father love you?"

"I wouldn't call it love, more like obsession. I was promised to him, and I'll be his forever. Love has little to do with it. But that's neither here nor there anymore. When I was younger than you, I fell in love. Nothing but disaster followed, for me and for everyone I loved."

"Mama, I didn't know."

Mama's words shocked Julia. She'd never had an inkling that her mother kept such secrets. She wanted to ask questions. Hear everything. But the look in her mama's eyes stopped her.

"I won't stand by and let the same thing happen to you."

"It won't."

Mama's eyes narrowed and a hard, determined look came over her face. "No, it won't."

A sudden chill bit Julia's neck, and she threw a glance over her shoulder to see if a storm had come up. But the summer sun shone through the open door with the usual ferocity of June in Missouri.

When she turned back, Mama had closed her eyes and turned her face to the wall as if asleep.

Julia sat at her mama's bedside as the Missouri sun heated the house toward scalding, yet still she shivered.

"Con! Connor Sullivan, where are ye?"

Shamus Murphy's bellow reached Con as he dressed for vespers in his rooms at the back of the church. Afraid something had happened to Ryan or

Jason, Con threw his robe over his head and hurried toward the church in his stocking feet.

"There ye are. I was afraid ye might be gone on one of yer pilgrimages to perform good deeds."

Since Shamus was smiling, not weeping or raging, Con relaxed a bit, but when he saw Kathleen hovering at the back of the church, his tension returned.

"Why is Kathleen here?"

Con knew how frightened Kathleen became whenever she left home. How Shamus had gotten her here, he had no idea. From what he'd heard, she had refused to get on a horse since she'd returned several months ago.

"Me years in Ireland fightin' the fight make me a prize in a war composed mostly of boys. Me old friend Tom, General Ewing that is, has secured me a captain's commission with the Fourth Kansas Cavalry."

"What?" Con pulled his gaze from Kathleen, who huddled in the corner of a pew in the darkest portion of the church.

"I've decided not t' wait around fer the Bushwhackers t' come t' me. I'm gonna take the fight t' them. If me boys can do it, then so can I."

"What about Kathleen?"

A shadow passed over the old man's face and he turned sad eyes upon his daughter. "It is fer Kathleen that I go."

"I don't understand."

"I stayed out of the fight at first fer the boys. Ryan was out fightin' the fight and Jason was so young, I couldn't leave him. Then Kathleen came home and—" His voice broke and Con put a hand to his elbow.

Shamus cleared his throat and straightened, throwing off Connor's comfort. "She nigh to broke me heart. Me little girl so quiet and changed. I couldn't leave her."

"Of course not."

"But I'm doin' her no good. She still does not speak. She'll nod or write a bit if she must. But she won't tell me what happened. I wonder if she knows."

Shamus glanced at Kathleen again, and this time his face shifted from sorrow to shame. "I have t' do something t' pay them back for all they've done t' me and mine."

"Who?"

"The damned Rebs, the Bushwhackers, the Coltons most of all."

"Shamus, I'd leave the Coltons be."

"Ye would, would ye? Well, that's why ye wear a skirt, Father," he sneered. Con blinked, surprised at the fury in the old man's voice and the sudden madness sparking his eyes. He'd known Shamus was hurt and angry and desperately missing his wife, but he hadn't realized how close the old man was to slipping over the edge. The human heart and mind could only stand so much loss and pain.

"I've brought her t' you."

"What?" Con seemed to be stuck on that single word.

"Ye take care of her like she was yer own sister now. The war'll be over soon enough, once I get me hands on a gun."

"She can't stay here. With me."

"Of course she kin. She needs sanctuary. This is a church."

"But—but—Shamus, I can't have a young woman staying with me."

Shamus scowled. "And why not?"

"People will talk."

"About what? Yer a priest, fer cryin' out loud. And near a member of the family t' boot. She's like yer sister. Yer all she's got."

Con glanced at Kathleen and his heart broke. She no longer resembled the girl he'd grown up with. Though she was older than he by five years, together they'd run through the brush, playing childish games, laughing, singing. Kathleen had been a beautiful girl, her hair a cross between sunshine and fire, her eyes bluer than the sky in July, her skin like cream, peaches the shade of her cheeks. But even more beautiful than her face had been her heart and her soul. Kathleen had loved life, lived it with fury and passion.

Now she merely existed, her hair dull, her eyes lifeless. She did not speak; she no longer laughed. Con had tried to reach her, but he could not. Perhaps if he'd been a better priest, he might have helped her. If he'd been a better man, she wouldn't be like this in the first place.

Though he'd forgiven the Bushwhackers who killed his family as a good man of God should, he still prayed every night to find forgiveness in his heart for those who had killed the Kathleen he loved. So far, his prayers had gone unanswered.

"Connor?"

"Yes?" Con came back from his memories to find Shamus waving a hand in front of Con's face.

"I'm talkin' t' ye, son. Where were ye?"

"Right here, Shamus." Con clasped his hands, a habit from so many years spent praying. He prayed now. What should he do? A glance at Kathleen and he knew. He could not deny her anything, or perhaps he could not deny himself a chance to try again to help her, though he'd most likely fail, as he always did. Still, she'd be here, and that was what he truly could not deny. To himself.

Con indulged himself for a moment, silently cursing Ryan. In keeping a vow, Ryan had broken a promise and set something in motion that could not now be stopped. He recalled Ryan's words of impending doom. Con felt it now, as well.

"All right," he snapped, and then took a deep breath to calm his voice. Shamus did not seem to notice. "I'll take care of her until you get back. What about the farm?"

"I sold all the stock, closed up the house, and Kathleen brought all her things, such as they are anymore. If ye can ride by once in a while and make certain the damned Coltons haven't moved in, I'd be grateful."

"And if they do?"

"Send me word. I'll be with the boys and we'll come directly."

Con nodded, though he would never send word to the Murphys if such a thing occurred. That'd be like setting a match to dry grass.

He narrowed his eyes, considering. Was that what Shamus had in mind? If he left the farm, and the Coltons showed up, he'd have good reason to bring the wrath of the entire Federal army in Kansas down upon them for thievery.

Well, Con didn't plan to be in on Shamus's game. He'd take care of Kathleen, as a good priest should. Con looked up as Shamus led her over, placing Kathleen's cold, limp hand into his.

And he'd try to forget how very much he'd loved her long, long ago.

Chapter Eight

The unease that fell upon Julia by her mother's bedside increased as the days passed, and she often found her parents with their heads together, whispering. Then her father would ride off on secret rides, and Mama would not tell Julia where he went or what he did.

She worried that Del had spilled her secret, and that her father plotted Ryan's demise. Though she'd threatened Del with dire repercussions, she didn't know if she could turn him over to the wolves—even if he was one of them. What good would it do to hurt Del if the truth had already been told? Despite her up bringing, Julia had no stomach for vengeance.

Mama, who had always been Julia's best friend—her only friend until Ryan—had suddenly become a stranger. She'd gotten over her fever, hauled herself out of bed for the first time in over a year and gotten dressed. She sat on the porch and watched the brush as if expecting a visit, or an attack. She refused to allow Julia to help her, and Julia wanted to scream and rage and cry at the loss of everything familiar. Instead she went about the duties remaining to her and kept her mouth shut, waiting to be punished for a crime she was uncertain she had committed.

Nevertheless, when punishment came, Julia was not prepared.

Her father brought Ted Chandler home for supper one day. That in itself was not odd. If a partisan company lurked in the vicinity, her father might ask one of the boys home to carry food out to the rest. Though Ted came alone, he did not look as though he'd just come out of the bush. Instead, his pale blond hair was still slicked to his head from a recent bath, and he wore his Sunday best. Just sixteen, the same age as Del, he looked even younger without his guerilla clothes and multitude of firearms. Shyly he glanced at Julia, then away, as her father urged him to sit down at the table.

"Look who's come to see us," her father enthused. As if they couldn't see for themselves.

Julia frowned and glanced at her mama, who made her way slowly to her chair. Mama wouldn't look at her, and the chill that had cling to Julia for far too long increased until she rubbed her arms and shuddered. Something was going on here. Something she did not understand. Something she doubted she would like.

Dinner was a strange affair, her father speaking too loudly for the small party and too jovially to be natural. Mama didn't talk at all. She didn't eat either. She just sat at the table and stared at her plate. Ted nodded when spoken to, ate heartily and glanced at Julia far too often. Julia watched them all and continued to shiver.

When the meal ended, Ted came around the table and pulled back Julia's chair. "Would you walk with me?" he asked.

Julia looked at her father. His joviality was only for Ted since he narrowed his eyes, scowled at her hesitation and jerked his head toward the door, ordering her to go. She looked at Mama, whose face remained carefully blank, but her eyes had filled with doubt.

"Mama?" Julia asked, uncertain of the undercurrents between them all.

"Go on, child. I'm fine. Ted has something he'd like to tell you."

Ted put his hand beneath her elbow and guided Julia toward the door. Both her mama and her father nodded as if she and Ted were doing something extremely clever. Julia went along, though her mind couldn't seem to grasp what was happening. Had something terrible happened to one of her brothers? But if that were so, her father would not be smiling, false though his smile might be.

She stepped from the house and into the pleasant coolness of approaching night. After a humid, heated day, the sinking of the sun provided release and relief. The ball of red still hung in the western sky, bright against a horizon streaked with orange, pink and violet. Julia loved this time of day. Too bad she couldn't enjoy it tonight.

Ted led her past the barn and outbuildings, out of sight of the house, yet not too close to the brush. With a shy smile and a shrug, he let go of her arm and contemplated the setting sun. "Storm on the way," he said.

"Really?"

Nodding, he pointed at the sky. "See how the horizon is purple, but the line between the sky and the ground moves?"

"Yes," Julia agreed, though she watched Ted and not the sky. He'd rarely said more than three words to her in his life, and those had been "thank you" or "Yes, Miss Julia." She was amazed to discover him capable of a decent conversation, even if it was about the weather.

"That wavy purple line means a thunderstorm is coming in from the west."

Julia made a noncommittal sound. A walk. A talk. The weather. This situation smelled suspiciously like a courting ritual. Or so she'd heard, since she'd never been courted. But why would a sixteen-year-old boy, who'd pledged his allegiance to the guerilla way, come courting a twenty-year-old woman whose life was devoted to caring for her sick mother?

"What did you want to tell me, Ted?"

Crimson crept from his collar to his chin, making his watery blue eyes shine in an eerie way. "Has something happened to one of the boys?" Though her brothers could be vicious, they were still her brothers, and she didn't want them dead, or worse, captured.

"No." Ted's flush faded, bit by bit. "Or leastways not that I've heard. Colonel Quantrill took his men north. No word of any skirmishes."

"Then what?" Julia's voice was too loud and they both started, but she was getting mighty sick of all the secrecy.

Ted straightened, as if he'd been called to attention, looked into her eyes and grabbed her by the shoulders. "This," he said, and kissed her.

Julia's eyes went wide with shock, and she found herself unable to move or breathe. His eyes fluttered closed and he sighed, obviously enjoying himself, and his fingers dug into her shoulders, pulling her closer. His lips were hard on hers, too hard she knew now, and when he pushed his tongue into her mouth she gagged and tore away from him. Before she could think, she slapped him as hard as she could.

Ted might have been young, but he was guerilla bred. By the time Julia's fingerprints glared red against his pale cheek, he'd pulled his gun and pressed the barrel beneath her chin. She stared into his eyes, fascinated with the change from shy, innocent suitor to vicious killer.

"Just what the hell do you think you're doing?" she whispered, not wanting to shout and bring her father into the fray—or get her head blown clear off her shoulders.

Ted did not bother to lower his voice. "Taking what's mine."

She would have gaped if he hadn't had the pistol pressed so tightly to her jaw. "What?"

"You're mine."

Julia laughed, probably not a good idea, but she couldn't help herself. "I don't think so. Just because we danced one dance doesn't mean you can kiss me, Ted Chandler. You'd better put up your gun before my father comes out here. He won't take kindly to your pawing me, and the gun will surely cause a scene.''

Ted stepped closer, trailing the barrel of his gun down her neck, a twisted caress, until the cold metal pressed against her breastbone. Julia held very still, staring into his face, trying to gauge her chances of grabbing the gun and smacking him over the head with it. From the look in his eyes, those chances were mighty slim. He leaned forward and whispered into her ear, ''I don't think your father will care, seeing as he's the one who gave you to me.''

Julia jerked away from the heated drift of his breath across her ear, prepared to give him a proper set down. One look into his face and the words froze in her throat. She'd mistaken the depth of Ted's commitment to the guerilla way. In his eyes she saw the same deep-down mean she'd seen in many an eye in her lifetime. What he wanted, he would take, and right now he seemed to want her.

She backed up a few steps, to remove the cold, hard barrel of his gun from her chest. Ted smiled, not the shy, sweet smile she'd seen on him all his life. Instead, he smiled a new, nasty smile that made her turn and run all the way back to the house.

Julia burst inside to find her mama crying and her father standing nearby, an annoyed look on his face. In the past, Julia would have run to her mama and done whatever she could to ease her pain; this time she kept her distance.

''Is what he said true?'' she demanded.

Her father scowled. ''Can't ya see your mama is upset?''

"I'm upset! He said you gave me to him. Is that true?"

Mama sobbed and threw herself facedown onto the bed. Julia's father looked from his wife to his daughter, hesitated, then clenched his fists and crossed the room. Julia refused to let him intimidate her. This was her life they were talking about. Up until now she'd been told, and believed, her duty lay in taking care of her mother. Now the very man who'd told her that had given her away like a worm-filled sack of flour.

He stood so close Julia had to crane her head back to see his face. "Your mama said you've been mooning over that Murphy boy. And she ought to know. I even heard a rumor he was at the dance ya went to. Next thing I know you'll run off and whore for him, then come home with a brat in your belly. I won't have it. I won't let ya make me a laughingstock in this county, girl."

Julia felt as if everything she'd ever known as truth had been a lie. Her mama had betrayed her. The Federals weren't the enemy; the enemy was right here. Suddenly Julia was so angry she couldn't see anything but red.

"It's all right for me to whore for someone of your choice. Just make sure it isn't a Murphy, is that it?"

"Who said anything about whoring?" her father sneered. "You're gonna marry Chandler, just as quick as I can make the marriage happen."

"Marry him? I will not. He's sixteen years old."

Her father grabbed her by the shoulders and shook her. Julia's head snapped back so hard the world wavered. She blinked to clear her vision, and her father shouted into her face. "I don't care if he still wets his pants, you'll do what I say, when I say it, ya hear me?''

She yanked herself free of her father's hands. "I hear you.''

"Del's the one who brought Ted to me. If Del picked him, he's gotta think Ted'll do right by ya.''

She'd wondered what Del's revenge would be, but this was beyond anything she'd imagined. A lifetime shackled to a man such as Ted was pretty severe punishment, even for a traitor. She should have expected as much from the man Del had become, despite her best efforts, but somehow she had not.

Julia spared a glance for her mama, who was still crying upon the bed. For the first time in her life she felt something other than love or pity for the woman who had borne her. Right now all she felt was betrayed—and trapped.

Julia turned toward the door. Ted stood in the doorway, gun safely back in its holster, nasty smile still in place. The trap's door creaked further closed.

She had to find a way out of this; someone had to help her. And she knew just who.

Since their da had shown up and taken command of their unit, Ryan's and Jason's satisfaction with the military had been fading fast. Not that their da was a bad commander. He was just a little obsessed.

He had became more so with each passing day in which they did not encounter a guerilla unit. He rode them from one end of Bates County to the next, through terrain so rough horses and men were scraped and bloody from the bushes and burrs. How the Bushwhackers could find a trail through the mess that was

Bates County, no one could understand. But Shamus Murphy planned to be the first Kansan to discover their secret—and their camp.

Once Ryan had revered his da like most boys. His father was the biggest, the strongest, the smartest and the best. But Ryan had grown up; Shamus had grown strange, and though Ryan had vowed to revenge himself upon those who had wrecked their world, the increase in the depth of his father's hatred frightened him at times. It was as if the man he'd known all his life had disappeared and another had come to take his place.

Still Ryan did as he was told, as a good soldier and son should. But he felt itchy, twitchy, as if something was happening that he should be in on. The constant riding, the searching but never finding, did not help his unease. Neither did the message a young boy brought from Father Con for Ryan.

Come quickly. Tell no one.

"Damn." Ryan couldn't think of anything else to say. What kind of message was this? He scowled at the paper. Trouble? Death? Sickness? Who?

Since Kathleen was with Con, Ryan had to go. Not that he'd ever considered ignoring such a summons. If there was one thing Con was not, it was a nervous man.

But tell no one—what did that mean? If something were wrong with Kathleen, shouldn't Da and Jason come, too? Ryan threw the paper into the fire and went to find his father. If Con said tell no one, then no one he would tell. Ryan just needed to come up with an appropriate lie to get permission to ride to the church on the hill, and hope he didn't get himself shot along the way.

Con prayed. For guidance. For strength. For some kind of sign. What was he supposed to do?

The Colton girl had shown up on his doorstep, pale and shaking, but not a tear in her eye. She'd said Ryan had told her to come to Con if she needed help. Damn Ryan Murphy. Con had never helped anyone in his life.

Still, he'd sent a message to Ryan immediately. If the army were camped near enough, he should be here before morning. In the meantime, Con had put Julia in to sleep with Kathleen.

Two women in his bed. God did have a sense of humor. Why was the joke forever on Connor Sullivan?

He'd been with Kathleen for over a week. She still had not spoken, though Con had spoken to her quite a bit. Why he thought he might be able to reach through her pain he did not know. He wasn't much of an advisor. He wasn't much of anything. If he'd had the courage to defy his father once long ago, Kathleen would not be the way she was now. But recriminations would do neither of them any good.

Perhaps Kathleen being here was a sign in itself. Her face, lined with pain, her hair grayed by agony and her eyes dulled with forced oblivion showed Con what happened when love was denied. With Kathleen as an example, how could he deny the love of Julia Colton for Ryan, despite the avowed enmity between their families? He of all people should know a heart must be followed, no matter the consequences.

Since his mother's death, Ryan had matured into a man far different from the one Con had expected. The joyous, adventuresome boy who wanted to be everyone's hero had become a solemn, silent man guided by a vow he never should have taken. What had happened at the Colton farm had only added more guilt and recriminations to those Ryan already carried within him.

If Ryan continued on the path he'd set, he would surely die. But in his friend's eyes that night at the dance, Con had caught a glimpse of the old Ryan—whenever Ryan had looked at the Colton girl. She'd looked at Ryan as if he could change the world, or at least her world. Perhaps that was what Ryan needed. Someone to believe in him absolutely, to believe him capable of anything, and then he would be. Someone to forgive him everything, then maybe he could forgive himself.

If Julia Colton could bring back the Ryan of old, could she save Ryan from his self-destructive path? If Con believed in God and all he'd been taught to follow and to teach others, then Con had to believe in the power of love over the power of hate. And if he didn't believe in God, he might as well die now. For God was all he had left.

Con muttered and shifted, his knees aching from the hours spent on the marble floor. "A sign, Father, just once, please God, give me a sign," he begged.

The door of the church banged open, and an icy breeze that promised thunder, lightning and hail swept down the aisle and extinguished the candles on the altar. Con sat back on his heels and waited, but if God was speaking, Con was unable to hear.

Then he noticed the breeze had ruffled the pages of a book that lay open between the candles. Slowly he got to his feet, hoping against all hope he'd at last been given a sign from above. He relit one candle, leaned over the book, read the entry and began to smile.

The ceremony of marriage. A pledge of love before the world.

God had answered. At last.

Julia awoke alone, amazed to have slept at all after running through the night to the church on the hill and telling her tale to the priest, Ryan's friend. She'd been terrified he would order her to honor her mother and father, pat her on the head and send her back home to marry Ted. The longer she had to think on the idea, the more nauseated she became. She would not marry Ted Chandler. She'd die first.

In the light of morning, her vow of the night before seemed a bit melodramatic, though that did not mean she would not keep it. Being bound for life to a boy who would pull a gun on a woman and who called her *his* like a prize cow would not do. Kissing him again was out of the question and anything more intimate an impossibility. But how, dear God, was she going to make her father and Mama see the light?

Julia sat up in bed, and a quick glance revealed Ryan's sister had left the room already. When the priest had brought Julia here last night and introduced the two of them, the irony had not been lost on her—a Murphy and a Colton sharing a bed for the night. Heat flamed her face when she recalled the face of a Murphy she'd rather share a bed with.

Julia paused, realizing she did not know Kathleen's married name. The priest had introduced her as Kathleen Murphy, as if she had been and always would be that in his mind. It was, perhaps, as if her years as a married woman had never existed, or were best not spoken of.

Kathleen, the victim of a Bushwhacker attack, no longer spoke. Still, she had nodded solemnly and pulled back the bedclothes in invitation after Julia had been introduced. A blush of shame had ignited in Julia's cheeks that this woman who had suffered and lost more than Julia could imagine, would accept lying down next to the enemy without a quiver. The world could take lessons on forgiveness from Kathleen Murphy.

Last night, with the candle extinguished and while Kathleen slept, Julia had stared into the darkness and thought about the three Murphy children. Each possessed startlingly beautiful blue eyes, very similar in shade, shape and lurking shadows. But each suppressed the shadows in a different way. Jason laughed and joked and grinned, but the sadness never fled. Kathleen did not speak, solemn and sure were her eyes, but the agony lurked there, too. And then there was Ryan. He tried to drown his pain with words of anger and violence and vengeance, but he only pushed the shadows deeper within.

Julia shook her head to clear her mind of the image of Ryan's eyes. She could not lie in bed all day in her shift when any moment someone might trace her here and drag her home—or worse. Hurriedly Julia dressed and went in search of Father Con.

She couldn't find him or anyone else. She seemed

to be alone, and the thought frightened her. If her father found her here, he would say sanctuary be damned and drag her right home. Or he might bring Ted along and force her to marry the little cutthroat right there. She could refuse, but she had no doubt her father had ways of making her concede, despite her resolve.

With little else to do, Julia sat in the front pew and stared up at the stained-glass window of the Virgin holding Jesus. Though she'd seen many representations like it, for some reason this morning the mother and her dead son made Julia wince and turn her gaze away from the sight of so much pain.

"Julia?"

The voice from behind her made Julia leap to her feet and spin around, terrified she'd find her father, or Ted, waving a gun in her face. Instead, Ryan stood in the aisle.

She blinked, but he remained. Tired, rumpled, muddy, still he was the most beautiful thing she'd ever seen, even attired in the Federal uniform she'd known he wore yet had never viewed him in. With a choked cry she ran toward him, throwing herself into his waiting arms.

"What are you doing—"

She stopped his question with a kiss, pressing her body against his, heedless of the mud on his uniform, or the guns at his waist that bruised her hips. She wrapped her arms around his neck and lost her fears in the wonder of his embrace. She purged the memory of another's mouth upon hers, making new memories with the man of her heart. How long they stood there in the middle of the sun-drenched church she did not know. She only knew when she broke the kiss that her face was wet with tears, and the dirt on his cheeks had turned to mud.

He frowned at her tears, reaching up and tracing a track with his thumb. "What's wrong?" he whispered, at once fierce and gentle.

She shook her head. "It doesn't matter. You're here now. That's all that matters."

He started to move away, but she clung, making his frown return. He knew her so well already, knew she did not usually cling, but right now she needed to be held. "Please, for just another minute, hold me."

He did, and he didn't ask questions she wasn't prepared to answer. He held her against his chest and rested his chin upon her head. The steady beat of his heart beneath her cheek calmed her own racing heart until the two beat as one. She never wanted to move again but she had to.

As she pulled back, she glanced up into his face and was surprised to find a look she had not seen there before. It was a combination of the secret, heated look he'd worn at the creek, the look she understood now as desire, but he also looked at her like Del used to, when she'd strayed too close to the brush or the open field where a sniper might hide. Ryan wanted to protect her, and the knowledge started a warm glow in her stomach.

She smiled softly and reached up to cup his cheek. The protective look disappeared and the heat soared. This time he kissed her. This time the kiss was not meant to soothe. She gave herself up to the passion that should not be between them but was, kissing him back with all the love that brimmed in her heart.

So involved were they in each other, they did not hear footsteps approach, did not hear anything but their own whispered sighs of desire until the voice echoed through the church. "From the looks of this, I take it you'll be marrying her, Ryan Murphy."

Ryan looked up, narrowed his eyes at the speaker and growled, "Marry?"

The shock on his face made Julia's heart break, and she tore herself from his arms to run past Father Con and out of the church on the hill.

Chapter Nine

"I'm impressed, Ryan." Con turned from the doorway, where he'd watched Julia run away and not even tried to stop her, then walked down the center aisle of the church, his face darkening with disgust and anger. "What Kathleen and I accomplished since Julia arrived here last night, you destroyed in a matter of minutes."

Ryan ignored him, trying to move past Con and follow Julia. Con grabbed him by the shoulders and shoved him into a pew. Not expecting the move, Ryan fell hard but came up with his fists clenched. "Don't mess with me, Con, I've ridden all night through the mud and the muck. At your request, I might add."

Con reached out and shoved him a second time. Ryan stumbled back a step, his legs hitting the pew so he promptly sat down again. "Are you crazy?" he shouted. "If you want to fight, let's go outside. Though why you'd want to I don't know. The last time we did this I flattened you."

Con slapped a hand on either side of the pew at Ryan's shoulders, effectively trapping him. "Shut up," he said. "For once you're going to listen to me."

Though everything in Ryan screamed for him to get up and go after Julia, Con's anger stopped him. He'd been wishing for years for some life to return to Con's eyes; now that it had, he couldn't abandon the miracle. Forcing himself to relax, Ryan sat in the pew and waited.

"Fighting's not the answer to every problem," Con said.

Ryan raised his eyebrows. "And I thought you were Irish," he said with a snort.

Con ignored his attempt to lighten the air. "Sometimes you've got to find another way."

"Your way?"

Sighing, Con straightened, then took a seat next to Ryan on the pew. "My way is my way. You have another choice."

"You've really lost me here. I came as you asked, though it wasn't easy to tell no one. I lied to my father."

"Good."

"Good?" Ryan glanced sideways at Con, who had become quite interested in his own hands, which were clenched as if in prayer. "And this from a priest. What happened to 'Honor thy father'?"

"Forget about that right now. We're going to listen to a different prophet today."

"Which one?"

Con unfolded his hands, straightened and stared up at the stained-glass window in front of them. "Christ," he whispered.

"Now you're taking the Lord's name in vain. I think you're slipping into Hell ahead of me."

Con turned toward him with a scowl. "Would you quit making jokes? Jesus said, 'Love your enemies.'"

"I've heard that."

"Shut up."

Since Con said the two words from between gritted teeth, Ryan shut up. Something had worked Con up awful high.

"I wasn't around when your ma died." Ryan went still, but Con continued. "I imagine you were mighty confused since you went off and joined the Jayhawkers. A mistake, but everyone makes them. If you'd learned from it, perhaps it wouldn't have been so bad."

"I did learn. I left them."

"To hate in other ways, other places, using a different name. But hating and fighting and vowing vengeance on the world hasn't helped, has it?"

Ryan's shoulders ached from the night ride and the tension brought by memories. He stared straight ahead as all amusement faded, and his stomach began its familiar burn. "I'm not done yet."

Con ignored his words. "That girl who ran out of here loves you. Despite who you are and all that you've done and every reason she has to hate you, she loves you. She's got trouble, and you're going to help her."

In the midst of shifting his shoulders to relieve the pain, Ryan froze. "What kind of trouble?"

"Marrying trouble. Do you love her?"

It was Ryan's turn to stare at his hands, which were clenched between his knees. He remembered Julia's lips, her strong, slim body beneath his hands, his name upon her lips and her name on his. "I don't know."

"Could you love her?"

Her name, his name—there lay the problem. "I don't know."

Con mumbled something beneath his breath that sounded suspiciously like a curse. "What *do* you know?"

Ryan pondered the question. *I know the vow that's shaped my life, the vow I have to fulfill if I'm to live with myself, is a vow against those she's been raised to protect. I've already hurt her family enough, but if I recant my vow, everything I've believed is a lie. Honor and duty and promises to keep. Yet if I never see her again, I'll never feel anything again. And I'm terrified if I love her and then lose her, I'll become exactly what I hate—a soulless, vengeful murderer.*

Instead of sharing those words with Con, Ryan drowned them out with other, angrier words. "I know that not more than a few weeks ago you told me to stay away from her. Told me she was the enemy and I courted my own death. Now you want me to marry her. Why?"

"Because I'm thinking maybe I should follow what I've been taught. Let an eye for an eye go the way of the Old Testament and start turning the other cheek."

"Fine for you. I'm a soldier in the middle of a civil war. Turning my cheek will not only get me killed but the rest of my men, too."

"I'm not talking about the war, I'm talking about the Coltons. I'm talking about Julia. And you. Maybe if the two of you choose love over hate the rest of them will learn from you. You could heal a lot of wounds, Ry."

"You want me to marry her." Ryan sighed, confused, uncertain. His heart wanted one thing, his body the same, but his mind argued. His stomach rebelled. "Then what will I do with her? She can't stay with me, or go to the farm. Even Kathleen's here with you."

"She can stay here, too. I'm running a regular asylum." He winced. "I'm sorry. I didn't mean that the way it sounded."

"I know." Ryan gentled his voice, forgiving what need not be forgiven. There had always been something between Con and Kathleen, though what it was Ryan had no idea—and had never found the courage to ask. "What will marrying Julia solve?"

"Maybe nothing more than her problem right now. But isn't that enough?"

"What exactly is this marrying problem?"

"Her father's trying to force her to marry someone else."

Mindless fury swept through Ryan. He smelled sulfur and ash, war and death. He couldn't see straight for the surge of battle that took over his blood. She was his, no one else's. She'd been his since the first moment he saw her, bloody, muddy and scared to death, but still fighting for her life. Despite his thoughts, his feelings, his fear made him fight the inevitable.

"How will marrying her solve that problem?"

"If she's married to you, she can't marry anyone else."

"They could force her."

"I'm the only priest left in four counties. I can't marry her to anyone else if she's married to you."

"They could get a minister."

"She'd still be married to you."

"They could kill me."

"Have to find you first."

Ryan was running out of arguments—for Con and for himself. "Can't this wait? I'm a little busy right now."

"This is your fault."

"Mine?"

"Her parents suspect her fondness for you. Because of that, to keep you two from doing something foolish—"

"Like marrying each other?" Ryan interrupted.

Con's lips tightened. "Because of you," he said slowly, looking into Ryan's eyes all the while, "Julia's father is going to marry her to a sixteen-year-old guerilla who likes to put pistols to women's heads."

Ryan straightened his back, unclasped his hands and stood. The ache in his gut dissipated as he glared down at his friend. "Someone pulled a gun on her?" Ryan rested tingling fingertips on the grip of his Colt. "Who?"

"Marry her, Ryan." Lifting his gaze from Ryan's hand to his face, Con smirked. "You know you want to."

"Who, Con?"

"I'm not telling you so you can go out and kill the kid, be a white knight charging to her rescue, a temporary hero. You do something permanent, and you do it now before it's too late."

Con left him alone, to contemplate past and future vows, present and forever promises.

Julia didn't know where she meant to run when she ran from the church. She'd already run *to* the church and *away* from home. Should she run back home now that she'd seen with her own eyes her secret dreams were just that—hopes without any substance or prayer of coming true?

She stopped when she reached the edge of the hill, glanced back, but no one followed, and she breathed a sigh of relief. She had no need for anyone's counsel or comfort but her own right now.

Despite the earliness of the morn, the sun beat hot and furious on her uncovered head. The brightness of the glare shone off the roofs of homes on either side of the hill.

What had she wished for in her heart of hearts? That Ryan would charge in as he'd done once before and rescue her. What would he do with her then? He was a soldier in the service of an army that wanted to crush all those who believed as her family did. With his sister residing at the church and all the menfolk off to war, he no longer had a home fit for a woman. If her family had their way, not only would he never have a home again, he wouldn't be alive to mourn its loss.

She admitted to herself that she was a dreamer. She

always had been. She'd had nothing else to fill the lonely days of her life. Mama had been her friend, but Julia had needed more than that. Though her days had been filled with work, her mind had been filled with wishes and hopes and dreams. She had been ripe to fall in love with the first man who paid her any mind, who listened and talked to her, the first man who resembled the hero she held in her heart.

She had been foolish to hope Ryan might feel the same for her. They were natural enemies. Perhaps she could have ignored his name, but he, it seemed, could not ignore hers. She had no experience with men or the world, and she would pay for that lack with the loss of her innocence—of the heart, if not the body.

What would she do? She could not marry Ted. Even if her love for Ryan was unreturned, hopeless, she still loved him and could not give herself to another. But she feared what Ted might do. She'd seen in his eyes before she ran that he would make her pay for this rebellion. He might be young, but he was mean and would only get meaner. She would not go quietly toward this damnation. She would fight until not a breath remained in her body. Perhaps she had been raised to honor her family first and all else later, but she would not do what they wanted of her now. She could not.

And that left her—

"In big trouble," she muttered.

"You came to the right place."

Julia knew the voice now, the quiet strength beneath the words, the soothing tone that did not match the world-weary look in Father Con's eyes. He had his own demons, this man who was Ryan's friend, but he put them aside to do what he could for everyone.

She turned and smiled. She'd seen him with Kathleen, and he near crushed her heart with the tenderness he had shown for the broken woman. If anyone could reach Kathleen Murphy it would be Father Con.

"You say I came to the right place?" Julia returned. "And why is that?"

He came to stand beside her, staring first to the east and then to the west. "You're caught between them, despite who you are. So am I."

"And how do you live with it?"

"I try my best to do what's right."

"And just what would be right for me?"

"Only you can answer that, Julia."

"I love him. I shouldn't. It would be easier for everyone if I hated him."

"Hate is always easier, but never right."

"No? It isn't right to hate the man who helped make my mother an invalid? She'll die soon. That makes him a murderer."

"Does your hatred change anything? Or does it just hurt more people in the end?"

"Do you always answer a question with another question?"

"It's my job."

She laughed. He was a charming man, though she doubted he meant to be. Her laughter died, and she glanced at him; a heated wind picked up her braid and flipped the length over her shoulder. Absently, she flicked her hair back. He turned to her with a quirk of his black brow. "I couldn't marry Ted, even if it would keep peace in my little world."

"I know. It isn't my place to tell you to defy your father, but I'm hoping if you and Ryan set an example, perhaps some of the strife between your two houses will die."

"Something will die, all right, but I doubt it will be the strife. Besides, I saw Ryan's face when you said the word *marry*. He was horrified."

He shook his head. "Surprised, maybe. Give him some time. He has more ghosts than you think."

Julia gave him a sober glare.

Father Con stared at her, though she doubted he saw her at all. "We all do," he murmured and left her alone to contemplate her fate.

He would marry her. Ryan argued with himself awhile longer, but in the end he gave up, despite the fact that the cons far outnumbered the pros. He'd lost the argument before he'd begun. He didn't want to win.

He'd most likely die for this. Slow and painfully, but he'd be doing the right thing, the only thing, he could do. She was in trouble because of him, because he'd been unable to deny his need to see her. He should not even have thought of her. He had been selfish and foolish, but he would not make her pay the price for his mistake when there was something he could do to keep her safe.

He went looking for her and found everyone else. Con sat in his study, writing a sermon on the power of love for Sunday's mass. Kathleen worked in the kitchen, baking a cake that looked suspiciously of the wedding variety. When Ryan came in, she smiled at him, and though the smile didn't reach her eyes, still she smiled. At least she would forgive him for what he was about to do, or if not forgive, she understood. Da would do neither. In fact, Ryan would be lucky if his own father didn't whip him to death instead of the hanging noose he expected once Julia's brothers got wind of this.

He continued to search the grounds of the church on the hill, alone. It appeared she did not want him to find her, and he couldn't say he blamed her after what had happened earlier. She'd looked to him for salvation, and just like once before, he had failed when she needed him the most. He had a second chance now, and he would not fail again.

In the late afternoon, when the heat became unbearable, Ryan removed his uniform coat and climbed the steps to the belfry. Though he'd figured the summer's heat had heightened the temperature in the tower to the bacon-sizzling range, he was surprised to discover the thickness of the stone walls kept the heat at bay. Shadows shrouded the small platform, and a light breeze played through the small opening. He sat down with his back against one wall, prepared to talk himself out of his earlier course— and there she was, on the opposite side of the bell, her dress unbuttoned to the waist, her chemise spilling out, the hair at her temples curling from sweat, fast asleep.

So he watched her as she slept, and forgot every argument he'd ever had for not marrying her and making her his forever. Even in sleep her inner strength was visible from the determined set of her mouth, to the slight line between her brows that showed her serious bent. Yet when awake, she could smile or laugh with equal ease. If he did not make her his wife he might never see her smile or hear her laughter again.

He would not let her go. He would not let her marry any other man, especially a man who would crush her spirit and take her will. The things about Julia he admired the most were her courage and her optimism. She might easily have given in to the demands of a hard life, to the hatred preached by her father and the viciousness practiced by her brothers. But she'd fought on, with her dreams and her will, to remain strong and gentle and kind.

He did love her, mistake though it might be, and he always would.

She opened her eyes then, stared straight into his. He tensed, expecting her to run, or shout, or spit at him. Instead she smiled, a sleepy, sensuous smile that made his throat close and his loins harden. He went still, afraid if he moved time would march on, and he wanted this moment to last forever.

But nothing lasts forever, and as she came fully awake he could see the memories tumble forward, dulling her smile, shadowing her eyes. She sat up and fumbled with the buttons of her gown, an embarrassed flush spreading from her chest up to her cheeks.

"I thought you'd go away."

"If you hid long enough, you mean?"

"Yes." She finished the last button, but the blush still heated her face. She kept her eyes averted.

"No. I wasn't going until I talked to you."

"About what?"

"Us."

She made a derisive sound and continued to contemplate the plank floor beneath her. "There isn't any us."

"There can be."

"No, there can't." She sighed, deep and sad, and traced a fingernail across a flaw in the wood. "I know I dream too much. I didn't have much else but work and dreams. Silly things, dreams. My mama always told me I'd fall in a hole someday while dreaming and never know it till I starved to death down there."

He didn't want her to stop dreaming, become beaten down and despairing like other women. "Dreams aren't silly. Sometimes they might be frightening, but never silly."

She flicked a glance and a frown his way. "Frightening?"

"Yeah. I've had some whoppers."

"Nightmares?" He nodded. "I'm sorry. I don't have nightmares. None I can recollect, anyway."

He smiled. "I'm glad."

They remained silent for a long while. Ryan didn't know how to begin, what to say, if he should say anything. The silence moved from companionable to awkward. Julia bent her legs as if to stand.

"Wait," he blurted, putting his hand out to stop her and knocking the bell. The heavy brass fixture swayed, and the knocker scraped across the inside, making them both wince.

"We'd best get out of here before someone rings this. We'll be deaf if we don't."

"Just a minute more," he said. "Please?"

She hesitated, her green gaze reminding him of a cat that had just been kicked but was too stubborn to run away, waiting to see if an apology would follow, but expecting another kick just the same. "A minute," she allowed.

"I made a mess of things before. I was surprised. Tired."

"You don't have to explain, Ryan. You owe me nothing. I can take care of myself."

"I'm sure you can. But—"

He stopped, uncertain again. Would she be angry if he said he wanted to take care of her? If he said he felt responsible for her predicament, honor bound to ease her troubles if he could, guilty over the past and anxious to amend the future. He didn't want her devotion, her dependence, her gratitude. Perhaps her forgiveness, but freely given and not owed. He wanted her to remain just as she was, except with a different name. His.

"Ryan? We should go down."

"Aw, hell, Julia. I'm no good at this."

"What?"

He leaned back against the stone wall, stared out at the descending sun. "Soft words. Tender touches. Roses and poetry." He looked back at her and shrugged. "I'm not that kind of man."

The wariness in her eyes faded as a gentle smile transformed her face. "You've done all right so far. I remember your touches, every single one, and they were quite tender, the words you whispered all the poetry I've ever wanted to hear. I'll remember them and you forever."

"That sounds like goodbye."

"It is." She stood.

Panic flared inside him, loosening his tongue. "No. Don't go. Please." He stood, too, making his way around the platform until he stood next to her. The wariness had returned to her eyes, the kicked-cat look again. He reached out a hand that shook just a bit and smoothed the curling hair at her temple away from her eyes. When his fingertips brushed her skin, she shivered, and a tiny gasp of surprise escaped her mouth. He had to taste that mouth or die with wanting to.

He pressed his lips to hers, drinking her sigh, drowning in her scent, roses and tears. She didn't respond at first, but when he continued to kiss her, then whispered her name in a choked, pleading voice he barely recognized as his own, she gave a sob of surrender and wrapped her arms about his neck, kissing him back with a desperation that matched his own.

He wanted her so much he ached with it. His hands swept over her back, her waist, paused beneath her breasts. She moaned and arched against him. The beat of his heart sounded in his head, a primitive drum blocking out sense and reason. He wanted her. Now.

The cool breeze shifted, bringing the scent of flames and ashes, remembrances of a world gone mad. His ardor receded. They broke apart to stare out the window. On the horizon, smoke billowed, and the sun bled red, reminding them of all that awaited. She leaned against him, limp, and he held her as they watched the smoke and the flames mingle in the distance.

"Marry me, Julia," he said without taking his gaze from the smoke-filled horizon.

"Yes," she answered, and the wind howled.

Chapter Ten

Julia stared into the mirror as her soon to be sister-in-law fixed her hair. She didn't look any different—for a dead woman.

She had lost her mind. That was a fact. When her father learned of her insanity, he'd put her away forever, if he didn't shoot her first. Or Ryan.

Julia winced. Kathleen, who must have thought she'd stuck Julia in the head with a hairpin, made an apologetic sound and patted Julia on the shoulder. Julia reached up and took Kathleen's fingers in hers, holding them until Kathleen leaned down and their gazes met in the mirror.

"Am I making a mistake?" she asked, though she knew Kathleen would not answer. "I'm selfish. I love him. More than I ever thought I could love."

Kathleen smiled and her eyes filled with tears. She

moved away from the mirror and scrubbed at her face with the back of her hand.

Julia turned around and stared at Kathleen's back. "You felt that way once, too, didn't you?"

Kathleen did not turn around; she did nod.

"And you lost him. That's why you won't speak." Another nod.

"I'm sorry, Kathleen. I can only imagine what that might be like." And the same could happen to Ryan. Today. Tomorrow. Next week. He could die in the real war, or he could die in the war between their families. Either way he could die, and then she would want to do the same.

"Damn," Julia whispered, her eyes stinging. "I should run far away. From here, from him. That's the only way to keep him safe."

"You can't keep him safe." Father Con's voice from the doorway made them both start and turn his way. "And love is a risk, but once a man loves a woman, he shouldn't ever let her go. Not for his family, not for his safety, nor any other reason I can think of. Life is too short, and getting shorter every day."

Though he spoke to her, or so Julia thought, Father Con stared at Kathleen. Kathleen smiled at him, as a mother would smile at a wayward child, and then turned to hold out her hand to Julia.

"You seem to have some strong opinions on love, for a priest," Julia observed as she and Kathleen followed Father Con toward the church.

"I was a man once."

"You still look like a man to me."

His footsteps faltered; his back tensed, but he recovered and continued toward the church without comment.

Julia forgot all about Father Con when she stepped into the church. "Oh," she breathed, unable to find words for her joy.

The altar was alight with candles, their warm, welcoming glow casting a dreamlike quality over the scene. Someone had gathered wildflowers and strewn them about the steps leading to the altar. Pink, yellow, red, the colors muted by the candlelight, their scent hung heavy on the air.

Ryan waited for her, his uniform miraculously cleaned of mud, his golden hair freshly washed and combed flat to his head, his face a combination of expectation and uncertainty. His eyes met hers and she hesitated, caught in his gaze as she'd been caught many times before. Everyone else in the world disappeared until nothing existed but the two of them and all that simmered between them.

Kathleen tugged on her hand, making Julia realize she'd stopped dead between the hallway and the church. She smiled sheepishly and followed as Kathleen led her toward Ryan. When they reached him, Kathleen took his hand and placed Julia's in it. She kissed both of them on the cheek and stepped back.

The ceremony was unlike any Julia had ever dreamed of, when she'd dreamed of such a moment. Though the man she pledged her heart, her body and her life to was the hero of her dreams, the absence of her family weighed on her heart. The knowledge that they would not have been here even if they'd known what she was doing cast a pall over her happiness.

Still, when Ryan finally answered "I do," in the

commanding voice she adored, her heart seemed reborn. When her turn came to pledge herself, she looked straight into his blue eyes and answered without hesitation. He smiled, a rare smile that reached his eyes, and squeezed her hand. He had not released it for a moment since his sister had placed it into his keeping.

"I don't suppose you have a ring," Father Con asked.

Ryan's smile fled, and he stared at the priest in shock. "Ah—I, well, I wasn't expecting—"

"Never mind. Let's get this done."

A hand appeared between Ryan and Julia's heads, the long, slim, white fingers holding a gold band. Ryan turned to his sister. "No, Kathleen. That's yours."

She scowled, grabbed his hand and placed the ring in it, folding his fingers closed and nodding at Julia before she stepped back again. Ryan opened his hand and stared at the circlet in his palm. He looked first at Father Con, who seemed pleased, and then at Julia, a question in his eyes.

A chill ran down Julia's back as she stared at the band. A symbol of the marriage between Kathleen and her husband, whose name Julia didn't even know. It was a marriage that had ended with the loss of a husband's life and a wife's sanity. Julia was ashamed to admit using such a token for her own marriage frightened her, but she didn't have the heart to refuse the kind offering. She had never been superstitious and now was no time to begin.

Her mouth felt made of stone, but Julia forced a smile and a nod, then held out her left hand. The thankful expression in Ryan's eyes dispersed her shivers and her premonition. Father Con blessed the ring and pronounced them Mr. and Mrs. Ryan Shamus Murphy.

"You may embrace the bride," he intoned.

Their first kiss as man and wife was more passionate than any they'd shared before. Nothing mattered but the flare of heat, the mindless pleasure, the ache and the need and the love.

Ryan kissed her and she could think of little else beyond him. And the wedding night.

Ryan and Con sat in Con's study and drank a toast to the bride with the communion wine. Blasphemous, Ryan was certain, but alcohol in any form was scarce these days. He'd do penance later. Right now he needed the drink.

Julia had fled the church with Kathleen, a bit pale and shaky. Ryan understood. He felt the same way.

"You'll take care of her then," Ryan said, holding his glass up to the candlelight. The deep red reminded him of the streaks through Julia's black hair. How would the strands feel cascading over his naked chest? Would the scent of roses rise from her hair, or merely from her lips when he kissed them?

He quickly put a stop to those thoughts. He'd only make himself insane if he continued to imagine them naked, together. He had to return to his company, and he'd best be on his way.

"I told you I'd keep Julia with me and Kathleen," Con said, not seeming to notice Ryan's preoccupation, or if he had, for once refraining from comment. "Once Colton traces her here, he'll be mad. But if she's under the protection of the church, I don't think he'll fight me.''

"If he does?''

"I'll think of something.''

"You'll send for me.''

Con shrugged. "I'll send for you.''

"Do you really think my name will keep her safe?''

"The Kansans won't touch her.''

"And the Bushwhackers?''

"They won't hurt one of their own.''

"Even if they think she's a traitor?''

"Southern code, my friend. Women are off limits. Besides, her brothers might be vicious, but their honor would be tainted if they let anyone hurt their sister. Though they might decide to make her a widow.''

Ryan raised a brow at the subtle warning, then tossed back the remainder of his wine. "They can try.'' He stood. "I'd best tell her goodbye.''

Con, who had stood when Ryan did, reaching for Ryan's empty wineglass, froze with his hand in mid-air. "Goodbye? You think you're leaving?''

"I have to get back. I told Da you were sick, and you'd sent me word you weren't able to protect Kathleen.''

Con turned and set the glasses on a nearby table, his deliberate movements revealing a sudden intensity. "I'd never let anyone hurt her. No matter how sick I was. Even if I was dying.''

Ryan contemplated his friend's rigid back, the suppressed anger in the priest's voice. "I know that, Con, that's why she's here. I told you I had to lie. But my lie will hold up for just so long. I need to go back.''

Con swung about and faced him, determination in his eyes. "Not tonight you're not. You have to make love to your wife."

Ryan snapped his mouth shut, stared at Con a moment, then said, "What?"

"Tonight, Ryan. Consummate the marriage. It's not valid otherwise."

"And who's to know if I do or I don't?"

"That's easy enough to verify if anyone feels the need."

Ryan clenched his fists at the idea of anyone verifying such a thing with his wife. *His wife.* Julia was his and he was hers. That knowledge soothed the ever-present burn in his stomach as only her presence usually could.

He hadn't thought Julia's family would attempt to invalidate the marriage through legal means. They'd be bent on murder for certain, but they'd been bent on murder for years. Now that he'd married her, he would make certain she stayed his, but there remained one problem.

"You're right, Con. But . . . I, ah, can't—"

Con's eyebrows raised and his mouth twitched. "Really?"

"I don't mean I can't. I mean, not here. In church."

Con's lips spread into a full-blown grin. "I don't care where, just do it."

"She deserves a proper place. A proper wedding night."

"She deserves a decent life and a man who loves her. That's you."

Ryan winced. He'd failed a woman he loved once before, badly. He would not fail again.

Despite his hopes of candlelight and flowers, he would have to make do with what he could manage. Ryan sighed. He couldn't say he didn't want to make love to his wife. That would be a lie. He'd just had images of a week spent in bed, alone, learning every inch of Julia's body and having her learn every inch of his. Where could he take her that was private and safe?

"I have an idea," he said.

"About time," Con returned. "Sometimes I wonder about you."

Ryan strode toward the door. As he passed Con, he gave his friend a good-natured shove. "And sometimes I wonder about you, Father."

Ryan slipped into the hallway before Con could retaliate and hurried to fetch his wife.

For some reason, Julia hesitated to leave the church on the hill. Though she'd been there but a day, she felt safe and at home—more so than she'd ever felt in her own true home. Though Father Con was a priest, he was a big, strong one who carried a gun in the pocket of his robes that he thought no one knew about. Julia knew a lot about guns and the men who carried them. He might be a messenger of God, but Connor Sullivan would use his gun if need be. He exuded confidence and power, except when she'd caught him looking at Kathleen. Then his gentleness and slight air of confusion had endeared him to Julia even more. She would trust Connor Sullivan with her life.

And Kathleen Murphy wouldn't hurt a fly on the wall. Julia kissed and hugged her new sister-in-law goodbye, blinking back tears when Kathleen pressed some of the wildflowers into her arms. They could be friends, Julia thought, despite the difference in their names.

Julia blinked in shock. She was a Murphy now; their names were the same. There would be hell to pay for this, and she'd make sure she paid it, not Ryan. For tonight, though, she would be a bride. Time enough to be a Murphy tomorrow.

Since she'd come to the church on foot, she rode in front of Ryan, on his horse. Her husband. The very thought sent gooseflesh down her arms. Fear? Anticipation? Lust?

She sent a longing glance back toward the two figures silhouetted in the door of the church. Con and Kathleen each lifted a hand to wave goodbye. The glow of candles at their backs made Julia shiver with premonition, but she turned forward, determined to meet her new life head-on.

Whatever had been burning in the distance smoldered now. She'd expected Ryan to ride off and see where the fight was, leaving their wedding night for another time, but he had come to her with a resolute set to his chin and told her to pack a bag for one night.

The man she'd first met by the creek had returned—raised her enemy, vowed to vengeance, pledged to the life of a soldier. Was marriage enough to bridge their differences? Could she forget how he'd begun his path to vengeance, what he'd done to one she loved, and continue to love him? Only time would answer those questions.

Ryan had not spoken a word of love, only of responsibility and obligation—he'd left unspoken his guilt and, perhaps, a desire for forgiveness. While his willingness to help those in need, his devotion to duty and his belief in honor and truth and right had brought her to love him, those qualities could also make him unable to ever love her. The mistakes of the past could rise up to threaten them both at any time.

Julia pushed those fears from her mind. If he did not love her yet, she knew very well that he wanted her. That wanting was uppermost in her mind right now. She felt it, too, but what should she do?

Mama had neglected to tell her the specifics. Since Julia had never been courted, never had a beau, only become betrothed yesterday without her consent, she supposed Mama hadn't seen the need, but right now Julia wished she'd asked more questions.

"Julia?"

Ryan's breath sent a warm shaft of air past her ear, and a flame of desire ignited beneath her breast. The knowledge that soon she would learn the meaning of all the feelings she'd had for Ryan since the moment she'd first seen him made her even more aware of every touch, every breath he took.

"Julia?"

"Hmm? What?"

"You understand we need to . . ."

His chest rose and fell on a sigh, pressing against her back. She leaned against him, wanting to feel every inch of him against every inch of her. Her buttocks were cupped between his thighs, and his gun pressed into her spine, though why his gun would be there she had no idea. Her face heated when she realized it wasn't his pistol that pressed at her spine. She resisted the urge to arch against his hardness and see what might happen.

"Julia? You understand what tonight means? What we have to do?"

"I-I think so."

She'd lived on a farm for twenty years; she'd seen animals mate. She recalled the time her father's prize stallion had mounted their mare. She bit her lip. Once Father had seen her watching he'd ordered her into the house, but she'd seen enough of the process and heard enough from inside the house to be frightened all the same. Certainly Ryan didn't have a male organ that resembled a stallion's?

She straightened so she could no longer feel that part of him against her back. He tensed at her withdrawal. After a moment he ventured, "Did your mama ever explain things to you?"

"Things?"

He muttered beneath his breath, a string of curses Julia had heard before. She was a Colton, after all. Make that a Murphy.

"Man and woman things. What married men and women do together in bed at night. Or in the daytime, if they're of a mind to."

"Daytime?"

She couldn't see his face, but she could hear the smile in his voice. "If they're of a mind."

She was a woman, not a child. She wouldn't allow him to think any less of her because she'd been raised innocent, away from most of the world, exposed only to menfolk, their killer friends and one sick woman. "She didn't spell things out word by word. Mama's a lady."

"Damn."

"There's no cause to curse, Ryan Murphy." She sniffed, like a lady. "I've seen animals. That should suffice."

"Not even close, darlin'. I'm not an animal." He lifted his mouth from her ear, but she heard his murmur just the same. "Or at least I'll try not to be."

Suddenly, he reined up his horse. "Here we are."

"Where?"

Despite the bright, sunny day they'd had, clouds now obscured the stars and the moon. Night had descended in earnest. Though they'd been riding for awhile, Julia's eyes still could not make out anything beyond the horse's twitching ears.

"Home," Ryan said.

Julia started, fearing he'd brought her back to Mama and Father. Father would shoot him first and worry about questions if they ever found the body. She needed to tell them what she'd done, alone, and then she'd run like Hell.

"My home," he said when she remained silent. "Yours now, too. Or it will be, when the war's done and we can all go home."

They'd stopped in front of the Murphy cabin, deserted now with all the men off to war. Julia stared at the sorrowful, lonely exterior and knew the truth.

This could never be her home. She could never belong here. Ryan might want her. Kathleen might befriend her. Jason might tolerate her. But Ryan's father would forever despise her, and there would always be her family, on the other side of Colton-Murphy Creek, to make their life a living Hell. She might be able to ignore what Ryan had done, but her brothers and her father would never forget or forgive.

"This is a mistake," she began.

"No." He shifted and jumped to the ground. "It's done now. No going back."

"We could. We could go back right now and this would all go away. You go back to your troop and I'll go home."

His face darkened. "And marry that guerilla your pa picked out? Let him put guns to your head whenever he's of a mind?"

She didn't answer. The picture was too clear—and too true.

He reached up and yanked her from the horse. She fell forward with a startled cry, but he didn't let her go, instead setting her on her feet in front of him with such care her head spun. "Then in the night when you lie in bed with him, and he touches you, kisses you and makes you a woman, will you think of me?"

Despite the darkness of the night she could see him quite clearly. The lines about his mouth, the spark of fury in his eyes, the need underlying his words that forced the truth from her mouth even though she knew she should deny him. "Yes," she whispered.

"Like hell." His gentle hands at her waist turned hard as he yanked her against him. "You're mine. Now and forever, and I'm not letting any Bushwhacking bastard touch you."

He lowered his head and kissed her, harder and longer and more completely than he had ever kissed her before. If anyone else but Ryan had touched her with such fierceness, she would have fought with all her might. But this was Ryan. The love of her life, the second part of her soul, her golden hero come to being. Nothing like any of the men she'd ever known. He could be strong, but he could be gentle. She found herself caught up in his passion, lost in the storm of emotion that flowed from him like a heated summer rain.

They stood in the yard and kissed until both of them were breathless, aching, sweating. Then the sky erupted into sound and fury and light, and the rains of summer drenched them to the skin.

Ryan stood with the water streaming down his face and began to laugh. She'd never heard him laugh. The sound captivated her so, she stood there staring instead of running inside, allowing the warm, welcoming rain to cleanse the scent of despair from her skin.

He stopped laughing to open his mouth and let the rain fall in, and then he swallowed and looked down at Julia, his face still alight with mirth. "If there's one thing I know, Julia Colton Murphy, it's that this . . ." He paused and lifted her from the ground to swing her around and around in the midst of the rain and the thunder.

"This will never go away," he shouted. "Never."

He kissed her again as the raindrops ran like tears down their faces, then climbed the steps with her in his arms and entered the home that could never be hers.

Chapter Eleven

Julia began to shiver as soon as Ryan set her on her feet. From the damp or the man or the place, she couldn't tell. She still held the flowers Kathleen had pressed into her arms tightly against her chest. They were drenched, just like her, and their fragrance wafted upward, so strong her head swirled and she swayed.

"You're freezing." Ryan steadied her before stepping back, then turning away to start a fire. The room was sparsely furnished. A stove, a table and a bed in one corner, with other rooms waiting down the dark hallway. Julia's gaze skittered away from the bed and all it implied, searching for Ryan.

She stared at his back as he bent and fed the flames. Ryan Murphy was so many men: the vengeful, grieving boy who had chosen the wrong path toward healing; the strong, competent young man of their first meeting; the honorable, duty-bound soldier who had arrived at the church; the laughing, joyous groom of a moment ago; the seductive, passionate man of her secret dreams. She loved them all.

To her surprise, the room heated quickly. Her damp clothes became sticky, uncomfortable. The scent of wildflowers overwhelmed her. She moved, crossing the short distance to the table to put them down. Ryan turned, their gazes caught, held, and the silence thickened to match the heavy, damp air.

"You should get out of those wet clothes."

She blushed. "I can't reach the buttons." Kathleen had helped her dress. In fact, she wore Kathleen's dress. Most likely Kathleen's wedding dress, a rich, leaf-green silk, with a full skirt and a tight bodice, buttons down the back. Luckily Kathleen was larger than she or Julia never would have been able to wear the fitted gown without a corset.

Ryan smiled. Julia stopped breathing. She'd known he was handsome, but she'd never seen him smile like this before, his lips curving with true pleasure and his eyes lighting from within to kindle an answering light within her.

He crossed the room, slowly, as if giving her the chance to run if she was of a mind to. She held her ground. She'd wanted him so many times and so many ways. At the creek she'd wanted a rescuer, and he had come. At the dance she'd wanted a beau, and had come. Yesterday, she'd needed a hero, and Ryan had come. Now she wanted him as a man, and though she was a bit afraid of what was to come, she was more intrigued than frightened. Ryan would never hurt her. He would die first.

He reached her side and looked down into her face. Mesmerized by the difference in his expression, she merely stared back. The shadows from the fire played across his face, but his eyes for once held not a hint of sorrow. They held only attraction and need.

Placing his hands upon her shoulders, he turned her about. Slowly at first, then with greater speed and less agility, he freed the buttons from the nape of her neck to the base of her spine. Despite the warmth of the room and the cover of her chemise, the air pressed cool upon her back. He slipped the sleeves down her arms, gave a tug past her hips, and the dress pooled at her feet.

"Th-this is Kathleen's dress. I should—"

"Should what?" His mouth against her neck, she forgot what she should do. Her head tilted to the side to give him better access, and he shocked her by sucking, then nipping her skin. The coolness disappeared as flaming heat took its place.

He yanked at the petticoats and they went the way of the dress, revealing pantaloons, garters and stockings. Her shoes were buried beneath yards of green silk and white cotton.

"Too many clothes," he murmured, gracing the opposite side of her neck with the same kiss he'd gifted the other.

"Yes, too many," she gasped. Her nipples hardened painfully, thrusting against the scratchy lace of the chemise.

"Lucky we have all night."

Unable to deny him anything since she could not

seem to think at all, when he took her hand and led her toward the bed in the corner of the room, she went without a murmur.

It was cooler there, away from the fire, but her skin was so warm she barely noticed. He gave her a tiny push and she sat on the edge of the bed, then he knelt at her feet, like a suitor, or a prince, and she reached out to stroke his golden hair.

Soft, amazingly so, and thick. The strands slid through her fingers, each one humming across her sensitive skin. She'd never felt so alive.

Her shoes fell one after the other with a clip-clop. His fingers glided up her stocking-covered calves until he reached her garter. She caught her breath when his hand brushed the inside of her thigh. No one had ever touched her there.

He hesitated, glanced up, uncertain. Her fingers, still in his hair, flexed, and he smiled, then rubbed his head against her hand like a cat. Holding her gaze, he rolled one stocking down and threw it the way of her shoes, then did the same with the other. Amazingly, he did not join her; instead he picked up her foot, like a prince, and began to rub the chilled skin. No one had ever rubbed her feet, and she could not believe how wonderful the caress made her feel. Some of the incredible tension that had drawn her tight as a fiddle string flowed away. But the touch of his fingers on her sensitive flesh made her want to feel those clever hands all over her body.

"You must be cold, too," she said.

His mouth twitched. "Not hardly."

She blushed at his words and the look upon his face. If he felt the same as she, he was no longer cold.

187

"I meant, you should get out of those wet clothes."

He raised one brow. "Would you like to help me?"

"H-help y-you?"

He frowned as her voice quivered. "You don't have to. I just thought you might like to. It's part of—" He shrugged, dropped her foot and stood. "This." A nod toward the bed indicated what *this* he spoke of.

"A-all right." She stood, her movements jerky and stiff, and raised her hands toward the buttons on his uniform jacket. He stilled them with his own, holding her captive against his chest.

She lifted her gaze to his, confused to find him as tense now as she. "What's the matter?" she whispered.

"I want to do this right."

"Don't you know how?"

"Very funny." His chest rose and fell beneath their joined hands. "I've never been with a woman the first time. I mean *her* first time. I don't want to make a mess of this. I don't want to hurt you, but I want you so badly. You're all I've thought about, dreamed about since I saw you. And now you're my wife, and I'm scared to death."

"Scared?" Julia was amazed. "My family will never look for me here. We'll be all right."

He snorted. "I'm not afraid of your family. I'm afraid of you."

"Me?" Surprise made the word come out a startled laugh, but the earnestness in his eyes convinced Julia he told the truth. The thought that Ryan could be frightened of her gave Julia a strange sense of power and peace.

He pulled her to him, holding her tight against his chest. "I've tried to do what's right, but sometimes I don't know what right is. My mother died because I tried to do the right thing, and I was wrong. Your mother's an invalid for the same reason. I'm scared something will happen to you, too, and I won't be good enough, or strong enough, or here enough to stop it."

He really was scared, and for some reason that knowledge made her think him more admirable than ever before. If a strong man could be frightened, yet brave and true despite that, he was a very special kind of man. But then, she'd known that already.

Julia put her arms around Ryan's waist and held on to him as tightly as he held on to her. "I'll be fine. We'll be fine." She rubbed his back, soothing, comforting. "It's all right."

But he would have none of her comfort. "I told you I've dreamt of you. Ever since I met you I've had nightmares."

"That makes a girl proud."

He ignored her attempt at humor. "I feel like disaster's on the way. Hanging over us like a great, black storm cloud."

The storm outside chose that minute to thunder so deep the house shook. The rain slapped against the roof harder and the wind whistled.

"See?" he said.

She pulled back and looked up into his face. The shadows had returned to his eyes. The haunted look that was so much a part of him had returned to his face. "Forget the storm. Forget the dreams." She cupped his cheek in her palm and he turned his head into her caress. "This is our night. We're safe here. We're married now and no one can change that. No one." She began to unbutton his coat. "Think of me now. Only me."

Her hands were more steady on his buttons than his had been on hers, and she made short work of his coat and shirt. The light dusting of golden hair across his chest fascinated her, and all the fears and memories and dreams faded as she learned the contours of her husband's body. Once she'd watched him stand naked in the moonlight, and she'd wanted something, though then she had not known what. Now she knew. She'd wanted to touch his strong, hard, man's body with her soft, supple woman's fingers. Now she could and she made the most of her opportunity.

He held still while she explored him. His arms quivered and the muscles of his chest became taut, but he remained quiet and unmoving, giving her courage to continue as she wished to. She ran her fingertips through the hair on his chest; it was different from the hair on his head, darker, not as soft, but just as fascinating. Her nail flicked against a hardened nipple; his moan of delight told her she had not hurt him, only pleasured him.

She recalled the way he had suckled her neck, the intense pleasure the act had given her, and she leaned forward to place her mouth to his skin. He gasped and his hands on her shoulders clenched, but they held her closer, did not push her away, and she continued to explore the shape of his chest with her lips.

"Come here." His voice was a growl, but she wasn't afraid, could never be afraid of this man who had defied his family for her. Just as she would have to defy hers for him. She pushed aside such nerve-wracking thoughts as he took her hand and led her to the bed.

They sat and she took a deep breath, the movement raising, then lowering her breasts, catching his eyes. Slowly he leaned forward. She raised her lips for his kiss, but his mouth settled upon her nipple, and he suckled through her thin chemise.

The pleasure was so intense she fell, backward, onto the mattress. He followed, somehow baring her breasts and yanking the chemise free of her body so she lay naked beneath him.

No one had ever seen her naked. With five men in the house, she bathed in her chemise, so even Mama, sitting in her sickbed, had not seen Julia without covering since her childhood. Even so, she did not feel embarrassed. This was Ryan, her Ryan—rescuer, friend, husband, lover—and she wanted him to know every part of her body and soul.

He learned her contours with his hands and his mouth, whispering nonsense against her skin as he made her writhe with new and wonderful sensations. Her hands fluttered over his bare back, halted at the waistband of his trousers, and she frowned at the obstruction, yanking at the buttons as she met his every caress with her own.

He left her for a moment and she cried out, bereft, but when he returned, he was as naked as she. Pulling the counterpane over them, he created a cocoon of warmth and love.

Her hand brushed his hardness, and his breath hissed in through his teeth. She pulled back, afraid she had hurt him this time. He was so swollen he must ache. But his mouth curved against hers, and he caught her retreating fingers, brought them back to curl about him.

"Touch me," he murmured, his lips against her breast doing dark, secret, wonderful things, so she did.

The night darkened; the storm deepened, and still they learned the secrets of pleasuring each other. Damp with sweat, her skin hummed with awareness, every inch of her body, every thought in her mind focused on something that lay just out of reach. Only he knew what it was. Only he could give it to her.

He touched her gently, dipping inside her and stroking with his thumb a tiny, hardened bud at the juncture of her thighs. When he flicked the nub and suckled her breast, her entire body went rigid, and she convulsed, over and over, falling apart in his arms as he stroked her and kissed her and whispered her name.

Before she was entirely herself again, he raised his body over hers, and probed at her throbbing passage. She opened for him, amazed that the ecstasy she'd thought had shattered her could return with such speed and stronger than before. He slid inside, and she understood they were not finished. They had only begun.

She opened her eyes, watching him as they became one. His eyes were closed, his jaw set so hard she reached up to stroke the tension free. His neck was corded with muscle and his shoulders bunched. She ran her fingertips down his chest, brushing his nipples, and his body surged forward. She let out a startled gasp as a tiny burn ignited inside her.

His eyes snapped open. "I'm sorry," he said. "Only once and now I'll never hurt you again. I promise."

Then his mouth descended to swallow her moans, and his body moved in and out of hers, faster and faster, bringing back the magic, stringing her tighter and tighter, taking her places she had still not been and this time going with her.

He pushed into her more deeply, held very still, and a surge and pulse inside made her cry out as her own release washed over her. She did not know how long they lay there, one body, one heart and soul. *One name.* She never wanted to let him go, and when he shifted away, she clutched him to her.

"Stay," she said.

"I'm too heavy."

"No, you could never be too heavy."

He smiled and moved anyway, pulling her close and wrapping himself about her. Then, with the steady, soothing sound of his breath at her ear, she fell asleep holding his hand.

Artillery awoke Ryan, too close to ignore. During the night he'd gotten up to take care of his neglected mount and pondered the glow of distant flames on the western horizon. They'd been far enough away then, but no longer. Now the battle looked to be headed this way.

He tried to disentangle himself from his wife, but she held on tight. "Where are you going?" she mumbled. "It's not even daylight yet."

"The sun is up and I hear artillery."

She opened her eyes, listened, frowned. "No, that's

thunder. I haven't heard a cock crow, or even a lark to sing the sun awake. Come back to bed." She kissed the side of his neck and he lost his will.

"Fine." He yanked her naked body across his, kissing her with the joy and abandon that had returned to him last night. "I don't care if the entire Confederate Army is at the door. As long as you want me here, I'll stay and gladly die in your arms."

She stilled, pushed against his chest, straining upward. He focused his attention on her breasts, which were suddenly in his face, but before he could give them the concentration they deserved, she rolled away, yanking the sheets from his body. The cool air hit his flushed skin and killed his desire.

"No, you're right," she cried, panic igniting in her voice. "It's artillery." She ran to the window, trailing sheets, pulled the shutter back. Sunlight spilled over her face. She turned to him, her eyes wide with fear. "Get up. We have to go."

Ryan sighed. Women. There was no pleasing them. He climbed from bed. Naked he stood in the middle of the room and looked for his pistols. His gaze lit on the gunbelt draped across the back of a chair. He retrieved his pants and then his guns, and though two pistols would be useless against an enemy force, he buckled on the belt. If the guerillas were at his door, he and Julia were dead anyway, unless it was Quantrill and the Colton boys. In that case, Julia would live. Maybe.

He glanced at her, and his mouth went dry with desire. She sat on the bed, green eyes wide in a fear-paled face. Her black hair tumbled across the white sheet she held over her breasts, the red streaks reminding him of blood at dawn. If her brothers saw her here like this—well, he didn't want to think about that. Not now. Not ever.

"Let's hope I can get you back to the church before someone finds us."

Her chin tilted up and some of the color came back to her face. "I can get back myself."

He bent, scooped up her underclothes and tossed them to her. "I have no doubt you can, but you're not."

She caught her chemise with one hand, the other clutching the sheet as if it were all she owned in the world. He tried not to laugh at her modesty. He'd seen and touched and kissed everything beneath that sheet last night. She had nothing to hide from him. Not anymore.

"If I run into guerillas, I'll be safer alone."

"And if you run into Jayhawkers, Federals or the Border Patrol, then what?"

In the midst of pulling her chemise over her head, she lost hold of the sheet, and Ryan got a good view of her full and luscious breasts. He stiffened and gritted his teeth. He had no time for that now. Another blast of artillery, closer, punctuated his thought.

Her face appeared through the chemise, scowling. "I'll tell them I'm Mrs. Lieutenant Ryan Murphy and they'll leave me alone. Or better yet, they will escort me where I'm going."

She had a point. Still he wasn't letting her out of his sight until he saw her safe with Con and Kathleen.

"No more arguing. We don't have the time. I know for certain if either side finds us here, we're in for it." He buttoned his shirt in short order and put on his coat. When he turned back, she wore the dress she'd brought along, the gray-blue one she'd run from her home in, and held Kathleen's wedding dress in her hand. As he watched, she ran her fingers along the skirt, and smiled a smile that made his heart thunder.

"What is it?" he asked.

Startled, she glanced at him. Her eyes were wet. "I was just thinking of Kathleen and all the dreams and hopes she must have had when she wore this dress. Now I have them too. I only hope—" She stopped and rubbed at her eyes impatiently. Kathleen's wedding band glinted on her finger.

"You only hope you don't end up like her or worse," he finished.

She nodded but did not speak, then put the dress into her bag, carefully, reverently.

Ryan began to button his coat while Julia got her shoes on. "I don't know what happened to Kathleen, exactly. She and Stan lived up north of here. She came back to this cabin alone. We heard from her neighbors that Bushwhackers killed Stan." Julia winced. "We don't know why she doesn't talk. Maybe we never will."

"I'm sorry. For all I know my brothers are responsible. If not, they would have been if they could have. That's how they are. They don't know any different. They don't want to."

Ryan sighed. "It's not your fault."

"No? I believed what I'd been taught, the Kansas folk were evil. The only contact I had with them was when they burned the house and hurt Mama—" She broke off when he flinched, then put a hand out, which he ignored. "I'm sorry, Ryan."

"You have nothing to be sorry for. You should hate me. I don't understand why you don't."

"I did."

His heart thudded once, hard and painful, but the look on her face held no hate, only love. He asked the question that had been on his mind for a long time, a question he'd been afraid to ask because the answer mattered so much. "Have you forgiven me, then?"

Her soft, gentle smile told him more than words. "I'm not the one whose forgiveness you need."

"But you don't hate me," he pressed.

She shook her head, looking at him as if he were a child of monumental innocence, her expression one of amusement and great love. "Before he died, the priest at our church always said hate breeds hate. Look at my father, then look at his boys, and you'll see he's right. I don't want to be a part of that anymore."

"You aren't. You're the most loving woman I've ever known. You're nothing like your brothers."

"Sometimes. There were other times I hated, just like them. Honestly I'll admit I hated the Jayhawkers more for ruining my life than for hurting my mama. I was selfish and childish."

"So what changed you?"

She stood, crossed the room to stand before him. "You." Raising up on her toes, she pressed a soft, sweet kiss to the corner of his mouth. "You rode in on your golden horse and you showed me the truth.

You treated me kindly even when you knew whose daughter I was. You defended me to my brother, and you saved me from a lifetime married to a man I don't love and can't respect. You showed me a dream can come true—there are men in this world who can be gentle and strong. You made a mistake, but you've never denied it or lied about it, and I think you've punished yourself on the inside for that night more than me or my family could ever punish you on the outside. I'll love you forever, Ryan Murphy, and that's a fact."

He stood there speechless at the fervor in her voice. When she took his hand and led him toward the door he followed like a first-year schoolboy led to his seat by the teacher. He'd known she saw him as some kind of hero, and he'd enjoyed the feeling that gave him. But the magnitude of her devotion also frightened him. If he failed her—

"Wait." She paused, her hand on the door. "Let me check first."

She nodded, backing up. He opened the door a crack. No one was in the yard. Motioning for her to stay put, he stepped onto the porch. The morning smelled new from the summer storm, yet ancient with the scent of gunpowder drifting in on the western wind. He could hear the sounds of a battle, close yet far enough away to assure their safety for the time being. Ryan retrieved his horse, and they went on their way.

Although it was still early morning, the day sweltered already. Julia leaned against Ryan's chest, and the heat of the morning carried her scent to his nostrils. He breathed deeply, hoping to affix that scent in his mind so he could pull out the memory and experience the peace she gave him when he was back in the midst of the war. Would the horrific burn that roiled in his gut go away forever now that she was his wife? Or would a return to the world that was his, the world in which he'd struggled for so long, resurrect the driven, vengeful man he had been? Just because he regretted what had happened to her mama didn't mean he'd given up on his vengeance. She'd said she would love him forever, but she did not really know him for who he was. Did he know himself anymore?

Ryan pushed aside the questions and the memories for the moment. Right now he couldn't recall ever feeling so at ease. The muted clop of the horse's hooves against the dirt road sounded in time with their hearts, which seemed to have been beating as one since their first kiss. Ryan laughed in silence. He'd never figured himself for a poetic kind of man, but Julia did funny things to his mind, as well as his body.

Rounding a curve in the road shattered their peace. Julia saw them first. She went rigid, sat up and put her arms out to her sides.

"What the hell?" he asked, then he heard the shout and the shot.

"Charge. Kill 'em, boys. Kill 'em."

She was trying to shield him with her body, to keep the guerilla troop they'd surprised on the road from seeing his blue uniform. She'd been too late.

Ryan wheeled his horse and darted into the brush.

He hunched his back, protecting her from the shots that would come. The trees and the foliage were summer thick and slapped against his arms and legs. Julia gasped as a branch scraped her neck, and Ryan tugged her closer.

The guerillas were hot on their trail; the brush was their territory. Ryan allowed his horse to find the best way, but he had no idea where they headed. Julia straightened, her gaze darting to the left and the right. A bullet whizzed past them, too close, and Ryan tried to shove her head down, but she resisted.

"Stay down," he hissed in her ear. "They're trying to kill me."

She shook her head, stubbornly refusing to duck. Then she yanked the reins from his hands and turned the horse to the left.

"What the—?"

"I know where we are."

"You do?"

"It isn't just the Reb boys who know this brush; the Reb girls know it, too."

So Ryan held on and let Julia guide the horse. She did seem to know her way, and soon the shots from behind them stopped, and the sound of hoofbeats faded. Ryan risked a glance over his shoulder. He could still see the brush moving way back, but he could no longer see any horses.

They skidded down an embankment, the horse nearly sitting down and unseating them both, but Julia was able to keep him upright. They crashed into a creek, waded downstream a ways and climbed the opposite bank. Seconds later, they burst through the brush onto another road—directly into a Federal patrol.

Fifteen pistols stared them in the face.

"Whoa," Ryan called, taking the reins from Julia.

She let him. Her hands were icy cold despite the heat of the day, and she held herself so still, he wondered if she'd been scared to death. "Shhh," he breathed into her ear.

The guns that had been drawn were holstered when they saw his uniform and he identified himself to the officer in charge.

"What are you doing out here, Lieutenant?" the captain asked.

"Surprised a party of Rebs back on the main road. They might be showing up any time now."

The attention of the troop, which had been focused too closely on Julia, turned to the brush.

"The whole area's goin' up in flames, Lieutenant. Haven't you heard?"

"What?"

"They executed Jim Vaughn in Kansas City."

Julia's gasp of horror brought the captain's intelligent gaze to rest on her face. He narrowed his eyes and contemplated her. She stared right back and lifted her chin, though Ryan could see her hands twisting together until they bled white.

Ryan had heard before he'd left camp about Vaughn. He was one of Quantrill's men, captured by Federals while getting a shave in Wyandotte, Kansas, and sentenced to execution. Quantrill had done everything he could to obtain Vaughn's release, offering three Federal prisoners for the release of that one man. But General Buell had refused, sticking to the no-quarter law for partisans, and hung Vaughn anyway.

"I heard they'd begun to round up guerilla sympathizers in the area and take them to Kansas City." The captain nodded at Julia. "Prisoner, Lieutenant?"

"My wife, sir."

"Your wife?" The captain frowned and shook his head. "I could've swore I'd seen her before. On this side of the border. I rarely forget a face. Might I inquire as to your maiden name, Mrs. Murphy?"

Ryan saw Julia's hands begin to shake before she clenched them to stop the telltale sign of fear. If the captain heard the name Colton, she'd be in his custody in a heartbeat. "My wife doesn't go out much, sir. I'm taking her to stay with my sister."

"Well, the Rebs have gone loco 'cause of Vaughn. Some of Todd's men surprised a troop yonder. Killed 'em all, then left a note in one of the dead men's mouths. Said 'Remember the dying words of Jim Vaughn.' "

"What were they?" Ryan asked.

" 'You may kill me, but you'll never conquer me, and taking my life today will cost you a hundred lives and this debt my friends will pay in a short time.' "

"So the guerillas are set to crown Vaughn a martyr," Ryan murmured, "and make his vow come true."

"Looks that way. Now we're gonna go and look for that Reb troop who chased you, Lieutenant. Wanna come along?"

"I'd best take my wife to the church on the hill to meet my sister."

The captain, who had turned toward his men to

issue orders, stopped and turned back with a frown. "The church on the hill?"

"Is that a problem?"

"The Rebs have taken over the area. All the roads to the church are in their hands. You can't get through."

"Hell."

"Exactly. You'd better take your wife home, Lieutenant. Those Rebs are mighty mad."

With a whoop and a holler the troop drove into the brush. Julia and Ryan sat on the horse, silent for a long time.

"Take me home," she said.

"You can't stay at home. There's no one to protect you. That's why we took Kathleen to Con."

She made a disgusted sound deep in her throat, then twisted in the saddle so she could see his face. "Not your home. My home."

"No. You're not going back there. What do you think they'll do when they find out you're my wife?"

"I'm not going to tell them."

"What about your fiancé?"

"He's with Todd's troop. You heard the captain. If they've killed a Federal patrol, they've hightailed it north and east. By the time they come back here, I'll be with Kathleen and Father Con."

"You won't go near that church until the troops have retreated?"

"Of course not. I'm no fool. Even if they are my brothers' friends, they're still animals."

Ryan stared into her eyes. She wasn't frightened. Not like he was. He didn't know what to do.

"You won't stay home."

"No. But I want to see Mama, Ryan. I need to say goodbye."

He sighed. "All right. We'll go there."

"Not you!"

"I'll let you off at the creek."

She hesitated, then nodded and turned to face front. It seemed they reached the creek too quickly, and she slid to the ground. He followed.

The water had risen, spilling over the banks and muddying the red earth. Her skirt brushed the ground, and she held the material up with one hand, looking as if she meant to dance, or curtsy. Ryan smiled at the image, then pulled her into his arms.

The kiss was not goodbye, even though it felt that way. She held on to him as if she never wanted to let him go. He understood the sentiment. When he tasted her tears he pulled back and brushed one away with his thumb. She made a sound between a laugh and a sob and put her hand up to catch his, pulling his fingers away from her cheek to place a kiss at the center of his palm.

Then she looked at him from sober, swimming eyes, withdrew the wedding band from her finger and placed the ring into his hand. "I'd better not keep this for now."

Ryan closed his fingers about the metal, still warm from her flesh. The sense of doom he usually felt upon awakening after a nightmare swamped him suddenly, and he tightened his hand until the circlet of gold caused a burning pain in the center of his palm. "I don't like this."

"Neither do I." She blinked several times, then

opened her mouth as if to say something else. When a choked sob came out, she spun about, lifted her already muddied skirts and ran away.

His heart went with her.

Chapter Twelve

Julia's eyes burned. At first she thought they were tears of sadness at leaving Ryan so soon after they'd married, but when she topped the rise separating Colton Creek from Colton fields, she saw what made her eyes burn in truth.

Smoke.

She ran through blackened fields of corn, her heart pounding with fear, her lungs burning from the acrid air. She burst through the small copse of trees between the house and the fields, and her knees almost gave way.

The house still stood, unharmed, though the barn was a smoldering wreck.

Cautiously, she walked across the yard, hesitated on the porch. What if . . . ?

Julia straightened, refusing to give in to the panic

that threatened. It would do no one any good if she lost her sense to fear. Throwing back her shoulders, she opened the door.

The bed was empty. The thunder of her heart began again. "Mama?" she called, scowling when her voice shook like a child's.

Suddenly she was yanked inside, a gun pressed into her ribs. Once she would have fainted. Now she merely turned and looked at her captor.

"Where the hell have ya been, girl?" her father asked.

She ignored the question. "Where's Mama?"

"Out back. Usin' the privy." He tightened his grip upon her arm. "Now answer me, where ya been?"

"At the church on the hill."

He narrowed his eyes, stared into her face, searching for a lie. Julia stared right back. She had told the truth, just not all of it.

"What'd ya go there for?"

"To think."

"Hmph. Well, while ya were thinkin', the damned Federals burnt our crop and the barn."

"I see that." From the proximity of the troop she and Ryan had encountered, she knew exactly who had done the burning. No wonder the captain had asked her maiden name. "What happened?"

"The boys were in county and mighty mad about Jim Vaughn dyin'. So they started a ruckus. But the damned Federals came here lookin' for 'em, and when I wouldn't tell which way they'd gone . . ." He shrugged and the barrel of the gun he still held at her ribs shifted. Julia winced.

"Sam, put up that gun!" Mama ordered from the back door.

He glanced at his wife. His hand on Julia's arm tightened, then released, and he stepped back so she could come inside. Julia ran to her mama and threw her arms about her.

Mama sighed, long and deep, then smoothed Julia's hair. "You came back," she whispered.

Julia looked up and saw the sorrow and guilt in Mama's eyes. "Yes."

"I'm glad."

"Now that she's here and I don't have to go drag her home, I'll be leavin'."

Julia released her mama and turned around to see her father picking up a knapsack and holstering his pistol. "Where are you going?"

He grinned. "Off with my boys."

Julia glanced at Mama, who shrugged and made her way slowly back to the bed.

"But—but—what about Mama?"

"You're here. Do your duty. I've got to do mine."

He started out the door, but Julia ran forward. "Wait! You're going to leave us here alone?"

"You've been off all night, here and there, all by yourself, and ya made it home just fine. Me and the boys will be in the area; we'll check on ya. There's your gran's pistol in the drawer and plenty of ammunition. The crops are burned, the horses gone. Nothin' to steal and nothin' left for me to do here."

"Except protect your wife and daughter."

His face flushed red and his hands clenched. When he took a step toward her, Julia backed away in spite of herself. These days, she always said too much. "I have a duty to join the cause and revenge myself on the bastards who burned me out. If we win, I'll get the Murphy farm too. Quantrill promised. I heard all the Murphys went off to join up, even the old man, so if they all die . . .'' He smiled his blood-chilling smile and patted his pistol, ''then there won't be any arguments at all. Protect your mama now, girl. If anything happens to her, it's on your head.'' With a nod to his wife, he turned and walked off into the brush.

Julia stared at the empty doorway long after he'd gone. Her father had gone off to kill her husband, and she could do nothing to stop him. For if she told what they'd done, she'd seal Ryan's fate. Her father would not just kill him if he saw him, he'd hunt Ryan down like a mad dog, and he'd make certain every partisan was in on the game.

She could not run off to the church on the hill as she'd promised her husband. Turning, Julia stared at her mama's back. She was trapped in her old life— trapped by love and honor and duty—all the things that bound her to the Coltons and made the name Murphy one she should hate.

Julia rubbed her aching forehead. Right now she did hate someone by the name of Murphy. She hated herself.

Ryan galloped into camp—or into what had been camp. Overturned tents, smoking wagons and a row of dead soldiers awaiting burial told the tale of attack. Those left alive dug graves and packed what hadn't been destroyed onto the remaining horses.

His gaze searched frantically for his brother and father, and his chest ached with fear. Had he been absent again when he was needed the most? Had another of his family died because of him?

"Where've ye been, boy?" The sound of his da's brogue made the breath Ryan held rush out in relief. Halting his horse, he turned and saw his father emerging from a tent riddled with bulletholes.

"Sir." Ryan saluted. His gaze darted about, searching for Jason, halting on the bright red head of a soldier digging nearby. Jason glanced up, and his solemn face told Ryan more than words. Things were not good, and Da was mighty mad.

"Lieutenant!"

Ryan's gaze flicked back to his father. "Yes, sir!"

"I asked ye where the hell ye've been."

"Taking care of a personal family matter, sir."

"And how is that personal family matter?"

"Fine, sir."

His da nodded, obviously relieved. But in the next instant he ordered, "Get down off that horse and help the rest." His ability to dismiss thoughts of Kathleen with such ease showed again how very much he'd changed in the last few months. "We could have used ye here last night, boy, but I know ye had t' go and take care of things at the church."

Ryan winced at the thought of what he'd been doing while his comrades had been dying. He slid down from his horse. "What happened?"

"Bloody bastards attacked at dusk. Came through the brush like ghosts, they did, and overran us whilst we ate our evenin' meal." He shook his head. "Killed the sentries. Slit their throats, the murderin' scum."

Ryan picked up a shovel and took a place next to another soldier. He began to dig; the thud of the tool into the muddy red earth and the sight of the dead men all around him made him sick—the burning again.

"I hear the Colton farm got burned last night."

"What?" Ryan glanced at his da, who watched him too closely.

His father smiled, a thin, telling smile, as if he'd just learned the secrets of the universe. "Burned their crops and their barn. Took their animals and their store. Left the house standin', though. Federal forces ain't completely heartless—the old woman is too sick t' put out on the road. But interestin' thing—the girl was gone. Might ye know somethin' about that, me boy?"

Ryan returned his attention to his digging lest his da see the lies in his eyes. "No, sir."

"Hmm," was his da's only comment before he walked off to give orders.

Ryan continued to dig, but his mind roiled. He should never have let Julia out of his sight. But he could do nothing now. If he rode off to her rescue he'd only end up arrested, shot or hung for desertion, and then he'd be no good to her at all. He'd wait until tonight, then slip away and make certain she was safe.

The task at hand was dirty, bloody and miserable. Each soldier Ryan lowered into the ground seemed to stare at him with accusation. He had slept with the enemy.

Gently he closed their eyes, yet their voices taunted him.

Traitor, they whispered. *We died because of you. You were making love while we were dying for our country.*

211

Jason stopped next to him. "What happened?"

Ryan glanced over, then back. "Nothing."

"The whole county's up in flames, you're right in the middle of it and nothing happened?"

"That's right."

For once Jason didn't pester him, and for that Ryan thanked God. He didn't know what he would have said except more lies. Instead, he berated himself until the guilt inside him festered to a boiling, raging inferno of fury.

Ordered to break camp to go in search of those who had attacked them, Ryan did so eagerly. Double time, they rode deeper into Bates County, then turned off the main road, heading through the brush. Each man kept a wary eye on every clump of trees, every mound of earth. The Bushwhackers had been digging caves in the sides of the hills. They would cover the cave with logs, old board and brush, put a fireplace in the back with a chimney made of sticks or mud. Usually they cooked only at night to avoid smoke, so that during the day their hideaway was nearly undetectable by any who did not know the location.

Ryan had been with the Border Patrol long enough to detect those caves, so he rode closest to the low-slung hills. Jason rode at his side but continued to remain blessedly silent. Ryan did not have the energy to lie to his brother this morning, and he did not think he should tell Jason the truth about his absence. At least not yet. Too much was at stake, too much depended upon the secret he and Julia had begun last night. If her father, or his, found out the truth too soon, either one or both of them could die.

The ramifications of his marriage hit Ryan with the

force of an ice storm. He was married, for better or worse, until death did they part, to a Colton. Her brothers and father would want him dead. Her mother would despise him until her dying day, which thanks to him would be soon. His own da would kick his ass from Hell to Sunday. Ryan rubbed his eyes against the beginning of a pounding headache.

A bullet tore through the top of his hat. The brush erupted into screams and gunshots. Jason knocked him from his horse, and the two of them went down hard in the mud. They rolled until they reached cover, then yanked their pistols free and searched for the enemy.

"There." Ryan pointed. "In that hill."

Jason nodded and began to return the fire coming from the cleverly disguised cave. Ryan had missed the hideout while thinking of his own problems.

He pushed aside the usual guilt and recriminations to take care of the matter at hand. He'd begged for the chance to fight and now the time had arrived. They'd found a Rebel base and could wipe it from the face of the earth. Vengeance would be his, in some small part, for the men he had buried this morn, the men whose blood still stained his hands. Would he ever be able to wash away the blood? Perhaps, but only with the blood of the enemy. Despite these thoughts, Ryan hesitated.

Suddenly Jason cried out and put a hand to his forehead. When he drew it away blood covered his palm and ran down his nose. His eyes rolled upward and he slumped forward, unconscious.

"Jase?" Ryan's voice quivered. He reached out a

hand that shook as well and touched his brother. "Jason!" No response.

Ryan couldn't breathe; he couldn't think. He stared at his brother's still, bloody face—a nightmare come to life—and was back again in northern Kansas, staring at his mother's body. The beginning of the nightmare all over again.

The battle still raged around them. The Rebels, knowing they were trapped, that their ammunition would run out soon and that they would be shot like foxes in their burrows, attempted escape. Fury surged through Ryan's veins, hot and red and bubbling. With a howl of rage he erupted from his cover and ran forward, pistols blazing.

Later he would not remember the specifics of what he'd done, only that when the sound of gunfire ended, he stood surrounded by dead partisans, pistols empty.

"Holy Hell, Ry, are you crazy?" Jason's voice, just above a whisper, startled him. Turning, Ryan looked into his brother's ash-pale, blood-streaked face.

Jason was alive.

The relief that rushed through Ryan made him stagger. Jason put a hand to his shoulder, and when Ryan looked into his brother's face, the expression there cleared his mind a bit. Jason stared at him as if he were a monster. Ryan looked down at his hands and found them bloodier than ever before.

He stared at the fallen Bushwhackers. He knew none of them, yet the sight made bile rise in his throat. Not a one was over the age of twenty. Some revenge for his mother's death. None of these kids could have been among the men who had killed her five years before.

He risked a glance at Jason, who had stopped looking at him entirely, and then shoved his pistols back into their holsters with shaking hands and walked away. He ignored the slaps on his back and the words of respect from his comrades.

What was the matter with him? He was a soldier in the midst of a bloody civil war. People got killed. That was the point. If it hadn't been these boys, it might have been him, or Jason, or one of the others. Would that have been preferable? Yes, the partisans were young, but they were the enemy. In a war you couldn't choose your enemies, any more than you could choose your own killer.

A trickle of wet ran down Ryan's cheek. He swiped at the tickle with the back of his hand, and stared dazedly at the fresh blood. He rubbed his blood into the dried brown stain of his enemies' blood; he doubted it would ever wash free of his hands.

Night fell. No moon. No stars.
Black. Still. Like his soul.
Ryan slipped away from camp and into the brush. He was taking a chance. If he met up with an enemy patrol, he would be killed. If his father found him gone, he'd have questions to answer, more lies to tell. Still, he had to go. He had to see her. Touch her. Let her love, her strength, her goodness soothe the fire in his belly.

He ached, he hurt, he burned, and only Julia, his wife, could soothe away all the pain. He would gladly die for the chance to be held by her tonight.

215

Everything he knew that was true and right had been turned upside down today when he'd stared into the faces of the boys he'd killed. Sure those Bushwhackers would as soon have killed him and Jason as looked at them, but Ryan hated himself all the same. All his life he'd been taught to follow orders, yet today when he'd followed them—above and beyond the call of his honor and duty—he'd felt worse than ever.

They'd spent the hot, muggy afternoon burying the dead in their caves. Ryan had washed enemy blood from his hands in Murphy Creek, as well as his own blood from his forehead where a bullet had nicked him. Still he felt dirty, trapped. Julia's touch alone could cleanse him; her love could set him free.

When he arrived, the house stood dark, silent, but he knew where she slept. As he'd done once before he removed his boots, scaled the wall and slipped across the roof to her window. Open, despite the stillness of the night, the air hung heavy with damp heat and the scent of death. Would he ever be able to get that smell out of his nose and mouth?

Ryan went through the window, crossed the room and stood over her bed. She slept in her shift; damp with sweat, her nipples clinging to the cotton. Her hair, braided but coming loose in sleep, curled with the heat. He took a moment just to look at her, to fill his roiling mind with her image and breathe the scent of roses until the stink of death receded. He'd known coming here would heal him.

Down on his knees he went, not wanting to frighten her from sleep. He put his lips to her ear and whispered, "Julia."

The next second he stared down the barrel of a Colt Dragoon. Damn, she was fast. Where had she hidden the thing?

"Ryan?"

"Expecting someone else?"

"No." She uncocked the gun and placed the pistol on the nightstand, then sat up. "What are you doing here? Is something wrong?"

Something was very wrong, but he didn't want to talk right now. Instead, he yanked off his jacket, tore free the buttons of his shirt and shucked his pants in short order while her face went from concerned, to surprised, to pleased. She held her arms open for him, and with a sigh of relief he gave himself into her embrace.

His hands were dark against the white of her shift. *Murderer of innocents,* the ghosts of his victims shrieked. He drowned their catcalls with the sound of rending cotton as he tore the undergarment from her body. She gasped, startled at his violence, but she did not flinch or try to get away. Instead, without words, she understood his need for her and opened her body to him.

He made the agony recede with the taste of her breast, the scent of her skin. He filled his evil hands with the purity of her flesh and drowned his memories and his pain in the depths of her body. When they both shuddered release as one, damp from their exertions, she kissed his temple, ran her fingertips up and down his back and held him to her heart.

"Shh," she murmured, her fingers in his hair. "I'm here." She stroked from temple to nape. "We're together." Another kiss on the tender skin of his eyelid. "It's all right."

He relaxed against her, letting her hold him and stroke him and make him want to live again. When their hearts slowed to the steady beat that was theirs alone and the sweat on their bodies cooled in the whisperlike breeze, she reached for his hand, held on when he would have withdrawn and asked, "What happened, love?"

He didn't want to tell her, though she had to know the truth. Couldn't she smell death on his skin? He could. Couldn't she see the blood still on his hands, though he'd washed them until they stung? He did.

Ryan sat up, turned his back to her and put his head into his hands. "I killed today, Julia."

She took a deep breath, a hitch in the middle showing her fear. "Who?"

"Bushwhackers." He snorted in derision. "Kids. I was so angry. When I got back to camp they'd been attacked and I wasn't there. So many died. I felt—"

"Guilty."

"Yes. I wanted to make them pay. We found them in the brush. Jason got nicked. So much blood—I went crazy, started shooting. Killed them all."

Now she would scream and shout. Now she would hate him.

Amazingly, she touched him. Cool, slim fingers running up and down his spine, flat, callused palm cupping his shoulder, soothing his pain. "I'm sorry. About your friends. About the Reb boys. I can't say I'm happy to know you killed, but this is war and you're a soldier."

"I don't know what's the matter with me. Why am

I shaking? I've been wanting to kill them all for so long. They killed my mother.''

"I know."

He straightened, glanced over his shoulder. Though the night was dark, his eyes had adjusted so he could see her face, but not the expression in her eyes. She sat up, too, naked, unashamed, her dark hair tangled and tumbled about her face. "What do you know?" he asked.

"Your mama was killed by Rebs and then you all came south."

He turned away from her again. It was time she knew the whole truth of his heroics, or lack of them. "There's more to it than that."

"Isn't there always?"

"I was the man of the house when Da was away. But when Ma needed me the most, I wasn't there."

"What happened?"

Ryan's mind drifted back five years. The day his vow of vengeance had been taken. The day his childhood had ended. He had not allowed himself to think of that day for a very long time.

"Da had gone to Kansas City to try and get the Federal soldiers to patrol closer to our farm. We were getting pushed out bit by bit. Nothing big, a crop trampled or burned here, a cow stolen or shot there. Ma told Jason and me to go pick berries. She wanted to make a pie for when Da came home. She told me to watch Jason real close. He was my responsibility. She counted on me to keep Jase safe.'' Ryan swallowed the lump of pain in his throat and kept on. ''We came back just in time to see the Bushwhackers ride up. Ma stood on the porch with the shotgun. She saw me, and the glare she gave me, I knew she meant for me to keep Jase out of the way.''

"She was right," Julia said. "They would have killed you. That's what they did. That's what they do.''

"I know. I had my guns, but there were at least ten of them. I guess I thought they'd leave when they heard there were no menfolk around. Jase and I hid behind the Osage orange hedge between the fields and the house. I kept my hand over his mouth. He never could shut up. Not then, not now. I couldn't hear what they were saying at first.'' He paused, remembering— the heat of the afternoon, the scent of berries in the sun, dust and death and destruction. "One of them shouted, 'What's yer name, Jayhawker bitch?' I got mad, hearing them call her that, started to get up. Then everything went slow; I couldn't seem to move fast enough. Ma said, 'You can call me Mrs. Murphy.' 'Murphy?' one shouted. 'You're one of them abolitionist scum.' '' Ryan shook his head. "Ma never could shut up either. She lifted her chin and said, 'Yes, sir, I am, and right proud, too.' Jason was struggling, and I looked away for a minute to make sure I wasn't smothering him. And they shot her.''

Julia's indrawn breath gave voice to the pain in his heart. "The gunshot echoed and echoed. Before I even looked up, I shoved Jason's face into the dirt so he wouldn't see, but I knew. They'd shot her, just because of who she was, what she believed. She'd died for that, while I sat there hiding in the brush.''

"They would have killed you both if they'd seen you. You did what your mama asked. You kept Jason safe.''

"I was a coward. Hiding in the bushes while my own mother got shot."

"I'm so sorry, Ryan. I'm sure there are a hundred stories just the same on both sides of the border. You think there's a feud between our families? It's nothing compared to what's been going on across this border for a long, long time. The whole cursed war is a blood feud. Hatreds run deep and they run long and no one cares who dies as long as it's the enemy. That doesn't make it right, but it's the truth."

"I swore as I buried my mother I'd make them all pay."

"Will killing every Missouran you find bring your mama back? It's the men who killed her who were wrong. I would think you of all people should know that hurting others doesn't make you feel any better."

"True, but I can't let killers—even your brothers and their friends—just run rampant across Kansas. I have to stop them any way I can."

"Killing them won't heal what's wrong inside of you. It'll only make it worse. Has only made it worse."

He didn't answer. Couldn't. He didn't know any more what was wrong or right. Because *they* killed, he should? Because *they* did wrong, he could make things right by doing the same? He had been taught that, believed it for a very long time, but suddenly what had always made sense seemed ludicrous. Still he knew nothing else.

"I know they're killers," she persisted when he remained silent, "but they're my brothers, my father."

"They're the enemy." He recited the words without his usual fervor.

"And what are you?"

Ryan sighed and began to dress. When he stood at the window, he turned back to find her wrapped in the sheet, sitting on the side of the bed, the face that had contracted with joy when she'd first seen him now sharp with confusion and sorrow. She was as confused and as sad as he. Not knowing what else to say or do, he fell back on what he'd always believed.

"You're going to have to choose, Julia. Either you're my wife or their sister and his daughter. You can't be both."

"No, you'll have to choose. Either you're my husband or my enemy. The man I married would never hurt my family."

"Dammit," he exploded, though he kept his voice low. "You're a Murphy now. Act like one."

Her eyes narrowed. "Fine," she spat. "Next time I see my mama, I'll just shoot her for you. Like you would have done that night if you'd been close enough, right? Would that make me worthy of your precious name?"

Before the last word was out of her mouth, she gasped at what she'd said, put her fingers to her lips. But it was too late. Her eyes filled with tears. "Ryan, I'm—"

"Sorry," he finished, his anger fading This was an impossible situation. The situation would always be impossible—as long as the war raged. He gentled his voice. "We're both confused. This is . . ." He spread his hands, indicating them, the bed, life in general.

"Impossible," she muttered.

His answer was merely a sigh.

She stood, crossed the short distance to him and allowed him to hold her. "You wouldn't shoot my brothers or my father would you?"

Ryan clenched his teeth at the resurgence of anger. She wasn't going to let up on this. "Julia, please, what do you want me to do? If they see me, they'll be shooting."

"I know. I just . . ." she shrugged, the movement shifting her head against his chest, sending the scent of roses and tears across his face, reminding him of the choices they both had to make. "Just promise me you'll try not to get into it with them if you can."

Ryan hesitated, then shrugged. He could promise that. He didn't want to shoot her brothers or her father if he didn't have to. "I promise."

Her sigh of relief brushed her breasts up and down his chest. He clenched his teeth again, against lust, not anger this time. He would never get enough of her. Not if they had a lifetime.

If.

"You'll go back to Con and Kathleen soon?" he asked.

She stiffened, pulled back. "I-I can't. Mama—"

Ryan scowled. "You two can't stay here alone. Take her with you. Promise me you'll go to the church, or I'll drag you there myself and to hell with any Rebs in my way."

She nodded. "All right. As soon as they retreat, we'll go."

He kissed her softly, lovingly, hoping to impart without words what lay in his heart. Since Ma had died he'd never said, "I love you" to anyone. He was

223

terrified that if he tempted fate with his love, disaster would strike the one he loved, as it had struck both his mother and Kathleen. So he kept his love to himself and used his body to tell her what he felt.

When he pulled away, Julia's eyes remained closed, and she swayed against him. He smiled. She understood. "I don't know when I'll see you again."

Her eyes snapped open, the desire fleeing as fear replaced it. He hadn't said *if* but they both knew he'd meant *if* as well as *when*.

He stopped her fears with another quick, hard kiss. Then he was out the window, across the roof, onto the ground. Ryan was halfway back to camp when he stumbled over the enemy.

Chapter Thirteen

The smoke alerted Ryan to their presence. Otherwise his horse would have walked right over their hideaway and alerted them. But when he smelled the smoke yet saw no light, Ryan knew one of the Bushwhacker caves lay nearby. He left his horse behind and crept forward until he could hear voices. Then he crept forward a little more until he could make out the words. One of them was "Murphy," and Ryan blinked in surprise, then listened even harder.

"Them damned, thievin' Murphys are in that camp. I saw the red-haired one bright as day when I scouted earlier. Tomorrow, before the sun is up, we run 'em down. No quarter for any Federal. Same deal they give us. But leave the Murphys for me and my boys."

The last sentence gave a face to the voice: Sam

Colton. Julia's father. His father-in-law. *Hell.* What should he do about this? Obviously all the Coltons were in this cave, as well as some other partisans, and they planned an attack on his camp tomorrow. An attack on him and his family most of all.

He couldn't attack them now, alone. Even if he got some of them, they would overrun him and the camp would be caught unawares. He should return to camp and rouse his troop, bring them back and slaughter the Bushwhackers while they slept, just as they planned to do to him and his.

But he wouldn't. He couldn't. These were Julia's brothers and father and—vicious killers though they were—he couldn't bring the wrath of the Federal army down upon them like this. If they were killed in open battle, so be it, but he could not, would not, have their blood mingled with the other blood already staining his hands. Such an action would murder the future for which he now lived.

His sole course of action was to slip away, return to camp and alert his father of this information. He'd have to admit he'd been absent without permission, but this kind of intelligence would get him off on that count. They could all pack up and disappear before the Coltons and their murderous crew arrived.

Crawling backward as quickly and as silently as he could, Ryan hurried to do just that.

Julia overslept the next morning. When she opened her eyes, sunlight spilled across her bed, hot and bright. Blinking against the glare, she rubbed her face and tried to remember why she'd awoken so happy.

A single name answered all her questions, fulfilled

all her hopes and dreams. *Ryan.* He had been here last night, and though he had been dirty, bloody and heartbroken, he had come to her for comfort. She smiled at the memory of how they had comforted each other.

The smile faded at the realization that dawn had come and gone, but her mama had not called her. Was Mama—? No. Not that. Not yet. They had not made peace between them.

She dressed as fast as she could. Throwing a beige muslin day dress over fresh undergarments, she ran down the stairs still braiding her hair as she called, ''Mama? Mama?'' The panic in her voice heightened as she neared the kitchen and heard no answering call. The emptiness of Mama's bed made Julia's heart thud ever faster.

Julia burst from the front door onto the porch and nearly tripped over her mother, who sat in Gran's rocking chair staring out at the brush—pale, shaking, but alive.

''Mama?'' Julia went down on her knees next to the chair. ''What's the matter? You frightened me half to death.''

Slowly, as if the effort were too much for her failing strength, Mama turned her eyes from the brush and stroked Julia's hair with her bone-thin hand. ''I love you, child,'' she whispered.

Julia blinked back tears. This sounded too much like goodbye, and she was not ready. Mama needed her. Mama loved her. Mama had been her whole life for her whole life—until Ryan. Julia laid her head in Mama's lap, and her tears soaked her mama's night-dress.

"I love you, too, Mama. I'm sorry I ran away and left you."

"Never mind that. I have something to tell you."

"I have something to tell you."

"Hmm," Mama murmured, still stroking Julia's hair. It had been so long since her mama had soothed her. Julia couldn't remember the last time Mama had been able to do more than let Julia take charge.

"I-I-I got married," Julia blurted. The hand in her hair paused, clenched, and Julia almost jumped up and away, fearing a slap, though her mama had never raised a hand to anyone in her life.

"The Murphy boy." Mama did not question; she already knew.

Julia hurried on, before her courage went south. "I love him, Mama. He didn't mean to hurt you. He was crazy with grief over his own mama's death and he rode with the wrong men. He's so sorry, Mama. He just wants to be forgiven."

As did she. Julia held her breath and after a second's hesitation, the hand resumed its stroking, and Julia relaxed. She'd been forgiven, just like that. She should have known that no matter what she did, Mama's love would never waver.

"I loved someone once, too." Mama's voice had taken on the flat, emotionless tone she often used when something touched too close to her heart. Julia sat back, looked up and saw Mama had returned her gaze to the brush, as if she waited for someone. Her face as devoid of emotion as her voice, Julia, who knew her well, knew an inferno of pain burned beneath that cool exterior.

"Who, Mama?"

"I was young. Younger than you. Pretty then. Stupid. Betrothed by my father, just like you. And then I met *him* and knew I could not marry another. I ran off with him. Married him. Loved him for one glorious night before we came home to tell my family. My betrothed was there. I believed being married protected me. I underestimated my father's anger and my betrothed's obsession with me and the land my husband owned."

"What happened?" Julia whispered, but she knew, even before her mama said the words.

"My father held me back while my betrothed killed my husband."

"Dear God, no," Julia breathed, her active imagination bringing the scene vividly to life in her mind—except in her mind she saw Ryan and herself.

"Yes. My husband owned the land the Murphys bought. My betrothed—"

"Father?" Julia interrupted.

"Who else would be so obsessed with that cursed soil? Any other man would have let the place go, but not Sam. He thought it was his, just like I was his, and no one would take either from him. So he killed the only man I'd ever loved. He figured I'd done him a favor marrying his enemy; then I would get the land. But he had a brother, off in Ohio, and the farm went to him."

She took a breath, shallow and rattling, and then continued, though her voice had become rough, with overuse or excess emotion, Julia could not tell. Throughout, her mama's eyes remained dry. "Even then Sam didn't give up, the hatred just festered. He taught it to his boys so that by the time the Murphys

229

came he had his own private army trained to take the land from them. He's always been full of anger, but when I was hurt . . . the guilt of it made him . . . crazed. The Murphys were easy to focus on—to hate. But he's crazier than I've ever seen him. It scares me. Now he's gone off to use the war to take back that damnable piece of land.''

''How could you have married him, Mama? How could you marry him when he killed the man you loved?''

Mama's lips trembled, the first sign of pain she'd allowed herself since beginning. Her face went from gray to snow white, and when she looked at Julia, her eyes were harder than she'd ever seen them. ''I had no choice. I should have told you this long ago, explained to you how going against the family for your own happiness leads to disaster. And I'm not just talkin' about yourself. I'm talkin' about the one you love. If you really love him, you should leave him go. Never tell your father or your brothers what you've done. Unless you want him dead.''

''They're already set to kill him, Mama. He's a Murphy. My being one, too, won't make any difference.''

''You're a fool, child, and I never would have figured you for one. Yes, your father and your brothers are set to kill all the Murphys. This time they'll get that land if they have to die tryin'. But if they find out you betrayed them, any promise your father made to me long ago will just be words spit in the wind.''

Before she could explain, the sound of distant gunfire erupted, and they both started and turned their gazes toward the brush. Smoke trailed toward the sky, and on the early morning breeze drifted the scent of gunpowder and the shrill screams of the dying.

"Looks to be a bloody battle this morn," Mama observed, her face once again bleak, her voice lifeless.

Julia stared at the smoke trail and shook, despite the inhuman heat of the day. Not only had her mama's revelations made her sick with dread, but the location of the battle increased her fear. Was Ryan in the thick of the killing?

She'd known her father meant to get rid of the Murphys if he could. But the fact that they were protected by the Union flag had made her hope for the best. The story her mama had just told her revealed her father as a cold-blooded murderer willing to do anything for a piece of land. She'd thought his obsession more recent. Now she knew that his hatred went back further and reached much deeper. Father Con's belief that a marriage between Colton and Murphy might settle the feud now looked to be nothing more than another unanswered prayer.

She would never be free; Ryan would never be safe.

Julia turned to ask her mother's advice, only to find that Mama had slipped into one of her deathlike sleeps. The gunfire in the distance grew louder. Smoke blew across Julia's face, burning her eyes, making her cry.

What on earth was she going to do?

Things had not gone as Ryan planned. Instead of packing up and slipping away, his da decided to stay and fight. No amount of argument could make him retreat. Not when they had the advantage. Especially when he knew the Coltons were coming. Shamus Murphy never ran from anyone—least of all a Colton.

He'd not even asked Ryan where he'd been or why; he'd been too ecstatic to hear the news. Jason had stared at Ryan long and hard, unsmiling, considering, but had said nothing, and Ryan had been grateful. He didn't know how he would explain everything.

On their father's orders Ryan and Jason lay in the brush on the far side of the camp along with the rest of their troop. Just as the sun peeked over the horizon, the Bushwhackers exploded from the brush, howling the Rebel yell. As ordered, the Federals did not fire until the enemy had darted into the tents, found them empty and come back out to stand in the center of camp, exposed.

"Fire!" came the order, and fire they did. But the Bushwhackers were wily and dove back into the tents for cover.

"We've got 'em now, men!" Ryan's father shouted. "They'll never leave here alive. Charge!"

Just as they rose from their cover, a volley of shots from behind made them all hit the dirt again.

"Hellfire and damnation," Shamus cursed. "There's more out there and they've gotten behind us."

Reaching over, he cuffed Ryan on the ear. "Why didn't ye tell me they'd come with reinforcements?"

Ryan colored, feeling a fool. "I told you what I heard, Da."

"Captain, t' ye. Now we'll have t' fight hand t' hand. Let it be on yer head then." He turned away from Ryan with a scowl, dismissing him. "Each man fer himself. Fight yer way out!"

Mayhem ensued. The camp became a frenzy of battle, the brush even worse. In the close quarters and with the odd mishmash of clothing worn by the guerillas, it was difficult to determine friend from foe. Jason ran off into the dense smoke and Ryan tried to follow. Someone rushed at him from the side, and he shot without thought, heaving a sigh of relief when the man who fell at his feet was a stranger. Mistaken identity would take many lives this day.

Jason's howl of triumph drew Ryan through the murk just in time to see his brother jump over a prone body and race away. Ryan followed, attacking again and again as he made his way forward. The Rebels seemed to be multiplying amid the smoke and the gunfire.

Panic consumed Ryan. One of the last promises he'd made to Ma had been to protect Jason. She had died because Ryan kept that promise. To break it now would make Ma's death a hollow sacrifice.

He fought his way to Jason's side. They were far from the rest; the rush of his own blood and the war drum that was his heartbeat in Ryan's ears drowned the cries of triumph and terror in the distance. The thickness of the smoke made every breath a struggle. Ryan glanced at Jason, whose chest was also heaving with exertion. Sweat soaked Jason's uniform, ran down his face, mixing with the ash and soot, making him look every inch the dangerous warrior, completely different from the Jason Ryan had known. Seduced by the battle, by blood lust and victory, Jason had changed from a boy to a man in the space of a moment.

Ryan blinked against the sting in his eyes, knowing

that when innocence was lost, it was lost forever.

"Jason," he began, his voice the voice of a stranger.

Before he could finish, though he had no idea what he'd meant to say, the smoke parted and a man approached. No mistake about this man, he was guerilla from the tip of his feathered hat, past the bright, multicolored fabrics of his guerilla shirt, to the toes of his knee-high boots. Even if he hadn't worn the uniform, Ryan knew the face.

Del Colton—with a knife, his guns tucked into their holsters. Was he out of ammunition?

"Son of a bitch," Ryan muttered.

"That's what I hear about you," Colton sneered. "I've been lookin' for you, Murphy."

Jason's lip pulled back in a snarl, and he leveled his gun at Del. "No, Jase!" Ryan shouted.

Both Del and Jason gaped at him. Ryan couldn't believe he'd spoken himself, but he couldn't allow his brother to shoot Julia's favorite brother in cold blood.

"I don't want to do this, Del."

"But I do." He smiled, though the effect was not pleasant. Del was in the midst of battle fury, too, and just aching to kill someone, no matter the odds. "I've been dreamin' about it since I caught you with my sister. She might be dazzled by your pretty face, but I aim to mess it up some before I kill you."

"Let it go, Del. I have nothing against you."

Del's expression bled from angry to vicious. "I've got plenty against you. Plenty. My mama lies abed day in and out because of you. If that ain't enough, my pa says you violated Julia."

"I'd sooner die than hurt her."

"Glad to oblige. Now use that pistol or draw your knife, you yellow bastard. I'd like nothing better than to kill you where you stand."

Jason's gun clicked as he cocked the hammer. "Jason, stay out of this," Ryan warned.

"But—"

"Stay out of it!" Ryan shouted.

Jason didn't argue, but he didn't leave and he didn't put up his gun. Ryan had no choice but to try and talk Del out of his course, though he doubted talking would do a bit of good when the air hummed with blood lust and battle rage. Still, Ma had always said he had a knack for soothing man and beast—and Del Colton was a little of both.

Ryan maneuvered so he stood between Jason and Del, blocking Jason's shot. His brother growled in disgust, but Ryan ignored him, keeping his eyes on Colton. Del caressed his knife like a lover.

"I apologize for anything I've ever done to hurt your family," Ryan said. "You can believe me when I say I want nothing but peace between us from now on. I hold the name Colton as dear as my own."

Del and Jason snorted at the same time, then glowered at each other. "I don't have time for this shit." Del made a move.

"Ry, get out of the way!" Jason shouted.

Ryan lunged, grabbing hold of Del's wrist before he could attack. They struggled. Though Ryan was taller, older and heavier, Del was wiry and strong, full of hate. Ryan's love for Julia had weakened his hate but strengthened his will to live.

Concentrating all his energy on keeping the knife

from plunging into his chest, Ryan didn't expect Del to kick his feet out from under him. He fell backward, hitting the dirt so hard that his breath left him. Del followed. The knife scraped along Ryan's neck, drawing blood.

"First blood," Dell grunted.

"Let—this—go," Ryan managed.

Del's eyes, black in color and in spirit, went darker still with hate. "You ruined Julie. Her body, then her mind. You're gonna die squealing in your own yellow blood, cryin' for your mama like the weakling you are. And when you're dead, Julie will get her mind right, marry Ted and be one of us again."

Infuriated, Ryan lifted his legs and sent Del flying head over heels toward the earth. Ryan ignored the pain in his ribs and the sting on his neck, leaping to his feet and crouching for the expected attack. Del lay at Jason's feet, too still. Jason stared at Colton with a curious look upon his face, his gun still cocked in his hand. Then he glanced at Ryan, eyes wide.

"He landed on his knife, Ry."

A jolt of fear went through Ryan's chest, and he ran the few feet to Colton's side, flipped him over. A wave of nausea hit him so hard he staggered.

"Dammit." Ryan fell onto his knees next to Del.

The knife embedded in Del's chest and the amount of blood staining his brightly colored guerilla shirt left no doubt that his time on the earth drew to a close, yet he found the ability to yank the knife free from his own chest. Blood pulsed from the hole in time to the beat of his fading heart. He grabbed Ryan's hand, fingers slippery but strong, and slapped the bloody blade into Ryan's palm.

"You've sent me to the worms, you Yankee bastard. I curse every Murphy, you hear me? Every last one of you. I wish you would all know misery worse than this."

Then Delbert Colton's eyes glazed with death, and Ryan stared at the fresh blood on his hands, unamused by the irony that Del had just cursed the sister he'd sought to defend.

Suddenly, Ab, Ben and Clark Colton burst through the flaming brush, their father at their heels, to find Ryan covered in Del's blood, holding the knife that had killed him.

Chapter Fourteen

His troop near decimated, Shamus Murphy was in a fine fury. The fact that his bloody sons had been reported missing didn't make him any easier to deal with.

"If none of ye can find me boys, I'll damn well find 'em meself." Growling a stream of curses, he plowed his way through the living and the dead, stalking into the brush alone. No one dared follow.

The Bushwhackers had retreated, dragging their dead with them. The troop of Federal soldiers had made a fine account of themselves. They'd been bushwhacked, to be sure, but Shamus Murphy did not take a whupping lying down. As soon as he found Ryan and Jason, they'd be off, the three of them and whoever was able to ride, in pursuit of those murderin' hooligans.

He should have joined the war long ago. All those years mourning his wife had been wasted. He'd never felt more alive than when he was avenging her. In his mind, the enemy had all become one. Bushwhackers, Rebs, Missourans, Coltons. They would pay and they would pay dearly for killing the woman he had worshipped and driving mad the little girl he adored. Sometimes, in the heat of the night, Shamus wondered what his gentle wife would say if she saw what he'd become. But then, his wife had always been a saint. Shamus Murphy was far from it.

A rustle in the brush up ahead made him slow, draw his gun and crouch out of sight. Even when he identified the speakers, the subject of their conversation made him continue to hide.

"I thought we were dead for sure, Ry. When all those Coltons came burstin' through the brush."

"Me, too."

"Why do you think they didn't attack us?" Jason asked.

"Luck," Ryan said, withdrawn. "Or lack of ammunition." His heart did not seem to be in the conversation. Come to think of it, Shamus recalled, Ryan's heart had not been in much since his ma had died—except for revenge and soldiering—and since he'd met that Colton bitch he seemed to have lost even that.

"If they hadn't stopped to check Del they would have fallen on us like mad dogs, you think?"

"Yeah, I think."

"Why didn't you let me shoot Del when he first came through the brush?" The two of them stopped, several yards away, and Shamus froze. Ryan hadn't killed a Colton when he could? Something was wrong with that boy. "He just about got you with that knife," Jason continued. "Was it because of the girl?"

Shamus strained his ears for the answer.

A sigh, a muffled curse, then a single word that infuriated a father's vengeful heart. "Yeah."

"She's a Colton."

"She's my wife."

Shamus nearly gagged. Silence, heavy and hot, hung between the two boys. "Your what?"

"My wife."

"Are you crazy? Da'll kill you."

Ryan made a disgusted sound, and he and his brother appeared on the path as they walked back, though they were not able to see their father. "You're the one who told me I should do whatever I had to do to be with her."

"*Be* with her, not marry her."

Ryan stopped, whirled on his brother. Shamus crouched lower. His boys were but a few feet away. "Oh, it's all right to see her. Maybe violate her like a good Jayhawker should. But don't *marry* her."

"You aren't a Jayhawker." Jason's voice was petulant. "Not anymore."

"Jayhawkers, Federals. What's the damned difference?"

"We're soldiers, like we always dreamed we'd be. Fightin' the good fight, Ry, for justice and freedom."

"There is no good fight, Jason." Ryan spread his arms wide. "This is all there is, and it isn't good. It's a taste of Hell. I feel like I'll never be free of this."

"Well, shit, Ryan, what happened to you?"

"I grew up, finally, and you should, too. I've been a fool, and I have no one to blame but myself. I'll do my duty in this damned war. I want it over as quick as I can make it over. Then I'm takin' my wife, if she can forgive me for killing her little brother, and I'm leavin' this place. I've had a bellyful of hate."

"You didn't kill Del. It was an accident."

"He's still dead."

Silence reigned for a moment, and then Jason said in a little-boy voice, "What about Ma?"

Shamus glanced at his oldest son's face in time to see the pain before Ryan controlled his eyes and his mouth.

"What about Ma?" His voice held a warning Shamus heard, but Jason must not have.

"You told me we needed to make them pay for killing her. As many as we could."

"And I seem to recall you telling me, not so far back, that Ma wouldn't want that."

Jason sighed. "She wouldn't. But she's dead and I still hurt over it, Ry. I thought maybe doin' something to revenge ourselves on them would help."

"Yeah, I thought so, too." Ryan stared west, stroking his lip with his thumb. "But it doesn't."

Shamus could tell by the look on Ryan's face that his boy was not remembering his ma. He was remembering *her*. If Shamus hadn't hated the Coltons before on principle, he hated them now because of that traitorous woman who had taken his son away. Women; they were all Jezebels, intent on seducing a man from his purpose and duty.

Except for Mary Margaret Murphy, of course. His own dear Maggie had been as sainted as the Virgin

241

herself, and she'd understood the passion for freedom that had driven him first from Ireland to America, then across the land to Kansas. She'd shared his passion. Hers had rested in freedom for the slaves; it was something he'd never understood but had been willing to go along with for her sake. Together they had fought for their passions. Maggie had died for them, and Shamus would never forget that. Even if his son had.

"What good does killing them do?" Ryan asked. "The more of them we kill, the more of us they kill. There's a whole lot of widows and orphans and no one wins."

"What about our farm?"

Ryan glanced at his brother and his face softened. "I don't want it if I can't have her."

Jason gaped, most likely as surprised with the gentleness on Ryan's face and the fervor in his eyes as Shamus was.

"I don't understand you, Ry. Da taught us that a man's nothing without his home, his family, his land. You believed it, too. Now you're telling me you'd throw it all away for a woman you met just a few months ago?"

"Yeah."

Ryan stalked off in the direction of camp. After a long moment, Jason followed. Shortly after, Shamus stood, staring after them as fury coursed through his veins. He fingered his pistol and considered his options.

His flesh and blood had betrayed him with the enemy. His oldest son. His warrior. Not only that, but if Ryan had his way he'd contaminate his brother's mind, too. Then where would they all be?

All that had gone before, death and destruction, loss and pain, his wife's life and his daughter's mind, would be for nothing, which Shamus could not allow.

Ryan had turned traitor. He would give up the farm, the land that was their life, for that Colton whore. Shamus wouldn't let him. But how could he keep both his farm and his sons?

He remembered an order that had just come down from General Ewing. All families believed to be aiding and abetting the guerillas could be rounded up and summarily imprisoned, and once in prison, it was a very short trip to the cemetery.

Shamus Murphy smiled; problem solved.

Midnight came. Julia sat at Mama's bedside and watched her sleep. She'd been able to carry Mama inside and put her in bed without much effort, which only revealed how very close to death Mama was. All that remained was skin-covered bone and a weakly pumping heart.

Voices outside made Julia's own heart thud with fear. She snatched Gran's pistol off the table, cocked it and crept to the door. Disappointment filled her. Whoever approached wasn't trying to keep quiet, so Ryan was not on his way. Who was it? Federals, who didn't care if their approach was heard? Or her family and their guerilla friends?

She nearly fired on them when they burst through the trees, riding toward the house hell-bent. But the moonlight shone off a white feather in Ab's hat and then she heard her father shout, "Girl! Get your ass out here."

Julia uncocked the pistol and glanced at Mama, but even the approaching riders and her husband's shout had not awoken her from this deathlike sleep. Julia slipped through the door and onto the porch.

She breathed a sigh of relief to see that only her brothers and father had come. No Bills, no James boys, or any of the rest.

"What's the matter?"

"This," her father growled and shoved a blanket-wrapped lump from his horse.

The body hit the ground and lay still. Terror struck her dumb for a moment. But the need to know burst through her fright into a single word. "Who?"

"Who do you think? Look around, girl, anyone missing?"

His words penetrated her paralysis. She'd been so afraid they'd killed Ryan and brought him home to gloat. But a glance at the faces lined up in front of her showed Julia the truth. "Del?" she asked, knowing the answer even before she ran to the body and pulled the blanket away from his face.

He looked so very young framed by the dark, coarse wool. His black hair made the whiteness of his face shine even more pale in the moonlight. His eyes were closed, inky black lashes casting a spiderlike shadow upon ghostly cheeks. For a moment Julia could not think, could not believe what she saw could be true. Then a tear fell from her eye onto Del's face. It slid down his temple, blended with his hair, and memories rushed forth.

Del as a baby, laughing and fun, her own personal doll. Del toddling after her when she took care of Mama, clinging to her skirts, lifting his hands to be picked up and rocked. Del in Colton Creek, giggling, naked as the day he'd come into the world, splashing Julia as they played together. She'd thought she'd put that Del to rest when this one had been born, but now she knew she never would. Del had been her boy, and she loved him despite everything.

"How?" she asked, stroking his cold, cold skin. "Who?"

"Your lover."

Julia's hand froze on Del's cheek, and she spoke from the pain in her heart and the confusion in her soul. "No, he promised."

The growl of fury from her father made Julia realize what she had said and she gasped, jerked her hand from Del and covered her mouth—too late to keep the telling words from their escape.

Her father leapt from his horse and walked toward her. The clink of his spurs against the hard-packed dirt thundered loud in the deep silence of the night. He stopped right next to her, and then she saw his eyes. Hatred glowed there, as bright and hard as the hatred that he reserved for the enemy.

He hit her across the face with the back of his hand, and she fell over the body of her brother. Ab, Ben and Clark gasped, but they did not interfere. Julia's cheek throbbed. Slowly, she pulled herself upright and faced him again.

"You traitorous, lying whore." He hit her in the mouth. Her head snapped back, and she smelled blood seconds before she tasted it upon her lip.

"Pa!" Ab protested. "That's enough."

Her father didn't even acknowledge Ab's words. He hovered over her, fists clenched as if beating her would somehow revive Del. Julia kept her gaze on his, trying to discover by the shift of light across his eyes when he planned to hit her again. "I should have known the day I learned you were in your mother's belly that you would be no better than her. I should have killed you like I killed your father."

Julia gaped. This man wasn't her father?

Sudden understanding hit her like a blast of sunshine, and through the agony of Del's death came a tiny spark of joy that this man who had always despised her was not who she thought him to be. The man her mother had told her about was her father, the man Mama had loved, the man this man had murdered in cold blood before her mother's eyes. And all for a dirt farm across the border.

Anger cut through Julia's fear. So much hate, so much pain, so many dead and for what?

"You talk a lot about killing," she spat. "How you're going to kill me and Ryan and the rest of them, but they're still alive and one of you is dead."

He kicked her, like a cur, and Ab jumped from his horse to grab his father's arm before he could hit Julia again. "Stop. Both of you," Ab said.

Ab's intrusion surprised Julia. No one in the family had ever stood up to her father before. For Ab to interfere now he must think Sam meant to do worse than beat her silly.

Sam Colton wrenched free of his son, reached down and yanked Julia to her feet. He put his face so close to hers she could feel his breath across her cheek. "They knew we were coming. You knew where we were since ya'd brought supplies. Only you,

Julia. You told that Murphy boy and now your brother is dead. It's on your head.''

"I didn't tell him anything. Just because the Murphys were in the battle doesn't mean Ryan killed Del. He's not a savage like you.''

He laughed in her face. "This said about the bastard who fired your house down about your ears. You stupid, stupid girl. I found your precious Ryan standing over your brother, Del's blood on his hands, this still in his fingers.'' He grabbed her hand, slapped something cold and hard into her palm. Julia looked down and froze. Del's knife, crusted with blood. "Just him and his brother standin' over Del. Two against one and Del's gun was empty. Ryan Murphy killed Del and he's gonna die.''

Julia dropped the knife with a mew of pain. She wanted to collapse right there and wail until she couldn't wail any more. Had Ryan done such a thing? Yes, this was war, but Del was her little brother. Ryan had promised.

Sam let her go and she did collapse, but he wasn't through with her yet. "Get off my farm. The next time I see you, promise to your mother or not, I'll kill you.''

Then he and the boys rode off into the night without another word.

Julia lay alone, surrounded by the dark, the dead and the dying. Her heart had shattered in more ways than she could explain—numb, yet on edge, in agony, yet unable to give voice to that agony. Perhaps if she could cry she would be able to stop the sizzling burn in her stomach from increasing until her entire gut seemed to be aflame. But she could not seem to bring forth any tears. She could only hold her brother and rock him as she had rocked him when he was her baby, while she tried to understand that the man she had loved and married had murdered her boy.

Perhaps Sam lied. She could no longer think of him as Father, and that knowledge soothed her somewhat. She didn't share blood with such an obsessive, hate-filled man. She wasn't truly a Colton. But could she be a Murphy if what Sam said was true?

Hours passed and she grew chilled holding Del. No matter how she tried to warm him, his skin grew colder, his limbs harder. She would have to bury him come morning, but for now she would keep him close.

Horses approached, and she stared at the Dragoon that lay a few feet away, but she couldn't make herself move to retrieve it. A boot came down on top of the pistol, then a hand swiped the gun away. Slowly Julia raised her gaze and met eyes as hate-filled as Sam Colton's. But these eyes were blue, not black—as blue as his uniform, and the grin upon his face made her think of Satan himself.

"Get up," Shamus Murphy ordered.

Julia shook her head to clear away the confusion. Why was he here? What could he want? Why did he stare at Del as if her dead brother had given him a precious, coveted gift? She glanced at the other Federal, who still sat his horse. She did not know him. He stared straight ahead, mouth twisted into a grimace, as if he'd been ordered to do something distasteful but had to do it just the same.

"Get up, I said. Are ye deaf, woman?"

Murphy yanked her away from Del and to her feet, shook her a bit until she struggled to be free. Then he let her go and strode toward the house.

"Wait!" Julia ran forward. "My mama's sick. Sleeping."

"Well, she can sleep all the way t' prison, but t' prison she'll go."

"Prison?" Julia blinked and turned to the second man. He kept staring straight ahead; his frown deepened.

"Aye, prison. Anyone found aiding the renegades goes t' prison. Grab what ye need and come along."

"We haven't done anything."

Murphy nodded at Del's body, and his Satanic grin returned. "How'd ye get that if it wasn't brought by a Bushwhacker?"

"It's my brother. We have to bury him in the morning."

"I know who it is, girlie. Me son killed him."

Julia winced and her bruised cheek throbbed at the movement. She had hoped against hope Sam lied. Now she'd heard the same from Murphy. Ryan had murdered her brother.

"He wouldn't. He promised."

"War's hell," Murphy sneered. "Now get yer things or ye'll have none. Wake yer ma or I'll wake her fer ye."

"No. You can't. She's ill." Desperation filled Julia and pushed away the odd inertia that had overtaken her. If her mama went to prison she would die in misery. Julia couldn't bear to lose another she loved so soon. "Please. Talk to your son. He—we—I—"

she broke off and glanced at the other man. Nothing. She looked back at her father-in-law.

He smirked. "Aye, I heard all about the two of ye. We all did. Ye made fer some fine entertainment fer the men last night. They don't get t' hear about such a hot piece as yerself. Probably not considered gentlemanly to share such things, but then, Ryan only wanted ye fer that anyway, so why worry about manners?"

Julia flushed at the implication. He couldn't mean— Ryan would never—But how could Murphy know about them if Ryan hadn't told him?

"My son was right pleased with ye. But he's had ye now and he's gone on his way." He continued to smile, and Julia wanted to claw the expression from his face. "I'm surprised ye believed all his sorrowful words that he was 'oh so sorry he'd hurt yer mama.' After all these years with the feud betwixt us, I'd think ye'd be smarter than that, girlie." He shook his head, still smiling, and Julia lost her urge to claw him; she lost her will to stay upright at all as he continued. "He would have come himself t' take ye off t' Kansas City with the rest of the Bushwhacker women, but he's the best guerilla tracker we've got. After he finished gettin' the congratulations fer killin' such a dastardly criminal as yer brother, and tellin' us all about the kill, he went on t' trail the rest of yer kin and finish 'em the same as this." He shoved at Del with his boot.

Julia heard a growl and realized the sound came from her own throat. Her hands curled into claws. "Don't touch him again."

Shamus laughed. "All right then. We'll leave 'im

fer the scavengers. They have t' eat, too." He grabbed her by the arm, bruising her, and dragged her toward the house. "Now do as I say, and this fine young man will take ye where ye belong."

Julia yanked her arm free. She wasn't leaving her brother for the coyotes. Murphy, thinking she meant to do as told, let her go. Instead she swung her elbow into his gut. His breath whooshed out and he doubled over. She brought her knee up and clipped him on the chin. He hit the dirt like a dead body.

The soldier on the horse pulled his gun, cocked it, but Shamus Murphy halted him with a wave of his hand. Julia stood, ready to fight or die. Murphy caught his breath, stood and rubbed his chin. The light of derision in his eyes had shifted to curiosity. "Damn but ye fight dirty."

Julia narrowed her eyes, lifted her fists.

He dipped his head in acknowledgment. "Yer fer prison still. Easy or hard, it's yer choice, but ye'll go."

"Fine, I'll go. But you'll bury Del first."

Murphy's heavy eyebrows shot up. "And if I say nay?"

Julia smiled, and from the frown her expression caused on Murphy's face she knew she'd mastered the art of the evil grin. "I was raised a Colton. I know this brush like I know the touch of my mama's hand. I'll escape, and you can bet when I reach Quantrill, Kansas will bleed like it's never bled before."

"Ye'd leave yer mama behind?"

Julia looked straight into those blue eyes, so like the eyes she'd loved, and she lied as well as Ryan Murphy's eyes had lied to her. "Yes."

251

"Hmm." Murphy considered, still rubbing his chin. "If we bury the Bushwhacker, ye'll go t' prison without a fight?"

"I will."

"Ye swear on yer father's life?"

She had learned hours before the truth that set her free. Her father was already dead. Easy enough to swear on his life.

"Certainly," she answered.

The lack of concern in her voice nearly betrayed her. Murphy scowled, hesitated, but when he looked into her eyes he nodded, sealing the bargain, then moved off to bury Del.

Julia almost laughed aloud. This was so easy. Why had she ever thought she could not lie? All you had to do was hate enough, and you could say anything, do anything to get what you wanted.

Julia walked toward the house, making her plans. She would go along to prison and make certain Mama was safe and well. Then she would escape, someway, somehow.

If it was the last thing she ever did, she would make Ryan Murphy pay for every dream he had destroyed.

Chapter Fifteen

If July had been almost as hot as Hell, August was hotter. Not only because of the heavy heat that made breathing difficult and comfort long forgotten, but because of the place Ryan had been sent with his men—north and then east, straight into the heart of Bushwhacker territory.

Patrolling Bates County to keep the peace was no longer necessary. War had spread across the land in an all-out assault, mirroring the war in other parts of the country. In early July, Vicksburg at last fell to Grant. During the same week, Lee lost a mighty battle at an obscure little town named Gettysburg. The tide was turning for the Union—everywhere but in Kansas.

Directly after the battle at their camp, Ryan's father had ordered him to take the troop and track Quantrill;

253

then Shamus had ridden off with one of the youngest recruits on some hush-hush mission. When Da returned, the recruit did not, and Shamus Murphy refused to answer any questions. After the first order to "Mind yer own business, Lieutenant, and do yer job," Ryan had done just that.

Several weeks after the death of Del Colton, Ryan still led men through the weeds, and he hadn't even seen the rump of a partisan horse. The Bushwhackers had gone to ground somewhere. Somewhere other than here.

Too hot for a fire, which was against orders anyway, the troop ate hard biscuits and jerky at day's end. Jason appeared from the indigo night and slumped next to Ryan. "I'd give my right toe for a cup of coffee," he grumbled.

Ryan nodded but didn't answer. He was sick to death of talking to Jason, and the rest of them, too. Sick of most everything about the army. He found it hard to recall why he'd been aching for a soldier's life. Was anything you dreamed ever as magic as the dream? Funny how a few short weeks on the trail with no hot food, little water and no coffee beat a man down. Ryan felt on the edge of humanity sometimes, on the edge of sanity.

The only thing he ached for now was his wife. Julia's image was the sole thing that kept Ryan from becoming like the rest of his men. They reminded him of a pack of starving wolves—tantalized by the scent of meat, knowing it was out there somewhere, just beyond their reach, but they could not find it. When they did, they would tear their quarry into bloody shreds. Shamus Murphy was the leader of the pack.

The madness that had threatened for so long had erupted, like thunderclouds on a hot, hot day. Ryan had tried to broach the subject of their father to Jason, but Jason had changed, too. Or maybe it was Ryan who had changed. Whichever was the truth, Ryan no longer felt connected to the brother and father he had loved all his life.

Ryan leaned back his head and focused on the moon. The pure silver sheen reminded him of Julia—the night he'd sworn on the moon that his word was true. Then he'd lied to her—promising he would not hurt her family. A stupid promise, but sometimes Ryan wondered just how smart he was.

He wished he could see her, wished he could have been there when she learned about her brother, wished he could explain what had happened and hold her while she cried. She would have cried. He'd seen how she'd looked at Del that night of the dance. Del had made her angry, and she'd taken Ryan's side, but she had a softness for that one, and his death would hit her hard. Ryan still reeled from it.

Every time he closed his eyes Ryan saw the blood on Colton's guerilla shirt, felt the slick, bloody knife in his hand, heard the rasp of Del's curse, smelled his death in the air. Whenever he fell asleep Ryan remembered Sam Colton's voice moaning, "My son, my son. What have ya done to my son?"

Ryan looked at his hands and sighed with resignation. Every time he glanced at his palms he saw the red, red blood staining his flesh. When he blinked, the stain was gone, but the memory and the guilt remained. Julia's little brother was dead.

Would she understand? Would she forgive? And if she did not, would he want to live?

"Did you hear we're headed out in the morning?"

Jason no longer adopted Da's brogue to tease, perhaps because Da had changed too much to be funny, or maybe because Jason had changed too much to enjoy teasing. Still, Jason never ceased talking to Ryan, even when Ryan's responses were downright surly.

"We head out every morning."

Jason hit Ryan in the shoulder. "We're headed west this time. Then south."

Ryan tilted his head and scowled. "Why?"

Jason met Ryan's scowl with a grin, as usual. Was it only Ryan who could see that the light no longer danced in Jason's eyes? Or did Ryan see the changes because he was the one who heard Jason moan every night, the one who listened to Jason cry in his sleep? The flesh wound Jason had sustained across his scalp had healed, but deep inside Jason carried an open wound, and Ryan, with a similar wound of his own, had no idea how to help his little brother to heal.

"Quantrill ain't here," Jason said. "Anyone can see that. Don't know why Da insisted we stay way the hell over here for so long, but the men are getting so restless he's got to take 'em somewhere for a fight."

Ryan grunted, though his heart beat faster and his breath sped with excitement at the news. Southwest meant Bates County, or at least closer to it.

Love. Peace. Gentleness. He needed them with a desperation he'd never felt before, but would he find them in the one who awaited him there?

"Julia," he whispered, and her name was no longer just a name but a prayer.

He kissed her as he'd always kissed her, with wonder and love. His lips, soft yet strong, traveled her body, made her shift, moan and ache for more. His large hands spanned her waist, smoothed over her hips, touched her intimately as only he had touched her. She arched, sighed, tensed, reached for him, but he was not there.

"Julia," his voice whispered. His breath, or was it the wind, stirred her hair. Love bloomed within her, chasing away the burning pain in her stomach.

Pain over Del's murder and Ryan's betrayal had turned to thoughts of vengeance, the need to punish. Julia could almost laugh at the silly prattlings of peace and forgiveness that she had tried to press upon Ryan during their days at the creek. No wonder he had listened with a slight curve to his lips, as if pondering a misguided child. That was exactly what she had been.

She understood Ryan's hatred now, and he would understand hers. Even while she plotted her revenge upon him, she missed him, and her yearning for his touch found life in her dreams.

She clung to sleep and to the dream, for only in dreams could she find the peace that had once been hers, the hope of a future she had found in Ryan's arms. But her future looked bleak and his arms were no longer there, even if she could have borne to let him touch her in the light of day. Sometimes the pain, in her gut and in her heart, was so bad she could not eat. Julia moaned, shifted, awoke.

The dank smell, and the heavy heat that cooled in the midst of the night to almost bearable; the low murmur of the Federal soldiers outside, safe and away from the danger of the dilapidated building; the sighs of the women all around told Julia that her dream had given way to reality's nightmare.

Prison.

She and Mama had been in Kansas City for a week. The trip north had passed quickly. The elder Murphy and his minion rigged a travois for Mama and then the young soldier, who'd identified himself as Private Jonas, hustled them north as fast as he could while Murphy fled to destinations unknown. Jonas had been quiet but tough. Julia hadn't been able to escape, even if she could have left Mama. Jonas had tied her hands together by day and her hands and feet by night.

When they reached Kansas City, Jonas produced transfer papers and became one of the guards at the prison. At first the women were confined in a building on the levee, but the place became too rat-infested even for Rebel sympathizers, so the prisoners were moved to a building on Grand Avenue and confined to the third story.

There were nine women and girls in the prison with Julia and her mama, all of them awaiting banishment from Missouri for guerilla activities, none of them over the age of twenty. Three were Bill Anderson's sisters—Josephine, Mollie and Janie. Janie was only ten years old. Mollie was sixteen and had been sweet on Del. When Julia told her of Del's death, Mollie had gone white and turned away. She had not done much but lay on her bunk and stare ever since. Julia understood Mollie the best.

Having the Anderson girls there made Julia think they would not be confined long once Bloody Bill got wind of it. But being rescued by him, being in his debt, made Julia wonder if she'd be better off here, despite the way the ceiling sprinkled wood chips and the walls creaked in the wind.

Mama still lived, but just barely. The days and nights on the road had weakened her so she could no longer walk without the aid of two of the women. A single week in prison had turned her into a shallow-breathing corpse. Ryan would pay for this, too.

Julia's real father was dead, her mama near enough. Her love was a lie. So was her life. If she didn't have vengeance, she would have no reason to go on. But she did, and she would—until justice was served. No matter how long it took.

I have notified the military authorities of the unsafe nature of the prison on Grand Avenue, but no one will heed my warning. None of the Bluecoats will even stand guard within the structure as pieces fall daily from the ceiling, and the walls creak so loudly they nearly drown out the cries for mercy from the women incarcerated there. It is my belief the entire structure will soon collapse. Perhaps if you were to speak with them, Father Sullivan, they would heed your counsel. At the very least, you will be here to pray for the dead and comfort the maimed. Sincerely, Doctor Joshua Thorne, Chief Surgeon—Kansas City.

Con leaned back in his chair and studied the letter he had received that morning. Even if he hadn't recently learned that Julia and her mother had been dragged to a Kansas City prison, common decency demanded he answer the call of his father's old friend. His occupation ascertained it.

In the kitchen he heard Kathleen preparing dinner. He would have to take her with him. He couldn't leave her here alone, and there was no one left in the neighboring counties to leave her with, even if she would be parted from him. If he dressed her as a boy and they traveled fast, and well armed, with the Lord's care they would arrive in Kansas City safely.

Con scowled. The Lord had not been listening to any of his other prayers lately, why would he listen now? Con had spent the last month praying ardently for a release from the torture that was Kathleen Murphy. Why was God testing him like this? Hadn't he proven years ago by walking away from her and never looking back that he was God's disciple? Why now, when it was too late to change anything, did God bring her back into his life and like this? Day and night they were alone together, and she needed his friendship, his counsel, his love. The love of a shepherd for his flock, not the love of a man for a woman. The woman he had always wanted but could never have.

Con crushed the letter in his hand and swore. He had taken vows. Not only to God but to his father. He could not break them, even if she would. But when she looked at him, smiled at him, she did so with the eyes of a sister, the mouth of a mother. She had never seen him as anyone other than Con, her little brother's best friend.

Heavy boots stamped through the church. Spurs clanked against the marble floor. Con came to his feet, grabbed his gun and hurried into the hallway.

Kathleen's snow-white face and wide, terrified eyes appeared in the kitchen doorway. He motioned her back and cocked his gun. They'd been invaded many times by both armies in the last month. Con had strained his vows in deed even more than he'd strained them in thought. But he would allow no one near Kathleen, even if he must use the gun he should not even possess.

Every time a soldier came into the church, Kathleen hid for a day or more in her room. The crack in Con's heart tore deeper each time. Once she had been wild and carefree. Nothing had scared her, nothing had stopped her from living and laughing. Now every man but him and her own family sent her back into a world he could not reach. She barely lived and she never, ever laughed.

A soldier appeared in the arch between the church and the hall leading to the house. Bluecoat—familiar blue eyes. Con sighed in relief, uncocked the Colt.

"Ryan."

Without a word of greeting, Ryan strode down the hall, grabbed Con by the shoulders and stared into his face. The stark terror in Ryan's eyes sent a shaft of fear through Con. Ryan was never afraid. Or at least he never let his fear show.

"Is she here?"

The question, uttered in a hoarse, desperate voice, told Con the source of Ryan's fear. He had been to the Colton place.

"No."

"Ah, God!" Ryan spun away, put his hands to his head, knocking his cavalry hat to the floor. "I knew I should have come back here and taken her away."

Con raised his eyebrows, stooped to pick up the hat. "Disobeyed orders? Deserted your men?"

Ryan's hands fell from his head, clenched into fists at his sides. He turned back to Con. His gaze fell on the hat in Con's hands, stuck on the insignia of the United States Army, then skittered up to meet Con's own. "I've had a bellyful of the army. Of hunting and stalking and killing. I don't know why I ever dreamed this was the life for me. It makes me sicker than I was before I started."

"You've changed. Learned. Grown up. Because of Julia."

"I killed her brother."

A cold wave of dread washed over Con. "You what?"

"An accident, but he's dead. I can't stop seeing his face, and hers, whenever I close my eyes."

Con swallowed, reached out a hand for comfort, but Ryan flinched away. He did not want comfort, he wanted to hold his guilt close to his heart and let it fester, as he always did. Con let his hand drop. "This is war, Ryan. People die."

The fear in Ryan's eyes flared again. "If Julia's dead, nothing else matters. I never told her I loved her. Hell, I never tell anyone. I'm so damned scared they'll depend on me too much, and I'll make a mistake, and they'll die because of me. Like Ma. But if Ma saw what I'd become, she'd kick my ass for being a coward of the heart."

"So tell Julia you love her."

"I can't," he said through his teeth, jaw bulging as he ground them. "She's gone."

"To Kansas City." He took Ryan's hat and

slapped it onto his own head. "They're holding guerilla sympathizers in a house on Grand Avenue. I was
on my way there at the request of the doctor in charge
when you barged in."

Ryan growled deep in his throat and swiped the hat
away from Con. "Why the hell didn't you say so?"

"I just did."

"You're taking Kathleen with you?"

"I wouldn't leave her here."

Ryan stared deep into Con's eyes. He must have
found what he wanted to find for he gave a slow nod,
then turned to leave. Con stopped him with a hand
on his arm. "What are you willing to do to get her
out?"

"Whatever it takes."

"Break promises to the dead?"

Ryan winced. Con wanted to as well. He was a fine
one to speak of breaking promises.

"Do you enjoy ripping out my heart and stamping
on it?"

Con used Ryan's own words against him. "Whatever it takes. If you have to keep a vow, Ryan, keep
a vow of love over hate. Your vows of marriage over
your vows of vengeance and war."

"I just want her safe."

"Will you lie? Perhaps cheat? Or steal? Deny your
father, refuse your name? Then run like Hell once you
have her. Love is important. Life. Your marriage. Do
whatever you have to do."

Ryan nodded, then put his hand over Con's,
squeezed, and Con knew this was goodbye. "Tell
Kathleen I love her," Ryan said.

"I will."

"And while you're at it, Con, tell yourself."

Ryan grinned, a smile near enough to the grin of his youth to cause Con's eyes to sting with the memory. By the time his gaze cleared, Ryan was gone.

Ryan made good time to Kansas City. Fear kept him riding long past exhaustion. He'd already slipped away from his troop, leaving a note for Jason that said he'd gone to check on Kathleen, lying to his brother, who would in turn lie to their father and the United States Army. Ryan couldn't have cared less. All he wanted right now was Julia.

Kansas City came into view and the weight on his chest lightened. Whatever it took, he would free her, make her understand about Del, and they would start their life together. Just making that decision had stopped the desperate sizzle in his stomach. His mother would be proud of him. Why hadn't he seen a gentle soul such as Ma would never have condoned his thirst for vengeance? He had been blinded by grief, tempted by his father's obsession, won over to hate by the madness of this time, his surroundings. But his mother would have been sorely disappointed in him. As disappointed as he was in himself.

The town was overrun with Federals—Bluecoats everywhere. It was easy to ask one the location of the women's prison, and shortly thereafter Ryan reined up in the middle of Grand Avenue.

He frowned at the structure in front of him, then glanced about, wondering if he'd come to the wrong place. No, the soldier he'd asked had said the prison stood between Thirteenth and Fourteenth streets. Though several other houses were on this block of

Grand Avenue, only one belonged to General Bingham, and on the front porch of this dilapidated house the name Bingham was prominently displayed. Several guards stood in the front yard, shifting from one foot to the next, talking, smoking and staring at the third story, where the women were said to be housed.

Ryan approached the man with the highest rank. "Captain." He saluted. "I've come to transfer one of your prisoners."

The captain returned the salute. "Papers?"

"I—ah—"

Lie, cheat, steal, Con's voice whispered.

Ryan straightened and looked the captain straight in the eye. "I lost them at the river ford. Horse went lame and dumped me. Papers ruined. But I'm to take a Julia Colton to Lawrence immediately."

The captain puffed on his cigar as he considered Ryan. Great billows of evil-smelling smoke drifted toward Ryan, making his eyes water. He choked back a cough.

"No papers, no transfer."

"But—"

"It was hell gettin' these women here. Few of 'em fought like she-cats all the way. They're as dangerous as any Rebels. Now that we've got 'em, I'm not lettin' any of 'em go. You want one, get the papers." He turned away.

"Sir!"

"What?" The captain turned around scowling, chewing on his cigar like it was a fine beefsteak.

Ryan hesitated. Should he tell the truth? Would that help or hurt his cause? If he couldn't get Julia out of here, would the knowledge that she was his wife endanger her life with the she-cats the captain spoke of? Then again, he'd seen Julia fight; she could most likely hold her own.

"Lieutenant—? What the hell did you say your name was?"

"Murphy, sir."

"Murphy? That's the name on the order to incarcerate the Colton tramp." He rustled in his pockets, yanked out a tobacco-stained sheet, peered at it, nodded. "Murphy, Shamus, Captain." He looked up, chewed harder on his cigar. "Who the hell are you?"

Ryan couldn't find his voice. This explained Da's disappearance after the battle in Bates County. What he couldn't understand was why. Da hated the Coltons, but to make a special trip just to ascertain that the Colton women went to prison was above and beyond even Da's realm of hatred. Then he remembered the madness in Da's eyes and realized he did not know any longer what his father had become capable of.

"Lieutenant?"

"I'm Ryan Murphy, sir. The captain is my father. He sent me here. There's been a mistake." His voice trembled.

"Yes, there has. No papers, no girl." The captain spat his cigar onto the ground next to Ryan's boot.

Ryan took a moment to talk himself out of beating the captain senseless. When he spoke he was relieved to find his voice level and calm instead of raging, like his stomach. "Can I see her?"

The captain's eyes narrowed. "What the hell for?"

"She's expecting me. To take her to Lawrence. I'll need to explain the delay."

"Who cares what she thinks?"

"This is a mistake, sir. She's the wife of a Federal officer."

"Hmm, spread 'er legs for a Yankee. Them women are meaner than hornets in the summer sun—they'll kill her if they find out."

"That's why we need to get her out of there. Can I at least tell her I'll be back?"

The captain shrugged. "Go ahead. But you can't go inside the house."

"What?"

"It's unsafe. Gonna fall down any minute, sounds like. We stay out here. No Federal officer allowed on the premises."

Ryan found he couldn't speak for a moment, his shock was so great. When he did, his voice was low, hoarse, desperate. "That's barbaric. You have to get them out of there."

"No orders, no movin'."

Impatience combined with fear made Ryan want to take the captain and shake the man until he recovered some sense, but experience told Ryan such an action would be wasted. Instead, Ryan took a deep breath and strove to be calm. "How can I talk to her if I can't go inside?"

"Like we do. Back window. Third story. If the window's shut, throw a rock and one of 'em will open up. That's how we feed 'em, too. Use a bucket and a rope."

Escape plan number two dissolved before his eyes. Ryan's mind spun as he walked toward the rear of the house. He had to get her out of here. But how? Tell her to jump? With all the Bluecoats in Kansas

City, they'd be caught and hung before they reached the city limits. Sneak back and knock out the guards? He doubted he could best the ten men who milled about the prison grounds.

He took off his hat and wiped the sweat from his brow. It looked as if the only way to ascertain the safe release of his wife would be to obtain the legal papers needed for her release. He could do that. He'd find the officer in charge of the Kansas City regiments and convince him to release Julia, but first he would talk to his wife.

Feeling like a lovesick boy, Ryan picked up a stone and tossed it at the widow. Seconds later a young girl appeared. She was far too young to be imprisoned and Ryan's face flushed with shame. He wanted to yank off his blue coat and never put the garment on again.

"Hello?" she called. "Could you send up a clean chamber pot? Miss Julia's been throwing up in ours all morning."

The sweat on Ryan's brow turned to ice, and tiny white dots danced in front of his eyes. He blinked, swiped a hand across his forehead and forced himself to speak. "Is she sick?"

The little girl shrugged. "Every day." She leaned farther out the window and lowered her voice to a conspiratorial level. "My sister says she's in a family way. There'll be trouble when Miss Julia's pa and brothers find out. She ain't married—though I can't quite figure how she got a baby in 'er when she ain't married. Ma always said married comes first."

"Get her," Ryan croaked.

"Sure, mister. You feel all right?"

"Get her," Ryan repeated. "Now."

"All right. You don't have to be so mean."

The girl disappeared from the window. Ryan waited, then he waited some more. When he was about to stamp around front and shoot his way through a Federal division to get upstairs, Julia appeared at the window.

Her eyes widened at the sight of him, then narrowed as an expression came over her face he had never seen there before. Even in the early days when they had first met she had never looked at him like that. She had feared him; she had been intrigued by him; she had wanted him; she had loved him.

But never had she hated him.

Chapter Sixteen

"Have you come to gloat?" She leaned out the window, spreading her arms wide. "Here I am, in prison. Just like you wanted. Did you tell all the guards how easy it was to get me in bed? Don't leave any Federal ignorant of your prowess, please. I suppose they'll be up here wanting me on my back, too, if they have the stomach to come inside this wretched place."

Ryan did not know what to say to this woman who looked as though she might spit upon him at any second. Ghost pale, fading bruises at her eye and lip, hair unkempt; her hands shook. She talked in riddles. He could understand if she berated him for killing her brother. She had to know that truth by now.

"Julia, I don't know what you're talking about."

She wrinkled her nose as if she smelled something foul, then braced her hands upon the windowsill.

270

"Was the marriage even real?" She had lowered her voice to near a whisper for the question, but her laugh, a high-pitched, hysterical sound that made the hair on the back of Ryan's neck prickle, was too loud. "Wouldn't that be a fine joke on me, along with all the rest?"

"Of course the marriage was real." His voice rose along with his anger and confusion.

"Shut up," she snarled. "I know you want me dead, but at least let me die with dignity. If these women find out I'm a traitor, they'll murder me in my sleep. Mama, too. But then, you've wanted that all along, haven't you? I've been such a fool."

"I don't want you dead. I came to get you out of here."

She laughed again, the same frightening laugh. "Sure you did. That's why you sent your father to take me and Mama to prison. Get me out of the way."

"I did not."

"Then how did your father know about us?"

Ryan didn't know the answer to that. He had told no one but Jason, and Jason would never have revealed that. "I don't know, Julia, but I swear I didn't tell him. He must have got it into his head to get you and your ma off the farm. He's been acting crazy for a long time now."

As crazy as you're acting, he thought.

"I don't care about why or how. Mama told me family came first and if I forgot disaster would follow—for myself and those I loved. She was right. Mama's always right. I'm a traitor to my family, my country. I deserve prison. I deserve to die for letting you touch me. For loving you." She leaned forward, and this time she did spit but missed him by a mile. Her words were right on target—an arrow straight to his guilty heart. "You killed my brother, you son of a bitch."

"I did. I didn't mean to. An accident . . ." He broke off, hearing himself, realizing he babbled like a guilty man.

She stared at him, her eyes full of hate, her arms wrapped around her stomach, as if hiding a secret. He knew her secret and it both frightened and exhilarated him.

"I don't believe you," she stated in a flat, dead voice. "You always hated him, hated all of us. Why I ever believed you were sorry about Mama, I'll never know."

He could tell by the wildness in her eyes and the tremor in her voice that there was no use arguing with her now. He would do what he had come to do, and try to make her understand the truth later. "Fine. Don't believe me. But I'm getting you out of here. You and my child."

If possible her face went whiter. Her hands flew to her mouth, and she whirled, then raced away.

The little girl came back to the window. "You made Miss Julia puke again. Go away." She slammed the casing shut.

Ryan stared at the closed window for a long time. She hated him, but he loved her. He still had not told her, not that she would have believed him, but he would. Just as soon as he got her out of here. If he had to, he would throw her over his shoulder and carry her away kicking and screaming.

She couldn't hate him any more than she already did.

Soldiers came in and out of the first floor throughout the next day—an oddity in itself since none of the Federals wanted to risk being trapped in the poor excuse for a building when it fell. Loud thumpings and strange scrapings drifted to the prisoners on the third floor, giving hope to some that the enemy had fixed the insecure foundation wall. Others, Josephine and Mollie Anderson especially, feared they were removing the solid part of the foundation that held the prison upright.

From the taunts the guards had leveled at the women during the time they'd been prisoners, Julia had to agree with the Anderson sisters. These men hated the guerillas, Anderson and Quantrill the most. They wanted vengeance, and since they couldn't seem to get their hands on either of the two Bills, they'd take their vengeance wherever they could.

Julia lay on one of the few bunks allowed the prisoners. Her mama lay on the other a few feet away. Between the two bunks stretched their arms, fingers linked for comfort and strength. For the first time she could recall in her life, Julia had none of either to give.

Ryan's visit had drained her. His treacherous words had reopened the wound in her heart. His face had caused the love she thought dead to revive. His knowledge of her secret had caused her to lose what small amount of food and water she'd managed to keep down. She'd been sick the remainder of that day, most of the night and again this morning. Her gut was scraped raw and her head pounded. The intense heat of the early afternoon made things worse.

August 13, 1863—just another day in Hell.

Thank the Lord none of the women had heard their conversation. They still treated her like a pathetic, disgraced girl. Funny, if they knew she was actually a proper, married woman, they would hate her. But to be pregnant and unwed in the midst of this war was a cause for sympathy. As long as the father was a partisan. Julia had never said anything about the father. And she never would.

A question continued to plague her: Why would Ryan come to Kansas City if not to release her? She pushed her curiosity aside. He could as easily have come to make certain she died, and the fact that he'd gone away yesterday and not returned only gave weight to the second belief rather than the tiny spark of hope in her heart.

When he came for her, if he came for her, she would not go. She did not have to go anywhere with him ever again. Though a short while ago she had feared Anderson's arrival, now she hoped one of the two Bills would come before Ryan secured her release; then every Bluecoat in the vicinity would die.

Nausea swirled through her stomach, lightened her head, made black spots dance in front of her closed eyes. Ryan would die if he were still in Kansas City.

She hardened her heart, willed the weakness away. He was none of her concern. He was a murderer. A liar. A cheat. A thief—of her innocence and her love. He deserved whatever he got.

He was also the father of this baby everyone insisted she had in her, and she could not seem to make her heart listen to her head on this matter. But she would. She cursed beneath her breath and rubbed her hand over her still flat stomach.

"Child?"

Julia turned her head, met her mama's gaze. "Yes, Mama?"

"A baby is a wonder of God, and when you make one with the man of your heart it is a miracle of love only a mother can understand."

Damn, but her mama could hear a worm wiggle in the night if she set her mind to it, and it seemed she'd been of a mind to hear her daughter's conversation with the enemy.

Julia tightened her lips against the angry words threatening to spill free. She had given; Ryan had taken. That wasn't love.

"Do you know how I survived all these years without your father? Years spent in the bed of the man who had killed him, bearing children for that man, children who broke what was left of my heart?"

Julia didn't want to hear Mama's pain, but she did want to hear about her father. She shook her head, mute with the anguish on Mama's face. They had not spoken of her father, except for Julia to tell Mama how she'd learned the truth from Sam.

"I survived 'cause of you, child. You're all I have left of him except faded memories. In your strength of will I see him. Your eyes are mine, but your hair, that streak of russet, is his. The set of your chin— his. The only thing you got from Sam Colton is your intolerance of the Kansas folk, and I don't think you ever truly felt that way."

"Think again, Mama."

"You think you hate him, but you don't."

"He killed Del."

Mama closed her eyes and sighed, swallowed. When she opened them again, her gaze was determined. "I loved that boy, too. I carried him; I bore him in blood and pain. I watched him become one of them, but I loved him. He was fated to die by the sword. That was the life he lived. One thing I've learned, you have to forgive or the hatred eats you alive. You're the one who suffers, not them."

"He'll suffer. You can count on that."

Mama tightened her fingers on Julia's, a weak twitch of bone within skin. "Don't become one of 'em. If you do, they've won. Don't make my sacrifice worthless. Let me die knowin' your father will live on in your child. That I was able to raise his daughter without hate."

"You ask too much, Mama."

"I don't. I ask for one thing. Love over hate. If you think about it, you'll understand and do what I ask."

"How can you ask this of me? You of all people? Ryan rode with the men who hurt you."

"I was hurt past fixin' long before the Jayhawkers came that night."

"You've forgiven him, then?"

"Long ago. Holdin' on to the past only makes the present more of a torture. From what I've heard that Murphy boy had good reason to hate us all. But he needs to get past his hate, and so do you."

Confusion filled Julia, and anger followed soon after. "I don't understand you. I trusted you with my dreams, and you betrayed me to your husband. Nearly got me hitched to that bastard Chandler. I would have lived the same life as you. How could you have thought that was best for me? Even after I told you about Ryan, you told me to give him up.''

''I was wrong. I was worried about you, about what Sam would do to you if he found out. I thought I would save you from a life like mine if I stopped your love for that Murphy boy before it went anywhere. I should've known love like that is too far gone from the very first sight.'' She sighed, closed her eyes, and her face took on a peace Julia had never seen there before. When she spoke, Julia understood where her peace came from. ''It was too late for me and your pa the moment we lit eyes on each other. We were star-crossed—fated for disaster. I knew it, but I couldn't stop lovin' him anyway. The more you deny the feeling, the stronger the pull. It's the same for you, I see that now.''

Julia sighed, let her hand fall away from Mama's as she stared up at the ceiling. ''What was his name? My father?''

''Ray.'' Mama's voice caressed the name. Julia felt betrayed by the simplicity of that single word. Such a plain, dull name for a man who had been at the center of so much pain, love and destiny.

She should know better than to dwell on a name. What was in a name? By any other name the man would still be her father.

''Ray what?''

''Julian.''

Heavy silence fell between them. Julia turned her head and met her mama's eyes. Together, they smiled.

Mama seemed to sleep, but Julia could not. After awhile she got up and made her way to the window. She sat next to the opening and breathed in the heated afternoon air, hoping to still her nausea. When two Bluecoats stepped out back to smoke, the way they put their heads together and spoke low made Julia lean away from the sunlight so they could not see she listened.

"Wall should go down some time today," one said, lighting his cigar. "Then we'll be free of 'em."

The second nodded, leaning over to use the light. He blew out a trail of foul-looking smoke, then laughed and clapped his friend on the back. "Damn that Murphy wasted his money. I would have done this for free."

"Me, too. But the money doesn't hurt. Wonder who he wants dead so bad?"

"Said it was a family matter." The second man shrugged. "Who cares."

They laughed again and walked away.

"I saw that man give the Yankees money."

Julia started at the voice next to her elbow. She turned her head and met the solemn gaze of Janie Anderson. "What man?" she whispered.

"The one who made you puke. After I told him to leave, he talked to the captain, gave him some money, then rode away."

Julia swayed, put her hand to her head as the blood left. Janie grabbed her arm. "I thought you should know."

Julia nodded, fighting the threat of faintness. She'd so badly wanted to believe Ryan had come for her, she'd actually been looking for him at the window.

She was a fool. He wanted her dead just like his father had said.

She didn't have time to cry over lost love now. She had to do something before the damned Federals killed everyone in the prison just to get to her.

An ear-splitting shriek erupted. Dust and wood rained down upon her and Janie. Women screamed as the earth moved. Julia leapt to her feet, ignoring the wave of dizziness and the stab of nausea the movement brought to her and thrust Janie away from the window. The child ran to her older sister.

White dust hailed down. Julia choked when her lungs filled with it. A piece of the ceiling hit her on the head. She fought further dizziness. Damn, she was too late to do anything but die. Julia moved toward her mama, fighting the shifting floor and the hysterical women.

They were trapped like horses in a burning barn, and like those horses, some ran mad. While horses might run straight into the fire, here the women ran straight toward the locked doors, slamming into the wood, hurting each other more than the falling ceiling and shaking building had yet to do. They turned and ran toward the windows. Glass spewed as the windows broke, spraying the closest women with shards.

Blood streamed. Screams flowed. The storm of wood and dust increased. Julia glanced up just in time to see the roof collapse inward, falling slowly in her direction. She threw herself on top of Mama right before a heavy beam fell inches away, crashed through the floor and spiraled downward. The bunk they lay upon slid toward the hole. They fell, and fell, and fell.

They hit bottom. Julia took a deep breath, unable to believe they were still alive. Then the rest of the ceiling fell on them.

At last the screams stopped.

Con and Kathleen arrived in Kansas City in the late afternoon of August thirteenth. The sun still burned in the sky; the heat was intense and heavy, causing a haze to hover over the city as if doom awaited all who entered there.

Shaking aside his strange sense of foreboding, Con reflected upon the trip. They'd gotten all the way here without incident—much more than he'd hoped for when they left the church on the hill. For some reason, the land between Bates County and Kansas City was devoid of partisans. Certainly they'd seen some Federal troops. But his vestments and explanation of where he and his mute altar boy were going had gained them nothing more than a grunt and a wave onward.

Con glanced at Kathleen. After he'd told her what they were doing, she'd gotten into the spirit with more enthusiasm than he'd seen from her. When she'd first emerged from her room clad in the too-large work pants and faded work shirt he'd found in the barn, her rear end looked a bit too shapely for a boy. But the large shirt hid her tiny breasts and when untucked disguised her rounded posterior adequately. Thank the Lord his last stableboy had been very big. After braiding her faded, red-blond hair, she hid the mass under a floppy straw hat, which helped to shade her face, too pale and refined for a farm boy if anyone looked too closely.

She'd swallowed her fear of riding a horse. He took her compliance as an indication that she was improving, though whenever they saw soldiers she shook and had trouble breathing until long after they were gone. Even now, when soldiers ran past them up Grand Avenue, she flinched at the sight of every one.

"I can take you to a hotel, Katie." She glanced at him with huge, frightened eyes. "You wouldn't be by the soldiers there. You'd be alone. I'd come back when I finished."

She moved her head, left, right, left again, and her mouth thinned into a stubborn line. Con sighed. He should leave her at a hotel, but curse his love for her, he could not. She wanted to stay with him, and he could not deny her that, even though her need for him stemmed from fear.

"Come on then," he said, more gruffly than he had ever spoken to her before. "Let's get this done."

He hoped Ryan had already secured the release of Julia and Mrs. Colton and was long gone from here. If not, Con would use whatever influence he had with Dr. Thorne and whatever other means necessary to help the two people he'd joined together before man could tear them asunder.

A gasp from Kathleen made Con reach for the rifle in the spider on his saddle. As his fingers touched the gun, he saw what had upset her and withdrew his hand. When he rested it upon the other over the reins, his skin had gone cold. The foreboding that had overwhelmed him at his first sight of Kansas City returned full force.

The Federals had been running up Grand Avenue for a reason. A house had collapsed and lay in rubble about halfway up the avenue. Con didn't need to look at the street signs to know the building was, or rather had been, the prison.

Bluecoats buzzed about the ruin like bees about a fallen hive, and with as much hope of restoring the house to its original state. One man stood in the midst of the disorder shouting orders. Con jumped down from his horse, threw the reins to Kathleen along with a look that said to stay there and headed for the Queen Bee.

Dr. Joshua Thorne had aged since Con had last seen him, but he still recognized his father's dearest friend.

"Connor?" Thorne asked, holding his hand out for Con's before Con could answer. "Even without the garments of your faith, I'd have known you anywhere. You look just like your father."

Con nodded. Every time he looked in the mirror his uncanny resemblance to his father held him to his vow as much as the vow itself. "I see you were right, Doctor. The prison collapsed."

"I wish I hadn't been right this time." Thorne turned and stared at the wood and stone pile. "This is a disaster." He flicked a hand at the buzzing Bluecoats. "Word is, they collapsed the wall."

Con gaped. "On purpose?"

"Yes."

"That's murder."

"Murder's a fine line in times like these."

"I say the line's been crossed here."

"I'd agree. They won't realize the mistake they've made right away. The dead women are the least of their worries. When Anderson hears of this, he'll hit

282

Kansas like Satan himself. One of his sisters is dead. The youngest is crippled for life, and she's only ten years old.'' The doctor sighed and rubbed a hand over his eyes. ''Sometimes I can't believe what people do to each other in the name of a cause.''

''How many others are dead and who?''

''Hard to say. The guards don't exactly know how many women were inside. So far five dead. Several may be crippled. I've got an old woman who was half-dead when she came to prison. She survived this, and she's still holding on by a wish and a prayer.''

Sounded like Julia's mother to Con. But what about Julia? ''Any of them paroled recently?''

''Paroled?'' The doctor snorted. ''Hardly. General Ewing is notorious for sticking to his own orders. He ordered Bushwhacker sympathizers jailed, women and children alike, and he isn't going to parole any of them.''

The doctor's words sent a sick feeling through Con's stomach. Where the hell was Ryan? Had he even managed to get to Kansas City? Julia lay, if not beneath the rubble, then dead beneath those blankets or crippled in the nearest house that had been set up for a hospital. Con had to find out which one. ''I'll help any way I can,'' he offered.

''I appreciate that. You could give last rights to the ones beneath the blankets yonder. Then help out in the hospital. We'll need every hand we can find.''

A cry went up for the doctor and Thorne loped off to help without a backward glance. Con headed for the blanketed bodies.

For a long moment he stood there. He did not want to lift those blankets and see dead women and children. He did not want to find Julia Colton Murphy beneath one of them. How would he ever tell Ryan?

Damn, but he hated this job.

A hand slipped into his, warmth against his chill, strength in the midst of his weakness. Con didn't have to turn his head to know Kathleen stood at his side. When he continued to hesitate, she bent down and gently pulled back the blankets from each face. None were Julia.

Together they sighed relief, then turned to the task at hand. Not a one of the dead was over twenty. Kathleen caressed each cheek with the back of her hand, closed staring eyes, smoothed away lingering dirt. Con knelt next to her on the ground. She lifted her face and her cheeks shone wet in the glare of the setting sun.

Con raised his hand and brushed her cheek as she'd brushed the cheeks of the dead. She smiled, a sad lift of her lips that tore at the crack in his heart where she lived. Frowning, he traced his thumb across those lips, fascinated with the return of her smile.

She stilled at his touch. Her gaze lifted to his and panic flared in the blue pools of her eyes. She stood, backed away and stumbled. He reached for her, but she put up her hands in a gesture to ward him off. She had seen his love in his eyes.

Con wanted to die.

"Katie," he murmured, holding his hand out palm up, a peace offering to a terrified wild thing. "I won't hurt you. It's all right." She shook her head and he feared she would run. "Don't. Don't go. I have to help these women. I need you. Do you understand?"

She looked away, her gaze touched upon the rubble, skittered off the milling Federals, then returned to his. The panic had receded, though the wary, wild look still lurked. She nodded, and he turned to give comfort to those who no longer needed it. The story of his life.

Latin fell from his lips as he put the dead to rest, quickly, efficiently, as he'd done many times before; then he covered them again and headed for what remained of the living.

Julia wasn't hard to find. There were so few left alive. She lay on a bunk next to an older woman. Mrs. Colton, obviously, who looked more dead than the women Con had just prayed over. Only the thin rattle that came from her lips with each breath proved she still lived.

Covered in blood and wood chips and dust, Julia's breathing was shallow but even. A quick examination revealed that she had received medical care of the leanest kind. Most of the blood came from a gash on her head that had been cleaned and bound haphazardly. If she woke and hadn't lost her sense, she might live, though she'd have a mighty fine scar across her forehead to remind her of a stay in prison.

Con heard mutterings and realized the sound came from him, not praying as he should be but cursing beneath his breath. He stopped himself and glanced at Kathleen.

"She's alive," he said. She did nothing but stare back at him with her newly suspicious eyes. He fought the urge to curse himself. He had to worry about Julia now. He would soothe Kathleen's fears and suspicions later.

"Get her out of here." The hoarse, desperate whisper came from Mrs. Colton.

Con left Julia and came around the bunk to kneel at her side. Her grasp on his hand was surprisingly strong for the near dead.

"She's all right, ma'am. I believe she'll live."

"If you get her out of here, she might. You have the power. Tell them she died, then take her out. Quick, before she wakes up and fights to stay with me."

Con frowned, confused. "Why?"

"Take her to the Murphy boy. It's their only chance to live a life together. Once the guerillas find out about this they'll come down on Kansas like the Horsemen of the Apocalypse."

"I know. But the guerillas won't hurt their own women. They'd take you out of here."

"That's why you need to get Julia away. She's got a babe in her. If my husband finds out—"

"He'll kill Ryan."

She snorted and then began to cough, violently. Red foam flecked her lips, and Con dabbed the blood away with his handkerchief. "That's old news. If he finds out she's got a Federal brat in her belly, he'll kill her and the baby, too."

"He wouldn't."

"Yes." She grasped Con by the collar, drawing him so close her breath puffed against his chin. "He would. Now you take her out of here and send her on her way. Tell her I'm already dead if you have to. I will be soon enough."

"We'll take you, too."

"No. I've had enough for this lifetime. I just want

to lie here now and sleep. Get her out of here, then send a message to that Murphy boy's troop. I think he must have gone back there after he came to take Julia away yesterday.''

"He *was* here?"

"Yeah, and they had a doozy of a fight. But she loves him, even though she's confused right now.''

Con glanced at Kathleen, who shrugged. He agreed. He had little choice. If he left Julia here there were many ways she might die. If he took her away, she had a chance to live with Ryan as they were meant to live. Con had hoped their marriage would soothe the hatred between their families; now he hoped it could soothe the hatred between them. If so, perhaps their child could bridge the chasm between those left alive at the end of the war. If there were any.

Leaning down, Con pressed a kiss to Mrs. Colton's forehead. She smiled. "Tell her I love her," she whispered. "I'll always be in her heart as she's in mine."

"I will," he promised.

"And tell that Murphy boy to quit livin' in the past.''

Con raised his eyebrows. "You've forgiven him?"

"It's not me whose forgiveness he needs.''

Con nodded. "You're a wise woman, ma'am.''

She merely smiled and closed her eyes.

Con had just wrapped Julia's body in the blanket, flipped the end up over her face and lifted her into his arms when Dr. Thorne walked into the hospital. He frowned at Con and hurried over.

"Another one dead?"

Con held his sigh of relief. He would not have to

tell that lie, merely agree to it. He nodded.

"Damn it to hell!" Thorne exploded, then scowled. "Sorry, Father."

"Never mind. I know this woman. Julia Colton. I'll take her body back with me. I'm sorry to leave so soon, but I've been called home on an urgent matter."

Thorne hesitated, shrugged, nodded. "Thank you, Father. I appreciate your coming to help."

"A favor, if you would?"

"Certainly."

"I need to send a message to a soldier in one of the Kansas regiments. A life-or-death kind of message. Do you have a dependable man?"

"Of course." He turned and motioned to one of the young soldiers who followed in his path. Someone called for him in a desperate, hysterical voice. Distracted, Thorne ordered, "Percy, take Father Sullivan's message wherever he asks. Guard it with your life."

"Yes, Doctor!" The impossibly young man saluted. Thorne began to return the salute, made a face and turned on his heel. He walked away muttering, "I'm a doctor, not a soldier, dammit."

Con paused a moment to write a message for Ryan. *Julia not dead as reported but safe and with me at the church on the hill. Come quickly. Con.*

He stared into the young man's eyes. "This is a matter of life and death. I charge you, in the name of God and the United States Army, give this to no one but Lieutenant Ryan Murphy with the Fourth Kansas Cavalry. Do not read it, and if you are captured, destroy it. Understand?"

The young man's face paled. He swallowed, then

he straightened with pride and determination. "Yes, sir!" He saluted and blushed. "I mean . . . yes, Father." He started to cross himself, stopped.

Con sighed, grabbed the boy's hand, shoved the paper into his palm and bid him Godspeed. Then he and Kathleen took Julia's body and disappeared into the Kansas night.

Chapter Seventeen

"Hell, no, Lieutenant! Partisan sympathizers will not be allowed parole under any circumstances." Brig. General Thomas Ewing, Jr. glowered at Ryan from atop his horse. In the general's eyes Ryan saw not a hint of mercy.

Ryan had spent the better part of the previous afternoon locating the general several miles outside of Kansas City, hunting of all things. Ryan had left for the camp at first light, only to arrive after the general had ridden out. At last the general returned, and Ryan received an audience near suppertime.

Ewing had replaced General Blunt as district commander after the infamous Westport ambush, where George Todd and his partisans had killed fourteen troopers in retaliation for the execution of Jim Vaughn. Ewing, a brother in-law of William Tecumseh Sherman, was aggressive, ambitious and immovable. Still, Ryan tried once more.

"Sir, the woman in question is my wife. There's been a mistake."

"No mistake. Julia Colton is the sister of some of the most vicious Rebel guerillas on horseback. Even if she is your wife, I couldn't set her free to aid and abet the enemy."

"Why would I lie, sir?"

"Why, indeed? If I didn't know your father personally from his old abolitionist days and recognize you as his son, I'd think you were a partisan spy, have you shot right here and now. But since there isn't a man more devoted to winning this war than Shamus Murphy—hell I gave him his commission myself—it is my opinion the woman bewitched you." The general tightened the reins as his horse sidestepped. "Happens to young men. Nothing to be ashamed of, unless of course, you let things go too far. Pillowtalk and the like. Wars have been lost over that sort of nonsense."

The general looked as though he planned to expound on the issue for awhile, but they were interrupted when an orderly rode through the camp on a winded and frothing horse. He pulled up and saluted the general. "General Ewing, sir, the partisan prison in Kansas City has collapsed. Number of deaths unverifiable at this time. The officer in command requests you return immediately."

Unable to breathe, Ryan continued to stand at attention. The general flicked a glance his way. "Things have a way of working out, Lieutenant.

You'll be better off if she's dead. Now get back to your troop. That's an order."

Without waiting for Ryan's salute, the general rode off in the direction of Kansas City. Ryan rode in his wake.

He reached the remains of the prison as the sun died and the moon was born. The half light cast ghostly shadows across the ruins and a strange, heated haze seemed to have captured the city in its grip, lending the entire area a ghoulish cast.

The rubble lay deserted, the lack of activity revealing more than words could say. No one remained alive beneath the tomb of wood and stone. The sight of General Ewing and his entourage already riding away to the west reinforced that belief.

Ryan's mind had stopped thinking further ahead than the next moment the second after he'd heard of the prison's collapse. If he thought any further he would be unable to go on, and go on he must, until he knew the truth. His haunted gaze swept the area, fixing upon the house next door, ablaze with candles and life. On heavy legs he traveled there and ducked inside.

The moaning women, the blood and beds revealed a makeshift hospital. In the corner, human-shaped lumps beneath blankets revealed a makeshift morgue. He winced. Was she—?

That thought he cut off before it could bloom. *Move forward one step at a time and no more,* he told himself. That was the only way he could go on.

Another sweeping glance and his gaze lit upon the doctor, occupied in setting a woman's broken leg. The bone protruded grossly from the flesh, splinters visible. If she survived, and that was not likely with such a wound ripe for gangrene, she would be lame. Ryan approached the doctor, stepped closer to see the patient, relaxed when he did not know the face, then moved in to help hold her down.

He'd assisted in such disasters before. In the bush the men often did their own doctoring, but he'd never before been on hand to assist a woman wounded by war. One day earlier and he might not have been able to bear her screams. Tonight, numbed by terror, he held her still without flinching until she fainted; then he awaited the doctor's attention.

"Thank you—" The doctor glanced at Ryan's uniform. "Lieutenant. Can I help you?"

"I'm looking for my wife."

"Wife?" He frowned. "There are only partisan sympathizers and Federal soldiers here."

"Julia Colton."

The minute he said her name, the doctor's face changed, and Ryan knew.

No.

The word sounded loud in his head, where someone screamed it over and over again, but slipped from his mouth a mere whisper.

"I'm sorry, Lieutenant. She died a few hours ago. Her mother's still here, but I'm afraid she can't speak or be moved. She's lost consciousness. I doubt she'll recover. This is a terrible situation. Terrible. And the repercussions will be worse. Anderson's eldest sister is dead, the youngest crippled. This has been a horrible injustice, and is sure to spark tremendous retribution. Kansas is going to burn."

Ryan didn't care. They could all kill each other and

good riddance. He needed to know one thing. "Where is she?"

"A priest took her. Said he knew her family and would take the body home. Connor Sullivan. Do you know him?"

Ryan nodded, relieved. He'd forgotten Con and Kathleen were on their way. Con would take care of Julia; he would bury her in the best way and place. Ryan was grateful that he did not have to look upon his wife's dead face. He was such a coward. Blindly, he stumbled from the room, and then the house, to fall to his knees in the brown grass outside.

He'd failed again. As always, he had tried to do things the right way and been wrong. Once he'd done what his mother had told him and she'd ended up dead. Now he'd tried to follow the legal channels for Julia's release and the same thing had happened. The single time he'd done the "wrong" thing, married Julia, it had turned out to be the most right thing of his life.

In the midst of his pain, Ryan heard another voice—a dying, screaming, cursing voice. *I curse every Murphy, you hear me? Every last one of you. I wish you would all know misery worse than this.*

Ryan had never believed in curses and the like, but he did now. He'd rather be dead like Del than living in this misery.

People walked past him, into and out of the hospital, but no one paid any mind to the soldier who knelt and wept upon the lawn. He sat in the grass and stared up at the moon and remembered every moment he'd spent in her company, every word she had spoken, every touch they had shared. Then he thought of the child they had made, the child who had died with Julia, and Ryan knew what he must do.

Agony rocked Julia's world. Pain exploded in her head, so bad her stomach roiled. She moaned, and a man's voice soothed her, gentle hands comforted her.

"Ryan," she whispered, then wondered why his name brought a separate wave of misery, before sleep claimed her again.

She awoke to thunder. Lifting heavy, itching eyelids, she stared in confusion at the indigo sky streaked with bolts of lightning. The air filled with the tang of spent electricity and the mellow promise of rain. Other impressions crowded her mind in rapid succession. The jolt and rattle of a wagon, the scratch of the straw beneath her, the sound of horses jangling in their harnesses.

A cool, gentle hand touched her brow, and Julia turned to meet familiar blue eyes. So like his, yet completely different. For in Kathleen's eyes Julia saw true compassion and affection. Ryan's eyes had lied.

Her mouth formed a question, though she didn't give voice to the words. Kathleen wouldn't answer. Instead Julia struggled up, wincing when pain shot through her head sharper than the lightning in the sky. She fell back, groaned, and the sound brought the wagon to a stop.

Father Con's face appeared above her, upside down as he peered over the wagon seat. He smiled. "Glad to see you've rejoined the living."

"What happened?"

"You've been in and out of consciousness the entire trip back to Bates County."

Julia frowned. That long? It seemed like she'd only just . . . What had happened?

Con saw the confusion on her face. "You don't remember?"

Julia thought hard, though the effort made her head ache madly. She put her hand to the pain, encountered a bandage, and suddenly memories burst before her eyes.

Ultimate betrayal. Screaming, falling, pain, darkness.

"Mama?" she whispered.

Con's quick glance at Kathleen made Julia's heart contract with fear. She sat up, fought the pain and the black, swirling dots that threatened to send her back into the void and turned to look at Father Con.

"Is she—?"

"Not dead. At least not from the prison collapse—thanks to you." A shadow of sadness passed over his face. "Quite a few were killed. You're lucky to be alive."

"Where is she?" Julia demanded. Con looked uncomfortable, and Julia knew why. "You left her there? How could you? A man of God." She turned her attention to Kathleen. "And his angel of mercy."

"Julia, you don't understand. She's dying."

"She's been dying for years. Sometimes I think she'll outlive us all." Julia gasped and put her hands to her mouth, shocked to hear such bitter words spill from her lips. Had the bump on her head addled her completely?

"She made me swear I'd take you to Ryan."

"No!" Julia shouted, eliciting a frown from Con and Kathleen and a moan from herself at the volume.

"Why not?"

"He had his father send me to prison. He paid the guards to collapse the wall. He wants me dead."

"Not Ryan. You're mistaken."

She heard again Janie's voice. *I saw that man give the Yankees money.*

Julia winced. When would the pain of his betrayal fade? She scowled at Father Con. "Ryan Murphy is a liar and a murderer. He begged for forgiveness for a sin he's never regretted. He promised not to hurt my brothers, then he killed Del."

From the expression on Con's face, Julia could tell he knew of Del's death already. "I think you're wrong about his sins. He regrets them all, and he's tortured himself over them ever since. I'm sorry about Del, but this is war, and I'm sure Ryan had no choice. As for Ryan having you sent to prison, I think I'd lay the blame for that at Shamus Murphy's door. Ryan came to get you out as soon as he heard."

"That's what he said. But then he left and the prison collapsed."

"You sound as if you believe he was responsible for it."

"He was. I heard some of the soldiers saying Murphy paid them to collapse the prison. To get rid of a family matter. That would be me."

Con looked taken aback. Then he straightened, shook his head. "No. You must have heard wrong. I can't believe even Shamus would go so far."

"Not Shamus. Ryan. Janie Anderson saw him paying the guards."

"There has to be a mistake. I've sent word to Ryan

that you're with me. We'll clear this up when he arrives.''

''He'll send someone else to kill me, or come himself.''

''You're behaving irrationally, Julia. I've heard women in your condition can become this way.''

''My condition,'' she spat. ''Is nothing secret?''

Con blushed. ''I'm sorry. Your mother thought we should know.''

His words brought back Julia's pain. ''Mama,'' she whispered, and tears flowed down her cheeks. She seemed to cry about every little thing lately, uncharacteristically, and determined to control herself.

Lightning flashed, close enough to make the horses skitter. Con turned his attention forward. When he'd calmed the animals he glanced at her again. ''Ryan should be here in a day or so.''

''He won't come,'' Julia said. ''Not for me.''

Con sighed and turned away. He obviously thought the baby had made her irrational. Well, they'd just see who was right. If it hadn't been for the baby, she wouldn't care about dying. Without Ryan and the promise of their future, life looked pretty damned dim. But the baby gave her one ray of light in a suddenly dark and empty world.

Con clucked to the horses and the wagon moved again. Julia watched the familiar terrain roll by. Bates County loomed empty—the men gone into the brush, the women gone to prison. The entire region held the aura of an ancient graveyard, long relinquished to the elements and the ghosts.

''Turn here,'' she called.

Con threw a curious glance her way, and she

pointed down a path through the tangled brush.

"My old home. We may as well go there before we all get soaked."

Con hesitated, glanced at Kathleen. Julia understood. "We'll be safe. The boys and Sam are off burning Kansas by now. They won't come here until they're done, if then."

With a shrug, he turned the horses and wagon down the overgrown path, taking Julia Colton Murphy home.

"He's not here, ye fool. Give over that message."

Shamus Murphy had had enough of the messenger who'd come riding into camp looking for Lieutenant Murphy and no one else. The young man looked done in and frightened. Shamus had to hand it to the boy; he held on to that piece of paper like it was God's gift to creation. The more the kid hung on to the message, the more Shamus wanted to read the words written there.

"I'm his damned father, ye moron, and a captain t' boot. Give over that message and get back t' yer unit. That's an order!"

At last the boy held out the creased and grimy paper. Shamus grinned, returned the salute and waved the young man out of his tent. Then he opened the paper.

Julia not dead as reported but safe and with me at the church on the hill. Come quickly. Con.

Shamus cursed. The little whore hadn't died in the prison collapse last week as he'd planned. He'd paid good money to send her there, even more to assure that the unstable building actually fell. Trust Connor Sullivan to come to the rescue.

The paper crushed in his palm, Shamus fought to think past the fury boiling in his heart. If Connor was sending Ryan a message, then Ryan wasn't in Kansas City as Shamus had thought. Strange. Since Ryan had been missing for a week, he'd figured that was where his son had run off to, there to discover his father's duplicity and never be heard from again. But God had smiled on the secret, it seemed, though He had not seen fit to send that devil girl to Hell.

The sound of a horse thundering into camp sent Shamus to the opening of his tent. He breathed a sigh of relief. Ryan had returned. His son looked ill, the golden stubble on his face darker than the white of his skin, his hands shaky upon the reins, blue eyes brighter for the purple circles beneath them. He'd had bad news.

Shamus lifted his hand, opened his fist, stared at the paper and smiled. As Ryan dismounted, Shamus tore the message into tiny bits and let them blow away into the storm-scented night.

Ryan stared at his father over the short distance separating them. Anger nipped at the edges of his inertia, bringing the pain of Julia's loss rushing back. He closed his eyes for a moment, forcing any emotion away. If he allowed his fury at his father to burst forth into angry words, vicious questions about why Da had sent Julia to prison, he feared the screams of agony and the tears would burst forth, too. What was done was done, those who were dead could not be resurrected. All you could do was join them.

He had come to that conclusion during the week he'd spent wandering back to his unit. Or at least he thought it was a week. He couldn't seem to remember very clearly what he'd done or where he'd been since the night he'd learned his wife and child were dead. Not until he'd neared his troop and spoken with one of the pickets had Ryan realized so much time had passed. Not that it mattered. Nothing mattered.

Ryan turned away from his father, who would want an explanation for his disappearance, and headed for his tent. Before he made it inside, the camp guard hailed a rider. Seconds later a messenger rode into camp. Ryan's father read the paper, then looked up with a wide smile and contemplated his troop, all of whom had come out of their tents at the sound of the messenger.

"This is from General Ewing." He waved the paper in the air. "He's headed out from Kansas City with three hundred men of the Eleventh Ohio, chasing after Quantrill and a passel of partisans who are retreatin' toward Missouri. The bastards just sacked Lawrence. They've killed over a hundred and fifty and scorched the town from the face of the earth."

Ryan was not surprised. Retribution just like the good doctor in Kansas City had predicted, and now the Federals would chase the Bushwhackers down and kill them. Retribution just went on forever. But this particular form of reprisal fit into his own plans quite well, though he didn't plan to kill. He planned to die.

His father continued to speak. "We've been ordered north and east t' trap Quantrill and the rest between us and Ewing's cavalry. Pack up. We leave as soon as we can get our arses on our horses."

301

Ryan ducked into his tent. Jason was already packing. He glanced at Ryan, disappointment ripe in his eyes. Ryan sighed. He was a disappointment to everyone he loved.

"What?" he snapped, tending to his own packing. He wouldn't need any of this in a few hours, but he didn't want anyone to know that yet.

"I was worried."

Ryan hesitated; then his shoulders sagged with defeat, and he turned to put a hand on Jason's shoulder. "I'm sorry. Everything's fine. Now let's chase down those murderers and be done with it."

Jason frowned. "That's not like you, Ry."

Ryan turned away from the confusion, pain and love in his brother's eyes and began to pack. "What isn't like me?"

"I thought you wanted to stop killing. You're married to one of 'em, by God. I figured you'd grabbed her and ridden off."

Ryan winced, glad he'd turned away so Jason could not see the pain his words had caused. He *should* have grabbed her and ridden off, but he'd failed. He would not fail now. He belonged with her, and he would be with her again.

"I can't keep track of what you believe or want or are anymore, Ryan."

"Neither can I," he murmured and then retreated from the tent.

The breeze had shifted and now came from the North, bringing the odor of death and destruction. Ryan breathed deeply, recalled the scent of roses and tears, then retrieved his horse and rode to the head of the column to join his father.

His da watched him warily, his hand near his pistol. Ryan's lips twisted. Did Da think he would kill him for what he'd done to Julia? What would be the point? Ryan had only one death on his mind, and he figured that death would be punishment enough for Shamus Murphy. When he learned his manipulation of Ryan's life and his inability to let go of foolish hatreds had cost him his son, Shamus would understand many things, or so Ryan hoped.

"Let me scout ahead, Da. You know I'll find them if anyone can."

His father smiled at him, pride shining in his eyes for the first time in a long time. "Ye do that, me boy."

Da was proud Ryan wanted to kill the damned Missourans, but Ryan only wanted to find them first so they could kill him. Then he could be done with this place, with killing and hating and the promise of eternal loneliness. If he died he could be with Julia, and perhaps in the afterlife she would forgive his being absent when she needed him the most. Perhaps in the better place people did not hate based on where they lived, or what they believed, or what their parents believed. And if no afterlife existed, that was all right, too, because he did not deserve to live when his wife and his child had died.

Jason rode up. "Da, I don't think he should go alone. I'll go along."

A cold sweat broke out on Ryan's brow, and the blood deserted his face. "No, you won't," he ground out.

Jason reached over and grabbed Ryan's arm before Ryan could ride away. Ryan jerked from Jason's grasp with a snarl. "Leave me be, Jase, or I swear I'll knock you flat."

"You can try." Jason narrowed his gaze on Ryan's face, shook his head and turned to their father. "Something's not right with him. Can't you see it?"

Ryan let out an impatient snort, then he caught his father's eyes, and he straightened, attempted to look as if he gave a damn about anything.

"Ye have been actin' peculiar, son."

"Dammit, Jason, would you quit acting like a little old woman!" Ryan exploded. "I want to get them, all right? I want to get them now. They've killed too many, burned too much. It's time to make this end. I can't stand it anymore."

He bit off the rest of the words before he allowed too much to escape. Even so, Da grinned and Jason frowned. For just a moment Ryan wanted to touch Jason, to tell him he loved him, before it was too late. But to say such a thing now would only serve to make Jason more suspicious.

So instead, Ryan narrowed his eyes and said, "I'll find 'em, sir. Just keep *him* out of my way." Ryan kicked his horse into a gallop and left his family far behind.

Chapter Eighteen

Ryan ran right into a troop of retreating Rebels.

They weren't hard to find. South of Baldwin City the stench of burning crops and buildings made Ryan's eyes water. Black smoke billowed in the northern sky. The sound of rifle fire and galloping horses approached. Quantrill and the rest were burning their way toward Missouri. Little did they know the cavalry was on their tail and in their face.

From what Ryan could determine, the enemy regrouped on the other side of a neck-high cornfield. Ryan could ride directly through and into the front line of the partisans, die easy and quick. But if he didn't alert his troop to the presence of the guerillas, they could all die before Ewing backed them up. Ryan needed to wait until the rest caught up to him. There were so many ways to die in battle; he could find one.

He would not fail at death as he'd failed at life.

The second his troop appeared from the south, he held up a hand and indicated the flaming northern horizon. His da understood and gave silent orders to set up an ambush on the edge of the cornfield.

"Hold yer fire, men," Shamus hissed. "If ye shoot too soon, they'll go t' ground in thar and we'll have t' burn 'em out."

They did not have long to wait. The partisans, exhilarated with their success, came barreling through the corn at a gallop, screaming the Rebel yell. Ryan hated it when they did that. That damned screech set his nerves on end. Obviously the shouts frayed the nerves of another soldier, for a shot went off, too soon, alerting the guerillas to the presence of the enemy force.

"Son of a bitch!" Shamus shouted as the Rebels rolled from their horses, taking cover in the lofty cornstalks and returning fire. "Charge," he screamed. "Charge, I say."

Ryan didn't need to be told twice. He dove into the field at the head of the line, raced down a row, the drying stalks scraping against his face and neck, making it hard to hear where the enemy lay. They had all dismounted at the first shot and gone to ground, just as Shamus predicted. Horses raced to and fro. Ryan heard shots and screams, shouts and shuffles, but the lack of sight confused him, and he felt surrounded yet unable to locate an enemy.

Pausing, he allowed the sounds and the smells and the feel of battle to flow over him. Why did he search? Why had he pulled his gun? Habits died hard.

Ryan returned his pistol to its holster and waited

for fate to find him. He should have known fate would arrive with the face of a Colton. That he deserved. When Ab stepped through the corn, Ryan just smiled.

"Murphy, this is for my mother and my sister, you Bluebelly bastard." Ab raised his gun, then hesitated, frowned. "What the hell are you doin' here with your guns in their holsters? Pull your gun, you yellow bastard."

Ryan's smile faded and he sighed. Why couldn't anything be easy? "Just kill me, Colton. Do it."

For a moment Ryan thought Ab would go honorable on him, say he didn't shoot unarmed men, or some such thing. But in the end, Ab shrugged, cocked his gun and aimed at Ryan's head with a smirk.

"Ryan!"

At the sound of Jason's voice, horror iced Ryan's veins. He tried to shout, tried to turn—too late. Jason barreled into him, shoving him out of the way just as Ab fired.

Ryan hit the ground, looked up and saw Jason jerk as the bullet plowed into his chest. His gun fell. Jason followed. Before his brother's body had hit the earth, Ryan had grabbed his weapon.

Ab had already turned his gun in Ryan's direction. Ryan forgot his vow to die. All he knew was that this man had shot his little brother. He wanted to tear Colton limb from limb with his teeth and nails and hands. He wanted to hear the bastard cry in pain. He *meant* to kill Abner Colton. This time there would be no accident, no mistake. Ryan looked into Ab's eyes and fired.

Colton was dead before he knew he'd been shot.

Ryan didn't spare him another glance. All he cared about was Jason.

"No, please, no. Me, not him. Please." The words tumbled from his lips, a plea and a prayer. He held the hope that his brother would live this time, too, that the wound was not serious, that he would merely faint and come back to the world once more, but the moment Ryan looked into Jason's pale face and saw the fading life in his eyes, he knew.

In the distance came the call of advancing cavalry; Ewing's Eleventh Ohio closed the gap behind the Rebels. The partisans would be surrounded here if there were enough men left in the Fourth to keep them in the cornfield until Ewing's troops arrived. But even as the advance sounded from the north, a retreat called from within the field. Ryan didn't care if they got away to a man. Nothing mattered now.

"Why, Jase?" he whispered.

Jason grabbed his hand. "Why?" he repeated.

There was no answer for either of them and no time for explanations. The life in Jason's eyes faded before Ryan could say another word. He gathered his brother to his chest and whispered, "No, Jason. I love you." Too late again, always too late.

Ryan rocked his brother's corpse while the Rebels escaped into the Missouri brush; the Fourth gave chase and Ewing's men followed, leaving Ryan alone with the dead.

Morning dawned fresh, clear. Jason was still dead. So was Ab. Julia, too. Ryan blinked at the bright sun, amazed to find it continued to rise when the world seemed so dark. Life went on no matter how hard you wished for death.

He might have sat there all day but the flies began to buzz about Jason and Ab. He let them land on Colton, brushed them off Jason. When the crows started to circle lower and lower, he shot at them. More came. He had to bury Jason, if not Ab, and he knew just where he'd do it.

Several horses milled about the cornfield, masterless, their riders either dead among the rows or racing toward Missouri. Ryan caught one horse, then another.

Without emotion he numbered most of the dead Federal soldiers. Somehow, the ambushers had become the ambushed. Faces he knew, faces he did not, he couldn't seem to work up sorrow for any of them. Jason must be buried.

By the time he'd loaded both bodies on one horse and mounted the other, Ryan was soaked with sweat. He threw his uniform jacket into the field, followed by his gunbelt and pistols, then rode away from them and his dead dreams.

Ryan followed the path of the Bushwhackers. Behind him lay acres of scorched land and dead folk. Ahead lay just land and folk. The Rebels had stopped burning and pillaging once they'd engaged the Federals. Instead they had run for their lives toward the bush that was their home, their salvation. Ryan ran that way, too.

He buried Jason beneath a huge oak tree next to the house. He couldn't even say he had buried him next to Ma, since Ma lay at the old homestead, but at least they were together now. Ryan was alone. In trying to keep his vow to his mother, he had broken other promises, other vows, and brought about the deaths of the two people he loved most in the world.

Burying Jason made Ryan think of another burial—another grave. Con would have taken Julia home to rest. Not here, where she would never have felt welcome, nor been welcome, but to the home where she'd been born and raised, though she'd never felt welcome there either.

Ryan took Ab and wandered across Colton Creek. Memories assaulted him. Sun on the water. Laughter on the breeze. Secrets shared in the moonlight. The first time he'd seen her. The first time they'd kissed. Those memories seemed both forever and yesterday combined.

Ryan reached the house as the sun set, throwing blue-black shadows across the yard. Though the place should be as deserted as the Murphy farm, for some reason it felt occupied, yet he saw no horses and the door to the house remained closed as he approached.

Freshly turned earth mounded up from the grass and the world seemed to dip and roll before his eyes. He'd known she was dead, come here to see her grave, but until the evidence appeared before his eyes, he had still hoped she might live. How could she be dead when he felt her yet in his heart?

Ryan lifted his face as a warm breeze blew his hat from his head and tumbled it across the grass. If he didn't know better, he'd swear he could still smell her, roses and tears, on the wind. The breeze picked up, sailing his hat past her grave and into the brush. He let it go. He didn't want to wear anything that reminded him of what he had been, what he had done, all in the name of vengeance, using the excuse of war.

Dropping the two sets of reins, Ryan approached the grave. He stood at the base, uncertain. Should he speak to her? Should he pray? God, all he wanted was to be with her.

"Julia?" he whispered. "Can you hear me? I hope you can. I'd say I was sorry, but what good would that do now? I'll say again you were wrong. I'd never send you away. Never want you dead." His breath hitched in his chest and he fought against the pain. She had died thinking he wished her dead and he couldn't say he blamed her.

Damn the feud. Damn the war. Damn both her father and his. Damn himself for his vows and promises, none of which he seemed able to keep.

Ryan dropped to his knees, hoping he'd feel closer to her there, but he did not. "It's my fault you're dead. If I'd been more the husband you needed and less the soldier I'd dreamed of, I'd have taken you out of here without trying to do things the right way. Go through channels. Follow orders. I've been a fool. But you know that.

"I brought your brother home. Damn but I killed another one, Julia. Can't say I'm sorry for this one. He killed Jason. Jason died instead of me. Everyone dies instead of me." Ryan slammed his fists down on the grave and shouted, "Why can't I die?"

The wind whistled through the trees, a shriek in answer to his own. Ryan rested his cheek against the sun-warmed earth, and he knew what he must do.

Slowly he pushed away from her grave, drew his knife from his boot. The sun's last rays bled across the blade and, fascinated, he stared as the blood-red light played with his reflection. He looked half-mad, hair sweat-stiff and sticking up, face white, eyes wild. His thoughts chased themselves about his mind, tumbling from his mouth like a lunatic serenade.

"Coward. That's what I am, letting the damned Bushwhackers have at me. If you want to die so badly, Ryan Murphy, do it yourself. Do it now and quit your everlasting whining. Take one last vow, to die, and keep it."

He folded both hands firmly about the hilt, positioned the blade against his heart. "Julia, there are so many things I didn't say. But I'll tell them to you soon, my love. Soon."

Ryan tightened his grip, then closed his eyes. He took a deep breath.

He smelled roses and tears, stronger than ever before. A shuffle from behind him made him flip the knife forward and spin about.

"Tell me now, Ryan, all those things you didn't say."

He stared, blinked, dropped the knife in the dirt. Was he dead? Ryan looked down at his shirt. Still white and crusted with dirt and sweat and blood, but not his own. He looked up again.

"Julia?"

She wore a white nightgown, stark against the dark swath of her hair, unbound and trailing past her waist. A bandage, also stark white, circled her head. She stood as if uncertain on her feet. But the most telling sign that this was no dream lay in her eyes. He no longer saw love or trust in those green depths.

He didn't care. She was not dead, but here and warm and alive and real. Or at least she smelled real.

312

He climbed to his feet, took a step forward. She tried to step back, cried out in pain and began to fall. He swept her up, held her tight. She *was* real, thank God.

"Put me down," she spat.

He carried her toward the house. "You're hurt."

"Are you happy?"

"Right now, yes. I'm happier than I can ever recall being. I thought you were dead."

"That makes two of us."

She glanced at Ab's body as they walked by the horses, then turned her face away. "Every time a Murphy shows up I find another dead brother."

Ryan didn't know what to say. She was right, and he understood now the fresh grave. Del, not Julia.

A movement in the doorway of the house sent visions through his mind of the remaining Coltons, Quantrill, Anderson and the James boys pouring onto the porch and shooting them both. Ryan shifted Julia to one arm so he could reach for his gun, but Con's voice allowed him to catch her again in both arms.

"You got my message, I see."

Ryan stepped onto the porch, noticed Kathleen hovering in the doorway. She beamed when she saw him and came forward to stand at Con's side. Without thought Con put his hand at Kathleen's back. Ryan frowned and looked at Con. "What message?"

"I sent word that Julia was all right and with me. That you should come." Con cocked his head, stared at Ryan in confusion. "But how did you know we were here? We only stopped because of the storm."

"I didn't get any message." A sudden image of his da came to Ryan, how he'd looked guilty when Ryan returned to camp, then how he'd torn a paper into pieces and let them fly away on the wind. At the time Ryan hadn't cared about anything but dying. Now he knew what his father had done and anger burned away the fog that had clouded his mind. "I-I thought she was dead. I—"

"Put me down." Julia shoved at his chest, and he let her go. She walked unsteadily to the nearby rocking chair and sat, putting her fingers to her forehead. When she encountered the bandage, her hand fell away.

The sight of her injury reminded Ryan of his own intended suicide. He swayed in shock and terror. What if he'd succeeded? He'd be dead and she'd be alive. God pity the fools of this earth.

Con was speaking, moving toward the house along with Kathleen. "What?" Ryan asked.

"I said you're here now, so Katie and I will go back to the church."

"No!" Julia went white. "He's come to kill me, don't you see?" She pointed at Ab. "He's killing us one by one."

"I'm sorry about Ab." Ryan took a breath and then plunged forward. "He killed Jason."

For a moment sorrow overtook Julia's expression; then it was gone, and she stared at Ryan with hard eyes once more. "So you killed Ab. I should have known. Vengeance just never ends for you, does it?" She stared past him at her brother. She swallowed. Her lips thinned, bled white. "He was my brother."

Con and Ryan exchanged glances. "You two have a lot to work out," Con said. "You need to be alone."

314

Julia turned pleading eyes toward Con. "I'm afraid."

Kathleen took a step toward her, but Con shook his head. Kathleen frowned at her brother and disappeared inside the house. Con shot Ryan an evil glare. Then he stepped to Julia and took her hand. "He won't hurt you. I know what you heard. I know what you think. But I believe he's an honorable man."

"I'm not," Ryan argued.

"Would you shut up?" Con whirled on him. "You were seen paying off the guards at the prison. She heard the guards say Murphy paid them to collapse the wall and kill her."

Ryan shook his head, bewildered for a moment. He had given the captain money to bring her hot food and water. But why would the man say he'd paid him to kill her? Then he remembered that his da had sent her to prison in the first place. He must have been the Murphy the guard spoke of. Another wound opened in Ryan's already bleeding heart. He would never forgive his father for the seemingly unending list of betrayals. Da's madness had passed the point of redemption.

Ryan opened his mouth to explain, but Con held up a hand to stave him off. "Don't tell me; I know there's an explanation. You'd better make her believe it or I'll shoot you myself." Con strode toward the door.

"Should you take Kathleen out alone with night coming on?"

Con hesitated in the doorway and his shoulders stiffened, insulted. "Just because I'm a priest doesn't make me helpless." He glanced over his shoulder.

"You wouldn't believe what I've done in the past few weeks. I certainly don't." Ryan opened his mouth to apologize, but Con waved the words away. "The Bushwhackers are riding for the Sni Hills with the Federals right behind. They'll never catch them, but they're trying. There isn't a guerilla or a soldier for miles. Except for you."

"Don't count me with them anymore."

Con lifted his brows, hesitated as if to question him, then shrugged. "I'll come by in the morning," he said and turned away.

Ryan returned his gaze to Julia. He could not get enough of the sight of her face. She sat on the chair, poised as if for flight, though how she thought to get away from him was a mystery. So much lay between them, and the majority was bad. How had everything become so complicated? They had loved; they had married. So many had died and now she despised him. Could they find the love again through all the pain and the hate, the deceptions and the deaths?

He'd spend his life trying if he had to. The only time he felt at peace was in her arms. He needed her more than he'd ever needed anyone or anything. She was the part of him he'd lost, or perhaps the part he'd never even had. He couldn't believe their love was dead. He would not believe that.

Ryan took a step toward her. She tensed, staring at him with wary, suspicious eyes. He had to find a way to make her believe again. He opened his mouth, still not knowing what he meant to say, but instead of speaking he went down on his knees next to her, put his head into her lap and circled her waist with his arms.

She stiffened, tried to push him away, but he held on, unable to let her go now that he'd found her.

"Please, let me hold you. Just for a moment. I know you're scared. I know you don't trust me. But, please, I need to touch you now."

She stopped pushing at his shoulders, but she did not relax or embrace him in return. Would she ever again?

The sound of horses riding away echoed in the descending evening. Con and Kathleen had left. They were alone.

Next to the rubble of a prison in Kansas City he'd lost his will to live. In a cornfield south of Baldwin City he'd become a man without a country, a man without a family, a man without a home. In discovering Julia alive, he'd found that all he'd thought lost still existed in her.

He pressed his cheek to her stomach, felt her belly clench, shivered as her scent flowed over his face. He remembered how her skin felt beneath his fingers and how her body felt beneath his. Having her again in his arms was something he'd prayed for but never believed would happen on this earth. Now that it had, he was terrified to set her free for fear she would disappear as the moon did at dawn.

"I'm cold," Julia said, her voice as strained as her body.

Ryan held her close for one moment more, then sat back with a nod. "I'll take you inside."

"I can get there myself." She lurched from the chair and nearly collapsed before he grabbed her. He bent to pick her up, but she growled a warning deep in her throat and tottered off on her own.

Damn, she was stubborn.

He followed her into the house, shut the door behind them. She stood in the fading light, pale, ethereal, beautiful. "Even if what you say is true and you haven't tried to kill me, I don't know if we can ever get past what's been done in our names."

"We can if we leave here. Start our own life, without their hate."

Hope lighted her eyes for a moment, then flickered out like a candle in a swift wind. She looked away as if she could not bear to keep him in her sight. "I'm still a Colton. I'll always be a Colton."

"I don't believe that. You're not one of them. You never have been."

"You're wrong. Even if I wasn't one by blood, I'm one by name."

"You have my name now."

"Do you think a few words said before a priest changes who I am? I'll tell you a secret my mama shared with me: I'm not a Colton. Sam wasn't my father. But I've learned it's not your blood that makes you who you are, it's how you're raised, who you love, what you live with. I've lived as a Colton for twenty years, and when it came down to it, my prattlings of peace and forgiveness were just that. When I saw Del dead, felt his skin so cold, watched him be buried forever beneath the dirt, I hated just like my brothers. I wanted revenge with a desperation that would make them proud."

Fascinated, Ryan stared into her eyes. She might have green eyes instead of black, but she was right, she could hate just like a Colton.

"Tell me something. Every time you look at me

won't you see one of those who killed your ma, your brother? You think I won't look at you and see Ab and Del? The time will come when neither of us will remember the love, we'll only remember the deaths. All we'll have left is lust. That's not enough for a lifetime.''

''What's between us is more than lust.''

''Is it? I don't know.''

''I love you, Julia. If you'd believe that, you'd believe I couldn't ever hurt you. I don't care what your name is, who your father is, or what you were raised to believe. All I care about is you. The woman I married, the one who made me want to live in the world again.''

''That woman is gone. I don't know who I am. I don't know what I believe. I don't know what I want.'' She wandered toward a crate near the bed, bent and picked up a book. She stared at it for a long moment, then gave a snort of laughter and tossed the book back into the crate. ''Once I believed in these fairy tales. Love at first sight, knights on white horses, rescue from this place. I didn't know anything beyond this place except what I read in books. But in these books men had honor, they kept their promises, they loved with their whole hearts and they gave up everything for their love. I wanted to meet a man like that.''

Ryan winced. He'd done nothing but break promises since he'd met her.

''Then, when I prayed for a hero, you came. You rode a golden horse, and you were so different from every man I'd ever known. Even though you were a Murphy, a man I'd been taught was the enemy, I'd never felt so safe, so alive, so important as when I was with you. I loved you, despite everything. I was foolish. I still am. I waited for so long for someone to love. Someone who would love me.''

''I do.''

She shook her head. ''I'm different now. I don't know if even love is enough to take all the hate and pain away. The magic has died. Life's not a fairy tale, not a dream. I don't know what it is anymore, and I don't know if I care to find out.''

Before he knew what he meant to do, he'd walked up behind her, encircled her waist with his arms and put his lips to her neck. She gasped, with shock or pleasure he could not say. But she did not struggle, and she did not tell him to stop.

He needed her. Now. Always. Forever.

Inhaling the scent of her hair, her skin, he traced his lips across the soft flesh that joined her neck to her shoulder. He could not get enough of her warmth. If he was near her long enough would the icy, dead place within him melt and revive? He had to find out.

Turning her about, he saw her eyes were closed against him. Bending, he kissed her, savoring her mouth, teasing her lips with his tongue, delving within when she sighed with longing. The kiss went on and on, evoking memories of pleasure, promising oblivion from pain. When he pulled back, his mouth hovering close to hers, she murmured, ''This won't solve anything.''

''I know. But I need you, Julia, and I think you need me. Please.''

She shook her head, squeezed her eyes shut tighter, as if she couldn't bear to look at him. His heart broke and he began to move away. She grabbed him by the neck and pressed her mouth to his. He tasted her tears—on her lips, on his. She tore at his clothes, scraped his chest with her nails, molded her palms to his waist with a desperation he understood, but it frightened him just the same.

"Shh," he whispered. "You'll hurt yourself."

She ignored him, yanking at his trousers until he stilled her fingers and undid the buttons himself. Frightened she would injure herself further, or hurt the baby, he carried her to the single bed in the room, yanked her nightrail over her head and lowered them both to the mattress.

She did not look at him. They did not speak. Instead they allowed their bodies to voice their needs and desires. When he rested deep within her—one body for a time—he could feel that their hearts no longer beat as one. Their souls no longer spoke to each other in a language all their own.

"Julia?" He wanted her to look at him, to see him as they reached the heights together. Her eyes remained closed. He slowed his movements, held still as he stroked her hair and whispered into her ear.

"The first time I saw you, fighting those Jayhawkers at the creek, I denied what I felt. You denied it, too. But our hearts understood we were meant to be together despite the hate between our families and the war. Don't let them win. If we let them destroy our love, there's nothing left worth living or dying for."

"I would have died for you," she said.

He heard the past in her words and fought the pain that knowledge brought him. "I'll take you away from here. From them. There'll be just us and the baby. Let me try again to be your hero."

She didn't answer, only clutched him closer as her release came upon her. Her body clasped his, bringing his own release, and they lay in each other's arms, entwined, as close as two people could be, yet more distant than lovers had ever been.

"There are no heroes anymore," she said and turned away, leaving him alone in the dark.

Chapter Nineteen

"Do you think she'll see the truth?" Con asked.

Kathleen smiled her Madonnalike smile and Con was comforted. He wasn't certain if he'd done the right thing, leaving the two alone, but Julia needed to learn to trust Ryan again, and she needed no distractions. He sensed a lot of anger in Julia. Right now she reminded him of Ryan, before Ryan met her. It was ironic, for Ryan seemed to have at last understood what was important in life and found strength and peace in love. With any luck, their love would soothe Julia's anger as it had soothed Ryan's.

They reached the church on the hill as a crescent moon ascended into the sky. Countless silver points of light made the heavens resemble a celestial pincushion. On nights such as these Con felt very close to God.

He glanced at Kathleen and all thoughts of God fled. He sighed, discouraged at the limitations of his life, the promise of years and years spent alone doing a job he feared he wasn't very good at—dying alone, the last of his name.

But his vows had been made to God, his promises given to the dead. Questions had begun to haunt him not only in the darkest hours of the night, but all day long, as well.

Con dismounted and moved to aid Kathleen. She slid from the saddle into his arms. He should have let her go, stepped back and tended to their mounts as he always did. Instead the moon made him reckless, and he continued to hold her within the circle of his arms.

The serene expression that had begun to replace the hunted look in her eyes fled. She stared into Con's face, a mixture of confusion and concern on her own. He smiled softly, sadly, and brushed the lock of white hair at her temple with his fingertips.

"Ah, Katie," he sighed. "I wish I knew what has hurt you so, and how I can make your pain go away."

Her forehead wrinkled and she tilted her head, studying him, waiting and watching, suspicious once more.

"I wish . . ." The words left his mouth and fell into the heavy silence between them. What did he wish?

She raised her hand and traced her thumb across the lines of his frown. He caught her fingers and pressed the knuckles to his cheek. That one small touch combined with the scent of woman and rainwater ignited his body in a way no man of God should experience. He never felt this way, except with her.

He wished he had a right to feel this way forever.

Con dropped her hand as if it were a serpent and stepped back. She stared at him with wide eyes, her breath coming heavy and hard, matching the pace and frustration of his own.

"I was so alone, Katie, until you came. I existed, but I didn't live. The war—" He broke off with a groan of frustration. "I hate the war. People dying all around us, women imprisoned, children cold and hungry. It's a travesty. Yet I don't want the war to end, because when it ends, you'll leave, and I'll only exist for the rest of my life. I wish . . ."

He looked up at the stars. One blinked brighter than the rest, and he allowed his secret wish to tumble forth. "I wish you were mine. I wish we could have a life together. As a man and a woman, a husband and a wife. I want children, and I want them from you." He closed his eyes, blanking out the heavens and the star that continued to wink, as if in mockery. "I resent everyone and everything that keeps me from you. Especially God."

He opened his eyes in time to see her flee as if the hounds of Hell barked at her heels. Since he'd gone this far, he threw the rest of his principles into the abyss and shouted, "Dammit, Katie, I've loved you all my life.

She disappeared into the church and Con cursed his weakness. She was his temptation. She always had been. From birth he had been promised to God. He had known it; she had known it, though she had never loved him in the way he loved her. That didn't make his feelings for her any less real; that didn't make him burn any less in the night. Still, he had to wonder why he continued to live when his entire family had died. That had not been the deal made all those years ago between his father and the hill spirit he had saved.

Leading the horses toward the barn, Con remembered the day his father had told him the truth of why Con had been pledged to the church. After Con had taken his vows and only weeks before his entire family died, Con's father had traveled to the seminary to speak with him.

"It's time ye knew, Connor, about a promise I made before ye were born. Swear to me, son, you will remain a priest. I know it is a hard life, especially for one such as you. I raised ye to know the importance of vows and promises, to understand a man is not a man if he cannot keep his word. I made certain ye knew that fer a reason."

"I've taken my vows, Da. I mean to honor them."

"Good. Now listen while I tell ye a story. D' not interrupt me."

The intensity on his father's face, the strength of his grasp upon Con's hands had made Con listen—even past the point of believability.

"Years before ye were born I became lost, huntin' in the Sni Hills. For days I wandered, afraid I would die there and never see yer ma or yer brothers again. Then I came upon a little person trapped by a fox."

Con raised his eyebrows. His father was from the Old Country and believed in such things. Who was Con to say fairies and pookas and leprechauns did not exist? He had not seen God either, yet he believed.

"I shot the fox, and the little man and I exchanged promises. For his life, he showed me the way out of the hills. In friendship he vowed the name Sullivan would live forever on this earth, as long as I pledged my next child to the church. Yer ma was past the time fer such things, so it was a promise easily made. Yet she conceived you, a miracle as it were. You, my son, you are my miracle.'' His father, never a demonstrative man, cupped Con's cheek with his palm and stared into Con's face with a face so like Con's own it was uncanny. "All of me family died in Ireland. I am the last. I will not let the cursed English wipe the name Sullivan from the earth. I made that promise to the pooka in the Sni and I have kept it. Now ye must do the same.''

Anger filled Con at the thought that he had been sacrificed for a promise to a mythical little person. But he had been raised knowing he would go into the Church, and even if he had been able to follow his heart and marry Kathleen Murphy, the time for such a thing was past. She was married to another and Con had vowed to serve God.

Con shook his head, dispelling the memory. While he'd thought of the past he'd taken care of the horses and strolled into the church. He sat in the back pew and considered his vestments.

What joke had been played on the Sullivan family? They'd been promised descendants for eternity, yet the entire family, save one, had been wiped out by Bushwhackers. The only Sullivan left was Connor, and he was a priest.

Had the pooka been a boogey instead? A wicked spirit instead of a benevolent one? Con snorted and rubbed at his aching eyes. If anyone could hear his thoughts, they'd think him mad.

The question that had haunted him since Kathleen

had come back into his life was this: How could the name Sullivan continue unless he continued it? And how could he do so if he remained chaste?

He could run—leave his church, his vows, his commitments behind. The promise of a new life beckoned. But could he live with himself if he denied everything he had been raised to uphold, if he betrayed everything he believed, if he took every promise he had made to God and to man and tossed them to the wind like they meant nothing at all? If he couldn't keep his vow to God, could he be trusted to keep a vow to the woman he loved? More important, did the woman he loved love him?

Con rose and headed for the back of the house. Right now he must assure Kathleen of his protection. She did not need to feel threatened by the very man she had come to trust.

He knocked on her door. No one answered. When he stepped inside his heart lurched.

Kathleen was gone.

Ryan remained awake all night, trying to think of a way to bridge the distrust between himself and his wife. Even while he'd been deep in her body, both of them in the throes of passion, she had not looked at him or said his name.

When dawn painted the gray sky with pink, orange and yellow veins of light, Ryan had still not figured out what to do. Either she trusted him or she didn't. She believed him or she believed someone else. She loved him no matter what, or she hated him forever. He had never felt so helpless or so desperate in his life.

But the day was young.

Julia turned to him in her sleep, and though he knew she did not realize what she did, Ryan pulled her close and savored the trust she gave him unconsciously, drawing from the small gesture a thread of hope for their future. He kissed the top of her head, cupped his palm over her flat stomach and imagined how her flesh would round and increase, how one day there would be a child born of their love. Somehow they had to find a way to make a world for that child without the hatreds of the past. He would not allow a child conceived in love to be raised in hate. Distracted by his thoughts, Ryan heard only the peaceful sound of Julia's breath against his chest and the laughter of a child not yet born.

The door to the cabin crashed inward. The room filled with Bushwhackers. Julia started up from her sleep, flicked a glance at him that revealed nothing. She calmly reached for her shift. Ryan faced Julia's father and a circle of Colts wearing nothing but a blanket.

Sam Colton's face was purple with fury, and in his eyes Ryan saw the same rabid madness that had consumed his own father. Both men had been pushed over the edge. It looked like there would be no return to sanity for either of them.

Ryan could understand Sam's anger. He would feel the same if he found his daughter in bed with a man, any man, let alone the enemy. But Colton didn't give him a chance to explain.

"Get away from her, Murphy," he ordered.

Ryan obliged, though he took the time to step into his trousers first. A quick glance at the others caught smirks on their faces. He recognized Jesse and Frank, Cole Younger and the young man whom Julia had danced with the night Ryan had first kissed her—her fiancé, Ted Chandler. He was not smiling. Neither were Ben or Clark—Julia's two brothers. They'd most likely seen Ab outside, and if Ryan hadn't been a dead man for that alone, being caught in bed with Julia had sealed his fate.

He was in deep trouble. Ryan had no idea how he would get out of this alive and in possession of his wife and child, but he had to try. And if he could not save his own life, then he must save theirs.

Colton turned his attention to Julia, who had managed to throw a day dress over her shift. "How many times have I told you, your sole purpose on this earth is to take care of your mama?"

"Every day for my entire life." She lifted her chin and stared him in the eye. "And I have."

"You left her in prison to die." Colton backhanded her across the mouth. She staggered but did not fall. Ryan started toward her, but the click of several Colts and Julia's glare made him stop.

She wiped the trail of blood from her chin and met Sam's stare head on. "You told Mama you'd never hurt me. I guess your promises are as worthless as you are."

Sam scowled and raised his hand again, then, oddly, he smiled and lowered it. "All my promises to your mama will die with her soon enough. I'll deal with you then."

Julia's face went white. "What do you mean?" she whispered.

He jerked his head toward the door. Julia ran, pushing aside every man in her way. They let her go, turning their grinning countenances to Ryan.

"So, boys, what do you say we have some fun with him before we kill him? Any man who fools with my daughter deserves what he gets, wouldn't you say?"

The grins spread wider. Ryan shot a glance at the door. He could hear female voices murmuring on the porch.

"From what I hear, she's not your daughter, Colton."

Colton's grin faded. He glanced at the other men. An embarrassed flush spread from his neck to his forehead. Ryan realized his mistake. He'd just revealed that Colton's wife had borne another man's child, humiliating him in front of his men.

Ryan took a deep breath, imagining the torture he'd just assured himself in one single, stupid sentence. More than likely Colton's embarrassment over that incident of his past had festered for years, contributing to his obsession and his madness.

The boy who had been pledged to marry Julia stepped forward and shoved his gun into Ryan's stomach. Ryan met eyes as dark and as devoid of human feeling as a rattlesnake's. "You violated my betrothed. You took what was mine and you made it worthless."

"Julia could never be worthless. If it makes you feel any better, I married her."

Emotion flared in the boy's eyes—fury, hatred. Ryan prepared himself to die, gutshot, but amazingly Colton stepped forward and yanked the gun from the kid's hands. "Back off, Chandler." He narrowed his gaze on Ryan's face, thinking. "This could work for me."

The kid started to argue, but Colton growled, "Back off, I said." He jerked his head at his sons. Ben and Clark moved forward and yanked the boy out of their father's way.

"You say you married her? Tellin' the truth?"

"Yes. I love her. We hoped some day both families would be able to put aside their differences—"

Colton smacked him in the mouth as indifferently as he'd hit Julia. "Shut the hell up. I loved Vi, and look where it got me. Cuckolded before the wedding just like Chandler here. Women are all alike. I don't care about your namby-pamby idea of love and forgiveness; I care about your farm. My farm. I want it back and I think I found my way to get it."

Ryan narrowed his eyes. He didn't like the glint of greed in Colton's gaze, but then, he never had.

"Where's your brother?"

Ryan's lips tightened. "Ab killed him."

At the mention of his eldest son, Colton turned away. "Good boy, that one."

"So I killed Ab."

Colton spun back, but instead of tears, anger filled his eyes, erasing the greed for a moment. Ryan recalled Colton's moans and tears over Del, and found it interesting that only a few weeks later the death of Ab caused anger and nothing more.

"And do ya want to snivel an apology for killin' him, too?"

Ryan looked straight into Colton's angry eyes. "No."

An eye for an eye. Ab for Jason, he thought. On the heels of those words came more. *What about turn the other cheek? If someone doesn't start doing that, the killing and the vengeance will never stop.*

Ryan blinked at the amazing thought, one he never would have considered a few months back.

"You'll pay for Ab soon enough," Colton snarled. "For Del, too. You won't die quick, Murphy. I promise you that."

Ryan shrugged. He'd been prepared to die for days. He had found his will to live again at the sight of Julia, but if his death could ascertain her life and the life of their child, he would gladly go without a qualm.

"Where's your father?" Colton continued.

"With his troop."

Colton nodded. "So all that stands between me and my farm is your father? If he's dead, Julia, as your wife, gets it all?"

Ryan considered Colton's words and spared a thought for Kathleen. What the man said was true; in marrying Julia, he had taken Kathleen's home from her. Though Julia would never put his sister out, he had no doubt Colton would, if he didn't kill her just because of her name. Since Colton seemed to have forgotten Kathleen's existence, Ryan would not remind him. Again, he thanked God for Connor and the knowledge that his friend would never let harm befall Kathleen while he lived.

Ryan turned his attention back to Colton. "Julia would own the farm. If my father dies and I do."

Colton laughed. "You will. Him, too."

"Then Julia," he paused and looked into Colton's eyes, "and our child, are the only Murphys left."

Colton's amusement died. "You put a brat in her

already? You Federals can't keep it in your pants, can you?''

"Can you?"

Colton hauled back and punched Ryan in the stomach with all his might. While Ryan gasped for air and prayed not to disgrace himself on Colton's boots, Colton hauled him up by the hair, and put his face close to Ryan's. "I married Vi even when I knew what she'd done. I raised Julia as my own, even if looking at her every damn day made me want to puke. Should have drowned her at birth for all the trouble she's caused. Blood will tell, they say, and she turned traitor even though I raised her up right. But she's brought me one thing—the farm that we lost all those years ago. So I guess I'll let her live. For now.''

Colton let Ryan go and he fell to his knees coughing. Ben and Clark yanked him to his feet.

"Hang him, boys. Out on the road, so the Federals'll find him. We'll wait for his father to come, and then we can shoot old Shamus, too.''

"Wait," Ryan wheezed as they dragged him toward the back door and away from Julia. "Without our marriage certificate, you can't prove Julia's the heir.''

Ben and Clark stopped, glanced over their shoulders at their pa. Colton crossed the room. "Where is it?''

"Safe.''

Colton nodded to Chandler. The kid walked forward, smiled into Ryan's eyes, then kneed him in the groin. This time Ryan did disgrace himself, all over the kid's shirt. It was almost worth the pain to see Chandler's expression.

"Where is it, Murphy? Tell me or I'll let him cut your balls off. Where yer goin' ya won't need 'em anymore, anyway." He guffawed and the rest joined in. "After what you've taken from Chandler, it's the least I can do."

"Take Julia—" Ryan paused to choke back a retch. Chandler stepped away to avoid another dousing. After several deep breaths, the pain receded. He tried again. "Take Julia to the church on the hill. Leave her with Father Con. I'll write him a message, and he'll give you the marriage certificate."

Colton considered the offer. Ryan could see Sam's mind spinning for a way to get around this deal. "Con might be a priest, but he's not helpless. Unless he has word from me, you won't see the proof. Do whatever the hell you want to me. I don't care, but I want Julia and my child safe with him. And don't think to use her against him. If she's hurt in the slightest way, you won't get that cursed farm."

"Fine," Sam growled. "Write the message, and I'll send Jesse to the church. No one'll dare mess with him." His annoyance gave way to a smirk. "I like this idea, Murphy. I don't want to see her face for the rest of my days anyway."

"And I'm sure she'd rather not see yours," Ryan drawled. Ben shoved him toward the table and the paper that had appeared on Colton's command. He wrote the note that would end his life and save Julia's, handed the sheet to Colton and then caught his father-in-law's gaze.

"Tell me one thing. How can a bit of land be worth so much? A lifetime of anger and hatred? The loss of your wife and two sons for possession of a dirt farm and a creek?''

"Ab and Del died for the cause—not the farm.''

"You go on believing that, Colton. Maybe then they won't haunt you in the night.''

Colton started to breathe heavy; his face went purple again. Ryan waited for the eruption. "That farm belonged to my family. Just because the enemy bought it don't make it theirs. What's mine is mine. Forever.''

Ryan shook his head. He could understand loving one's home, but to covet something the way Colton did was beyond him. People were important, not things.

Ryan's uncomprehending expression infuriated Sam all the more, and Colton stepped closer, lowered his voice to snarl, "Vi's gonna die soon because of you and Julia. If you two had hated each other like you were born to do, none of this would have happened.''

"Julia and I were meant to love each other. It's taken a lot, but I've learned. I'll choose love over hate any day.''

"Get him out of here," Colton growled.

Ben, Clark and the rest hustled him out the back door. His one regret was that he would die without seeing Julia one last time.

Julia's chest ached. Her belly burned. How could she feel so much love and so much hate at one time?

She held her mama in her arms and knew this time the end was near. All those other times when she'd feared Mama would die, Mama had rallied. This time there would be no miraculous recovery. Elvira Colton had reached the end of the trail.

"Mama?" Julia shook her. "Mama, please. Don't leave me."

Mama's face was waxy gray, her skin icy cold. She barely breathed, and when she did the rattle made Julia's heart leap in terror.

Julia leaned over and put her lips next to Mama's ear. "I love you, Mama. I'm sorry I left you there. They took me away when I was asleep. I never would have left you, Mama. Never."

Ice touched the back of Julia's neck and she jerked upward. Her eyes met those of her mama and together they smiled.

"I know that, child. I told the young priest to take you away. You need to be with that Murphy boy. Love such as yours deserves a chance to grow."

Mama had always been able to read Julia's mind, see into her heart, and right now was no different, it seemed, despite her imminent departure from the earth. She narrowed her gaze on Julia's face and frowned. "You aren't still blamin' him for me? You aren't still broodin' over your brother? You aren't still holdin' a grudge over the prison? 'Cause if you are, you'll stop it right here and now. Life's too short. Either you love or you don't, and if you love you'll forgive him anything. That's what love means."

"Mama, you're dying."

"I've been dyin' since I was born. You have to quit worryin' about me now. I'm off to be with your pa, and I'm glad. Seein' what's happened to you has made me see my past so clear. It took a lot of years, but I finally forgave your pa for dyin' to save me and you. Right noble of him, of course, but he still took the easier route. I had to live with Sam and the boys.

Remember that, Julia; dyin's easy, it's livin' that's hard. Now you go and you get your young man and have your baby and live a good life."

Julia shook her head. The emphatic movement made pain spread through her injured head and down her bruised jaw. She winced and remembered why she'd been hit. She had run off and not taken care of her mama. Sam Colton was wrong about most things, but about Julia's desertion he was right. She owed her mama that much.

"I won't leave you again, Mama."

Her mama frowned, closed her eyes for a long moment as if to gather strength, then yanked Julia closer. "What are you talkin' about? I want you to hightail it outta here and get to that Murphy boy before your father finds out about the baby. He'll use you and the child to get that farm. But first he'll kill your husband. History repeats itself too damn often. No one ever learns a thing."

"Ryan's here."

"He's here?" Mama struggled to sit up, fell back coughing. Blood appeared on her lips, and she pressed a stained kerchief to her mouth. "Are you a fool? Do whatever you have to do. Promise them anything, but get him out of here."

The intensity of Mama's voice reached Julia, and she glanced over her shoulder at the cabin. Julia had been so concerned about Mama, afraid she was dead, she had run from the place and not looked back. Now she stood and approached more slowly than she had left, only to find the cabin deserted. Terror spiked her heart, replacing the uncommon inertia that had been there since she'd discovered Ryan's duplicity. She ran back onto the porch.

"They're gone."

"You'd better find them," Mama whispered. "They'll kill him for certain."

Julia ran down the steps, stopped and turned back. "But, Mama, you're sick—"

"I'm going to die soon enough. You think havin' you stare at me while I leave this world is what I want? Now go and do what needs to be done. Don't let that Murphy boy play hero like your pa did and take the easy way out of this world. Make my life mean something. Learn from the past, child. For me, if not yourself."

Torn, Julia hovered between the house and the bush. When faced with Ryan's loss so many things became clear. Life wasn't a dream or a fairy tale; Ryan wasn't a golden hero on a white horse—and she didn't care. Those were the hopes of childhood. She was a woman now, and she had to act like one.

The sound of a gunshot forced her to move, despite the terror that made her legs heavy and her heart thunder. Julia lifted her skirts and raced, barefoot, into the brush.

Chapter Twenty

Julia ran as if her life depended upon her speed, and it did. If Ryan died, she would not want to live. How had Mama survived all these years with the man she loved gone before her? Just like Julia, if she hadn't had a baby to think of she would have joined her husband in the grave.

Please, oh please, let me be in time.

She prayed, she begged, she pledged anything to all the powers that were. Mama had been right. No matter what Ryan had done, she didn't care. She loved him and she always would.

She slowed as the brush thinned near the main road. Above the sound of her own harsh, terrified breathing she heard the unmistakable crack of flesh against flesh, curses and an occasional gunshot. Dear God, they hadn't killed him already, had they?

She peered through the scrub. She should have known her brothers would not let Ryan die so easily. Instead they had hung him from a tree—but not completely. They allowed his toes just to touch so he had to use his energy to keep himself from choking. Ben and Clark's idea of fun involved punching Ryan in the stomach, then laughing hysterically when he swung back and forth in the wind. Frank James and Cole Younger sat their horses, declining to take part in the festivities, looking a bit disgusted. Jesse was nowhere to be found. Julia didn't like that. Jesse was dangerous. He could sneak up on a body like an Indian.

She cast an uneasy glance about the brush but could detect no movement. She had no choice. Even if Jesse lurked somewhere, along with Sam, she had to do something soon.

Another gunshot froze her blood. She forced herself to look back at the road. The explanation for the random shots stood directly in front of Julia at the edge of the brush. His back to her, Ted Chandler shot at Ryan's feet, joining in Ben and Clark's hysterical laughter when Ryan had to scramble for purchase each time he yanked his toes out of the way of a gunshot.

"That tears it," Julia mumbled. Before Ted knew she stood behind him, she stepped out of the brush, yanked his pistol from his hand and smacked him over the head with it. He hit the ground like a sack of rocks.

She turned her attention to her brothers. Never too bright, Ben and Clark just gaped at her, giving Julia time to cock the pistol and train the weapon upon them. They had not bothered to take out their pistols while beating a strung-up man.

She flicked a glance at Frank and Cole. They watched her with interest. "You two stay out of this. It's family business."

They raised their hands in surrender, though both looked ready to lose their battle with laughter. "Toss those gunbelts over here, boys. Every one of you."

All four complied, though with great reluctance. Julia hurried over to Ryan. His eyes were closed. She wondered if he even knew she was there, so deep was his concentration on staying upright. Then he opened his eyes and smiled.

"I was praying I'd see you one more time." His voice was so hoarse she could barely hear him, but the love in his blue eyes shone brighter than a Missouri sky. "I wanted to tell you I love you."

Then he lifted his feet and the noose went taut.

"Damn it!" Julia swore. She yanked Ben's Bowie knife from his belt and sawed at the rope with all her might. "You ass," she muttered. "You can tell me that for the rest of our lives."

He fell to the ground. She fell with him, forgetting the gun in her hand and her brothers nearby. Instead she put her cheek to his bare chest, listening for his heart. All she heard was the cock of two pistols behind her.

She spun about, putting herself between the others, who had retrieved their weapons, and Ryan, but Frank and Cole had gotten the draw on the Colton boys. She nodded her thanks and the two men thumbed their hats.

Frank scowled at Ben and Clark. "She's your sister, what are you thinkin' to draw on her?''

"She's savin' that Yankee bastard," Ben snarled.

"Her husband. Family. Leave her be."

"He's a damned Murphy. It's a family feud between us and them. Won't be over till they're all dead and buried."

Frank pursed his lips. "Or you are."

Ben and Clark blinked, as if they'd never considered such an occurrence. Frank's lips twitched, and he glanced at Cole, who rolled his eyes. Then Frank turned back to Ben. "For all your family feelin' over this feud, you'd think you'd understand your sister's concern for a husband."

"I don't get your meanin'."

"I didn't figure you would." Frank nodded at Julia. "Sister, tend to your man. Best get him outta here before your pa shows up."

"Why are you helping me?" she asked. "I thought you hated the Yankees worse than anyone."

"I do. But I know true love when I see it, and I see it in you and him. It don't come along every damn day, sister, so you two run. Run far, run west. As long as this Yankee's not in the war, he's as good as dead."

Ryan stirred, moaned, and Julia turned back around as joy filled her heart.

He opened his eyes, blinked, frowned. His lips moved, and she leaned forward to hear his pained voice. "Are we both dead?"

"Not yet, no thanks to you."

"Your pa said he'd take you to Con. Why are you here?"

"For you. If you think I'm living the rest of my

life alone, you can think awhile longer.''

His glance flicked to the side, lit on their company, returned to her face. His smile was strained. ''I wanted to be a hero.''

''What good is a dead hero? I prefer a live husband. A very wise woman once told me, 'Dying's easy, living's hard.' True heroes choose life over death.''

''Love over hate?''

She nodded.

''You've forgiven me?''

She loosened the rope from his neck and traced the bloody trail it had left with her finger. ''There's nothing to forgive.''

''And your mama?''

''She forgave you long ago.''

''Then why don't I feel forgiven?''

''Because you have to forgive yourself.''

He pondered that for a moment, then his hand groped for hers. She took it, held on tight. She had just managed to help him to his feet, her mind frantically searching for a way to get a horse, when a voice froze them all.

''Ye'll be puttin' down the firearms, gentlemen, or we'll be pluggin' ye.''

Julia stared, amazed, as Shamus Murphy emerged from the opposite side of the road with five Federals. Frank and Cole scowled, considered the odds, then tossed their guns to the ground. Uneasy, Julia glanced at the brush behind her. No guerilla would ever give up his guns that easy unless he knew friends with more guns lurked nearby. She wanted to get out of here before they all started shooting.

Ryan held her close to his side, for her protection

or to keep upright, she didn't know. She didn't care. For the rest of her life, she would stay as close as she could to his side. Nearly losing him had taught her so much.

Shamus dismounted, his glance sliding over everyone in the road. Then he addressed Ryan. "Where's yer brother?"

Julia felt the force of Ryan's pain in the stiffening of his body. She knew his agony and suffered with him. "Dead."

Shamus went white, staggered, then drew himself upright by force of will. He dashed the back of his hand roughly across his eyes before meeting his son's gaze. "In battle?"

"Yes, sir."

" 'Tis a good way to die."

"No way is a good way, Da. Jason is dead, and I'll mourn him for the rest of my life."

"And well ye should. We'll spend the rest of the war makin' 'em pay. Together, you and me."

"Da, you frighten me," Ryan said. "I don't even know you anymore."

"Yer bein' foolish, boy. The only way to make the pain of Jason's death go away is to kill as many of them as we can."

"No, Da, you're wrong. I tried to make them pay for Ma, but it didn't help and I hurt a lot of innocent people. It wasn't worth it. No matter what we do, Ma's dead and Jason's dead. Sometime the hating's gotta stop."

"Not in my lifetime." Shamus swaggered over to his son. Reaching out, he grabbed Ryan's chin, pushing it from side to side. "Ye'll have a nice hangin' scar, boy. Ladies'll love it.'' He threw a smirk Julia's way and she stared back without a flicker of her eye. "Perhaps it'll remind ye t' keep t' yer own."

"It'll remind me of what's important."

His father's bushy white eyebrows made a *V* above angry eyes. "Which is?"

"Love."

"Aye, me boy. Love. Yer family. Yer land and yer home. Yer country and yer duty. Let's be off."

Ryan shook his head. "Love for my wife and my child."

"What child?" Shamus thundered.

"Mine. I'll not give up Julia or my child for anything or anyone."

Shamus squinted at Julia. His smirk returned. She tensed in expectation of his attack. When it came, she almost laughed aloud.

"Ye mean t' tell me, girlie, ye'll still be spreadin' for him even after he tried t' git ye killed?"

"Da—"

"No, Ryan." Julia put her hand on his chest, holding him back. She faced Shamus and said what she should have said long before. "I'm ashamed I believed your lies for even an instant. I never should have considered what you told me. I was shocked about my brother's death. Sick with the baby and scared for my mama."

"I didn't lie. I'll get ten Federal soldiers t' swear I'm tellin' the truth and the boy's lyin'."

This time Julia gave in to her urge to laugh out loud, and then tilted her chin and stared Shamus in the eye. "I don't care what he's done. I love him."

Murphy's face flushed purple. He turned to his son

and poked him in the chest so hard he left a red mark on Ryan's bare skin. "Ye come with me, boy. Leave the Bushwhacker whore alone. I'll not tell ye again."

Ryan shoved his father. Shamus stumbled back and Ryan advanced. "I won't tell *you* again. She's my wife. She carries my child. If we're not welcome here, together, then we'll leave."

Shamus stopped retreating. He pulled his chest up like a fighting rooster ready to strut and peck. "As of this day yer one of 'em. If ye lie down with the enemy, ye become the enemy. Yer a traitor, and as a captain in the United States Army it is my duty to list ye as such. If any Federal sees yer face, they'll shoot ye for a deserter."

Julia gasped. "He's your son. How can you say such things?"

"I have no sons." Murphy turned his back on them. "My sons died in the war."

"They did at that."

Julia wanted to scream her frustration at the sound of Sam's voice. He stepped from the brush, Colt cocked and aimed at Shamus. He stepped over Ted, who had just begun to moan and hold his aching head, with a sneer of disgust, then frowned at his sons.

"Why the hell isn't Murphy dead? I told ya to hang him *before* his pa got here. Do I have to do everything myself?"

"We were just havin' some fun with him, Pa," Clark whined. "Then she came and whopped Ted on the head, cut Murphy down."

"Ya let her get the best of ya?"

"You know how she is, Pa. She's tricky and mean.

347

Fights dirty. Didn't even give Ted a chance, just whopped him good. Anyways, Frank and Cole took her side.'' He looked at the two guerillas with the disappointed eyes of a pup scolded by its master.

Sam glowered at Cole and Frank, but before he could speak, Shamus cocked his pistol. ''Drop the gun, Colton. Ye're outnumbered here and ye're goin' t' hang.''

''I don't think so, Murphy.'' He cocked his gun. Five Federal pistols followed suit.

Julia and Ryan tensed, but before a war could erupt, with them in the middle, a rider burst through the brush and all the weapons turned that way.

''This place is more popular than New York City,'' Ryan muttered. Then he saw the identity of the rider and shouted, ''Don't shoot. He's a priest!''

Con reined up between the two warring parties, glanced around. He did not wear the robes of his profession; instead he wore traveling clothes—tan trousers, brown shirt, Palo Alto hat and a gun belt. The only priestly attire was his rosary, which clanked about his neck as he jumped to the ground.

''A priest with a gun?'' Frank James asked, keeping his own weapon cocked and trained on Con.

''In these times a man without a gun is a stupid man,'' Con replied.

''Or a dead one.'' Frank uncocked his gun with a nod. ''Lucky you're wearin' that rosary, Father, and Murphy recognized you, or we might have shot first and worried if you were friend or enemy later.''

Con shrugged. ''I'm sure my profession has saved my life many a time in this war.'' He crossed to Ryan. His gaze lit on the hanging scar. ''What's going on?''

"Showdown."

Con sighed. He closed his eyes for a moment as if to pray for strength, and then turned to address the combatants.

"Colton. Murphy. Haven't enough of your children died over this bloody feud? Do you have to kill every last member of your families before you're satisfied?" Sam and Shamus merely scowled and kept their guns trained upon each other. "Your children have found love. They found a way to end this hate. But you won't be happy until you destroy everything."

"I have no sons," Shamus gritted from between clenched teeth and shoved Sam.

"She is not my daughter," Sam returned, shoving back.

Con threw up his hands. "Fine, then you won't care if they leave now."

Both men turned to gape at Con.

"He's a deserter when he walks away from here," Shamus said. "A renegade just like these others."

"That all right with you, Ry?"

"Fine."

"She's not a Colton. Frickin' bastard," Sam snarled.

Julia lifted her chin. "I'm a Murphy now."

"If I ever see you again, I'll kill you." Sam flushed red and took a step toward her, but Julia was done with cringing. She would face all life had to offer and take the worst with the best from this time on. She stood her ground as he continued to rant. "Don't think to see your mama, if she's still alive. You've betrayed her. Leave now and don't look back."

Julia hesitated. To leave her mama without a good-bye . . . leave her to die alone with these men. She had pledged her life to her mama until death. With Mama's time so close, was it wrong to break that vow?

Julia glanced at Ryan and her eyes filled with tears. As always, he understood her pain without words.

"We'll take her with us," he whispered.

Con put his hand on her arm, a touch so gentle she knew even before he spoke what he would say, and her breath caught on a sob. "She's gone, Julia. I stopped at the house before I found you. He's just trying to break your heart."

The tears spilled from Julia's eyes. "He has."

Ryan took her hand. "We've done all we can. There's no talking to them. There never has been."

Julia nodded. He was right. Sometimes you just had to do your best and then let it go.

"Don't come back. If I see either of your faces, I'll kill ya," Colton fumed.

"Yer a traitor to yer country, yer family and yer name. I'll see ye in Hell, boy."

Con, Julia and Ryan retreated, the sound of Shamus's and Sam's last words following them down the road into their future.

Ryan felt as if he'd gone to heaven. Even though he walked away from everything he'd ever known toward an uncertain future, with no money, no prospects, no horse and no shirt, he was the richest man on earth. Julia's hand in his, the memory of her voice, strong and clear and proud when she'd said, "I'm a Murphy now," made everything worthwhile.

Once they were out of sight of the others, Con paused. He stared down at the reins of his horse, avoiding Ryan's gaze.

Ryan frowned. "What is it?"

"Kathleen's gone, Ry."

"Gone? What do you mean, gone?"

"Left. Packed up her things and—" He shrugged, spread his hands wide. "Gone."

"Well, we'd better find her."

"Not we. Me. You two had better head out before they change their minds and decide they'd rather see you dead now than later."

Ryan frowned. "But—"

"I'll find her." Con caught Ryan's gaze, held it. "I swear."

Ryan nodded, accepting the promise. Con slapped his horse's reins into Ryan's hands. "Take him. There are clothes, supplies and money in the saddlebags. I'll go back and get another."

"Where'd you get money? I thought you took a vow of poverty, among other things."

Con ducked his head and his black hair fell forward obscuring his eyes, hiding his thoughts. "I sold the farm."

Ryan sighed. The farm was the only link Con had to his old life. That he'd held on to it this long had made Ryan think the place meant something more to him than a bit of land in the North. "I'm sorry, Con."

"Don't be. There's no one left but me, and what will I do with it?" He took a deep breath, shook the hair from his face and straightened. "I figured with the war on I'd best keep the money for . . ."

"An emergency?"

"Like this."

"I'll never forget what you've done for us, Con. I'll never forget you."

"'Course not. Saved your ass again, didn't I?" Con grinned, though the expression didn't reach his eyes. Ryan wondered if Con's eyes would ever smile again. He shook Con's hand, but his friend drew him close for a hug.

Then Ryan turned to help Julia onto the horse. Tear tracks traced her cheeks, broke his heart. Con nudged him aside. "Let me," he murmured.

Con put his arms around Julia, pulled her close and stroked her hair. Then he leaned down to whisper something into her ear, something that made her smile, first at him and then at Ryan. Ryan breathed a sigh of relief. She would be all right. They both would.

Con helped her into the saddle. Ryan swung on, too. Horses pounded around the bend and all three of them froze.

Julia stiffened in his arms. "Bloody Bill."

"Of all people," Ryan said, and braced himself for another battle.

But the guerillas raced by them without much more than a glance, intent upon something in the distance. As soon as the partisans rounded the bend in the road, gunfire, shouts and orders drifted on the wind as those left behind battled each other.

Together, Ryan and Julia sighed. Nothing would ever change here no matter what they did. But at least they had each other, the baby and their lives. So many had so much less.

Ryan reached into the pocket of his pants and withdrew the symbol of their love.

"Julia?"

She turned her head; her hair brushed his cheek and the scent of roses and tears made him smile. When she saw what he held in his fingers, she smiled in return. She gave him her left hand, and he dropped the band of gold onto her finger for the second time, the last time, in their lifetime.

"See that you keep those promises," Con said.

Ryan took up the reins. Julia put her hands over his, and they turned the horse west. Con headed south. None of them ever looked back.

Epilogue

May 15, 1864

Dear Ryan and Julia,
  I returned home to find your letter telling me you had arrived safely. I was glad to hear you've found a place to live and work running the abandoned stage stop for Ben Holladay's mail line. Knowing you were safe and well brightened my spirit, which was quite bleak at the time. I'm sorry to say I have been unable to locate Kathleen. But I have not given up hope. On my way home I met up with some Cherokee Confederates. They told of a spirit woman who lives in the Sni Hills. She does not speak, and her hair has been touched by flame and ice. I am off to the Sni as soon as I finish this letter.
  I find I have done more good for folk in the

past several months on the road than I did in all my time at the church on the hill. It is my fondest wish that in finding Kathleen, I will also find the part of myself I lost long ago.

I regret to inform you that both Clark and Ben Colton were killed the day we walked away from them on the road. Ted Chandler, too, and several of the Federals. Your fathers survived.

Sam Colton took ownership of the Murphy farm upon the death of Shamus last week. Unfortunately for Sam, he only got to enjoy his victory for a short time. He was killed in a raid several days ago. I presided over his burial today. I suspect the two are still fighting in Hell.

Their deaths leave the two of you as sole heirs to the Murphy-Colton farms. I hope you will return when the war is over and make something good and right out of what went so wrong there.

With God's grace, Kathleen and I will be waiting for you.

Con

Julia looked up from the letter. Three years old now, the paper had been read so many times that the writing had faded, the creases so prominent they had torn through in places.

She stared out over the stagetrail coming in from the East. Dust kicked up and headed her way. She waited and watched, hoping Ryan had returned and not just another stage.

Despite Con's prayers, they had not heard from him or Kathleen again; neither had they returned to live in Kansas or Missouri. Julia could not bear to set foot on the blood-drenched land again. The memories were too painful.

Raising her hand, she traced the scar on her forehead. The mark from the Kansas City prison collapse had never faded, though her nightmares had. Whenever memories of that time overwhelmed her, she stroked the scar and concentrated on the multitude of joys that had been hers since that day.

A single rider materialized from the dust, and she let out a cry of joy when Ryan reined in before the combination stage stop and home they had made theirs in Nevada.

Paying no mind to the heavy dust that covered him head to foot, making his blue eyes shine brightly in a gray, ghostly face, Julia threw herself into his arms. They allowed their kiss to impart all their love.

Ryan broke the kiss, then wiped the dust from her mouth with the bandana he now used to cover the hanging scar that had never faded either. Grinning, he stepped back to cock an eyebrow at the bulge beneath her apron. "I did it again, didn't I?"

She grinned right back. "Yes, sir. That's what happens when you go away for three months. You miss me puking all morning long. Again."

"Sorry."

She laughed. So happy to have him back, the months of morning sickness and fear for him now faded into memory.

She took his hand and together they walked to the bench that had been built against the front wall of their stage-stop home. They sat and she looked at him with all her questions in her eyes. As always, she did not need to voice her concerns; they were his as well.

"I sold both farms to a young couple from Ohio. Got a good price. The place will be one farm now. Like we wanted."

"One in love, not hate."

He nodded, but his eyes looked east and not at her, and she knew he remembered what he had seen there.

"The place looked the same, but the heart's been ripped out of Missouri and Kansas. I don't know if anyone or anything will ever be the same."

"I'm glad we decided to let the farms go."

"I couldn't live there and not see Jason every day."

"And Mama and Del. Was the church on the hill still there?"

Ryan closed his eyes, and she knew the news was not good. "The new father said . . ." Julia squeezed Ryan's hand. He took a deep breath and rushed on. "Con's been listed as dead with the church. No one knew anything about Kathleen."

"I'm sorry, Ryan."

"So am I."

"Papa!"

Julia and Ryan turned at the sound of their daughter's voice. Just up from her nap, Ellie rubbed her eyes. With the enthusiasm of youth, she came running and threw herself into Ryan's open arms. He held her close and kissed her hair and then looked over her head at Julia.

Ryan smiled, and her heart lurched in just the same way it had the first time she'd seen him—all those years ago on the banks of that blasted creek. She'd left her home to be with him, left everything she knew behind and taken the name of her enemy. She'd learned what was in a name—absolutely nothing. Her years as a Murphy had been hard, but she'd never regretted a single one.

"I'm glad to be home," Ryan said.

"Home." Julia rolled the word about on her tongue, amazed to discover at last that the word matched a place in her heart. Home was not a farm or a house, not a county or a state. Home was Ryan and Ellie and the baby inside her. Home was in her heart.

Julia placed her hand over her stomach. Ryan's hand covered hers, and Ellie's made three. One home, one family, one name.

AUTHOR'S NOTE

The hatred between the people who live on the border of Missouri and Kansas has become legendary. Their war began five years before the Civil War when John Brown murdered several pro-slavery families in the name of the Army of the Lord. From then on the hostilities continued, taking on the characteristics of many a family feud. Jayhawkers and Bushwhackers alike killed on the basis of a person's family and beliefs, before, during and after the war.

The story of the prison collapse in Kansas City is unfortunately true. I added my characters to those known to have died or been maimed in that sad occurrence. Bloody Bill Anderson's oldest sister, Josephine, was killed in the prison collapse, and his youngest, Jainie, was crippled for life. This incident became one of the sparks that ignited the raid on Lawrence, Kansas, by guerrillas a week later.

The back of the guerrilla movement was broken at Albany, Missouri, in October 1864 with the death of Bloody Bill Anderson. Five days before, George Todd was shot through the neck at Independence. Quantrill lasted until May 1865, when he died during a gun battle in Kentucky.

Some of their followers joined General Sterling Price in a last-ditch effort to wrest Missouri from Union control. Others threw up their hands, handed in their guns and pledged allegiance to the Union so they could go home. Still others retreated to Texas, hoping to keep the Confederacy alive from there.

Though the American Civil War ended in the spring of 1865, a new war began—the war of the Southern outlaw against Union-held operations. The James-Younger gang, and others like them, rode throughout the West robbing trains, stages and banks, and remained a thorn in the government's side for years to come.

I hope you enjoyed *By Any Other Name*. In my next Love Spell romance I will return to one of my favorite settings—the Old West—where a widowed schoolteacher, a half-breed bounty hunter and an ancient, evil Comanche spirit battle for control of a little town in Texas. Look for *Dreams of an Eagle* in September 1998.

I love to hear from readers. You can write to me at: P.O. Box 736, Thiensville, WI 53092. A SASE is appreciated for a reply. Or check out my web site at: http://www.eclectics.com/lorihandeland/

An Angel's Touch
D.J.'s Angel
Lori Handeland

D.J. Halloran doesn't believe in love. She's just seen too much heartache—in her work as a police officer and in her own life. And she vowed a long time ago never to let anyone get close enough to hurt her, even if that someone is the very captivating, very handsome Chris McCall.

But D.J. also has an angel—a special guardian determined, at any cost, to teach D.J. the magic of love. So try as she might to resist Chris's many charms, D.J. knows she is in for an even tougher battle because of her exasperating heavenly companion's persistent faith in the power of love.

_52050-8 $5.99 US/$7.99 CAN

Dorchester Publishing Co., Inc.
P.O. Box 6640
Wayne, PA 19087-8640

Please add $1.75 for shipping and handling for the first book and $.50 for each book thereafter. NY, NYC, and PA residents, please add appropriate sales tax. No cash, stamps, or C.O.D.s. All orders shipped within 6 weeks via postal service book rate. Canadian orders require $2.00 extra postage and must be paid in U.S. dollars through a U.S. banking facility.

Name_____
Address_____
City_____ State_____ Zip_____
I have enclosed $_____ in payment for the checked book(s).
Payment <u>must</u> accompany all orders. ☐ Please send a free catalog.

DON'T MISS OTHER SPINE-TINGLING PARANORMAL ROMANCES!

Waitangi Nights by Alice Gaines. With her meager inheritance almost gone, young Isabel Gannon has little hope but to stake her future on a risky gamble. She accepts an offer to accompany a shipment of wild orchids to the lush New Zealand home of the darkly handsome Richard Julian. There she is determined to nurture the precious plants—and resist the lure of her employer's strong arms. But even as Isabel feels herself blossom beneath Richard's tender touch, she senses something else lurking on the exotic estate. A strange cry in the night, a mysterious light—something sinister that threatens to nip her newfound happiness in the bud. Now Isabel will have to unravel a web of secrets if she wants to preserve their halcyon days and savor the passion of their wild Waitangi nights.

_52153-9 $4.99 US/$5.99 CAN

Full Moon Dreams by Lori Handeland. Emmaline Monroe is not prepared for the deaths at the circus that occur on nights when the moon shines full and bright. Everyone has been warned to trust no one. But the lovely tiger trainer is finding her attraction to Johnny Bradfordini impossible to tame. Each time she looks into the handsome stranger's silvery-blue eyes, she feels pulled into an all-consuming passion—and an inexplicable danger.

_52110-5 $5.50 US/$6.50 CAN

Dorchester Publishing Co., Inc.
P.O. Box 6640
Wayne, PA 19087-8640

Please add $1.75 for shipping and handling for the first book and $.50 for each book thereafter. NY, NYC, and PA residents, please add appropriate sales tax. No cash, stamps, or C.O.D.s. All orders shipped within 6 weeks via postal service book rate. Canadian orders require $2.00 extra postage and must be paid in U.S. dollars through a U.S. banking facility.

Name_____
Address_____
City_____State_____Zip_____
I have enclosed $_____ in payment for the checked book(s).
Payment <u>must</u> accompany all orders. ❑ Please send a free catalog.

NATIONALLY BESTSELLING
AUTHOR OF *REJAR!*

DARA JOY

Tonight Or Never

They call him "Lord of Sex." He is a rake, a rogue, a
libertine, and a scoundrel. With his wicked sense of humor,
keen intelligence, and charming ways, the Viscount Sexton
is an expert in the art of seduction. But little does he know
his days of debauchery are about to come to an end. For
Chloe intends to have him for her own, forever. Now she'll
just have to get the stubborn devil to realize that they belong
together. And the feisty redhead has the perfect plan, for
what could be better than beating Don Juan at his own
seductive game...

___52216-0 $5.99 US/$6.99 CAN

Dorchester Publishing Co., Inc.
P.O. Box 6640
Wayne, PA 19087-8640

Please add $1.75 for shipping and handling for the first book and
$.50 for each book thereafter. NY, NYC, and PA residents,
please add appropriate sales tax. No cash, stamps, or C.O.D.s. All
orders shipped within 6 weeks via postal service book rate.
Canadian orders require $2.00 extra postage and must be paid in
U.S. dollars through a U.S. banking facility.

Name_____
Address_____
City_____ State_____ Zip_____
I have enclosed $_____ in payment for the checked book(s).
Payment <u>must</u> accompany all orders. ❑ Please send a free catalog.

SANDRA HILL

Sweeter Savage Love. When a twist of fate casts Harriet Ginoza back in time to the Old South, the modern psychologist meets the object of her forbidden fantasies. Though she knows the dangerously handsome rogue is everything she should despise, she can't help but feel that within his arms she might attain a sweeter savage love.

___52212-8 $5.99 US/$6.99 CAN

Desperado. When a routine skydive goes awry, Major Helen Prescott and Rafe Santiago parachute straight into the 1850 California Gold Rush. Mistaken for a notorious bandit and his infamously sensuous mistress, they find themselves on the wrong side of the law. In a time and place where rules have no meaning, Helen finds herself all too willing to throw caution to the wind to spend every night in the arms of her very own desperado.

___52182-2 $5.99 US/$6.99 CAN

Dorchester Publishing Co., Inc.
P.O. Box 6640
Wayne, PA 19087-8640

Please add $1.75 for shipping and handling for the first book and $.50 for each book thereafter. NY, NYC, and PA residents, please add appropriate sales tax. No cash, stamps, or C.O.D.s. All orders shipped within 6 weeks via postal service book rate. Canadian orders require $2.00 extra postage and must be paid in U.S. dollars through a U.S. banking facility.

Name_____
Address_____
City_____ State_____ Zip_____
I have enclosed $_____ in payment for the checked book(s).
Payment <u>must</u> accompany all orders. ☐ Please send a free catalog.

FRANKLY, MY DEAR...

SANDRA HILL

By the Bestselling Author of *The Tarnished Lady*

Selene has three great passions: men, food, and *Gone with the Wind*. But the glamorous model always found herself starving—for both nourishment and affection. Weary of the petty world of high fashion, she heads to New Orleans for one last job before she begins a new life. Then a voodoo spell sends her back to the days of opulent balls and vixenish belles like Scarlet O'Hara.

Charmed by the Old South, Selene can't get her fill of gumbo, crayfish, beignets—or an alarmingly handsome planter. Dark and brooding, James Baptiste does not share Rhett Butler's cavalier spirit, and his bayou plantation is no Tara. But fiddle-dee-dee, Selene doesn't need her mammy to tell her the virile Creole is the only lover she ever gave a damn about. And with God as her witness, she vows never to go hungry or without the man she desires again.

_4042-5 $5.50 US/$6.50 CAN

Dorchester Publishing Co., Inc.
P.O. Box 6640
Wayne, PA 19087-8640

Please add $1.75 for shipping and handling for the first book and $.50 for each book thereafter. NY, NYC, and PA residents, please add appropriate sales tax. No cash, stamps, or C.O.D.s. All orders shipped within 6 weeks via postal service book rate. Canadian orders require $2.00 extra postage and must be paid in U.S. dollars through a U.S. banking facility.

Name_____
Address_____
City_____ State_____ Zip_____
I have enclosed $_____ in payment for the checked book(s).
Payment <u>must</u> accompany all orders. ☐ Please send a free catalog.

Someone's Been Sleeping In My Bed

A Faerie Tale Romance

LindaJones

**WHO'S BEEN EATING FROM MY BOWL?
IS SHE A BEAUTY IN BOTH HEART AND
   SOUL?
WHO'S BEEN SITTING IN MY CHAIR?
IS SHE PRETTY OF FACE AND FAIR OF
   HAIR?
WHO'S BEEN SLEEPING IN MY BED?
IS SHE THE DAMSEL I WILL WED?**

The golden-haired woman barely escapes from a stagecoach robbery before she gets lost in the Wyoming mountains. Hungry, harried, and out of hope, she stumbles on a rude cabin, the home of three brothers; great bears of men who nearly frighten her out of her wits. But Maddalyn Kelly is no Goldilocks; she is a feisty beauty who can fend for herself. Still, how can she ever guess that the Barrett boys will bare their souls to her—or that one of them will share with her an ecstasy so exquisite it is almost unbearable?

_52094-X $5.99 US/$6.99 CAN

**Dorchester Publishing Co., Inc.
P.O. Box 6640
Wayne, PA 19087-8640**

Please add $1.75 for shipping and handling for the first book and $.50 for each book thereafter. NY, NYC, and PA residents, please add appropriate sales tax. No cash, stamps, or C.O.D.s. All orders shipped within 6 weeks via postal service book rate. Canadian orders require $2.00 extra postage and must be paid in U.S. dollars through a U.S. banking facility.

Name_____
Address_____
City_____State_____Zip_____
I have enclosed $_____ in payment for the checked book(s).
Payment <u>must</u> accompany all orders. ☐ Please send a free catalog.

A FAERIE TALE ROMANCE

VICTORIA ALEXANDER

Ophelia Kendrake has barely finished conning the coat off a cardsharp's back when she stumbles into Dead End, Wyoming. Mistaken for the Countess of Bridgewater, Ophelia sees no reason to reveal herself until she has stripped the hamlet of its fortunes and escaped into the sunset. But the free-spirited beauty almost swallows her script when she meets Tyler, the town's virile young mayor. When Tyler Matthews returns from an Ivy League college, he simply wants to settle down and enjoy the simplicity of ranching. But his aunt and uncle are set on making a silk purse out of Dead End, and Tyler is going to be the new mayor. It's a job he takes with little relish—until he catches a glimpse of the village's newest visitor.

_52159-8 $5.50 US/$6.50 CAN

Dorchester Publishing Co., Inc.
P.O. Box 6640
Wayne, PA 19087-8640

Please add $1.75 for shipping and handling for the first book and $.50 for each book thereafter. NY, NYC, and PA residents, please add appropriate sales tax. No cash, stamps, or C.O.D.s. All orders shipped within 6 weeks via postal service book rate. Canadian orders require $2.00 extra postage and must be paid in U.S. dollars through a U.S. banking facility.

Name_____
Address_____
City_____ State_____ Zip_____
I have enclosed $_____ in payment for the checked book(s).
Payment <u>must</u> accompany all orders. ☐ Please send a free catalog.

ATTENTION ROMANCE CUSTOMERS!

SPECIAL TOLL-FREE NUMBER
1-800-481-9191

Call Monday through Friday
12 noon to 10 p.m.
Eastern Time
Get a free catalogue,
join the Romance Book Club,
and order books using your
Visa, MasterCard,
or Discover®

Leisure
Books

Love
Spell